Crime Files Series

General Editor: **Clive Bloom**

Since its invention in the nineteenth century, detective fiction has never been more popular. In novels, short stories, films, radio, television and now in computer games, private detectives and psychopaths, prim poisoners and overworked cops, tommy-gun gangsters and cocaine criminals are the very stuff of modern imagination, and their creators one mainstay of popular consciousness. *Crime Files* is a ground-breaking series offering scholars, students and discerning readers a comprehensive set of guides to the world of crime and detective fiction. Every aspect of crime writing, detective fiction, gangster movie, true-crime exposé, police procedural and post-colonial investigation is explored through clear and informative texts offering comprehensive coverage and theoretical sophistication.

Published titles include:

Maurizio Ascari
A COUNTER-HISTORY OF CRIME FICTION
Supernatural, Gothic, Sensational

Hans Bertens and Theo D'haen
CONTEMPORARY AMERICAN CRIME FICTION

Anita Biressi
CRIME, FEAR AND THE LAW IN TRUE CRIME STORIES

Ed Christian (*editor*)
THE POST-COLONIAL DETECTIVE

Paul Cobley
THE AMERICAN THRILLER
Generic Innovation and Social Change in the 1970s

Christiana Gregoriou
DEVIANCE IN CONTEMPORARY CRIME FICTION

Lee Horsley
THE NOIR THRILLER

Merja Makinen
AGATHA CHRISTIE
Investigating Femininity

Fran Mason
AMERICAN GANGSTER CINEMA
From *Little Caesar* to *Pulp Fiction*

Linden Peach
MASQUERADE, CRIME AND FICTION
Criminal Deceptions

Alistair Rolls and Deborah Walker
FRENCH AND AMERICAN NOIR
Dark Crossings

Susan Rowland
CRIMINAL DECEPTIONS

Adrian Schober
POSSESSED CHILD NARRATIVES IN LITERATURE AND FILM
Contrary States

Heather Worthington
THE RISE OF THE DETECTIVE IN EARLY NINETEENTH-CENTURY
POPULAR FICTION

R. A. York
AGATHA CHRISTIE
Power and Illusion

Crime Files
Series Standing Order ISBN 978–0–333–71471–3 (hardback)
978–0–333–93064–9 (paperback)
(*outside North America only*)

You can receive future titles in this series as they are published by placing a standing order. Please contact your bookseller or, in case of difficulty, write to us at the address below with your name and address, the title of the series and the ISBN quoted above.

Customer Services Department, Macmillan Distribution Ltd, Houndmills, Basingstoke, Hampshire RG21 6XS, England

---

French and American Noir

Dark Crossings

Alistair Rolls and Deborah Walker

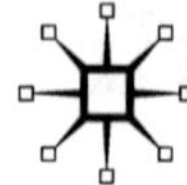

First published 2009 by
PALGRAVE MACMILLAN

Palgrave Macmillan in the UK is an imprint of Macmillan Publishers Limited, registered in England, company number 785998, of Houndmills, Basingstoke, Hampshire RG21 6XS.

Palgrave Macmillan in the US is a division of St Martin's Press LLC, 175 Fifth Avenue, New York, NY 10010.

Palgrave Macmillan is the global academic imprint of the above companies and has companies and representatives throughout the world.

Palgrave® and Macmillan® are registered trademarks in the United States, the United Kingdom, Europe and other countries.

ISBN-13: 978–0–230–53690–6 hardback

This book is printed on paper suitable for recycling and made from fully managed and sustained forest sources. Logging, pulping and manufacturing processes are expected to conform to the environmental regulations of the country of origin.

A catalogue record for this book is available from the British Library.

A catalog record for this book is available from the Library of Congress.

10   9   8   7   6   5   4   3   2   1
18   17   16   15   14   13   12   11   10   09

Transferred to Digital Printing in 2010

To Our Parents

Contents

Acknowledgements

We would like to thank the many individual people and institutions that helped to make this book possible. Our respective institutions, the University of Newcastle (NSW, Australia) and the University of Auckland (Auckland, Aotearoa, New Zealand), supported the project in a number of ways, through research grants and sabbatical leaves that enabled us to work together, or collaboratively at a distance, and at other times individually, on our respective sections of the book. The initial idea behind the project came when we met in Sydney, in 2002, at a bi-annual conference of the Sydney Society of Literature and Aesthetics. We thank the society for bringing us together and providing a platform for researchers like us, working out of quite different theoretical frameworks, and for encouraging the kind of open dialogue that fosters the development of new knowledge.

Early, abridged versions of several chapters in the book were first published in academic journals, and we should like to thank the following editors for kindly granting us their permission to reproduce in this book ideas previously published in the following articles: Professor Peter Goodall (Rolls, A. "Silk or Nylon: Boris Vian, Leg Fetishism and the American Way", *AUMLA Journal of the Australasian Universities Language and Literature Association*, 103, 2005, 93–108); Professor Brian Nelson (Rolls, A. "Throwing Caution to the French Wind: Peter Cheyney's Success Overseas in 1945", *Australian Journal of French Studies*, 43.1, 2006, 35–47); Associate Professor Hélène Jaccomard (Rolls, A. and Vuaille-Barcan, M.-L. " 'Merde à la fin! L'écrivain, c'est vous ou c'est moi?': Jeux de roles dans *Hygiène de l'assassin* d'Amélie Nothomb", *Essays in French Literature*, 43, 2006, 255–273); Alexandre Trudel (Walker, D. "From Honest Thief to Media Psychopath: American Culture through French Film Noir", *Post-Scriptum* 4, 2004, http://www.post-scriptum.org/sin.pag.); Professor Peter Goodall (Walker, D. "Reversing the Remake: Jacques Audiard's *De battre mon cœur s'est arrêté*", *AUMLA-Journal of The Australasian Universities Language and Literature Association, Special Issue*, 2007, 301–310); Hannah Brodsky (Walker, D. "European Dialogues with Hollywood: Classic French Film Noir", *New Zealand and the EU: Perspectives on European Cinema, New Zealand Europe Institute Research Series, Special Issue*, September 2008, 1–16).

Staff at a number of research libraries assisted us in accessing archival material. Deborah Walker wishes to thank in particular, the team at the Archives of the *Bibliothèque du Film* (BIFI) in Paris for their generous and professional support.

Special thanks to film maker Bob Swaim, who took time off a busy writing schedule to grant two extensive interviews to Deborah Walker and who generously provided the cover image of the book. Thanks to Tim Page of the Faculty of Arts, University of Auckland, for technical advice on formatting this image.

Alistair Rolls would like to add the following people: Associate Professors John West-Sooby and Jean Fornasiero of the University of Adelaide with their ongoing encouragement of my work on French noir fiction; Professors Murray Pratt (Nottingham Trent University) and Larry Schehr (University of Illinois) and Dr Marie-Laure Vuaille-Barcan (University of Newcastle), for their unfailing support throughout the writing of this book; Ross Chambers, Professor Emeritus of French and Comparative Literature at the University of Michigan, whose work has been a great inspiration to my own over the last few years; and finally, Associate Professor Chris Dixon (now University of Queensland), with whom I have shared more lunches at the University of Newcastle canteen than I care to remember and many evenings at 93 Bull Street that I wish I could...

A number of colleagues, friends and family read and commented on early drafts and provided much needed encouragement and inspiration. Deborah Walker extends warm thanks to Professor Raylene Ramsay (University of Auckland), Sylvie Solier, Neil Morrison and Pascal Sadoun in this respect.

Finally, many thanks to Clive Bloom and rest of the editorial team at Palgrave, who provided support, encouragement, constructive criticism and professional advice.

Introduction

This book grew out of a paradox; or rather, it grew at the intersection of a number of paradoxes. The initial premise was a reinvestigation, and potentially a reconfiguration, of the exchange of influence between France and the United States, which generated first 'noir' the term, and subsequently a critical discourse around a movable corpus of films and novels that have become known as French noir. The principal paradox lies in the troubling coexistence of two axioms: the films and novels that traditionally constitute French noir are indisputably American in influence; and, at the same time, so many of these works are so obviously caricatural and/or reflexive that their American pastiche is always already made universal.

The second paradox flows from the first: the modernist principles on display reflect concerns with the dissolution of the modern identity, a concern that is, on the one hand, universal and central to all artistic endeavour and, on the other, closely linked to our understanding of the French national identity.

Such icons as the films of Jacques Tati, for example, simultaneously present tales of everyman, of Modernization with a capital 'M', and powerful allegories of the loss of French identity.[1] Even that most potent symbol of the new, modern Paris of the mid-nineteenth century, the flâneur, has been universalized. He is a trope of Modernity, and Paris herself has followed suit: the association with global modernization has seen the French capital reconfigured, by turns, into the capital of modernity and the world.[2] In this light, there is something of a tradition of France and its icons both coinciding with themselves and extending beyond their own parameters into abstraction. Marianne is another example: she is so inescapably French that the Republic cannot be conceptualized without her; and yet, her image is easily and repeatedly reproduced as the symbol of her very antithesis, as Germania, Britannia, even Monarchia. Indeed, every country in Europe can be represented in Marianne's image. She remains, however, recognizably French. Even as she stands holding her flame aloft in New York, her revolutionary French heritage remains intact. And even if this last image, of a dual symbol of France and the United States, is the most striking and the most obviously relevant to this book, it is the concept of universalization that has underpinned so much of this study. Predicated as it is on pastiche and self-referential techniques, noir grows in the tension between work and text, torn between the influence of its creators and the intertextuality that is its interface with its consumers. Ultimately, therefore, our reading of French noir finds its Frenchness in the sensibility of its audience and readership; it is in its very understanding of itself as text, or as universalized product, that its national specificity can be recuperated.

The emphasis of this book will be to show that French noir (from the 1940s and beyond) functions not merely as one particular translation of an American hard-boiled tradition but as a reflection on the nature of recent French history, and especially the psychological trauma of the Second World War and its aftermath. In the first half of this book we show that French noir fiction is not the exclusive realm of authors merely born in France or whose first language is French, or who even write in French for a Francophone readership. Translation plays an important role in producing allegories of the contemporary French condition, a specifically French response to the humiliation of Occupation. In this light, for example, Peter Cheyney and James Hadley Chase become 'French' authors through their impact on French readers.

From this there emerges a new model of the evolution of French noir fiction. On the one hand, it remains undeniable that there is a constant communication and transference between French noir literature and its American counterpart. Even if we go back to the works of Charles Baudelaire we find this transatlantic conversation, Baudelaire's own noir voice, expressing itself through his translations of Edgar Allan Poe. And yet, there is also an argument to be made for an independent evolution of French literary traditions towards noir: a purely French story of negotiating not the otherness of the United States but the otherness of self. This is the ghost narrative of the metropolis past, which dogs the steps of all flâneurs, be they poets, *rentiers* or detectives.[3] If it will always be difficult to read French *polars* without taking into consideration the works of Hammett, Chandler and Cain, a Latin erotic tradition does exist and it extends beyond the *roman noir* into the French canon. For to reposition French noir fiction, to divorce it (if only temporarily) from the American hard-boiled thriller, is to open a new noir perspective, one that has less generic unity but which loses nothing of the mood that gripped French readers and cinema-goers alike in the summer of 1946.

One of the principal difficulties in defining noir lies in its dual application to film and fiction. Our own use of the term comes from studies of post-war French film and fiction, both of which played a substantial part in the development of noir in France. The popular success of Marcel Duhamel's Série Noire, which began in 1945, and the coining of the expression Film Noir shortly afterwards, led quickly to the adoption of the term 'noir' to cover the hard-boiled version of the detective novel or thriller and a certain set of films. The result is that while we may all claim to 'know what is meant' by Film Noir, we can really only explain it in terms of some sort of mood.

A closer look reveals that this paradoxical quality of noir is not equally extended to film and fiction. While film scholars such as James Naremore, author of *More Than Night*,[4] are concerned to dispel the myth of film noir as a genre, preferring to see instead a collection of films with a number of common concerns and motifs, those working on hard-boiled fiction are far happier to take generic concerns as their starting point. Woody Haut, for example, while drawing a distinction between pulp and hard-boiled fiction and noir film, in his book *Pulp Culture*, goes on to analyze the phenomenon of 'neon noir' in reference to crime fiction.[5] For his part, Geoffrey O'Brien, author of *Hardboiled America*, uses the word noir as a hook in his subtitle *Lurid Paperbacks and the Masters of Noir* but makes scarce reference to it thereafter.[6] All this is not to criticize the use of this problematic term but to suggest that defining noir is at the same time both a difficult task and one that is, implicitly at least, inevitable. In this book, we refer to novels and films that can easily be termed noir, but which reveal themes that are shared with other texts, not all of which so easily accept the appellation. In this way, the purpose of this book is to analyze what we consider to be films and novels of critical importance in the history of French noir, and our emphasis is on the analysis of key texts rather than broad generic sweeps.

The most enduring myth that this book seeks to dispel is that French noir was a post-war borrowing or simple translation into the French language of an American genre. At this point it will suffice to draw on the preface to Boris Vian's pseudonymous novel of 1946 *J'irai cracher sur vos tombes*, the text that perhaps more than any other appears to define this traditional view of French noir fiction. For if Naremore elects Vian as the incarnation of noir mood, it is due to the esprit governing this singular work, which by virtue of its status as a phoney translation (it purports to be the French translation of a novel by unknown black American author Vernon Sullivan) can be considered as a pastiche of noir itself. Ostensibly intended as a joke, the work nonetheless achieves noir status when, as a cult novel, it is reappraised as having genuine literary pretensions.

The joke lies in the way in which Vian plays with a dual literary tradition as well as the duality of race (an African-American man crosses the line and passes for white, and his black murder serves to answer an original white murder). Noir, therefore, becomes a troubled category: just as the colour of a man's skin is not a clear indicator of racial lineage, a novel's espousal of certain tropes and settings cannot usefully align it within a clearly defined tradition. What is on trial is the stigmatization of a whole breed of post-war, Paris-based literary creation as 'American'. Noir thrillers which were best-sellers were also beset by the suspicion of American influence, which prevented them from receiving the critical attention awarded to other novels—novels admitted unquestioningly into the French canon. In this light, there is little choice for Vian/Sullivan but to establish a new tradition, since the one in which his novel would logically fit, and with which critics of French noir have striven to align it in order to justify its literary quality, has, according to the author, rejected him: 'Sullivan was all the more willing to leave his manuscript in France because his previous experience with American publishers had shown him the pointlessness of trying to publish in his home country' (Sullivan 1973: 10). The preface of the novel indicates that the work's affinity with a 'more Latin erotic tradition' (1973: 10) lies equally in an underlying subtlety of style. The power of Vian's joke is to suggest that French noir is embedding itself, self-consciously, in a French literary tradition, and that American novels are aligning themselves with it and not vice versa.

Yet, all is subverted in Vian/Sullivan, and the hybridity of the novel's identity at the level of authorship is immediately satirized in the preface by an allusion to the debt that Sullivan owes to the American hard-boiled genre: 'You can, moreover, also find in these pages the clear influence of Cain . . . and of more recent authors, such as Chase' (Sullivan 1973: 10). Nevertheless, Vian/Sullivan's text goes further than these Anglo-American influences in terms of sadistic realism.

The novel's 'hero' Lee Anderson is simultaneously black and white. As such, it is exemplary of the way in which a novel is not only noir but actively *noired*. That is to say, that knowledge based on the phenomenological truth of what is before our eyes is simultaneously, and again paradoxically, counterbalanced by belief in a mythological reconstruction of events leading from the past into the present. Noir's dependence on these apparently mutually exclusive phenomena is at the heart of its fetishism.

The second half of this book deals with film: specifically the multiple 'crossings' between French and American film noir. Here, the industrial nature of cinema, as opposed to literature, together with the enormous economic and ideological stakes of film lead finally to an examination of the complex relationship between French and American noir in economic as well aesthetic and cultural terms: reflective of the uneasy ambivalence of the French towards the United States.

In a number of key French noir film texts from the 1950s on, including the screen adaptation of Vian/Sullivan's text, America functions as a sign, signifying French ambivalence towards processes of capitalist-driven modernization, and as a catalyst for an examination of France's own internal tensions. The result, we argue, is film that encapsulates and extends the essential points of this study in arguing for French and American noir film and fiction emerging out of the anxieties and pleasures of a complex and ongoing transatlantic exchange.

1
Fetishistic Noir: Charles Baudelaire and Léo Malet

If there is any consensus that emerges from the literature surrounding noir—be it Film Noir or *le roman noir français*—it is that the term has been used so frequently, with so many meanings and applications, that it has become almost unusable as a critical term. It is from within this incoherent framework of overuse on the one hand and, in some instances, critical oblivion on the other that a certain number of novels can potentially be considered—for want of a better expression—as classics of French noir fiction. Furthermore, despite, and to a certain extent because of, the difficulty of clearly defining French noir fiction (if noir is anything, it is essentially unclear) or tracing its origins, the readings of these texts will be made against a number of vexed assumptions. Most importantly, the novels examined here do not simply inherit a noir mantle; rather, to borrow from Sartrean discourse, they 'exist' noir. In place of the passive attributes of the adjective 'noir', our analysis will be underpinned by the more active verb 'to noir'. It will be shown, for example, how the French noir novel begins 'to noir' actively and self-consciously in the period immediately following the Second World War.

Such a position may seem reactionary, suggesting an alignment of the French noir novel and the launch of the Série Noire in 1945. It does not, however, mark a simple opposition to those who argue that the roman noir had wartime, or pre-war origins in France. Indeed, it is important to understand that the elements of French noir, together with a tradition of thriller writing, existed before Marcel Duhamel's project came into being. It is also important to recognize the difficulty of arguing for a specific starting point for a phenomenon whose very existence resides in the muddying of a number of long-standing literary lineages. And yet, those who seek to unseat Duhamel often wish to put in his place other equally contentious dates and contenders, foremost among which is Léo Malet, and particularly his novel *120, Rue de la Gare* (1943). While the legitimate pretensions of this novel to classic noir status will be weighed and, to a certain extent, postulated here, given its abundant usage of traditionally accepted motifs, it will be shown that there is a significant change in mood in France generally, and in Paris more specifically, between 1943 and 1945. This change is not merely historical; neither is it purely one of literary convention. Between *120, Rue de la Gare* and the launch of the Série Noire there is a shift that is both historical and literary. The Liberation of Paris does something to French nostalgia, something that had happened before in French literature, and which is somehow particular to French literature; and this something—this way in which texts can be said 'to noir'—is crucial to the readings of the novels chosen for the present volume.

The origins of French noir fiction

Two bold statements form a useful starting point for our discussion. Firstly, James Naremore sums up his discussion of the history of the idea of noir (referring in particular, although not exclusively, to Film Noir) with this description: 'Consequently, depending on how it is used, it [noir] can describe a dead period, a nostalgia for something that never quite existed, or perhaps even a vital tradition' (1998: 39). If we are to gain any insight at all into the importance, or even necessity, of the emergence of the Série Noire during that traumatic period when *les années noires* gave way to the Cold War, we must understand the ramifications of Naremore's expression of nostalgia: to noir is not to remember the past with longing or to harbour delusions as to the way life used to be; instead, it is to act in the present with no idea of what is to come and in full (if suppressed) knowledge that our memories of the past are longings and no more than that. The noir path lies between desire and knowledge; it is a way of compromising, and as such it is deeply fetishistic.[1]

Nostalgia will be a crucial concept in the interpretations of French noir novels that follow. In most detective fiction, be it the English golden-age whodunits of Agatha Christie, the wistful investigations of Georges Simenon's Maigret or the hard-boiled thrillers on either side of the Atlantic, there is a remembrance of things past, often a wallowing in better days. Indeed, this would seem to be an important hook for detective fiction's readership: a part of us all craves the unique perspective of rose-tinted glasses. And this is precisely where the nostalgia of noir begins to diverge from simple reminiscence and take on the fetishistic edge of mythologizing. When a work of French Surrealism, such as Louis Aragon's *Le Paysan de Paris*, laments the past glories of Paris, it falls in line with a nostalgic tradition extending back to Charles Baudelaire. Baudelaire, in his prose poems, and the Surrealists, with their attempted synthesis of the incompatible realms of the dream and the waking moment, act as fetishists. That is to say that they do not entirely confront the unpalatable truth that is presented to them. Instead, a kind of psychosis is erected whereby they fail to register the truth—except that they can see it, and still they choose not to believe it. The result is a dual, paradoxical state: they both know the truth and believe in an alternative state of affairs.

This convenient world-view allows the subject to ignore the present while simultaneously living in it and reconfiguring the past. The fetish, a goddess alighting amid a banal street scene in Baudelaire's case, or a moment of objective chance for Aragon or André Breton, acts as a symbol of the truth while simultaneously masking it.[2] It thus provides a way of negotiating reality by making room for a lie: in order to contemplate the harsh reality of the prosaic Paris of the present, the fetishistic poet invents a utopian vision of the past—the myth of old Paris.

In noir fiction, the 'noiring' of the text lies in the way that instincts replace knowledge or are used by the protagonist as a means of ignoring it. In the classic French noir novels of the post-war years (e.g., those that open the Série Noire), the immediate future and past reveal themselves in an equally blurred light. Whereas the harsh conditions of the Occupation seem to translate in Malet's fiction into a counter-nostalgic 'hope for the future' (a mythologizing of days to come), the tainted victory of the Liberation, with its overtones of dawning Americanization, forces rose-tinted glasses back on to the past.

Our second key introductory statement relativizes an attitude towards modernity that has marked so much literature, French or otherwise, placing noir in the specific cultural context of the time of its production:

> The plot is only the bare bones of the noir novel; it is fleshed out by social history...There is a need to move beyond the sphere of the individual and to understand those unexpected events, those accidents of history, inside the socially determined framework, that prove crucial and which are the modern equivalent of destiny.
>
> (Pons 1997: 7)

Jean Pons is clearly striving to draw a distinction between the traditional plot-driven whodunit and the essentially mood-driven thriller.
To the extent that it embraces the mood in which it is produced, the
noir novel is pointedly 'anti-social'. Not only is it vaguely and universally modernist in its critique of the present, it also bears the marks of
its era like so many scars on the flesh of its narrative.

The historical background to the dawn of the Série Noire is painted in
Marcel Duhamel's ironically entitled autobiography *Raconte pas ta vie*, in
which we find the oft-quoted reference to his discovery of Peter Cheyney
and James Hadley Chase:

> It's around that time that I visited Marcel Achard's home in rue de
> Courty. I cannot recall exactly what prompted me to go. Perhaps I was
> drawn by his infectious good humour or, quite simply, it was out of
> friendship.
>
> It was during that visit that he gave me three books to read: *This
> Man is Dangerous* and *Poison Ivy*, by an English writer called Peter
> Cheyney, and *No Orchids for Miss Blandish*, by a certain Hadley Chase.
>
> I read them. I laughed reading the first one; by the second I was
> really becoming interested; and when I came to the third one, I set
> out to translate it as I had done with *Tropic of Cancer*, just for fun at
> that stage. That ended up leading further than I could have thought.
>
> (Duhamel 1972: 491)

'Around that time' refers to the period of tension that immediately preceded the German retreat from Paris, a time where the occupying forces
and the Resistance were increasingly trading blows in the streets. This is
a troubled period in French history; it is the moment when people who
had previously praised the order brought by the Occupation now flocked
to the side of the Resistance. The truth, of course, as in all such situations, lies somewhere between the courageous acts of self-sacrifice and
the last-minute attempts to join the bandwagon. Duhamel's objective in
giving his account of a life lived through such times is quite clear:

> But what I'm telling you is that… I was there and I saw it, that's all.
> And if I'm speaking about it, it's because so much nonsense has been
> said on this topic and, at the same time, shame has caused a veil to be
> drawn over what really happened. We had to wait for the remarkable
> film *The Sorrow and the Pity*[3] to bring the truth out on a great number
> of points, notably the general atmosphere.
>
> (1972: 489)

It is our contention that, at the time of writing these lines, Duhamel had already settled his scores with the truth of the past. And the vehicle for his unveiling was a self-referentially veiled format: the French noir novel.

The three texts referred to above, which open the Série Noire in 1945, may be read as an allegory of France post-Occupation and of a period in which any glory that was won was done so with dirty hands. In its own way, Duhamel's autobiography resembles the works of the Série Noire, not only to the extent that it tells the story of its time (and he says of the future of detective fiction in general that 'if, like the Série Noire, it draws on real-life events and faithfully reflects its time, it will have the same fate as our society and will only change as it changes' [1972: 595]), but also in its focus on quotidian events and matters literary. There is no single defining moment of *les années noires* that comes across in Duhamel's account—the reader is instead witness to everyday tribulations recounted more or less in the order in which they were lived. And the most passionate description of the book is perhaps saved for Duhamel's encounter with Hemingway, whose presence among the liberating troops places American literature centre stage, providing a literary footnote to the famous images of jazzmen arriving on the heels of the departing German armies.

The final line of the book completes its ludic dimension, giving a noir twist to the narrative: 'And now, excuse me if I bid you my leave, but it is time for me to make myself some memories' (1972: 595). For this calculated distillation and colouring of remembrance, more than anything, expresses the esprit of the French noir novel: if a hard-boiled detective novel is a social critique, in which details small and large are all grist to the author's mill, then the novel that is truly 'noired' is one that revisits the past, refocuses on it and, through death and dishonour, makes it bearable.

In his essay on the *roman noir français* Robert Deleuse gives due prominence to the end of the Second World War and all the bad faith that accompanied it. He does not, however, specify how the reconfiguring of France's wartime history and the emergence of a certain type of literature are linked:

> 1945 is the year when France extracted herself, lock, stock and barrel, from full-blown Pétainism only to plunge body and soul into acute de Gaulle-mania. On 9 May the triumphant General solemnly proclaimed that 'the French command was present and party to the act of capitulation'. What he overlooked to mention was that the State,

in almost its entirety, was on the run ... from one château to another. This attack of amnesia on the part of Free France, which was destined solely to serve its own political ambitions, would cost the country fifty years of painful dirty linen, which even today we have still not finished washing. In terms of what is of most direct concern to us here, 1945 was above all the year of the Série Noire.

(Deleuze 1997: 59)

Deleuse neither makes explicit the importance of this juxtaposition of dates, nor is he inclined to lend too much importance to the place of Duhamel's series in the history of the *roman noir* in France. Reasons for this include the fact that his history is more concerned with the development of a type of fiction *within* France rather than a type of French fiction. His argument is that the two types of fiction share common ground, but that when the French noir novel comes into being, its descent can be traced back to a nineteenth-century tradition that is entirely French, including 'Balzac, Mérimée, Zévaco, Sue, Gautier, Hugo, Féval, Zola' (Deleuze 1997: 57). He is also keen to stress that the American noir novel does not enter France for the first time in 1945:

Totally American at the outset, the *roman noir* accosted the Old Continent from 1939 with the English writer James Hadley Chase and, four years later, with the French writer Léo Malet. In 1945 Gaston Gallimard allowed Marcel Duhamel ... to create the Série Noire. Contrary to certain misguided notions, however, it was not in fact in the Série Noire that the French *roman noir* ended up.... As for the American *roman noir*, contrary to a number of stories that have been bandied about, it was during the 1930s and not at the time of the Libération that it appeared in France in a collection entitled 'Chefs-d'œuvre du roman d'aventures [Masterpeices of the Adventure Story]', at whose helm was to be found the same Gaston Gallimard, who also created the magazine *Détective*.

(1997: 55)

Deleuse's comments must be read against the framework of a knee-jerk reaction whereby the French *roman noir* and the novels of the Série Noire are deemed to be synonymous. Claire Gorrara is another scholar to trace the distinction between noir fiction in France and French noir, as shown in Chapter 2 on Boris Vian and the Série Noire. The point must be made that Deleuse is dealing with a phenomenon called *roman noir*, which he basically considers to be a detective story, generally (and increasingly in the twentieth century) in the hard-boiled tradition, whereas we are investigating tropes within novels that make them 'noir', ways in which narrative can be said to be 'noired'. Like Gorrara, Deleuse considers French noir fiction—that is, fiction resembling the American hard-boiled thriller written by an author of French nationality—to begin with the first Nestor Burma novel:

> It was on a grey-green night [*couleur vert-de-gris*] that the French *roman noir* chose to make its first appearance hard-boiled style. Its first author, Léo Malet, was thirty-four... when, at the end of November 1943 under German Occupation, his famous *120, Rue de la Gare* appeared, giving life to the first French private detective of literary history: Nestor Burma.
>
> (1997: 58–9)

Clearly, it is not simply because Malet wrote what Deleuse calls a '*roman policier made in France*' (1997: 59) under the German Occupation that the latter uses the adjective *vert-de-gris*, the colour used to denote the German military uniform. His intention is to show that the type of novels that would be exemplified (and ultimately eclipsed) by the Série Noire and, above all, Duhamel's own translation of Peter Cheyney's *Poison Ivy—La Môme vert-de-gris*—had already begun to capture the popular imagination before the Liberation of Paris.[4]

The aim of this book is not to challenge Deleuse's balanced and thorough account of the development of the *roman noir français*. Indeed, a valuable precedent is set in the historical continuity that Deleuse traces back through what he sees as the American and French traditions. It must be borne in mind, however, that Deleuse's decision to nominate Léo Malet's *120, Rue de la Gare* as the first French noir novel, and thereby to posit this work within a chronology of influence extending back to the nineteenth-century literature of both France and the United States, leaves him in a perverse position. If the motifs evolving from the social realism of the hard-boiled detective novel can be traced back to the nineteenth century, and if 1945 is so pointedly rejected as a turning point, why should 1943 be invested with such importance? It is, therefore, all the more important that it be acknowledged at the very outset of this book that the position taken here has its own share of perversity. Our reasons for wishing to follow those other critics, whom Deleuse—not without reason—accuses of excessively concentrating on the years immediately following the Second World War, lie in what we deem to be a history of Parisian literary mythologizing of the past, which is at its height in the nineteenth century, and which, in our opinion, makes a significant comeback with the dawning of the Cold War.

Shades of light and noir

In order to trace the re-emergence of Parisian mythologies in French noir fiction, a closer look needs to be taken at some of the critical response to Malet's novels of the Occupation. On the face of it, Léo Malet's first novel under his own name has all the trappings of the novels that are analyzed here. As Claire Gorrara writes, '[w]ith its obsessive reworking of the themes of memory, loss and identity, *120, rue de la Gare* prefigures a moment of social and cultural transition for a nation still under the heel of the invader but soon to face the upheavals of post-war European reconstruction' (Gorrara 2001: 272). Indeed, Gorrara is in no doubt as to the importance of this work, referring to it as 'a watershed in the history of French detective fiction', a model 'for a specifically French roman noir' (2001: 271). And yet, it may also be argued that the very way in which Malet deals with the 'themes of memory, loss and identity' serves equally to set *120, rue de la Gare* apart from the first novels of the Série Noire, or at least to deliver a prototype from which they will develop in crucial ways.

While it foreshadows the translations of the novels of Peter Cheyney and James Hadley Chase published in 1945, inasmuch as it exploits the same kinds of dichotomies,[5] Malet's novel seems—not only through Burma's ultimate success in solving the mystery, but also via the very approach he adopts towards his investigation—to achieve a synthesis of the opposing elements that make up the theatre in which he must act. Peter Cheyney's Lemmy Caution, for his part, will fail to find a smooth synthesis; his will be the tortured path of the fetishist, his third way being trodden in an interstitial area of constant oscillation. While the 'grey area' of the post-war noir masterpieces represents an indecisive juggling between black and white, the grey of Nestor Burma is a toning down of the *années noires*, which appears based on both a touching and sincere belief in the past and a genuine confidence in better times ahead.

As already shown, nostalgia is a key element of noir, constituting, as Naremore suggests, an apprehension of the past, a desire to cling on to 'something that never quite existed'. In Malet's novel the past strikes a clearer contrast with the bleak present of the Occupation in a way that it will not do vis-à-vis the rather treacherous light of the Liberation. For the future will offer less hope once the Germans are gone and victory has been, to all intents and purposes, won. It is the unclear nature of this victory that forces a fetishistic negotiation of the past; the attendant feelings of ambivalence of the French people towards their Allied liberators make synthesis of the dichotomous elements of past and future impossible.

This slight but important change of perspective must be borne in mind when considering the way that 'Malet encourages [with his exploitation of the aforementioned binaries] the reader to interrogate the conditions of the Occupation in new ways' (Gorrara 2001: 274). For, as Gorrara points out, when Nestor Burma uses Surrealist techniques to solve the mysteries of *120, rue de la Gare* he moves between the dream and the waking moment, disturbing 'the boundaries between the real and the imaginary' (2001: 278). His victory, however, results in a successful intertwining of the two zones. As such, Burma's success in itself undermines his noir status because a noir victory is necessarily a tainted one. For this reason, Gorrara's assessment of the outcome of *120, rue de la Gare* reaffirms the novel's role as a crucial forerunner to the classics of post-war French noir fiction: '[his] reintegration into the charged atmosphere of the Occupation is achieved through his adaptability, a quality which means that out of all the characters introduced he is the one best suited to project himself into the post-war world as victor rather than victim' (2001: 282). Clear victory and happy resolution run counter to the fetishistic tainting that is essential to noir. The overwhelming feeling of realism that marks the 1945 vintage dictates that victory must be achieved by victims and through victimization, not in place of them. Victory itself becomes the victim of French noir fiction.

It is our contention that the masterpieces of post-war noir exist in the motion between continually juxtaposed opposites and not in the mere establishment of a binary narrative structure. For his part, Steve Smith concurs indirectly with Gorrara. The wavering between two poles to which Smith points in the title of his essay on two of Malet's novels (*Les Eaux troubles de Javel* and *Brouillard au pont de Tolbiac*, which date from 1957 and 1956, respectively) refers to the cold objectivity of the whodunit sleuth, at one end of the scale, and the emotionally involved, hands-on approach of the hard-boiled private eye, at the other. Malet's own blend of *roman noir* appears to incorporate aspects of both styles of detective novel. And it is in its failure to synthesize these that, in Smith's opinion, *Brouillard au pont de Tolbiac* falls outside the criteria of the noir novel:

> *Brouillard* is not in the final analysis an authentically noir text because, although he is exposed to the possibility, Burma does not fully face up to the choice between madness and death, on the one

hand, and detachment and compromise, on the other. The means of this avoidance is provided by Bélita, who functions as a sign of Benoît, a substitute object which permits access to Burma's former 'mad' idealism but only as a fantasmagoric projection. He is never, then, quite exposed to the vacuity of this fantasy, the 'nothingness' at the core of desire beyond a margin that frames the stability of his present identity.

(Smith 2000: 135)

This represents an interesting shift from a Nestor Burma who, in the years of the Occupation, mediates between black and white, eventually achieving synthesis, to one who, in the mid-1950s (the decade traditionally considered to be 'post-war' with all this entails in terms of French ambivalence towards the United States) points up the tension between the two sides of the dichotomy. In terms of our understanding of the verb 'to noir', however, this shift is actually *towards* noir. Lemmy Caution and the other 'heroes' of the first Série Noire novels and the other key early noir texts examined in the present study are noir to the very extent that they avoid the decisions mentioned above; their noirness lies exactly in this fetishistic attitude to the poles of knowledge and desire. Female characters who act as fetishes, such as Bélita in Smith's scenario, are French versions of the femme fatale in that they focus the protagonist's gaze on an illusion, blurring the black and white of truth and lie, present and past, myth and reality.

Smith notes an absence of nostalgia in Malet's post-war work. By nostalgia he seems to be referring to a desire for things past, and not necessarily for things as they might have been:

[I]n *Brouillard* the project of reconciliation [of public and personal] is threatened by the fact that both aspects of the story are linked together through the figure of Burma himself. The story does this, perhaps intentionally, by drawing on the scenario of Simenon's *L'Affaire St.-Fiacre*, but without the latter's tone of wistful nostalgia.

(Smith 2000: 129)

There is, however, a deal of nostalgia in the novels of the Occupation; and it is at times directly comparable to the wistful kind that characterizes the Maigret novels.

Unlike Lemmy Caution et al., Nestor Burma does not avoid the gaze of the females of his entourage. The femmes fatales, when they appear, are met face to face, and this is in spite of 'the erotic importance that

Malet accords to the underwear and to the stockings and suspenders of the women whom Nestor Burma meets' (Durozoi 1984: 178). The high heels and hosiery by which a woman is known in the Série Noire act as fetishistic objects, simultaneously veiling and highlighting her sexuality. By presenting such trappings before the eyes of the protagonist, the femme fatale offers him a means of negotiating his way between the present and the myth of the past. When Malet has recourse to the accoutrements of noir desire, it appears almost against his will, or as if he is making a conscious effort to conform to the rules of the *roman noir* (a kind of unity of costume). Thus, it is that a pair of heels lead Burma to discover the mysterious woman in *120, Rue de la Gare*: 'Then I saw with amazement that a high-heeled shoe, a woman's shoe, was sticking out under the folds of the curtain' (Malet 1943: 95). Hélène Parmentier does not remain long hidden beneath her fetish, however; Burma soon looks her directly in the eye: 'As my hand touched hers she slowly opened her beautiful, nostalgic eyes and looked at me in astonishment' (Malet 1943: 103).

Embedded in the narrative alongside similar motifs, the hunches that Burma takes may well resemble those guiding Lemmy Caution's investigations; they are, nonetheless, more calculated. When he chances his arm, therefore, '[r]isking [his] reputation and [his] freedom on a burst of intuition', it is not without the knowledge afforded by these beautiful windows onto the past: 'Her magnificent eyes moved me more than ever', and again '[Her beautiful eyes] with their nostalgic depths' (Malet 1943: 116, 119). Burma is quite simply less lost than the heroes of the Série Noire; for him the present is only bleak in comparison with the dependable values that are a past for which he longs, and a future that must necessarily be better than the present.

When Burma first sees the woman who he later discovers is Hélène Parmentier, she is standing in the middle of a play on words that will be the centre of both the novel's plot and its Surrealism:

> Her eyes, as though washed bright by tears, reflected an ineffable nostalgia.... She may have been twenty years old and admirably represented the type of woman that one only meets in train stations, nocturnal fantasies visible only to the senses of those fatigued by travel, and who disappear with the night that spawned them.
>
> (Malet 1943: 12)

This scene is set on a platform at the main railway station in Lyon, which is pointedly not the Gare de Lyon. Gérard Durozoi sees in

Léo Malet's detective fiction—and in particular his later series, the 'Nouveaux Mystères de Paris'—a popularized form of Surrealism comparable in importance to Jacques Prévert's *Paroles*. Textually speaking, the extract above is much more than a popularization of Surrealist tropes or referencing along the lines suggested by Durozoi; this brief encounter in a railway station can be interpreted as a sophisticated rewrite of a key scene from André Breton's *Nadja*, in which a train simultaneously surging out of the station and taking root on the tracks offers a fleeting glimpse of impossible synthesis (of motion or transcendence and immobility or immanence), the very essence of convulsive beauty. This is crucial: not only does Hélène's appearance suggest the presence of two parallel universes, one of everyday acts of train travel and the other of dream and fantasy, but it is also a moment of Surrealism when—for the briefest possible moment—these two worlds collide and become one. And all this is through the mediation of Burma's gaze. For although most of the art of Surrealism is a matter of juxtapositions, and of playful flirting in the zone between two sides of a binary opposition, there is always an underlying drive towards synthesis. That Burma should manage successfully to balance parallel worlds—to recall the past, and indeed to discover the true nature of past events, while walking in the city streets of the present day—makes him more than a flâneur. The flâneur of Baudelaire's prose poems is confronted by abstract truths and everyday existents, but they remain for him unworkable juxtapositions. Burma, on the other hand, fuses the two in such a way that his waking dreams communicate the keys to his cases. This is essentially what pulls Burma through his investigations, and it is effectively what separates *120, Rue de la Gare* from the noir novels of the Liberation era.[6]

Prose poetry and the fetish

Malet's work is illuminating in the way that it acts as a litmus test for the subtle but crucial change in the nature of noir brought about by the mood of Liberation in 1944. The Parisian focus remains the same; the difference lies simply in the question of mediation. It will be seen in subsequent chapters that the 1950s are generally considered emblematic of an ambivalent French attitude towards the United States. Teresa Bridgeman discusses this phenomenon in terms of the post-war Burma stories:

By 1954, the year in which the *Nouveaux Mystères* were launched, the German Occupation was physically over. Nevertheless, it still remained for this experience to be incorporated into an historical projection of French national identity, a process complicated by the growth of a cultural influence from beyond the borders of Europe.

(Bridgeman 1998: 60)

One of our principal objectives here is to signal that the post-war phenomenon to which Bridgeman refers is perceptible in works of French fiction as early as 1945. This post-war French experience (with all that this entails in terms of a blurring of national identity) and the development of a 'noiring'—as opposed to a simple mediation or synthesis—will be the guiding principle of French detective fiction from as early as the inception of the Série Noire.

Yet Léo Malet does not shift away from Parisian literary sources any more than he does from the capital himself. The shift is simply from the *point suprême* of Surrealist synthesis towards constant tension as expressed in certain nineteenth-century attitudes towards modernity. Bridgeman herself recalls Malet's own chauvinistic pride in the long French tradition of detective fiction, noting how Paris and its novels provide an extensive matrix within which French noir writing should be read:

> The deployment of an intertextual network of references can be seen as an explicit assertion of the place of the *Nouveaux Mystères* in the French tradition of *noir* and Parisian works, both reminding readers of this heritage and reassuring them of the participation of the texts and themselves in a shared national cultural identity.
>
> (1998: 60)

Noir, via its allegorical representations of republican iconography (see Chapter 2), will play a major role in the reconstruction of the French national psyche. To this end, Paris will become a key intertext. As Bridgeman notes, 'within the context of a dispossessed post-war readership, such references to other imaginary morphologies of the city serve as security rather than as destabilization' and 'Paris itself ceases to be a somewhat superficial backdrop to the action of the narrative, and becomes instead the central cohesive element of the text' (1998: 61, 63).

The change from Occupation to post-war detective fiction, as demonstrated by Gorrara, Smith and Bridgeman, runs parallel to the evolution of Baudelaire's conception of the poet as flâneur, which is itself a shifting response to the alienating face of modernity. François Rivière makes the link between Malet's use of intertextuality and the notion of Paris as mythology; Burma's Paris by night is thus 'doubly black [*noir*] as a result of the [wartime] *black-out* and doubly Parisian by virtue of mythological reverence' (Rivière 1995: 62). Durozoi, too, points the way towards a new poetics in Malet's work, one deeply rooted in the interplay of hard-boiled prose and Surrealist poetry:

> It is not appropriate to interpret this way in which poetry is transformed, this transition from the traditional format to detective-fiction prose, in banal terms by speaking of the introduction, into the detective genre, of a mere poetic 'atmosphere', with all that that implies in terms of loose description, more or less precious vocabulary and evanescent characters. Léo Malet's novels, and especially the Nestor Burma series ... are, on the contrary, extremely precise in their description (which we might refer to as their 'realistic' side); his characters are individuated and rigorously defined, and the vocabulary used is quite mundane. If they constitute 'another form' of poetry, it is not only as a result of specific methods but also because, within the specific framework of their plot, they teem with quotations, allusions and references, all the result of their author's past.
>
> (Durozoi 1984: 172–3)

The 'other form' of poetry that these novels espouse may well be considered a close relative to the prose poetry of Charles Baudelaire, in which Paris itself becomes synonymous with the prose poem, a convulsive and paradoxical form in which poetry and prose forever coincide without ever joining in synthesis. Thus, for Baudelaire, Paris is an impossible synthesis of its present form and a dreamscape made up of a mythologized past. Nestor Burma's Paris offers both sides of this opposition, '[i]n such a way that, for today's reader, [it] acquires a new quality: it progressively moves away from the Paris that we know by sight and becomes almost dream-like; or, more precisely, it is posited in an interstitial space, caught between the realms of the real and the imaginary' (Durozoi 1984: 175).

Ross Chambers has traced the fine distinction between Baudelaire's use of the flâneur poet as mediator of the binary structures of his poetry and art criticism on the one hand, and as witness to the tension between the two irreconcilable faces of the same coin on the other. Baudelaire is, as Chambers states, 'the prototype of what can be called the critical intellectual, who occupies an unaligned or third position'; this despite his persistence in 'interpreting the two-sidedness of the readerly city as a simple dichotomy—expressed particularly as a dichotomy of night and day' (Chambers 1999: 220–1). Reduced to its simplest terms, the development of Baudelaire's treatment of this poetic tension has to do with representation. As the poet moves—over the course of *Les Fleurs du mal* into *Les Petits Poèmes en prose*—from the fringes of voyeurism, from which he re-presents (belatedly, as omniscient narrator) the dichotomies of the modern city with artistic objectivity and the necessary mediation of memory, into the tortured path of the flâneur (both in and out of the action on the streets) he increasingly puts himself inside the poem, as the eyes of the reader, before which the city streets that are his poems are rendered immediate and raw present.[7]

It is for this reason that the metropolis of *Le Spleen de Paris* becomes, as Michel Covin argues (2000 passim), the very incarnation of the dichotomous structure inherent in 'prose poetry', a constant source of irreconcilable tension between the tropes of poetry and prose. Paris is a prose poem, therefore, because of the double-edged way in which it is negotiated. On the one hand, it is experienced as real in the sense that one can walk in it, following the 'natural' flows of its crowds— in this way one reads the city unreflectively, as a gawping *badaud*; on the other hand, it is also mythological insofar as one can step back from it, painting it from memory and infusing it with one's desire for it to have been other than it ever was—in which case one writes the city with the controlling power of the *voyeur*. So, just as the flâneur of Baudelaire's prose poetry has the particularity of combining these two positions *at the same time*, Paris, too, becomes an oxymoron: both the city that it is in situation, in real time (existentially), and one that it is, as it were, essentially (in the sense that it never really was at all). And this double-edged stance, which runs parallel to the concept of noir, is—as is noir itself—a response to modernity, such that in the aftermath of the Second World War in Paris a literature again emerged in response to 'historical conditions of accelerated cultural change that', as Ross Chambers describes when discussing the physical and psychological upheaval of the mid-nineteenth century, 'made the city uncannily readable by splitting it, in the eyes of its belated citizens, into an unconvincing presence haunted by an unrecoverable past' (Chambers 1999: 222). In this light, the nostalgia seen by Naremore at the core of noir becomes a way of dealing with an unpalatably real present by fetishizing the past, of looking between two untenable myths rather than confronting the truth. That is not to say that noir hides the truth from its readers; rather, it exposes the mythological underpinnings of modernity, revealing that truth itself does not so much lie behind as within the interaction of opposing narratives.

Baudelaire's fetishism, his poetic response to the trauma of the modern present, is the basis of the noir attitude of post-Liberation Paris. If Baudelaire is proto-noir, in much the same way as his surnaturalistic overvaluation of mundane objects has led to his being included uppermost among the forefathers of Surrealism,[8] then what tropes in his prose poems can properly be seen as noir?

In 'Le Crépuscule du soir' ('Evening Twilight') the present is noir, a veil through which dreams of the past can emerge in the fetishistic trappings that will become the hallmark of the femme fatale:

> or it may remind one of those curious costumes dancers wear, that reveal under dark transparent gauze the muted splendors of a dazzling skirt, just as the delicious past shines through the somber present; and the gold and silver stars sprinkled over it, represent the fires of fancy that shine brightly only in the deep mourning of the night.[9]

What is offered here is a noir reading praxis. This poem recalls the translucent stockings of the noir novel, which lead to a reconfiguring of the past, not in place of the darkness of the present but in full knowledge that the stars in the sky can only shine against a black background. Dusk is, then, not a synthesis of sombre hues (prosaic reality) and shining stars (poetic essence); rather, it shows the way in which the two interact.

And then there is 'Mademoiselle Bistouri' ('Miss Bistoury') who sees in all men the reflection of her own desire for a doctor:

> 'Well, you know, I've got a funny notion, and I don't dare tell him, the dear boy! I'd like him to come to see me with his instrument case and his apron, and even with a little blood on it.'
>
> She said this with perfect simplicity, as a man might say to an actress he was in love with: 'I should like you to be dressed in the costume you wear in the famous role you created.'
>
> And I still obstinately persisted: 'Can you remember the time and the occasion when you first felt this particular passion?'
>
> (Baudelaire 1970: 97)

This poem tells of the desire, born long ago, to dress the other as we should wish him to appear, to refashion the past in order to bring succour to the condition that is our present. This is a singular reflection of the male gaze that so often reads the female figure allegorically.[10]

'La Belle Dorothée' ('The Beautiful Dorothea') adds another aspect to the attributes of post-war noir fiction: Dorothea can be read as a poeticization of Marianne. She first transports Paris to the Mediterranean in a way that recalls Meursault's murder of the Arab in Albert Camus's *L'Étranger* (*The Outsider*):

> The sun overwhelms the city with its perpendicular and fulminating rays; the sand is blinding and the sea glitters. The stupefied world weakly succumbs and takes its siesta, a siesta that is a sort of delicious death in which the sleeper, between sleeping and waking, tastes all the voluptuous delight of annihilation.
>
> Meanwhile Dorothea, strong and proud as the sun, walks along the deserted street, the only living thing at this hour under the blue, a shining black spot in the sunlight.
>
> (Baudelaire 1970: 50)

Blinded by the light of day, the people of Paris gladly accept oblivion, all except Dorothea whose figure is cut in black against the blaze of the sky. This image of a woman refusing to submit beneath the weight of reality will reappear on the posters of Paul Colin in 1944 in the form of 'Libération'. Blue is also the first use of colour in the poem; it is followed in turn by: a 'red parasol', an 'enormous pile of hair that is almost blue' and 'her white smile' (1970: 50–1). Thus the colours of Paris are joined by their third element to make up the banner of the Republic. Dorothea's heroic role as Marianne is completed (since images of Marianne have often shown her partially or wholly naked) with a glimpse of her leg. The heels and stockings of the femme fatale begin to find their way back to Delacroix via this image:

> From time to time the sea breeze lifts a corner of her flowing skirt, revealing a superb and glistening leg; and her foot, like the feet of the marble goddesses that Europe keeps carefully shut up in museums, imprints its image faithfully on the fine sand. For Dorothea is such a prodigious coquette that the pleasure of being admired prevails with her over the pride of no longer being a slave, and although freed, she still goes barefoot.
>
> (1970: 50)

As Marianne, Republic and Paris, Dorothea is but one side of the coin; her shining mythological countenance forever drags in its wake the reality of the present (as poetry is here vehiculated through prose):

Dorothea is admired and pampered, and she would be perfectly happy if only she were not obliged to save up, *piastre* by *piastre*, enough to free her little sister who is all of eleven years old, and mature already, and so beautiful! She will doubtless succeed, the kindly Dorothea: but the child's master is too miserly to understand any beauty other than the beauty of his *écus*.

(1970: 51)

Myth and reality, poetry and prose, the Ideal of Beauty and the tawdriness of money: the one cannot exist without the other, despite the ineluctable thrust and increasing tempo of modernity.

Léo Malet couples the tension present in the prose poems and grafts it, for the first time by a French author, onto the model of the hardboiled detective novel. And while the first Burma novels differ, through their ability to synthesize, from Baudelaire's flâneur structure, Malet's texts bear many traces of the prose poems, which will pave the way for the more fully fetishistic *Weltanschauung* of 1945. In this respect, the arrival of the mysterious female lead on to the pages of *Nestor Burma contre C.Q.F.D.* (*Nestor Burma against Q.E.D.*), the sequel to *120, Rue de la Gare*, is worth quoting at length:

She burst out of the corridor sixty centimetres away from where I was standing quite still. I was pressed so close against the wall that it was impossible to avoid such an encounter in the event that somebody should rush suddenly out of the building. And the young woman had quite literally shot out. I had never seen anyone move so urgently. She was moving rapidly but rhythmically; her legs were slender and elegant, marvellously clad in a silk that was hard to come by at that time. Her high heels made not a sound. She was wearing a matching blue skirt and jacket under a short sheepskin coat whose golden tone seemed to blend into her auburn hair. I had only glimpsed her face. It had not struck me as at all unattractive. In any case, the whole look that I saw moving away was full of grace. When I had recovered from my surprise, however, I followed quickly in her footsteps. [...] Despite her hurry I had caught up with the young woman and was on her heels when suddenly a tremendous explosion shook the boulevard. [...] She span round abruptly as if she had been bitten by a snake. I started laughing. [...] She shrugged her shoulders and set off again.

(Malet 1945: 126–7)

The first thing we notice in this encounter in *Nestor Burma contre C.Q.F.D.* is the simultaneous juxtaposition and opposition of sudden, explosive motion and immobility. This again recalls the famous train on the platform in Breton's *Nadja*, on which the plot of *120, Rue de la Gare* turned, especially when one considers that this scene is serendipity itself. Burma shows a knack of orchestrating chance encounters: the young woman's positive action—her irresistible movement—strikes a sharp contrast with the negative lines of Burma's stillness; she bursts forth despite his positioning himself against such an eventuality and stands as an expression of speed that he has never seen before. This is an untenable fragmentation of the infinite, as expressed so frequently in Baudelaire's prose poems, in which eternal poetic values are continually shot through with shards of prosaic mundanity.

Burma's first gaze, after the shock of motion, is at the woman's legs. This scene at once recalls Baudelaire's gaze at the feet of the beautiful Dorothea and the rather more famous poem from *Les Fleurs du mal*, 'À une passante' ('To a Woman Passing By'):

> Around me roared the nearly deafening street.
> Tall, slim, in mourning, in majestic grief,
> A woman passed me, with a splendid hand
> Lifting and swinging her festoon and hem;
>
> Nimble and stately, statuesque of leg.
> I, shaking like an addict, from her eye,
> Black sky, spawner of hurricanes, drank in
> Sweetness that fascinates, pleasure that kills.
>
> One lightning flash…then night! Sweet fugitive
> Whose glance has made me suddenly reborn,
> Will we not meet again this side of death?
>
> Far from this place! too late! never perhaps!
> Neither one knowing where the other goes,
> O you I might have loved, as well you know![11]

Baudelaire's beauty is born in the hubbub of the city, only to dwell forever more in his memory. The love that he could and would have had for her becomes mythological in the infinity of representation. Like Baudelaire, Burma too will look into the woman's eyes (unlike the fetishist whose fixation on the legs serves to avoid the alighting of his eyes on the source of truth), detecting in them a hint of fear belied by her outward show of purpose and composure. Both passers-by fuse the 'sweetness that fascinates' and the 'pleasure that kills'; both will force a certain truth to emerge from the obfuscating background of the city streets. And as the Baudelaire of *Les Fleurs du mal* paints truth and beauty into his poems with the voyeuristic control of one who represents belatedly, Burma will concentrate on his past even as the present erupts all around him. Again, this is juxtaposition and opposition, but in Burma's case there will emerge the synthesis of the denouement. For this is what saves Burma; in the midst of a tumult of fetishistic symbols, he is able to see the whole picture, analysing the sum that is more telling than the individual parts. Thus, despite the show of legs and the richly Freudian trappings of the fur coat, Burma catches a glimpse of the truth, before which he does not shrink: 'I had only glimpsed her face. It had not struck me as at all unattractive. In any case, the whole look that I saw moving away was full of grace.'

Chapter 2 on Boris Vian's *L'Écume des jours* (1945, the same year as *Nestor Burma contre C.Q.F.D.*) shows how this same scene can develop into its exact opposite: Vian's protagonist, Colin, will follow on the heels of the same Baudelairian sources; he too will be ensnared by a pair of legs, a fur coat and a woman's hair.[12] In Colin's case, however, the revelation of the woman's face, far from allowing him to master the truth, will cause him to go into denial and revert to fetishism. (Immediately after their respective encounters with the face of the woman passing by, Burma will head downwards, avoiding the danger of the streets in a cellar serving as an air-raid shelter, while Colin will head upwards to a party.) Both Colin and Burma will know the truth, but only Burma will dare to hold its gaze. Indeed, for Burma the juxtaposition of fear and composure, of the Eternal's appearance in the present, is a vision of beauty. This is the difference with the prose poems, in which Beauty is continually tarnished by its descent into the streets of Paris. And so it is that Burma will doggedly pursue his investigation amid repeated references to Baudelaire.

One crucial thread in the plot of *Nestor Burma contre C.Q.F.D.* involves a dwarf's love for the beauty whom Burma has already seen alight in the streets. Every aspect of Burma's pursuit of the dwarf Mac Guffine (including the confusion of the latter's identity as an Irish Frenchman) is shrouded in contrast.[13] In order to locate the dwarf, for example, Burma has to consult with a Herculean associate whom he telephones from a bar:

Twelve really attractive girls—twelve, as announced on the door of the venue—scantily clad, and not as a result of the unavailability

of textiles, were parading on a stage to languorous accompaniment.
A seductive spectacle, but I was not there to watch the show. I ordered
a drink at the bar, drank half and went to the payphone.

(Malet 1945: 176)

Written during the Franco-American exchange of the Liberation, this
scene teems with the Franco-German polarity of the Occupation. All
is half and half: the girls are half-dressed and the drinks are half-
consumed. Burma is not there to fall into the trap of fetishism, however,
and takes his gaze into the telephone booth. Despite his attempted rejection of this blurring of his vision, his next step is into another binary,
the hotel of the two twins, and the very essence of noir: 'In the obscure
light of the street, the Hôtel des Deux-Jumeaux was darker still [plus noir
encore]' (1945: 177).

The story of the dwarf's love is one of knowing but continuing to deny
the truth. As such, it is a mixture of essential beauty and the existential
beast, both poetry and prose:

He had problems with his sexuality and little to be thankful for physically. He was a dwarf. He fell particularly strongly in love with you;
he worshipped you to such an extent that, five years later, he accuses
himself of a murder that he thinks you committed. Of course, you
never suspected this passion. Mac Guffine didn't declare his feelings.
What would have been the point? To the extent that he was a 'worm
in love with a star', he could only be rejected.

(1945: 226–7)

Indeed, Mac Guffine's love story takes the form of one prose poem in
particular. The refusal which he seeks to avoid, and yet which is implicit
in all his actions, is that of 'Le Fou et la Vénus' ('Venus and the Motley
Fool'):

At the feet of a colossal Venus, all of a heap against the pedestal,
one of those so-called fools, those voluntary buffoons who, with cap
and bells and tricked out in a ridiculous and gaudy costume, are
called upon to make kings laugh when they are beset by Boredom
or Remorse, raises his tear-filled eyes towards the immortal Goddess.

(Baudelaire 1970: 10)

This tale within a tale of impossible love is necessarily marked by the
paradoxical identity of the prose poem, which brings together opposed
elements (poetry and prose, abstract values and everyday existents) in

a tantalizing quasi-synthesis, which ultimately serves to present not a form of communication but a lack of it. By encapsulating this failed union between Venus and the fool, Mac Guffine functions as a microcosm of the prose poetic space in which Burma operates. Accordingly, all the key scenes of the novel, which the detective will pull together in his whodunit-style revelation, are marked by the same trope. For example, Burma realizes the truth (which has to do with cigarettes, as in *120, Rue de la Gare*) when, from the vantage point of his office window, he watches his Venus re-alight on the streets:

> Lydia Verbois was coming out of the building. She took a few steps, lost in thought as though sleep-walking. Then suddenly, as if from nowhere, a cigarette sprang from her lips. She inhaled deeply two or three times, still lost in her dream. Then she froze, came down to earth and must have realized just how provocative, in these times of tobacco shortage, her gesture appeared because she threw the cigarette away. Some kind of tramp, who was making his way wearily along the boulevard, picked it up with comical eagerness whilst the young woman blended into the crowd.
>
> (Malet 1945: 188)

The 'truth' of this scene is foreshadowed—and underscored—by Burma's ability to play on two levels: even as he walks through the streets, he is able to look back into the past. He can thus be present and belated without the one interfering with the other to the exclusion of the truth beneath the façade. In the above scene he looks on with the objectivity of the voyeur. When she takes out her cigarette, Lydia reveals her true beauty, or her Beauty as Truth; and having taken her essence down to the level of the street she suddenly realizes the power of the pose she has struck. Abandoning her statuesque mien, so redolent of Baudelaire's Venus, she disappears into the crowd while the proof of her role in the plot is highlighted by the counter-pose of a motley fool.

Hereafter, Léo Malet's use of fetishism revels in the stereotypical images of film noir. The point of such marked exploitation of stock imagery serves, perversely, to mask the non-fetishistic attitude of the protagonist. The only veil being drawn is that over the reader's eyes. Thus, when Lydia reveals her silk stockings, Burma is faking it: far from being fetishistic, his gaze is inward, and what he sees before him functions as a red herring for the reader alone:

> She stopped. She clenched her knee, lifting her skirt slightly. Under the sheer silk of her stocking could be made out the faint outline

of a bruise, a reminder of the ropes used by 'La Fuite' and his companion.

(1945: 194)

It will later be revealed that the bruising on Lydia's leg is not due to her having been bound. Here, then, it is the truth of the text that is veiled beneath the silk of Lydia's stocking. Leg fetishism functions throughout as a symbol not of Burma's incomprehension but of the attempts on the part of the woman to make him believe her lies. The role of the fetish is, after all, as much to symbolize as to veil; and Lydia's apparent attempt to lie can just as easily be read as a revelation of the truth. Under Burma's gaze, she ultimately falls into her own trap:

> She shuddered. Once more she hastily seized my hand. Her glistening eyes sought my gaze.
>
> 'You do believe me, don't you?' she asked imploringly.... Without withdrawing my hand, I drew up a chair and sat down.
>
> 'But that's just it,' I said reproachfully. 'You haven't told me everything.'
>
> She fell back into the armchair, overcome. She slipped down slightly on the cushion, and her skirt lifted, exposing her thighs. She paid no heed, but stared blankly at the coals in the hearth. Her eyes reflected suffering and resignation.
>
> (1945: 195)

In this way, Lydia becomes a flawed, and very French, femme fatale, and it is her own death that fate brings about at the end of the novel. Like Carlotta in Duhamel's translation of *La Môme vert-de-gris*, she will function as an allegory of the Occupation. As such, the following accusation is one that French noir novels will level at France herself:

> For three days you have been twisting and turning, not knowing whether truth or lies would be the best way to get you out of this mess. And you ended up using first one then the other, and at times a mix of the two ... You have acted capriciously, indecisively and spontaneously, however paradoxical this may appear, carrying out plans as they formed in your mind but always swapping them for others. Do you recognize yourself in this description? You ought to. Haven't you been plagued long enough now by these contradictory feelings?
>
> (1945: 196)

The noir twist to *Nestor Burma contre C.Q.F.D.*, published as it was in 1945, lies in Lydia's admission of her guilt and her Liberation at the hands of Nestor Burma. Her crime self-consciously manipulates Freudian imagery: she mishandles the phallus, wields power without knowledge and ultimately is freed almost despite herself: 'He fell, without a sound...I kept the revolver...I didn't really know what I was doing' (1945: 231). Unable to profit from her crime, she is released with Burma's consent and killed in a train derailment en route for Bordeaux.[14] In a final touch, Burma gives away the gold that is his reward for solving the case.

And so, Léo Malet, with this carefully controlled exploitation of fetishism, creates a markedly noired ending to a text whose mystery was solved through a counter-fetishistic approach. Within Malet's works, from *120, Rue de la Gare*, the Occupation classic, to *Nestor Burma contre C.Q.F.D.*, released immediately after the Liberation, there is a discernible shift towards a truly fetishistic form of noir thriller. This shift is not merely productive of mood but is also a response to the Zeitgeist. For in the very same year that Burma's love dies, France witnesses the birth of Duhamel's Série Noire and the advent of Lemmy Caution.

2

Liberation Noir: Boris Vian and the Série Noire (1)

David Platten writes that 'crime fiction is embedded in the French national culture' (2002: 5). This statement can be read with equal poignancy in reverse: national culture is embedded in French crime fiction. Indeed, one of the principal aims of this book is to investigate the possibility of simultaneously extending and refining the meaning of the term French noir fiction (and, implicitly, to consider its points of contact and departure from 'French crime fiction'). To this end, it is vital that the classic noir texts of post-war French literature be seen as an integral part of French national culture not in spite of their authors' status as non-indigenous authors but because of it. Indeed, the incorporation of non-French authors, via translation, into the French noir canon (or a noired French canon) functions as a discrete but telling parallel to the broader impact of American cultural and economic dominance on the French way of life in the second half of the twentieth century.

As novels written by non-French authors about ostensibly non-French issues, the early classics of the Série Noire have the necessary latitude to be able to function as powerful allegories of what were very much Franco-French concerns.[1] Indeed, the translation of the novels itself becomes a statement of intent on the part of their French publishers. The importance of text selection and creative and partial translation practice is no more innocent than the detectives and dames of the noir novels themselves. And so, when, in early 1945, Marcel Achard convinced Marcel Duhamel to organize the publication in French of three works of hard-boiled detective fiction, the texts were written by English authors: Peter Cheyney (*Poison Ivy* and *This Man is Dangerous*) and James Hadley Chase (*No Orchids for Miss Blandish*).

This is where Boris Vian first, and most famously, contributes to the development of French noir fiction. His lead role in bringing noir literature to France echoes that which he played in importing the sound of New Orleans jazz. And yet, in both instances, his role as importer must always be evaluated against his role as producer of literature and music as a French artist working in France. As far as classic French noir is concerned, Robert E. Conrath places Vian at Duhamel's right hand: 'With the help of a few friends, including Jacques Prévert and Boris Vian, Duhamel, had the idea of bringing together under the title of the Série Noire a number of novels written in 'hard-boiled' style' (Conrath 1995: 40). Gilbert Pestureau confirms this, pointing out that the three books that launched the Série Noire in 1945 were no sooner discovered by Duhamel than they were handed on to Vian, who read them both in translation and in the original English (Pestureau 1978: 256). While he may have had some reservations regarding Duhamel's rather liberal translation of Cheyney, he was struck by *La Môme vert-de-gris*, and considered that what it lost in 'its original flavour' by straying from the literal meaning of the English, it compensated for 'in vulgarity' (1978: 256).[2] In fact, Vian considered *Dames Don't Care* to be the best of the three Cheyney novels to have appeared in the original English in France at that time. He went on to translate this novel himself for the Série Noire; it appeared as *Les Femmes s'en balancent* in 1949.

Noir fiction in France, then, is born in translation, in the coming together of two languages and two cultural and literary traditions—and for the purposes of this study, 1945 is taken as the most important milestone in the development of this phenomenon. The hybrid form that emerges necessarily from such a fusion is rendered more complex in this case by the fact that Peter Cheyney and James Hadley Chase had one further point in common with Boris Vian: all three authors famously masqueraded as Americans. While Cheyney and Chase were both Englishmen who were taken to be American authors (by dint of their written style and also, doubtless, because the hard-boiled tradition has invariably been taken to be an American school).[3] Boris Vian became notorious for his persona Vernon Sullivan, under whose name he published *J'irai cracher sur vos tombes*. As a result, it is untenable to seek to place rigid nationalistic or geographical boundaries on French noir fiction (such as, e.g., to suggest that French noir is noir literature written by persons of French birth). The texts of the Série Noire had a huge impact on the Parisian scene after the Liberation, and this mood had at its core the ambiguity and negotiated identities that were born of Franco-American exchange.

Despite the popular legend that has built up around Boris Vian's role in the cultural life of Paris at this time, the full extent of his influence is only now beginning to be appreciated, as Raymond Queneau suggested would be the case.[4] Given the fluctuating success of his work—from a critical perspective at least, his novels fell into relative obscurity following a brief posthumous revival inspired by the events of May 1968, and are now once again experiencing something of a renaissance[5]—it is interesting to find that his contribution has not been lost on the scholars of film noir. Indeed, James Naremore, writing on the French contribution to American film noir, considers Vian's role to have been critical:

> The end of World War II in Paris gave rise to what might be called a noir sensibility; but this sensibility was expressed through many things besides cinema, and if I had to choose a representative artist of the period, it would not be a filmmaker. Instead I would pick the somewhat Rimbaud-like personality Boris Vian.
>
> (Naremore 1998: 11)

The dates within which Naremore posits the birth and flowering of this noir sensibility in American cinema (1946–59) are also, presumably not coincidentally, key dates in Vian's timeline: in addition to being the year in which the first wave of American films noirs broke over Parisian cinema screens, 1946 saw the publication of *J'irai cracher sur vos tombes*, and 1959 was the year in which Boris Vian died as he attended an *avant-première* of the film version of this very novel (see Chapter 6).

It is also interesting to reflect on the fact that the Boris Vian in whose work James Naremore is interested, this author who 'was approached by an editor who wanted to create a list of murder novels that would rival the popular, black-covered Série Noire, recently inaugurated at Gallimard' (Naremore 1998: 12), was posing as a translator. *J'irai cracher sur vos tombes* was offered to the French public as a translation by Boris Vian of the work of the previously unheard-of black American author Vernon Sullivan. Whilst the term film noir, as coined by French cinema critics, proved to be 'moody' and untranslatable, noir fiction in France thrived off translation to the extent that if a text was not translated from the American it was judged not to be noir at all.

What was it about this particular period of French history that lent itself to such extravagant cases of false identity? Noir itself depends on alienation, and, to a degree, on inchoate plots in which out-of-place people achieve unsatisfactory resolutions. As Naremore notes,

> [t]he discourse on noir grew out of a European male fascination with the instinctive (a fascination that was evident in most forms of high

modernism), and many of the films admired by the French involve white characters who cross borders to visit Latin America, Chinatown, or the 'wrong' parts of the city. When the idea of noir was imported to America, this implication was somewhat obscured; the term sounded more artistic in French, so it was seldom translated as 'black cinema.'

(1998: 12–13)

It is precisely within this coming and going across cultures that noir succeeds. And yet, to attempt to define noir in terms of such an exchange leads not only to dizzying complexity but to a delimiting definition of the films and novels that are its vehicle.[6] Noir does not simply create a mood; it captures one.

'L'Écume des jours' and the concept of French Noir fiction

In 1945 the French psyche is seeking refuge in blurred boundaries and border crossings. Noir steps in to filter the excessively bright light of Liberation that stung French eyes emerging from *les années noires* of the Occupation. This is more than moody verbiage: Paris had been trapped for four years between a rock and a hard place. The French identity had been squeezed out of the picture, lost somewhere between de Gaulle's London-based Free French rebellion and the culture of collaboration fostered under Pétain's Vichy government. In 1944 the signification of French patriotism shifted from the latter condition to the former, bringing with it a cathartic period that vacillated between euphoria and revenge. The difficulty facing historians of this period is to provide a logical reconstruction of the state of the French psyche from the Occupation, through Liberation to the onset of the Cold War. One thing is becoming evident, now that mythology has replaced empirical reality as the favoured means of conceiving of this epoch: this haze was less jazzy than it was noir. In its occlusion of right and wrong, of black and white (one good reason for not translating noir is that, perversely, it is rather more than a shade of grey; it is a confusion of black and white), noir foregrounds a harsh reality at the expense of delusional aspirations. Nothing is clear-cut in noir, just as for the French people of the time Frenchness itself had come adrift from any solid underpinnings.

Our claim here is that the key period for this constant re-evaluation is located before the Cold War was officially recognized as such. The success of the Série Noire grows out of a need to incorporate into the French national identity a share of America's success in the war and, at the same time, to apprehend that victory as an essentially tainted one. As Claire Gorrara writes, '[m]ore so than almost any other form of popular literature in France, the roman noir offers the opportunity to re-evaluate French national identity and cultural practice from the bottom up' (Gorrara 2003a: 9).

Historically, then, the Série Noire fills in a gap in discourse between the Liberation and the Cold War and between pre-war (detective) fiction and the popular success of noir itself, which becomes more widely understood in its association—and exchange—with film. Once again, because it cut across binaries, film noir filled a historical vacuum. Naremore describes this historical aspect in the following terms:

> This passion for literary toughness has an interesting relation to the social and political climate after the war. In the United States, the post-war decade was the period of Korea, the red scare, and the return to a consumer economy; in France, it was the period of colonial rebellion and parliamentary confusion leading up to the Charles de Gaulle government.
>
> (Naremore 1998: 23)

In order to see how this cultural phenomenon of an unstable national self-identity is portrayed by Boris Vian's noir fiction, our first step, ironically, will be to discard his American persona and to refocus on the project on which he was working under his own name even as he was hastily writing *J'irai cracher sur vos tombes*. For while it is interesting to study the most widely read of Vian's novels as a pastiche of noir fiction, which is how *J'irai cracher sur vos tombes* is traditionally considered, a more fruitful way of gauging the predominant mood in Paris in the years following the Liberation is to study the noir aspects of what may be termed 'mainstream' literature.

Christopher M. Jones, whose primary interest lies in the Sullivan novels, sees Vian's novelistic fate as being dependent on the favour in which America found itself in Paris. For Jones, Vian—the author of *L'Écume des jours*—is pro-US because he loves jazz and writes American-style fiction:

> Briefly [Vian] was beloved of virtually everyone, including members of the Sartre group who were emerging from the war in a position to dominate Left Bank intellectual discourse. Vian's Gallimard publication of *L'Écume des jours* in 1947 constituted an apogee of sorts. The novel mixed a unique sensibility with subtexts of American

jazz and Saint-Germain in-crowd ruminations and found favor with seemingly everyone who counted.

(Jones 1999: 137)

This apogee was, of course, tainted by the fact that *L'Écume des jours*[7] was a commercial disaster and that Vian failed to win the coveted Prix de la Pléiade. If Vian was pro-US, this attitude did not help his novel to succeed. We should, therefore, call into question Jones's assumption that Vian's success or failure hinged on the popularity of the United States. Such an opinion is founded on an agreed timeline for French anti-Americanism, which Jones views as a later phenomenon, thereby making it coincide with Vian's disillusionment with the novel form.[8] Vian is too often considered as a radical fan of America who, having been almost accidentally in fashion amid the dance parties of the Liberation, is snubbed in the ensuing anti-US bitterness and left out in the cold: 'Growing anti-Americanism cut at the very basis of Vian's self-image. By the Fifties Vian was living in relative isolation' (Jones 1999: 137). Whether or not Jones is correct in making this connection, his reading of *L'Écume des jours* as a jazz-soaked eulogy to the United States is a common, and in our opinion naive, interpretation. A noir reading of Vian's seminal text will allow a re-evaluation of Vian's attitudes as well as of the status of this particular novel as a politically motivated piece of prose.

On first appraisal the plot of *L'Écume des jours* may not appear to justify its inclusion within a body of French noir fiction, in which love stories are typically submerged in hard-boiled violence. The protagonist, Colin, is introduced to the reader as a man of means who only has to imagine a wish for it to become transformed magically into reality. His world is what David Meakin has called a 'desire-shaped universe' (Meakin 1996: 45–60). This unchallenged happiness is first destabilized when Colin meets and falls in love with his best friend's girlfriend, Alise. In order to take his mind off his love for a woman to whom access is denied (because she 'belongs' to another), he meets and marries an ersatz lover, Chloé. This is where Colin's free will—his ability to have what he wants—is exchanged (in what is a deliberate act on his part)[9] for determinism: Chloé is a construct, a piece of jazz music by Duke Ellington, that Colin conjures up. He therefore sets in train an infernal descent: his apartment shrinks; his money runs out; and, tragically, Chloé becomes terminally ill, dying at the end of the novel as a result of a water lily in the lung. This is a love story, but it is the story of a misdirected love. Love turns into death, and nobody goes unpunished.

This desire-shaped universe rapidly turns into a noir cityscape where dreams and ideals are replaced by gritty realism.

One of the most obviously noir motifs of *L'Écume des jours* is its fatalism; its characters appear helpless to overcome the situation in which they find themselves. As Paul Schrader points out, such a noir mood is not limited to the detective genre of the period: 'In 1946 French critics, seeing the American films they had missed during the war, noticed the new mood of cynicism, pessimism and darkness which had crept into the American cinema. The darkening stain was most evident in routine crime thrillers, but was also apparent in prestigious melodramas' (Schrader 1996: 53). While *L'Écume des jours* is itself not commonly considered to be linked to the detective-novel genre (critics preferring to link noir and the Sullivan texts),[10] few would dispute its status as 'prestigious melodrama'. Indeed, the novel can be said to be filmically noir. For if it appears not to share the obvious motifs of the detective thriller, which forms the backbone of the Série Noire, and which has furthermore become synonymous with French noir fiction, it is still made up of many technical elements common to film noir.

Most notably, the entire narrative push of *L'Écume des jours* is from a period of happiness, where dreams become reality, towards a gradual extinction of light, which acts as a backdrop to the entropic decay of the novel. The beginning of the text is marked by an exaggerated abundance of natural light. Two suns blaze through the glazed corridor that leads Colin from his shower into the story proper. As daylight is gradually lost, leading ultimately to the physical diminution of Colin's apartment, there is a key scene that shows Colin and his wife Chloé witnessing, by lamplight, the struggle of forces now beyond their control:

> In that place where rivers run into the sea there forms a bar that is difficult to cross and great foaming eddies where shipwrecks dance. Between the darkness of the night outside and the lamplight inside, memories flowed out of the shadows into the illumination. At first submerged then breaking the surface, they moved with flashes of white underside and silver backs.
>
> (Vian 1999: 109)

As will be seen later, noir lies in the troubled waters described in this quotation, which reflect the world of the noir hero where abstract values (truth, justice, love, knowledge) collide with more tangibly human forces (violence, anger, jealousy, desire). Inasmuch as Vian's novel showcases the movement from the former into the latter, it is the story of a noir becoming. Its very descriptive techniques lend themselves to this reading. Its use of lighting provides a good example: noir mood is most obviously signalled by the artificial lighting of night-time scenes. As Schrader notes, too much light would prove fatal to noir protagonists: 'Ceiling lights are hung low and floor lamps are seldom more than five feet high. One always has the suspicion that if the lights were suddenly flipped on the characters would shriek and shrink from the scene like Count Dracula at sunrise' (Schrader 1996: 57). *L'Écume des jours* seems to offer the negative of noir in this respect: the protagonists are born in light, only to see it flee from them. The deliberate play on light in the scene quoted above indicates a battle between the light of free will (and the tendency for dreams to come true) and the darkness of determinism (the ineluctable decline of the novel). This is a battle that Colin will lose.

And yet, it is not simply the case that the novel becomes noir in mid-narrative. For, although they are born of light, Colin and Alise—the text's central driving forces—are also children of the water. Colin first emerges from under a shower; Alise, for her part, is born to the novel on the ice of a skating rink. And while she is quite literally shot down in flames, Colin ends his struggle beside a watery grave. The quality of light in the novel also affects the quality of water: the lightness of *l'écume* (understood initially as bubbling froth) gradually gives way to a much murkier *écume* (or scum). In terms of noir mood, water is almost as important as the use of black and white; streets invariably glisten with puddles and rain. Again as Schrader notes, '[t]here seems to be an almost Freudian attachment to water... Docks and piers are second only to alleyways as the most popular rendezvous points' (1996: 57).

There are clearly sufficient grounds for suggesting that the structural elements of *L'Écume des jours* lend themselves to a noir reading. Furthermore, Vian's famous foreword suggests an obliqueness of light, a distorting of the picture, which couches the whole novel in noir terms: 'Essentially [this story's] production consists, in material terms, in projecting reality onto an irregularly undulating and distorted plane of reference in an angled and heated atmosphere' (Vian 1999: 21–2). For distortion is not, in fact, a removal of the art form from reality; rather, it is a way of representing reality, of demystifying the world. The gradual disempowerment of the characters in Vian's novel is a reminder that ideals have no effective role to play in a world where all is shades of grey. This is, again, a crucial element of film noir: '[O]blique and vertical lines are preferred to horizontal. Obliquity adheres to the choreography of the city... No character can speak authoritatively from a space which is being continually cut into ribbons of light' (Schrader 1996: 57).

In Colin's case, the erosion of his authority and the fragmenting of his light constitute a chicken-and-egg conundrum; whichever the reader deems to have come first, it is certain that the novel takes on the architecture of noir space in order for mood to occlude the protagonist's failure to take responsibility for his actions. The perversity of this will not be lost on those who believe that noir and Sartrean Existentialism emerge from a common world-view.

The shades of grey, which hold the key to our noir reading of *L'Écume des jours*, typify the tension inherent in the relationship between the United States and France. The contrary pulls of the narrative—the move from light into darkness—can be read allegorically as the shifting attitudes of a people thankful to the Americans for having liberated them from Nazi occupation and concerned that the US presence in Paris was morphing into just another shade of occupation. The importance of Boris Vian's novel as noir text lies in its historical relocation of this French ambivalence towards the United States. While much has been written in analysis of the ambiguous attitudes that were adopted by the French—intellectuals, artists, politicians and citizens alike—in their attempts to negotiate the increasing drive towards modernization (which in the years following the Second World War became increasingly synonymous with Americanization), there is a tendency to associate such uncertainty with cultural artefacts of the 1950s. In *Fast Cars, Clean Bodies* Kristin Ross concentrates principally on the literary works produced in the decade from the mid-1950s to the mid-1960s (and the effects on the French psyche of the Algerian War). For his part, Richard Kuisel, in *Seducing the French*, posits the origins of the tension caused by this dual attraction/repulsion towards the United States at the beginning of the Cold War. In this light, it is interesting to note that the signs of this ambiguity are already present in *L'Écume des jours*, which was published in 1947 but begun as early as 1945. For if the United States had already had its advocates and its critics among the French literati in the inter-war years, Boris Vian's first major novel, is clearly riddled by the dichotomy that would go on to mark the work of Paris's Left-Bank intellectuals for two more decades. It is, as such, a work very much before, of and about its time.

A glimpse of Noir: The motif of dames and stockings

The point where the text begins its steady decline is difficult to locate precisely. The following scene, however, is a crucial one. It shows Colin in a demoralized state: he has abandoned any attempt to concretize his love of Alise, and is about to go to a party (where he will find Chloé, who will embody this love as a life-sized token of his bad faith). The world is about to become noir, therefore, and the entrance into this new reality is via the seams of a stereotypically noir motif—a woman's leg encased in a stocking:

> The vague sound of the gathering at Isis's parents' place became audible as he arrived at the first floor.... Colin headed up the stairs, his nose level with the heels of [the] two girls. Pretty seamed heels in flesh-coloured nylon, high-heeled shoes made of good quality leather and slender ankles. Then the stocking seams, kinking slightly like long caterpillars, and the hollows sculpted behind the knee joint. Colin stopped and fell two steps behind. He set off again and could now see the stocking tops of the one on the left, the double thickness of the nylon stitching and the shaded whiteness of the upper thigh. The folds of the other one's skirt kept it flat and did not allow him such a distracting view, but under her beaver-fur coat her hips struck a fuller figure than the first girl's, causing an alternating right-left folding effect. Out of a sense of decency Colin looked down at his own feet, just in time to see them come to a stop at the second floor.
>
> (Vian 1999: 49–50)

Before embarking on a more detailed discussion of this literary exploitation of leg fetishism and its consequences for relocating the locus of the novel's fall from a state of grace, it is important to position this passage in its historical context. Noir fiction is a highly situated form of writing; it is at once a response to and a means of renegotiating historical reality. Vian's particular choice of material at this point is not a mere allusion to the Americanization of the fashion industry; the move of the female leg towards nylon parallels the shift in literary tastes towards the hard-boiled thriller.

Susannah Handley provides the following description of the first unveiling of the nylon stocking at the New York World's Fair in 1940: 'Du Pont was ready to show off its new nylon material at the Wonder World of Chemistry show with even greater confidence than in 1938 ... Du Pont's floor show—better known as a "leg show"—was judged "sexiest corporate show at the fair" by one impassioned observer' (1999: 43). It is crucial that Vian's own leg show uses this new material and not its naturally produced predecessor, silk, which had been adorning the legs of Parisian women since as far back as one could remember, and which was synonymous with stylish dressing and the sexual attraction that the female leg held for the male observer.[11] The ascent of the staircase to Isis's flat not only demonstrates Colin's attraction to modernity and this new American 'leg of tomorrow', but it also marks a break with tradition, a break that lies both at the heart of France's ambivalent attitudes to the United States and of Boris Vian's love story. For, as Handley's description shows, nylon stockings represent less American beauty than American dynamism, highlighting, by contrast, the antiquated ways of a France so recently liberated from Nazi occupation:

> Although the traditions of cloth-making were thousands of years old and the industrial revolution in Europe mechanized the textile industry beyond recognition, there was essentially something missing which gave European fabric innovation its stop-start character. Technology, in the textile context, was historically a dangerous and destabilizing beast and there was a certain wariness about breaking with tradition…In the United States, however, there was no conflict between the idea of newness and that of traditional culture. America's frontier mentality made it the natural home of reason-defying technical feats.
>
> (1999: 51)

Although the invention of nylon was a pre-war phenomenon—nylon stocking prototypes began in 1938 at Du Pont, and the first stockings were knitted in February 1939—'nylons' were not made available to the American public at large until May 1940 (although limited sales did begin in October 1939). If one also considers that no sooner had they gone on sale than the United States entered into the Second World War, with the result that Du Pont's nylon production was immediately and entirely commandeered for the war effort, then the coming of 'nylons' to Europe and their long-awaited return 'back home' may be viewed as an ushering-in of the post-war period. Although Boris Vian's vision in nylon would not necessarily have shocked the French public as something utterly modern, it is important to note that these new stockings were still very much capturing public attention some years later.[12] Richard Kuisel notes the shock recorded in *Le Monde* as late as 1949 to such manifestations of an increasingly ubiquitous American cultural footprint on French soil: 'Coca-Cola represented the coming American commercial and cultural invasion. Already "Chryslers and Buicks speed down our roads; American tractors furrow our fields; Frigidaires keep our food cold; stockings 'made by Du Pont' sheathe the legs of our stylish women"' (1996: 65).[13] The stairway that leads Colin, via the nylon-clad legs of two post-Liberation French beauties, to his future wife, Chloé, would appear to signpost the entry of the protagonist into the very heart of the love story. This would then be a wholly positive step for him to take. It can be shown, however, that historical studies allow the reader to re-evaluate Colin's ascent chez Isis.

> The debate about America during the Cold War also echoed prewar charges about 'America the menace.' It should be remembered that postwar France inherited a critical assessment of *américanisme* from the interwar years. If the literature written about the New World before the war often admired American dynamism, affluence, power, and even certain cultural achievements, on balance the collective judgement had been negative...
>
> (Kuisel 1996: 21–2)

The disparate voices condemning and praising the United States in France during the inter-war years are condensed in the body of Boris Vian's writing. For example, the youthful love of creative machinery, for which his work—rightly or wrongly—has become synonymous, is always tempered by its focus upon objects of personal rather than wider economic gain (*le pianocktail* of *L'Écume des jours* is a case in point). As for his great love of black American jazz music, this should not lead to any naive assumption that Vian saw the United States as a transatlantic Utopia: his jazz writings are starkly counterbalanced by the series of novels that he wrote under the pseudonym of Vernon Sullivan (in which Lee Anderson repeatedly draws a distinction between Americans and black Americans). Indeed, it should always be borne in mind that jazz itself was first and foremost a counter-cultural phenomenon within the United States. Finally, Boris Vian tends to elect the personal over the weight of society and the affective over the mass of technological progress.[14]

Kuisel describes an America that was already associated (from 1945 onwards) in the minds of the French with a thoroughly modern way of life, and which, as such, was both to be admired and viewed with suspicion. For example, America was on the one hand, 'hailed as the liberator of France, a close ally, and a democracy'; American culture on the other hand, 'was different—it recalled Hollywood, cowboys, and jazz. Above all Americans lived in a modern society: they were "modern people always taking the lead toward progress." This stereotype was quite stable from 1945 through the 1950s and long after that as well' (Kuisel 1996: 30). All the positive aspects of America—by which Jean-Paul Sartre and the intellectuals of Saint-Germain-des-Prés were genuinely fascinated—lay in its literary and film production. French ambivalence towards a US model of modernization does not simply arise from mixed feelings towards a uniformly presented neighbour; it can, on the contrary, be seen to reflect the very different images coming out of America itself. It is clearly possible to embrace jazz music, for example, without wishing to emulate US foreign policy. Such adulation (of jazz, dancing and quirky high-tech gadgets) is manifest in *L'Écume des jours*. Its position centre stage in the novel is so heavily signposted, in fact, that one is led to wonder if it does not conceal—or function as a screen memory for—a deeper mistrust that exposes a need for the reader to reinterpret the love story itself.

The first female character that Colin meets is Alise, the niece of his butler and girlfriend of his best friend, Chick. Interestingly, the first description of Alise begins not with her blaze of golden hair, which will become her trademark, but with her clothes:

> By a strange coincidence she was wearing a white sweatshirt and yellow skirt. She had on yellow and white shoes and hockey skates, and was wearing smoke-coloured silk stockings. White socks were rolled down over the top of her low-cut shoes which were tied with white cotton laces wound three times around her ankles.
>
> (Vian 1999: 36)

Alise is clearly a modern girl: the sweatshirt that she wears had only just arrived in the French lexicon. *Le Petit Robert* gives 1939 as the date for the arrival of the Anglicism *sweat-shirt* in the French language; furthermore it quotes the above passage from Vian as an example of its usage. Vian, too, is up with the times. This is only half the story, however, for sweatshirts, according to *Le Petit Robert*, are, just as are Alise's shoelaces, made of cotton. Alise is adorned with natural fibres. Her stockings are accordingly not made of nylon but of silk. Notes by Pestureau and Rybalka, which accompany the 1994 edition of the text, indicate that the substantive *fumée* [smoke] was a later addition to the original manuscript. As is typical of Vian's use of understatement in his writing, this addendum serves less to qualify and boost the status of the accompanying noun, *soie* [silk], than to act as a smokescreen (quite literally, in fact), distracting the reader's attention from the fact that the stockings are made of silk and, thus, stand in sharp contrast to those worn by the girls going to Isis's party.

The fact that Alise is natural and that Chloé, whom Colin eventually marries, is artificial is clear. It can also be argued that Alise is Colin's love object and that Chloé is merely a record, artificially created by Colin to assuage his love for Alise, a love that life appears to have made impossible. By focusing on the stockings, and especially the change in material that leads Colin to the next level of the story, we can read Alise as an incarnation of *la vieille France*, opposite Chloé's role as an exemplar of Americanization. For as an artificial woman, Chloé is based on a jazz piece by Duke Ellington; her fragrance is made of 'twice-distilled orchid' (one distillation incorporating essence of Alise and the other the comforting domestication of Colin's pet mouse). She may also be considered a chemical woman and, as such, to be part of the emerging science of fashion, of which nylon was the new champion:

> The Style News Service circulated the story of the heroines of the New York World's Fair, the Test Tube Lady (also known as Princess Plastics), who was shown emerging from a giant test tube and totally decked out in artificial materials, and Miss Chemistry of the Future, who modelled all-nylon 'lace evening gown, stockings, satin slippers, and undergarments'.... The 'startling symbol' of the new world was this woman clothed entirely in man-made materials, fibres, plastics and synthetic dyes.
>
> (Handley 1999: 43–4)

Handley explains how the invention of nylon changed the very dynamics of sexual attraction. For all her literary heritage, Chloé (as avatar of Marguerite from Alexandre Dumas fils's *La Dame aux camélias* and the living doll of *L'Ève future* by Villiers de l'Isle-Adam) is forced into existence by the hand of man in response to physical needs generated by the translation of Alise's natural allure. The very flesh-coloured appearance of the stockings worn by the girls who lead the way to Isis's flat points to the perverse nature of nylon: it is an artificial adornment of a natural feature, and its allure seems to lie in this very artifice. Whether nylon was originally designed to rival silk in the fabrication of hosiery, or quite simply to better it, is largely irrelevant. The fact is that nylon is a choice imposed upon Colin by the weight of Americanization. Colin does not ascend the stairs of his own free will; neither is he drawn to them by an act of *flânerie*, as is the case with his earlier arrival at the piscine Molitor where he first meets Alise (his current state is one of melancholia, and does not predispose him to the serendipitous encounters of objective chance): he is pulled up the stairs by the power of the crowd and the promise of 'pretty girls'.

The ineluctability of the rise of American values against traditionally French symbols can thus be compared to the insidious power of society over the individual. Chloé is a market-driven response to Colin's attraction to the unavailable Alise:

> Du Pont was dedicated to creating and promoting more and more new products, a policy described in 1940 by *Fortune* as 'forcing' nylon into being: 'It was developed under deliberate pressure, in line with Du Pont policy. If no new or improved products are forthcoming at reasonable intervals, then they must be made to appear ... [B]y synthesis, chemists make them [precious stones, etc.] at low cost ... even the rare perfumes which women use to 'attract the male' can be imitated with coal tar musk.
>
> (Handley 1999: 40)

Nylon, too, is insidious and ambivalent. As Vian synthesizes the technical and the human, and as Chloé fuses Colin's love of music and desire for Alise, the nylon stocking captures all that the French found to admire and fear in the United States: 'Nylon's launch in the intimate guise of stockings and lingerie was a perfect example of the successful domestication of a highly technical product. ... Nylons became a potent symbol of American technical know-how but they were also redolent of all the escapist glamour of Hollywood' (Handley 1999: 45). In the light of Americanization, the genuine tragedy of the novel may be said to lie not in the failure of the love story to endure but in Colin's betrayal of his love of the individual. The only character who acts with genuine autonomy in the novel is the girl with whom Colin is in love: Alise. By abandoning her in favour of a kind of mannequin, who appears to be moulded on Alise's individual traits, Colin conforms and causes the story to collapse in on itself. As Jean-Philippe Mathy explains, man's desires become shaped by the tensions regulating the society in which he lives (Mathy 1989: 462). The entropic shift of the novel follows Colin's ascent of the stairs and his simultaneous descent from a state of love of the individual to one in which he abandons the love of each individual (in the form of Alise) in favour of that of everyman (in the form of Chloé). In order to put this failure into the perspective afforded by our staircase scene, it is important to understand how

Colin's failure to love the individual may be analyzed in psychological terms.

As he mounts the stairs, Colin's gaze, too, ascends. It is checked, however, and remains fixed on the girls' legs, not accomplishing its journey. As a result, the female genitals remain covered. Freud describes the origins of the fetish as follows:

> The subject's interest comes to a halt half-way, as it were; it is as though the last impression before the uncanny and traumatic one is retained as a fetish. Thus the foot or shoe owes its preference as a fetish—or part of it—to the circumstance that the inquisitive boy peered at the woman's genitals from below, from her legs up; fur and velvet—as has long been suspected—are a fixation of the sight of the pubic hair, which should have been followed by the longed-for sight of the female member; pieces of underclothing, which are so often chosen as a fetish, crystallize the moment of undressing, the last moment in which the woman could still be regarded as phallic.
>
> (Freud 1961: 155)

The suddenly arrested ascending gaze is clearly present in Vian's scene. The fur coat, however, and the masking of the genitals would suggest that the screen memory is already in place: the passage from *L'Écume des jours* is an example of the female leg being observed by a viewer in whom a leg fetish has already formed.

The nature of the beaver fur, by which the genitals are apparently screened, is interesting in itself. *'Le castor'*—the beaver—was Jean-Paul Sartre's famous nickname for Simone de Beauvoir, and as such the term slots seamlessly into the novel's raft of caricatures of the personalities of Paris's Left Bank of the time. The fact that Boris Vian and his wife (at the time of writing *L'Écume des jours* he was still married to Michelle Léglise) were fluent in English—both were involved in translating American detective novels, such as Raymond Chandler's *The Big Sleep* and *Lady in the Lake*, for the Série Noire—would also suggest that he was aware of the connotations in that language of the term beaver (which *The Oxford Dictionary of Modern Slang* cites as being used to refer to the female genitalia from as early as 1922). The term *castor* is not without its slang connotations in French either: it can refer either to a man with a high degree of sexual potency or a male prostitute. The former meaning—when used to describe a coat adorning female shoulders—ties in with the fetishist's attempt to sustain his belief in the phallic woman whilst the latter would tend to suggest that Isis's flat is something of a den of iniquity, which is in itself an entirely defensible reading.[15]

If Colin is already a fetishist, it is logical to expect to find the origins of the fetish at an earlier point in the novel. In fact, one need only consult the previous page.

> Colin crossed the street. Two people in love were kissing in a doorway. He closed his eyes and started to run. He then quickly opened them again because he could see in his mind a great numbers of girls, and he was losing his way. There was one in front of him, heading in the same direction. He could see her pretty legs in white woollen boots and her long, slightly worn fur coat with a matching hat that set off her auburn hair. Her coat traced the fine lines of her shoulders and danced about her as she walked. 'I must get past her,' he thought. 'I must see her face.' He overtook her and broke down in tears. She was fifty-nine at least.
>
> (Vian 1999: 49)

The meaning of this passage is quite clear: Colin's obsession with the female leg is not caused by the sight of the woman's genitals. What terrifies him—to the point of causing him to revert to, and to fetishize, the view of the legs that preceded it—is the face of the older woman. Colin is appalled by this personification of ageing. So terrible is the idea of being 60 years old that he cannot even countenance the thought, and guesses the woman's age to be 'fifty-nine at least'. From this point on, then, the female leg will act as a screen memory that both veils and symbolizes the reality of ageing.

In terms of our reading of Americanization, Colin makes a trade-off. As a fetishist he is standing at what Ellen Lee McCallum has termed the 'unique intersection of desire and knowledge' (McCallum 1999: xii). Fetishism is a way of finding an acceptable way of living one's life when the world is not how one would like it to be and when one's belief that it might be better is flawed. The fetishist, therefore, vacillates between a state of mind based on concrete truth and one shaped by fantasy:

> It is not true that, after the child has made his observation of the woman, he has preserved unaltered his belief that women have a phallus. He has retained that belief, but he has also given it up. In

the conflict between the weight of the unwelcome perception and the force of his counter-wish, a compromise has been reached.

(Freud 1961: 154)

The compromise here lies in the knowledge that France is antiquated and the belief that she is young. Colin screens the face of old age, *la vieille France*, beneath the glamorous legs of youth. In adoring an Americanized fetish-France, Colin symbolically sends tradition to a grave to which the weight of the system and the American Way had already condemned it.

And yet to what extent does this reading ring true with the situation in which the French people found themselves at the end of the Second World War? Such an analysis of *L'Écume des jours* places Alise in the privileged position of true (mythologized) love object: with her silk stockings and natural fragrance, she is emblematic of traditional French values. The love that she and Colin feel for each other is not seized upon. Colin does not act on his feelings; rather, he goes with the flow of the novel and elects an easy way out. He negotiates a path between his love for the unattainable Alise and easy sexual gratification in the form of an available girl who is custom-built to fit all his specifications. This moment of fetishism reveals a hesitation between two myths (those of a French past and an American future); the female leg—an iconic noir image—represents the grey area of reality and the ambivalent feelings in regard to the modernizing of France. As McCallum points out, fetishism allows us to live through the impossible choices of a life consistently 'reduced to binary and mutually exclusive terms' (McCallum 1999: xi–xii). By choosing Chloé, Colin sets in train a man-made fatality that will lead to the destruction of the novel, Alise and, ultimately, love itself; by choosing Alise he would have nullified Chloé's very existence. Black or white. In the intermediary moment of fetishism, a third way was briefly glimpsed, then gone.

To gauge France's attitudes to Americanization in the post-war years, it is important to stay in the grey area. Indeed, not all layers of French society wished to see France so strongly attached to its heritage. The French voices of capitalism saw dependence on the past as weakness (and would have viewed Colin's apparent decision to say 'out with the old and in with the new' as wholly laudable). Speaking in relation to the impressive economic gains that marked the mid-1950s in France, commissioner of productivity, Gabriel Ardant, remarked in 1956: '[But] it's not always easy to opt for life, to choose imagination and reflection, to prefer new, and thus risky, investments, over outmoded, traditional outlays. Every Frenchman carries within him a formidable old man who is difficult to exorcise' (quoted in Kuisel 1996: 99–100). As shown, it is not an old man that Colin has on his back. While he is pulled by a desire—misplaced though it may be—against knowledge, towards modernization, leaving behind tradition, he will be forever dogged by regret in the form of the older woman. In terms of the love story, she may be interpreted as a symbolic representation of Alise, the girl whose love Colin spurned, and whose fate it is either to grow old alone or to die in a bid to galvanize the men around her. From a perspective of national identity, on the other hand, this woman, with her deceptively youthful appearance that fails to stand up to close scrutiny, embodies a decayed and fading Marianne.

The novel's denouement contains all the ambiguity of the fetish itself. Following Chloé's funeral in a paupers' cemetery, Colin is left grieving not beside her grave but at the edge of a pool, beneath the surface of which the reader is led to believe lies the water lily that had previously infected his wife's lung. Intermittently, he averts his gaze from the water's surface and contemplates a photograph. In other words, Colin is still torn between a bleak future and his past. His yearning for the past to have been different is twofold: his wish that his marriage had worked can be counterbalanced by a regret that he failed to take his love for Alise to a different conclusion. Indeed, as the novel draws to an end, it is not clear whose photo he is taking to his grave.

The lack of closure that marks the end of Colin's love story reflects the ambivalent attitudes that the French fostered in regard to the United States as early as 1945. It has been shown how a close examination of *L'Écume des jours* allows us to reassess the period of the Liberation through the lens of an ambiguity that has been seen as the hallmark of French popular culture in the Cold War era. In short, the history of mixed feelings between France and America can be shown to coincide with the launch of the Série Noire. Clearly, as Claire Gorrara notes, 'the success of certain genres at different historical junctures is predicated on the ways they embody the prevalent concerns of the day' (Gorrara 2003a: 7). Chapter 3 shows how the mood of the people and the literature they read in fact inform each other. Marcel Duhamel's success in liberated Paris is seen as an astute blend of 'giving his readers what they want' and painting a realistic picture of the times.

Deborah E. Hamilton has noted this same pattern in the more obviously satirical works of the Série Noire of the 1950s, in which there is a strong sense of melancholia and desire for a return to the good old days (the novels of John Amila and Auguste le Breton spring to mind). She describes the success of noir as follows: '[W]hereas the strong public taste for the hard-boiled format obliged authors to adapt their style to this form, it also provided them with a platform to question the assumed progressive nature of a post-war reconstruction fuelled in part by US policies' (Hamilton 2000: 233). The masterstroke of Marcel Duhamel was to do all this in 1945.

3
Allegorical Noir: Boris Vian and the Série Noire (2)

Chapter 2 showed how the years immediately following the Liberation of Paris were marked by feelings towards the United States that were not only mixed but deeply ambivalent. The French threw themselves with gusto into American jazz music, crowded into cinemas to watch American films and developed a passion for any book carrying the famous words 'translated from the American'. At the same time, they resented the presence on French soil of another occupying force, as if the GIs only served to reinforce the shame of defeat and Occupation at the hands of the Germans. There were basically two ways in which the French psyche could deal with these emotions: either, after an initial period of catharsis, these American cultural phenomena could be rejected; or, alternatively, they could be appropriated into French culture. Jazz and France to this day have a special relationship.[1] As for noir fiction, Robert E. Conrath has described how it seems designed to transcend national boundaries: 'The passionate and ambiguous relationship between [France and the United States] has turned the *roman noir* into a sort of floating signifier for all that was bad in our contemporary society' (Conrath 1995: 44). With this in mind this chapter examines how French noir fiction of the mid- to late 1940s can be read allegorically, allowing French readers to renegotiate their society and to come to terms with the end of the Second World War. And to begin, we return to Boris Vian, and in particular to the ending of *L'Écume des jours*, which fits perfectly into this noir mood.

'L'Écume des jours' as an allegory of the Liberation

The social-commentary reading of the end of *L'Écume des jours* is reinforced by the fact that it is recounted from the point of view of

Colin's pet mouse. If the mouse can be seen as a microcosm of the story, its loss being comparable to that of the principal human characters, it is equally true that Colin's story transcends his personal universe, becoming that of society as a whole. The message for the French people seems to be that while to hark back to the past is to overlook the wonders of the modern age, to seek to compensate for the memory of the Nazi occupation with the fruits of consumer society is a short-term strategy that can only lead to disaster. For not only is Chloé predestined to die in the same way that the notes of a record lead to its end, but her end is part of an acceleration of the pace of history. Entirely fashioned by society, she is a consumer product, built to break and bought to be discarded. And as with all such products, Chloé is a misplaced desire, standing in for life, filling the void left by days in the modern city.

The role of the mouse in *L'Écume des jours* has often been swept aside, considered a touch of humour to be enjoyed but not necessarily worthy of further analysis. It is a potentially rich symbol, however, and one whose possible provenance is open to speculation. For the purposes of this study it is our suggestion that the little mouse stands as a sign of the times. Firstly, Vian's adornment of his text with a mouse was something of a fashion statement on the Left Bank when *L'Écume des jours* was published. Gérard Henry, for example, notes how mice were used to accessorize the bobby-soxers in 1947:

> The newspaper [*Le Samedi-soir*, 3 May 1947] even provides their dress code: for the boys, tousled hair, shirt open to the navel, brightly coloured striped socks; for the girls, hair cut to fall straight down onto the chest, *some white mice in the trouser pockets* and a strict prohibition on make-up. It's a natural, almost unisex style, as launched by Juliette Gréco...
>
> (Henry, 2004—our emphasis)

This fashion was over by 1948, along with the vogue for Existentialism. The figure of the zazou was replaced as the pinnacle of fashion from 1947 onwards in favour of Christian Dior's New Look. This American-named style (the term was coined by *Harper's Bazaar*'s Carmel Snow), which included such dresses as 'Miss New York', ushered into Paris a wave of extravagance that shocked those who had lived through the hardship of the Occupation. Antony Beevor and Artemis Cooper record how a model, fated to enter posterity as *l'élégante de la rue Lepic*, was beaten and had her clothes all but ripped from her body by outraged Parisian women when the New Look made an impromptu debut at the street markets of Montmartre in March 1947 (Beevor and Cooper 1995: 315).[2] In this instance, an ostentatious display clashes starkly with the lived experience of the Parisian populace emerging from the rubble of the war. Dior's model receives a symbolic punishment comparable to that meted out to collaborators. Women, and the clothes they wear, are doubly symbolic in the aftermath of the Second World War: they point not only to a better, brighter future (Dior's New Look was also met with great acclaim in France and beyond, as one of its first major post-war exports) but also to scars that will take generations to heal. In this light, Boris Vian's Chloé is as short-lived as the fashions of popularized Existentialism, the zazous and the New Look, and the fate of the mouse is testimony to the apprehension with which the French looked to the future.

The French word for mouse, *une souris*, is also a sign of the times. Indeed, it is one of the more commonly used terms for a female character in the early novels of Duhamel's Série Noire. Vian's writing is famous for the way in which figurative terms revert to their literal sense. In this case a dame (*souris*) becomes a mouse (*souris*). The importance of this double meaning, or floating signifier, to use Conrath's term, becomes more readily understandable when one considers that Vian was writing *L'Écume des jours* just as he was discovering the work of James Hadley Chase and Peter Cheyney. Thus, while the work of Peter Cheyney is introduced into our discussion only after our analysis of the role played by Boris Vian in introducing noir fiction to France, the inspiration for the noir motifs of *L'Écume des jours* sprang, in all probability, from Vian's reading of the first works of the Série Noire. Our argument is that the urge to read American fiction in post-war France is, of itself, a noir act or, at the very least, a reaction to a noir mood that already held sway.

While the extent to which the development of French noir fiction depends on a complex textual interpenetration between France and the United States cannot easily be dismissed, it must also be remembered that this takes into account only the way in which noir mood is *produced*—noir mood, it must be remembered, is also a *response to* prevailing moods. It is our contention here that France, with its long-standing literary predilection for lamenting the loss of a mythical heartland (invariably crystallized around Paris, as seen in the poetry of Charles Baudelaire and, later, the Surrealists), was predisposed to noir fiction, and furthermore that the psychological damage wrought by the Second World War was, in literary terms, a revisiting of the modernization of the capital that took place in the mid-nineteenth century.

The particular use of leg fetishism in Duhamel's first translated title of 1945, Peter Cheyney's *La Môme vert-de-gris*, is discussed in the following section, as are the ramifications—in terms of conceptualizing French noir—of Duhamel's choice of title. Suffice to say that in *La Môme vert-de-gris* and *L'Écume des jours*, there is a third meaning of the term *souris* on which Vian and Duhamel both draw. For, *souris* also has more historically specific connotations that are crucial to an understanding of French noir: *la souris grise* was the term used by the French to denote a female officer in the Wehrmacht. The grey mouse in *L'Écume des jours* has often been deemed to parallel Chloé in the text, adding a dose of domesticity—and standing in opposition—to Alise. If one takes into account this use of wartime vernacular, and if Chloé and the grey mouse are linked, then Colin can be accused of sleeping with the enemy, which taints the euphoric, Liberation light in which critics have tended to bathe the novel. One may also consider the possibility that Alise herself (Colin's true love, not the woman for whom he settles in her absence), with her shock of blonde hair, is of Germanic origin. As Alise is the more significant female character of *L'Écume des jours* (indeed, she is arguably the text's protagonist),[3] we look to her as the centre of the novel's allegorical potential.

The reading of *L'Écume des jours* as an allegory of the Liberation of Paris is essentially double-edged: on the one hand, Alise symbolizes Germania (viewed in this light, she is *la souris grise*); and on the other hand, she can be interpreted as Marianne (standing in opposition to Colin and Chloé when the latter are viewed as collaborators or, at least, as characters withdrawn from active resistance against an oppressive regime).

Marie-Agnès Morita-Clément comments at length on the problematic love between the young French woman and the German soldier billeted in her house in Vercors's *Le Silence de la mer*. Writing in 1985, Morita-Clément points out that the opposite scenario—a French male falling in love with a female member of the occupying forces—is simply not written about: 'On the other hand, there are, at least as far as I am aware, no novels in which a French male becomes attached, for example, to a German secretary' (Morita-Clément 1985: 84). The fact that the French psyche has had difficulty in conceiving of a man failing in this way to carry out his duty of resistance (an attitude that fails to take into account the reality of life in *les années noires*) is also reflected in the *épuration* itself, which has become synonymous with the shaving of the heads of those who had allegedly engaged in 'horizontal collaboration'—an iconic retribution for a mythologized scapegoat. Only five years after the publication of Morita-Clément's study there appeared on French bookshelves the story of the love affair between Marc Danceny and Maria, an officer in the Wehrmacht. Robert Sabatier's *La Souris verte* (1990) is the tragic tale of a love affair that cannot succeed; it is also a sincere and touching account of the day-to-day endurance of the Occupation of Paris. While the love that Marc expresses for Maria is pure—and, indeed, lasting—the story is also one of the burgeoning of a young man's sexuality at a time when the artifice and deception of sexual attraction was further exacerbated by the new facts of life under occupation.

There are several interesting points of intersection between Sabatier's novel and *L'Écume des jours*. For instance, Marc's sexual initiation reveals the paradox of *La Souris verte*; this is not pure sexuality but sex in the city 1940s-style:

> At that point, whilst I stood still in embarrassment, my roses in my arms, she began painting her legs with a concoction, perhaps made of tea or chicory, which was coloured brown to look like stockings...Then she held out a brush and a bottle of black liquid and asked me to complete her work: fake stockings required a fake seam, which I was to trace on the back of her calves and thighs.
>
> (Sabatier 1990: 36)

In *L'Écume des jours* it is not only a seam on a woman's leg that Colin paints; he fashions himself an entire woman, arranging Chloé from a pallet comprising the golden-haired Alise and *la souris grise*. Chloé represents a composite French future, one negotiated by players external to events as lived in France. She is ushered into the novel on the heels of legs swathed in nylon: this is a sign of Liberation, of the US cultural dominance that was to begin as soon as the war was won.

During the Occupation years themselves, the appearance of nylon in Paris would have been more problematic. If *L'Écume des jours* is to be read as a retrospective critique of *les années noires*, then nylon still points away from Chloé as *souris grise* and towards her position among Allied ranks, where as Dominique Veillon points out, nylon stockings that found their way to France via the resistance were potent signifiers, '[constituting] a risk for the women who wore them (for the same reason as did English cigarettes for smokers) because they pointed in an obvious way to the links formed with the British or the Gaullists' (Veillon 2002: 138). Stockings also enhance the argument for reading Alise as *souris grise* in the text. Sabatier recalls the availability of luxury items, including silk stockings this time, to a German military that was busy profiting from all that was traditionally (and mythologically) French: 'Weighed down with occupation Marks, whose value had been greatly inflated, the German military exchanged their funny money for all that commerce had to offer (clothes, perfume, cloth, silk stockings, shoes, trinkets and so on) in what amounted to acts of organized pillaging' (Sabatier 1990: 19–20).

If the golden-haired Alise with her silk stockings represents Germany, then Colin's choice of partner may be framed as an act of resistance, of doing the right, even the patriotic thing (although patriotism was much-disputed territory throughout the war years) when his love was for a representative of the enemy. His decision to take Chloé as his partner is guided by Nicolas (who takes on the guise of de Gaulle) under the pretence that it would be inappropriate to select Alise as she already belongs to another man. The Occupation reading forces the morals of this choice to take on a historically specific political resonance. Vian may thus be seen to be noiring readers' expectations of a Liberation novel. His fairy-tale-like account is, in fact, brutally realistic once its veneer has been stripped back. The Occupation had been a long story of a people forced, in a sense, to survive by sleeping with Alise and putting aside their (patriotic) affiliation to Chloé.

Interestingly, Sabatier also draws on the theme of taboo (which is what keeps Colin from Alise). Marc is also drawn to a woman who belongs to another man, in this case his young stepmother. Daniéla's allure is linked to her perfume: 'Once we had arrived at the flat, Daniéla raised herself up on tip-toes, kissed my cheek and said: "Thank you, Marc!" I smelled her perfume. In reply I said stupidly: "What perfume is that?" She replied that she was not wearing any' (Sabatier 1990: 228). In *L'Écume des jours* Chloé wears perfume whereas Alise's fragrance is natural, and Colin's reaction to the latter's scent is expressed in almost identical terms to those cited above. At this time of painted legs, to be natural is to be not of one's time or simply out of reach.

This noir interpretation of the novel allows Alise's final acts of vengeance (not so much against those intellectuals who stood in the way of her love of Colin, but against a city that had opened its mind but not its heart to her) to be translated onto the schema of Liberation: as she beats her retreat she razes her enemies' city. Alise's torching of the bookshops becomes an allegory for the German withdrawal from Paris, a period of bitter fighting and no little scorched earth. This reading is essentially noir; it is a starkly realistic portrayal of France's all too recent past.

A more euphoric—and mythological—spin on this ending is produced if one considers Alise to derive her power from popular images of the iconic figure of Marianne. This reading looks not to the violence of the past, but focuses instead on Alise's resurrection. The discovery of Alise's hair in the flames becomes a ray of hope for the future. As already mentioned, Alise acts while other characters bow and accept (and even instigate) their fate; she prefers to go out in a blaze of glory, avenging her partner Chick (whose own death may be read as an allegory for the violent acts committed by the Gestapo and the *milice*) by killing the man who caused his downfall. She then proceeds to set fire to the bookshops of Paris. She flies from the text from the midst of burning ruins, leaving behind her golden hair, which the flames cannot consume because it is brighter than they are:

> A brilliant light, brighter still than the flames, shone forth from amidst the dusty ashes. The smoke disappeared quickly as it was drawn up towards the floor above. The fire had abated around the books, but the ceiling was blazing stronger than ever. On the floor, all that remained was this light. Dirty with ash, his hair blackened, Nicolas crawled towards it, struggling to breathe. He could hear the heavy footfalls of the firemen as they worked busily. Then, under a mangled iron joist, he saw the glittering blond fleece. The flames had not been able to devour it, for it was brighter than they.
>
> (Vian 1999: 189)[4]

This vision of Marianne rising from the ashes of Liberation combines the stories of the retrieval of the hidden busts of *la République* and the blinding light of Paul Colin's famous poster. The following scene, recounted by Maurice Agulhon and Pierre Bonte, tells of one particular bust of Marianne in the aftermath of the Occupation. The surprising resonance sheds new light on the discovery of Alise's hair:

> In the glorious sunshine, Marianne seemed to be shouting out in victory. For all that, she lost nothing of the slender, nonchalant grace of the painter's typical model. Less magnificent, perhaps, but moving nonetheless, was the reappearance in 1944, at Floure town hall, of the bust of Marianne that had remained hidden under a pile of coal.
>
> (Agulhon and Bonte 1992: 83)

While this provides a persuasive contextualization of the ending of *L'Écume des jours*, it does not fit as easily within a noir framework. In the former interpretation, in which Alise stands as a retreating Germania and not as a resurgent Marianne, the artificial Chloé becomes the rather woeful torchbearer for the Republic, while the fate of the *souris grise* (here to be read as the retreating German army, or the purging of collaborators) is decided blindly: the mouse rushes from the ruined apartment and, full of regret for the suffering of the man left behind, places her head in the jaws of a cat whose teeth will snap down on her neck when a group of blind children pass by and stand on its tail.

Chloé does not make it through the story at all. For her there is no Liberation, no party—only death and a burial in a paupers' grave. As an interpretation of the end of the war, this is indeed a bleak vision. And it certainly does not tie in with the understanding of Vian as an unthinking wartime reveller or as a naive supporter of all things American. Instead, it offers up an image of a Vian immersed in the mood of noir fiction. *L'Écume des jours* thus stands as a reminder that all is not black and white, and, more ominously, that Marianne is not back from the ashes but that the France of collective memory is gone forever, replaced by a global power struggle in which Frenchness will need to be disputed like a bone between dogs. Not only is Vian's anti-American message present, but it is discernible long before America has gone out of fashion.

Peter Cheyney and the grey-green dame

Writing of the French obsession with noir fiction, Conrath asks what becomes of a literary tradition when it is the object of inter-cultural exchange: 'What happens…when a genre that is misunderstood in its country of origin receives a more productive critical reaction in another country? And what happens when the writers and critics of this "adopted homeland" find an almost inexhaustible source of meaning in these texts?' (Conrath 1995: 39). One must certainly question whether something so widely accepted as American can remain so when it has been so successfully adopted and internalized by the French. Certainly, terms such as American and French, if they are to continue to have relevance in this context, must be shown to refer to readers' sensibilities and the context in which meaning is produced in a deconstructive sense.[5] It is this question that occupies the remainder of this chapter.

It cannot be denied that the words 'Série Noire' have become synonymous with French noir fiction. These famous books with their familiar black and yellow covers stand for all that is associated with noir: they fit into a 'hard-boiled tradition' and have plots involving violence, corrupt detectives and dames of dubious virtue; and they are often set in the United States. This has long been accepted as the world of noir. And yet, the final obvious hallmark of Marcel Duhamel's famous collection, which tends to jar with our understanding of the novels of the Série Noire as the standard-bearers of French noir fiction, is that they are often originally authored by Anglo-Saxon authors. As a result, the quest to define French noir fiction has led, understandably and perhaps inevitably, to the acceptance of a tacit code of critical double standards. Gorrara, for example, has sought to distinguish between authors of French noir (the first, in her opinion, being Léo Malet) and non-French authors of noir fiction that is widely consumed in translation by French readers (which is the case of Peter Cheyney's work). At the same time she uses the inclusion of French authors in the Série Noire (such as Serge Arcouët and Jean Meckert, whom she cites as being among the first to make the leap) as a mark of legitimacy, that is, a French author could be seen to have been accepted into the noir canon once he or she had been published by Marcel Duhamel. (This is indeed, as shown in Chapter Four, the reason why Vernon Sullivan has been seen as an author of noir parody while Terry Stewart has been integrated into the noir mainstream.)

It is clearly not the aim of this study to undermine the formative role of the Série Noire in the establishment of a recognizable French noir tradition: on the contrary, 1945, and the launch of the Série Noire, is a pivotal date in the history of French noir. Our contention here is that the novels of the Série Noire, inasmuch as they give voice to the motifs and tropes that constitute noir fiction, should indeed be given full recognition as exemplars of French noir. Furthermore, the legitimization of these motifs and tropes, which Duhamel's collection establishes, may be extended beyond the black and yellow borders of the Série Noire, and the work of Boris Vian is a perfect example of this assumption of a noir identity. Finally, and most importantly in the framework of this section, novels that feature in the Série Noire, and which are originally authored by non-French writers are also considered exemplars of French noir. Our reasons derive not only from the particularity of the translation project undertaken by Marcel Duhamel's team but also from the impact that the publication of these texts had in France and the mood that prevailed at that time, to which these texts spoke so poignantly. The key text to explore for all these reasons is the very first title to be published in the Série Noire: Peter Cheyney's *La Môme vert-de-gris*.

Poison Ivy is now something of a collector's item. Its French avatar, however, is easy to purchase: *La Môme vert-de-gris* was reprinted in France as late as 1982. Peter Cheyney is no longer a sine qua non of the

Anglophone discourse of hard-boiled fiction (as opposed to such writers as James M. Cain, Dashiell Hammett and Ernest Hemingway, e.g.); and yet his name is still much discussed in French academia. There are obvious reasons for Cheyney's erasure from the English canon: his writing is formulaic and, undoubtedly, hackneyed. His continued success in French lies in the quality of the translated text: with great deftness, Cheyney's translators produced texts that were arguably of more significant literary merit than the originals. Such attention to the quality of the product is the driving force of the Série Noire.[6]

The question of translating detective fiction in the immediate post-war years has given rise to an impressive body of work.[7] Marc Lapprand in his work on Boris Vian's 'parodic translations', for example, raises the issue of translating text for the needs of a specific audience. According to Lapprand, Boris Vian only began to translate Anglo-American detective fiction into French after he had begun to take himself seriously as a novelist in his own right. Production of fiction (in one's own name) and the translation of another's text, it would appear, go hand in hand. Boris Vian's case is seen to be more problematic still because, in addition to the novels signed in his own name and his translations (for Marcel Duhamel and others), he also produced four pseudo-translations under the nom de plume of Vernon Sullivan. Needless to say, the three varieties of textual production became intertwined in such a way that his translations are as much influenced by his own writing as the latter is influenced by Anglo-American crime fiction. Indeed, Lapprand suggests that Vian's interest in this genre led him to translate in such a way as to arouse a similar sensibility in his compatriots: 'In terms of reception, Vian directly aided the adoption of the detective genre in France. At the time the genre's status was still very much in the balance, and he remained faithful to its norms whilst at the same time working his own personal touches into his translations' (Lapprand 1992: 538).

In order to make this genre appetizing to a French palate, it was inevitable that the translators of the Série Noire collection should pay more interest to the French that they were producing than to the English that they were translating. Vian was no exception; his translation practice was, as Lapprand notes, more target-oriented (*cibliste*) than source-based (*sourcier*): 'Having had no first-hand experience of life in North America, he was able to give free rein to his imagination, and as he facilitated the shift from one language to the other he gave greater prominence to the target language than the original' (1992: 538). These words will be shown to apply equally well to the works translated by Marcel Duhamel himself. In fact, the French novels produced in the Série Noire will not only give French readers access to an imaginary America but also to a reappraisal of their own French imaginary. For Duhamel's texts will do more than tune into French feelings linguistically; they will bear the marks of history.

Lapprand notes how Vian emphasized certain historical references in his translation of Raymond Chandler's novel of 1943, *The Lady of the Lake*. For example, he renders 'Like they're doing all over the world right now' by 'C'est comme ce qu'ils font sur toute la terre en ce moment, *avec cette guerre* [*with this war*]' (Lapprand 1992: 540—our emphasis). This will undoubtedly be considered by readers to be a logical translator's addition; it resituates, for the French post-war audience, the wartime context in which Chandler's novel was originally published (in English).[8] What may appear more problematic is the issue of the more discreet, and more insidiously powerful, recontextualization effected by Marcel Duhamel and his team in the translation of the first titles to appear in French in the series, which were originally published before the war. In particular, it will be shown how Duhamel's translation of Peter Cheyney's *Poison Ivy*, which appeared in English as early as 1937, offers more than a few passing references to the Second World War. So much so in fact that, in 1945, the newly published French work offers a striking allegory of France's plight during and immediately after the war. As such, its status as 'translation' is every bit as vexed as that of any of Vian's works.

While noting the individuality of Cheyney's creation, Lemmy Caution, Claude Mesplède and Jean-Jacques Schleret point to the importance of being 'in the right place at the right time' in their consideration of Marcel Duhamel's noir project:

> One of the innovative aspects of these books lay in the incessant spiel of the 'hero' who commentates on his every action in fairly colourful language. This aspect did not escape Marcel Duhamel who launched his Série Noire collection in 1945 with Cheyney's first two novels. French readers were immediately hooked … Such success can only be understood by putting these works into the context of the post-war era. The 'free' ('*aérées*') translations of Duhamel and his team contributed greatly to this phenomenon by bringing a certain charm to the Lemmy Caution novels.
>
> (Mesplède and Schleret 1996: 94)

Mesplède and Schleret are right to put the word 'hero' in inverted commas, and this is a point that is discussed later. What is more noticeable, on the other hand, is that they fail to elaborate on what they mean by 'putting the works in the context of the post-war era'.

The reason for the successful timing of Cheyney's relaunch in France in 1945 hinges on the specific needs of his French readership. At the time of the Liberation of Paris in 1944 the French psyche had been damaged to such an extent by four years of Nazi occupation that concepts of truth, right and wrong, and notions of what constituted Frenchness had become severed from any stable landmarks. Conrath agrees that the time was right for noir; indeed, all Duhamel did was to provide (in an inspired move, no doubt) what the people were crying out for:

> When the first volume of the *Série noire* appeared in October 1945, France was licking its wounds. French readers were desperate for something that was both the product of a far-off culture, coloured with exoticism, and which did not directly enact the unthinkable horrors of the recent past. At the same time they were looking for stories and a narrative to convey a new range of feelings and emotions brought on by the war; they wanted a literature that could displace horror by making it human, more accessible, more individualistic and subjective.
>
> (Conrath 1995: 40)

From a psychological perspective, the French readers of the Série Noire valued these new hard-boiled thrillers because they could see in them, through the protective lens of translation, a model for renegotiating their own national identity. Our analysis of Peter Cheyney's popularity in France takes two parallel, if opposite, points into consideration: first, the allegorical reading of *La Môme vert-de-gris* offered here is the product of our particular thesis, our view that 'to noir' is to trouble traditional binary oppositions, and that noir itself is the product of a sensibility shift whose origins lay in the aftermath of the Second World War; second, it is our opinion that noir mood is not only a response to a prevalent mood and Zeitgeist, but that it is also manufactured, and as such that Duhamel, by operating a coloured—or noired—translation agenda, actively brought to popular attention a literary form that would become recognizable as French noir fiction. This dual ownership of French noir fiction—authorial production of and reader response to noir mood—is then shown to tap into a pre-existing legacy of nostalgia; that is to say that the French response to Liberation was to revert to a traditionally French mode of longing for a utopian identity, whose key literary exponents do not include Raymond Chandler and Dashiell

Hammett but Charles Baudelaire, André Breton and Louis Aragon. It must be remembered, therefore, that the French translations of these novels are worded in such a way as to make allegories of the Occupation and Liberation stand out against the more historically neutral pages of the original English. While the nostalgic reading offered here still functions in relation to *Poison Ivy*, emphasis is placed on the post-war reading experience and not on any would-be authorial intent of Cheyney himself, who, as previously noted, wrote his novel before the Second World War began.[9]

Given the post-war context in which it appears, *La Môme vert-de-gris* can legitimately be considered a classic of French noir fiction. It should be noted in passing that the term 'noir'—as in film noir—had not yet become popular parlance when Duhamel launched his series. As mentioned in Chapter 2, the very concept of 'noir' hinges upon a flow of critical discourse between France and the United States, and the coining of the term by Nino Frank both captures a mood, a shifting of identity and, at the same time, refers back to Duhamel's novels. In terms of film noir itself, the term becomes used by French critics in response to a wave of American films that came to Paris in the summer of 1946. As Raymond Borde and Etienne Chaumeton write later in the first major study of American film noir: 'In the course of a few weeks, from mid-July to the end of August, five films followed one another on the cinema screens of Paris, films which had an unusual and cruel atmosphere in common' (Borde and Chaumeton 2002: 1).[10] This American experience was then discussed by the French in terms of 'noir', a term that was subsequently taken up by the Americans themselves in relation to films sharing this bleakness of mood. It is our contention that the mood that was so prevalent in these American films caught on in France not because it brought 'a nice change' but because it struck a chord. As has already been stated, while noir is built around and creates mood, it also feeds off it. Speaking of the reception of American cinema in France in the late 1940s, Jill Forbes writes,

> [i]t promoted uncertainty about the truth of the image, about our capacity to distinguish black from white, and because it presented the individual as, at best, an explorer on the road to knowledge . . . [But] it also helped to provide the necessary means of mental reorganization, not so much a mind-set as a new image of the individual and the world, a means of looking at things with fresh eyes, recasting the same elements in a different, more satisfying, configuration, one that allowed the possibility of an alternative version of events

and which held out the promise that actions might be guilt-free. France had a culture in which, unlike that of America, psycho-analysis took root slowly and with difficulty. In that context, the American cinema, in the latter part of the 1940s, offered a therapeutic and more ambiguous view of things than the one envisaged by the propaganda-merchants of the US diplomatic service.

(Forbes 1997: 38)

When Lemmy Caution enters Paris it is not yet 1946. The French are still emerging from the Second World War. The babbling commentary of this off-beat detective does not read like a didactic tale, and Lemmy is no shining light or trustworthy patriarch. More analysand than analyst, Cheyney's protagonist confides in his readers, empowering them to engage with him in the struggle for justice in his noir universe. Given that Lemmy is neither hero nor anti-hero, French readers would have found in his struggle the same human weaknesses that had been brought into prominence during their experiences of the Occupation.

The noir mood of post-war Paris, which is so readily eclipsed by later images of the euphoric dancing of the zazous and bobby-soxers in the subterranean jazz clubs of Saint-Germain-des-Prés,[11] is perhaps most eloquently expressed in Paul Colin's poster of 17 August 1944, 'Libération'.[12] The image reflects the return to France of the beloved Marianne. This symbolizes the return of the Republic, which had been put aside under Pétain's regime, and the ultimate victory of France (female in terms of post-revolution iconography) over two patriarchs. Marianne is depicted rising up from the ashes of destruction to stand once again for French values. But these values are revealed to be damaged. The plunge from the darkness of *les années noires* into the bright light of Liberation is blinding, and Marianne has to shade her eyes from the future. As mayors all around France were retrieving busts of Marianne that had spent the war hidden away in cellars, a realization that things would never again be the same was an inescapable accompaniment to the celebrations of victory.

Cheyney's novels offer a dose of hard-hitting realism. This is a case of inoculation: he offers a small dose of what the people need. The French psyche could not leap straight back into a state of blissful normality. Indeed, *La Môme vert-de-gris* not only stands as a reminder that no return is possible for the Marianne of *la vieille France*; it also reveals such nostalgia for past glories to be based on an entirely phantasmagorical interpretation of history. Things cannot go back to the way they were for the simple reason that they never were how they are retrospectively imagined to have been. Lemmy Caution, Cheyney's 'hero', will dispel myths, treading a third way between the Manichaean choices that had been offered to the French throughout the Occupation, and which had arisen once again by 1947 in the form of the Cold War. Cheyney noirs reality, offering to his French readers a new Marianne, a female icon deliberately tainted and clothed in a protective fetish.

All Cheyney's leading ladies are essentially variations on a theme, and as such they lend themselves perfectly to their readers' need to invest them with allegorical significance. Instances of fetishism in the French translations of his novels correspond to the psychological need of the French public to draw up a screen between their eyes and the blinding light of reality. As shown in Chapter 2, fetishism is the tortured path that one treads when one's belief system is flawed and when one knows that things are not how one would desire them to be.[13] Thus Cheyney's women are just so many body parts. In his biography of Peter Cheyney, Michael Harrison quotes Allan Sinclair, who describes Cheyney's female characters as follows: 'They were all the Adolescent Boy's dream—and they all had the same figures, and wore "beige stockings of sheer silk". He was almost colour-blind to women's clothes' (Harrison 1954: 269). Such caricatural descriptions not only clothe Cheyney's female characters but also fetishize them, priming them for fetishistic interpretation.

Poison Ivy is the nickname of the dame Carlotta. And for a French reader, bathed in the renaissance of Republican iconography, Carlotta provides an allegory for France herself. Indeed, the French translation of this title alerts the reader to the novel's potential as an allegory for the emergence of France from the war. *La Môme vert-de-gris* is therefore not simply to be understood as the 'grey-green dame'. *Môme* is a common French substitution for the particularly hard-boiled term 'dame'. *Souris* is another term used in the same way. And, as shown, *une souris grise* was also the term used during the Occupation to refer to a female officer of the Wehrmacht. Similarly *vert-de-gris* is precisely the colour given to describe a German uniform. With her dual French and German resonance, Marcel Duhamel's Carlotta announces her fetish early; she will symbolize the French paradox: a desire for Marianne to return, coupled with the knowledge that she was only ever a mythological creation.

For the novel to succeed in France, the trade-off between knowledge and desire must allow for a French hand in the Allied victory and/or a tainting of that victory, against which the story of the Occupation will be just one among many ignominious tales of war. Lemmy Caution is an American agent who employs underhand tactics in defeating the (American-Italian) mafiosi: vacillating between hero and thug, he is pointedly not John Wayne. He flits continually across borders, including national boundaries. In this way, the novel has no geographical specificity; its waters are international, its space that of everyman. As such, *La Môme vert-de-gris* appeals to its readers indirectly and is thus ideally suited to Duhamel's allegorical project. This goes some way to explaining the choice of this singular novel as the inaugural text of the Série Noire. *Cet Homme est dangereux*, the third of the novels published in 1945, may well have been considered less readily adaptable to this end for the simple reason that it is set in France.[14]

The relationship between Carlotta and Lemmy is predicated entirely on fetishism. In the grubby world in which he moves, Lemmy wishes for Carlotta to live up to the myth of Marianne. His plight is comparable to that of the French people who, in their struggle for survival, have been condemned to place their trust in forces outside their control. His weaknesses correspond to a desire to view American supremacy with a dose of realism, as domination based on a combination of strength and luck, and not on some kind of divine right to conquer. Lemmy knows nothing; he plays things by ear, dealing in a harsh reality that is closer to Sartrean Existentialism than a traditional whodunit.[15] When Carlotta enters the text, Lemmy senses that she is flawed. His desire is that of the fetishist:

At that point I saw something that took my breath away and left me stunned. I saw a dame!...She was tall and moved like a queen with a figure to match....She had an oval face as white and as pure as marble...Beautiful?...Ah! I'm telling you that this dame had a mouth that was so perfect that you had to look twice to check you weren't dreaming.

(Cheyney 1945: 24–5)

Carlotta comes to epitomize the epistemological breakdown of the text. Knowing his vision to be misleading, Lemmy maintains his desire for her to be different in the form of the recognizable lexicon of fetishism:

So I stood there sniffing, and it was almost as though the dame Carlotta was there because I can tell you now that this dame's perfume will remain with me forever until after I'm gone....But I didn't discover anything except that the dame Carlotta has a classy lingerie collection and that she wears stockings so sheer that it was almost a sin to touch them.

(Cheyney 1945: 45–6)

The stockings represent Carlotta metonymically: they represent a phallic woman, a phantasmagorical icon of French power. This is the woman that Lemmy desires and the mythology that the French reader wishes to maintain: 'Deep down, I wished that the dame Carlotta was good, but my unfailing instinct—as women writers put it—told me that she was one of those dames who'd be quite capable of stealing your teeth while you were asleep' (Cheyney 1945: 50). This realistic negotiation of the narrative is accompanied by a surprisingly post-modern dissolution of Lemmy's fictional identity. Where one would expect a successful detective novel to lose its readers in a whirlwind of plot and deduction, Lemmy is just as concerned with engaging them in a succession of self-referential quips that appear to undo the very workings of the genre.[16] But then again, as Naremore maintains, noir is a mood and not a genre. Lemmy is aware of his failure ever to know or to understand—hence his fascination with desire—and this is necessarily accompanied by an empowerment of the reader. Thus, when we read the following line, we are called upon to challenge what exactly we understand ourselves to be reading: 'I told him that I had always been a fan of detective novels' (Cheyney 1945: 54). For it becomes increasingly clear not only that Lemmy is aware of his own status as protagonist but that he is also conscious of the extent to which his own tale is noiring the genre. His every action works to undermine the most fundamental basics of the Anglo-Saxon whodunit: by positing himself in a noired sphere between good and evil, the detective abandons both the objective omniscience of a Poirot or Marple and the moral superiority that comes with that certain sense of restoring things to their proper order.

It should also be noted that his idiosyncratic method of cracking a case, whilst individualistic, has little to do with the quest for an all-powerful truth. As such, Lemmy Caution exhibits the traits that Conrath suggests are the hallmark of the hero of the noir novel, who 'must fight alone to try, repeatedly and fleetingly, to establish his truth, that is to say, his freedom, his independence in the face of institutions who are trying to define it through the sheer force of their order' (Conrath 1995: 42–3). Perhaps the most important difference between the whodunit and the hard-boiled detective novel is the latter's consideration of truth with a small 't'. Lemmy Caution's truth is not an abstract value—it is not *the Truth*; rather, it is an example of textual productivity, a truth to be negotiated and constructed. Hence, the imposition of Lemmy's will is an active, writerly reading of the story of the *môme vert-de-gris*.

As has been seen, for the allegorical reading of the text to fulfil the psychological needs of a post-war French audience, the novel had to provide answers without those answers flowing from any necessary internal logic (for France's position in relation to the eventual Allied victory was all but clear); and neither could there seem to be any return to the comforts of tradition (as too much use had been made of too many traditional values under the Vichy regime for a sense of normality any longer to have credence). Thus, as both reader and protagonist alike flounder from incident to incident, Cheyney provides two scenes in which authorial power is ceremonially put to death.

Firstly, Lemmy is enticed on board a yacht following an invitation from Harberry Chase, the father of Willie *le pigeon*, a.k.a. Charles Chase, whose murder launches the intrigue. Harberry Chase wishes to expose his son's murder publicly by using a psychic to point the finger at the guilty party. In order for the psychic's powers to work fully, they must sail away from land-based interference. At the allegorical level, by taking the action into international waters, the text transcends national boundaries and makes the story universally applicable. Cheyney builds towards his murder of the author with a critique—delivered hard-boiled style—of the whodunit: 'Don't forget that most of what you read in detective novels is nonsense and that there aren't many detectives who discover things by sitting twiddling their thumbs' (Cheyney 1945: 149). In his contrasting view of how to get to the bottom of a case, San Reima, the seer, becomes both Poirotesque detective and the embodiment in the text of authorial power. Lemmy admits that such stories are a good yarn, and he himself is almost drawn in: '[San Reima] had a nice voice, soft with a fairly strong foreign accent, and the simple fact of his presence there looking at us had an almost magical calming effect' (Cheyney 1945: 156).[17]

When San Reima is shot dead by Cheyney's villain, Rudy, this signals—both in the novel and allegorically—the collapse of the status quo. Lemmy is left starkly in the contingent universe of noir. And with knowledge of the past and the future eliminated (in the form of San Reima), Lemmy necessarily reverts to a state of fetishism. Looking at Carlotta, he takes in her pose, which is primarily defined in terms of mood (the smoking dame), but focuses his desire (for his situation to be different) on her legs: 'At that precise moment I thought to myself that Carlotta had pretty ankles' (Cheyney 1945: 162).

Following Lemmy's escape from the yacht, the novel offers a second death-of-the-author scenario, in which, in addition to a further critique of the whodunit genre, we are presented with a veiled reference to the work of the other major English author writing in the Anglo-American hard-boiled style. The full name of the victim of the first murder in the novel is eventually discovered to be Charles Velas Chase, son of Harberry Velas Chase. The other author to make up the 1945 offering of the Série Noire collection was James Hadley Chase. As the role of Harberry Chase emerges as being pivotal to the plot of *La Môme vert-de-gris*, his role as patriarch begins to establish a referential discourse between Cheyney's novel and the work of James Hadley Chase. When Lemmy confronts Harberry Chase in London, the reader discovers that, far from wanting to avenge his adopted son's murder, the old man has been directing all the novel's criminal operations from the outset. Lemmy ignores Harberry Chase's smugness and delivers a self-consciously noired version of the whodunit exposure-of-the-murderer scene, at the end of which the ageing patriarch admits defeat, reaches for his revolver and is shot in the hand.[18] Cheyney thus uses his American gunslinger to castrate the principal figure of authorial power in the text, leaving power in the hands of Lemmy Caution, the protagonist to whom events happen and whose very modus operandi is characterized by a lack of control. In other words, the text sends up its own emergence on to—and unique status within—the literary scene, and Lemmy Caution becomes the very embodiment of what Naremore is referring to when he speaks of the 'European male fascination with the instinctive' (Naremore 1998: 12).

A brief comparison of the allegorical potential of *La Môme vert-de-gris* and the third of the three novels that opened the Série Noire, James Hadley Chase's *Pas d'orchidées pour Miss Blandish* [*No Orchids for Miss Blandish*], reveals a similar exploitation of female iconography. Whereas Cheyney's dame, Carlotta, though heavily fetishized, remains an active participant in events throughout *La Môme vert-de-gris*, Chase's beautiful heiress, Miss Blandish, is sequestrated and drugged, and remains the plaything of the Grisson gang until her liberation at the end of the novel. This plot provides a far more straightforward allegory for the Occupation. As a spoilt daddy's girl, Miss Blandish symbolizes a France torn away from an ageing and emasculated patriarch (Pétain) and left in the control of degenerate thugs. In the vision offered to the French reader by *Pas d'orchidées pour Miss Blandish*, Marianne is delivered from responsibility for the situation into which she is driven: she is not herself. While at first this appears to be a wistful, phantasmagorical reading of events—Marianne slumbers through her Occupation until

Liberation when she reawakens and becomes real again—with clearer distinctions between the forces of order and the cruel gangsters, the novel's ending delivers an uncompromising wake-up call to its French readers: Miss Blandish is rescued by Fenner the private detective but, unable to live with the scars of her ordeal once left alone, she commits suicide by jumping from her hotel window. Only in its tragic conclusion does *Pas d'orchidées pour Miss Blandish* stake its claim to be considered a noir classic.

At the allegorical level, Chase's noiring of the happy ending certainly paints a bleak picture for the future of France in the post-war world. And yet it is Cheyney who, by denying recourse to phantasmagoria, best exploits noir realism as narrative technique. Lemmy Caution succeeds in cracking the case precisely because he assumes his lack of knowledge and realizes that his desire is fundamentally flawed. If he succeeds in France, however, it is also because, having extolled a realistic view of the course of history, he manages nonetheless to give his French readers a sense of closure. For ultimately, the realism of blurred distinctions is a more effective means of delivering a satisfactory, digestible happy ending than an idealistic narrative that replicates the prevalent, schizophrenic tendency to apprehend the world in binary terms, and which serves only to compound despair.

The conclusion of *La Môme vert-de-gris* revels in noir: only by crawling through the dark does Lemmy find his way in: '[I]t was darker in there than a bottle of ink down a coalmine. I gradually got used to the darkness, however, and I moved a few steps forwards and found a door' (Cheyney 1945: 271). As a metaphor within the story, this underlies the naivety of the whodunit vision of detective work: in the real world there are no universal truths; such absolutes can only be constructed in the form of myths. As an allegory for Liberation, this search in the dark recalls the fact that the course of the Second World War hung in the balance; its ultimate conclusion cannot be retrospectively construed as ineluctable.

In terms of the mood of the text, Lemmy's decision not to light a match appeals to the oblique lighting techniques that are the hallmark of film noir. A shift from total blackness to sudden illumination would announce a polarization of the forces of light and dark, and it is precisely by giving himself up to the villains that Lemmy ultimately wins out. Victory is won through a mixture of tenacity on Lemmy's side and over-confidence on the side of the gangster; the author allows the detective no overwhelming superiority. Again, as an allegory for the French wartime experience, this victory through submission allows scope for inclusion of the work of the various Resistance groups whose efforts tend to pale into insignificance when compared to the irresistible Allied invasion force that landed in 1944.

Cheyney's masterstroke comes when Lemmy's instincts are put to the acid test. By handing himself over to the gangster Rudy Saltierra, he elects a course that is driven not by knowledge but by desire. He finally looks at Carlotta directly, forgoing his fetishistic negotiation of these two sides of the binary opposition and forcing a synthesis. In order for Lemmy to succeed, Carlotta must finally live up to his desires. This she does: 'I looked her in the eyes. For a few seconds I thought I saw them change colour' (Cheyney 1945: 281).

Just as Rudy is about to shoot Lemmy, Carlotta asks to be allowed to finish him off herself. Rudy hands her the gun, whereupon she turns on him and shows her true colours. Lemmy cannot win without Carlotta's intervention. Allegorically then, this reversal noirs the Allied victory in France. It is important to understand that—in terms of this noir reading of *La Môme vert-de-gris*—this does not imply a simple recasting of the ownership of victory (in which scenario, Marianne would not be liberated as much as she would liberate herself) but a tainting of that victory: Carlotta's intervention is made possible because of the murkiness of the waters. Only by blurring the distinctions between black and white can a realistic outcome be achieved. Only under the veil of fetishism can Cheyney's Carlotta disguise her power. By existing in the tension between knowledge and desire, she achieves tangible results.

In her discussion of Bernard Borderie's 1952 film version of *La Môme vert-de-gris*, Forbes suggests that the success of Dominique Wilms's portrayal of Carlotta lies in her caricatural persona: 'Everything about her is elongated—her legs, her frocks, her cigarettes and her vowels' (Forbes 1991: 90). Forbes also notes how the differences of nationality (between Wilms and the American-born, if not excessively American, Eddy Constantine) are exploited by Borderie in the sexual tension that he develops between the two characters. So charming is Constantine's Lemmy Caution that 'even the cold and distant Carlotta falls in love with him and betrays her gang' (Forbes 1991: 90).

In Cheyney's novel, on the other hand, Lemmy does not force Carlotta to change her desire; rather it is *his* desire—and his perspective, through which the French post-war reader is looking—that morphs to meet reality. Only when Lemmy ceases to desire Carlotta to be a myth (of beauty and goodness) can he appreciate her for what she is. In *Tropic of Cancer* Henry Miller reveals that the distinction between a French whore and an angel is in the eye of the beholder: 'Germaine had the right idea: she was ignorant and lusty, she put her heart and soul into the work. She was a whore all the way through—and that was her virtue!' (Miller 1993: 54). Carlotta, on the other hand, cannot be understood in the objective language of ideals; her 'heart and soul' are not relevant. In Cheyney's text, she must be experienced in the moment in order that her actions may speak for themselves.

In *La Môme vert-de-gris* Cheyney's lead woman is real: in Freudian terms, she is not a phallic woman. This makes her the perfect basis for Duhamel's allegorical transformation. Onto the Carlotta of the original English novel, *Poison Ivy*, is translated a female icon who noirs the myth of Marianne. The *môme vert-de-gris* traces a third way between binaries; her path lies between the double-cross of collaboration, whose grey-green colours she wears in her German-sounding cognomen, and the red, white and blue of French Republican legend. Her victory is made real by her interaction with her true ally. Allegorically, she both hesitates and acts as a point of intersection between France and the United States. To see the future in terms of mythological, jingoistic values in 1945 would have been to posit France outside events. Instead, France's new narrative is always already double, and nostalgic films and novels that seek to posit this modern reality against the myth of yesteryear would become widespread in the Cold War years. The success of *La Môme vert-de-gris* hinges, therefore, on Duhamel's ability to sell the French a version of the Liberation in which victory is won by real people at a real price.

4
Noir Strangulation (1): Terry Stewart and Vernon Sullivan

Strangulation is at the heart of noir. In terms of motifs, it is the coming together of sex and violence. At the nexus of textuality and sexuality, it is where the assertion of authorial control and abandonment meld together in a *danse macabre* fusing death and pleasure. Of all the celebrated examples of literary strangulation Lennie's, in *Of Mice and Men*, is perhaps the most famous. This murder is written indelibly into the landscape of thriller writing.[1] Indeed, it is referenced by no lesser figure than James Bond himself:

> Bond guessed that he would kill without interest or concern for what he killed and that he would prefer strangling. He had something of Lennie in *Of Mice and Men*, but his inhumanity would not come from infantilism but from drugs.[2]

While this observation from *Casino Royale* seems a little ironic—Lennie is, in many ways, far more humane than the calculating British agent— it is revealing that Steinbeck's novel should appear in a 1950s thriller. For all his humanity, the clumsy and deadly Lennie is undoubtedly a major source of inspiration for a series of killing sprees that marks the early years of the Série Noire. In fact, Lennie finds his way into French literature prior to the Série Noire, and still looms large today.[3] *Of Mice and Men* is a short novel; its characters do not have the time to grow old. They have become caricatures, larger than life and destined to extend beyond the parameters of Steinbeck's text. As Terry Stewart's Série Noire strangler, Ben Sweed, is warned, a man who kills with his hands is quickly traced. Obviously, all cases of death by strangulation from 1937 onwards on cannot be pinned on Lennie, but we can suggest that when he chokes the life out of Curley's wife he unwittingly sets in train an intertextual series of murders. If Bond is wrong in his assessment of the gentle giant, Lennie will live up to this reputation for inhumanity after his death. Intertextually, he will become one of the most prolific murderers of twentieth-century French fiction.

If it is commonly accepted that Boris Vian was a key figure in the development of noir literature in France, it is invariably assumed that the value of his contribution lies in the works that he wrote and published under the pseudonym of Vernon Sullivan. The ramifications of this attitude towards the work of Vernon Sullivan are at least double. First, those who have analyzed Sullivan from within the framework of Vian studies have tended to elevate his novels to the same literary status as those written in Vian's own name.[4] Second, and more importantly, the Sullivan novels are unquestioningly bracketed within an American literary lineage, the justification for which is generally Vian's much-cited love of US culture. Not only does this charge of zealous Americomania overlook both Vian's own comments on the negative aspects of American society, of which Duke Ellington and his music are clearly not representative, and the scathing anti-American sentiment present in his works, it also disregards the obvious critique of American society present in the works of the pioneers of the American hard-boiled tradition on their own side of the Atlantic. Gorrara, for example, notes how for 'American novelists like Hammett returning from the battlefields of the First World War, the American Dream had failed to materialize, leaving a bitter aftertaste of what could have been' (Gorrara 2003b: 591). While the rush on the part of the French in the years following the Liberation of Paris to read American novels and to view American films is well documented, the French tradition of noir in fact maintains a much hazier, and more realistic, focus on the United States.

The background against which the first of the Sullivan novels took form is anything but clear. Jacques Duchateau's pronouncement on the subject is, however, categorical: 'It was Jean d'Halluin who was behind *J'irai cracher sur vos tombes*' (Duchateau 1982: 67). The story of the wager that prompted Boris Vian to write *J'irai cracher sur vos tombes* [*I Spit on Your Graves*][5] in the space of two weeks in 1946 has become part of Vian folklore, and Duchateau's remark refers quite simply to publisher Jean d'Halluin's desire to have a best-seller to rival the success of Marcel Duhamel's opening gambit in his Série Noire. If a spin is put on the above quote, however, there begins to (re-)emerge a self-evident truth that has been all too readily circumvented: *J'irai cracher sur vos tombes* is a French novel written in Paris by a French author in what Vian playfully, but by no means innocently, referred to as a 'Latin tradition'.

Pestureau notes the incident, quoting an interview given by Vian to Gilbert Ganne: '[Jean d'Halluin] said to me: I'd need something quite erotic, something along the lines of *Pas d'orchidées* [*No Orchids for Miss Blandish*]. I said to him: Why are you looking for examples in America? There must be resources in our fine tradition of Latin erotic literature' (Pestureau 1978: 262).

In appealing to a Latin erotic tradition in his preface to the novel, Vian distances himself from such American authors as Henry Miller (who, arguably, could himself be said to be part of a Parisian writing tradition).[6] Indeed, Vian goes to some lengths, both in the preface and in the text of the novel itself, to steer away from American hegemony: references to France and the USA continually draw sharp distinctions between the two cultures throughout *J'irai cracher sur vos tombes*, to the point where it is clear that the novel's noir credentials cannot depend on any crossing of national boundaries (and the same is true of sexual and racial boundaries).[7] There is, therefore, a constant and heavily underscored vacillation between the two sides of a number of binary oppositions, but the tendency to pass over (and to become, as Jones is keen to stress, *un passe-blanc* (Jones 1999), a black man passing for white) only serves to reinforce polarities. It is this black-and-white tension that prompts us to consider in what ways *J'irai cracher sur vos tombes*, if it is to be analyzed as a work of literature, can properly be seen to be noir. The very success of noir in the post-war years lies in its ability to blur boundaries and to negotiate a third way through dichotomies. And, as demonstrated in Chapter 3, Peter Cheyney goes to great lengths to keep his novels in neutral territories by situating his plots in diverse geographical locations, keeping his characters on the move and, in the case of *La Môme vert-de-gris*, specifically locating his novel in international waters.

J. K. L. Scott suggests that in creating Vernon Sullivan, Vian goes beyond noir: 'In effect, Vian out-Herods Herod, creating a *roman noir* (or rather, a *roman d'un noir*) which is blacker than anything an American audience would have experienced' (Scott 1996: 215). Of course, if a novel is blacker than noir, it is arguably no longer noir at all. The impossibility of translating the term 'noir' hinges upon the fact that it captures a mood somewhere in between, in the movement between black and white. For her part, Gorrara points to the existence of a noir mainstream, suggesting that *J'irai cracher sur vos tombes* falls outside of it by dint of its overtly parodic nature. In suggesting that Sullivan not only parodies the American tradition of violent thrillers but surpasses it, Scott appears to wish to free the novel from the charges levelled against it (Sullivan was by many, he points out, 'perceived as a mere pornographer') by aligning it closely to the texts that Vian signed under his own name. He goes on to claim that 'there is no American crime fiction contemporary with *J'irai cracher sur vos tombes* which is so blatantly pornographic or graphic in its descriptions of sexual murder' (Scott 1996: 213, 214–15).

And yet, French literature has a strong tradition of such works, among which Vernon Sullivan fits quite comfortably; one might think of the works of the Marquis de Sade, Guillaume Apollinaire (in particular his novel *Les Onze mille verges*), Georges Bataille, Pierre Bourgeade and, more recently, Nathalie Gassel. So, it is possible to posit Vernon Sullivan on either side of the Atlantic. And if he is to be read as a follower of Raymond Chandler and Dashiell Hammett—and he was clearly well-versed in such writing, as were most of his literary contemporaries on the Parisian left bank—this does not necessarily make Boris Vian a naive disciple of the American dream. Rather than simply out-noiring noir, Vian-Sullivan offers a parody of a literary tradition whose defining mood is already parodic.[8] Indeed, the multi-layered parody of *J'irai cracher sur vos tombes* (it parodies the idea that a text must be *traduit de l'américain* to succeed via its staging of a case of an American novel having to be translated into French in order to achieve publication, and it offers reflexive commentary on the transatlantic exchange that generates the noir phenomenon in France, and which is already attaining mythical status) serves to remind readers that the American Dream itself is an allusion, rotting from within, and that the American tradition of hard-boiled fiction, as championed by Chandler, Hammett et al., was itself a reflection of this breakdown. Despite its parodic agenda, however, the novel remains 'genuinely' noir to the extent that its concerns offer its readership a bleakly realistic allegory for their own society. As Gorrara observes, '[i]ts obsession with racial origins reflects a general unease about shifting and unstable identities, anticipating the upheavals of European and French decolonization' (Gorrara 2003a: 36).

It is interesting to note that, while considering a key feature of early post-war French noir to be its potential for an allegorical critique of French national identity, Gorrara draws a distinction between Boris Vian (writing as Vernon Sullivan) and two other pseudo-Americans. In order to make her point that 'mainstream French hard-boiled detective fiction writers of the 1940s and 1950s' used a stylized America as a canvas on which to paint their concerns for French society (Gorrara 2003a: 36), she cites Serge Arcouët (writing as Terry Stewart) and Jean Meckert (writing as John Amila). While she does not explicitly acknowledge the distinction that she draws between these writers, her use of the term 'mainstream' appears to be derived from the principal difference between Sullivan and Stewart and Amila: of the three writers, Sullivan did not form part of the Série Noire.[9] As already mentioned, Vernon Sullivan was born from a wager, an attempt to rival Marcel Duhamel. Clearly, *J'irai cracher sur vos tombes* is reflexively parodic to a degree where it cannot legitimately aspire to the title of classic of French noir, in the way that works such as *Pas d'orchidées pour Miss Blandish* and *La Môme vert-de-gris* can, despite their being genuine cases of translation into French. It is, however, an important enough work—indeed, it can certainly vie for the title of most famous French noir novel—to warrant an investigation of its narrative strategies. Furthermore, a detailed analysis of *J'irai cracher sur vos tombes* in terms of French noir will reveal that it is more than a little problematic to draw a distinction between Sullivan and his contemporaries of the Série Noire.

The difficulty of locating a specific point of entry into noir has often been noted.[10] This notwithstanding, French noir literature certainly gains legitimacy from the establishment of Duhamel's Série Noire. When seen from this perspective, Serge Arcouët, via the intermediary of his pseudonymous creation Terry Stewart, becomes the first author of a recognized French noir novel when *La Mort et l'ange* [*Death and the Angel*] appears in the Série Noire in 1948.[11] The aim of this chapter is not, however, to argue a historical case for naming a certain date or text as the beginning of the French noir tradition; rather, our aim is to harness the legitimating force of the Série Noire in order to expose a powerful web of intertextuality between Terry Stewart's text and that of its more illustrious—or perhaps notorious—predecessor, Vernon Sullivan's *J'irai cracher sur vos tombes*.

J'irai cracher sur vos tombes has traditionally been read as a parody of a previously established tradition, that is, the American hard-boiled detective novel. Even the name Vernon Sullivan has been shown to be a clue puzzle for the initiated. Scott explains that the name Vernon Sullivan 'was a private joke; "Vernon" came from Paul Vernon, who also played in the Abadie band, while "Sullivan" was a veiled homage to the jazz pianist Joe Sullivan' (Scott 1996: 212). Although this is likely to be the case, it is important that the novel be interpreted as a novel and not as an insight into Vian's personal world. Too often critical judgement has been clouded by considerations of the particularly hectic pace of Vian's life. The warning pronounced by François Caradec in his afterword to Vian's *L'Automne à Pékin*, according to which the novel is not a *roman à clef* (Vian 1956: 297), is valid across Vian's oeuvre. For while there is clearly a strong ludic dimension to all his work—and it would be denying the obvious to suggest that Vian's texts do not contain allusions to his personal entourage—to seek to delimit any Vian novel's potential by taking these biographical points of interest as a truth by which all the work can be understood is to do a major disservice to the complexity of the text and the intertext within which it functions.

Without doubt, Vernon Sullivan has his place in the history of French noir fiction. In order for this statement to become meaningful, critically, any study of *J'irai cracher sur vos tombes* needs to focus first and foremost on the text itself. Most importantly, Sullivan's noir status should not be based on syllogisms or ambit claims: first, Vian was passionate about jazz, but this does not prove that he was blindly obsessed with all things American; and second, a close reading of *J'irai cracher sur vos tombes* suggests strong intertextual links to such novels as Jean-Paul Sartre's *La Nausée* and James Hadley Chase's *Pas d'orchidées pour Miss Blandish*. Furthermore, it is our claim that both these intertexts belong to a French literary tradition that lends the foundations to French noir. It is perhaps worth noting, if only to underscore the fickle nature of onomastics, that names used by Vian in his novels of the 1940s are also found in the works of James Hadley Chase from the same era. Just as Slim—the character from the film *Hollywood Canteen*, whom Colin is said to resemble in *L'Écume des jours*—is also the name of the most terrible of the Grisson gang and the tormentor of Miss Blandish, the name Sullivan reappears in Chase's sequel *La chair de l'orchidée*,[12] in which the Sullivans are two brothers who work as expert hired killers. There is thus an intertextual exchange, a kind of quid pro quo, taking place between the works of Vian-Sullivan and Chase. And while both Scott and Pestureau have named Chase as a literary influence on Sullivan, the way in which *Pas d'orchidées pour Miss Blandish* operates intertextually within *J'irai cracher sur vos tombes* has not been sufficiently developed. Neither has the fact that *Pas d'orchidées pour Miss Blandish* is one of the initial triptych of the Série Noire received the critical attention that it warrants.

This use of Chase's influential novel, which was very much the talk of Paris at this time, as a flagship for what would become one of the most famous literary series in French publishing, removes it from the American tradition, putting it squarely back into the realm of the Latin one that Vian discussed with Jean d'Halluin. As shown, Chase and Peter Cheyney are both interlopers in the American tradition; both were Englishmen passing themselves off as Americans (in the same way that Vian, Arcouët and Meckert were Frenchmen writing under American pseudonyms). Masquerade, it seems, is an important noir ingredient.

When one considers the various layers of pastiche involved in such projects as the Série Noire (with English authors imitating Americans, only to be imitated in turn by the French) it may appear a vexed proposition to talk of any national ownership of a defined writing tradition. The development of noir as a form of proto-postmodernism, however, certainly corresponds to a French sensibility. As Vian himself famously noted, since we are always disguised, we may just as well disguise ourselves, and thus we will be disguised no longer. It is precisely through this perverse, ludic and, ultimately, sincere expression of performative identity that a noir tradition predicated on intertextuality can be understood.

Vernon Sullivan does, therefore, draw on noir influences, but they are influences that have already been absorbed into a French tradition by 1946, the year of the publication of *J'irai cracher sur vos tombes*. Thus, in addition to wilfully extending a noir tradition (that is arguably French) Sullivan's novel also begins one (and, this time, one that is undeniably French). For Ben Sweed, the protagonist of Terry Stewart's *La Mort et l'ange*, is a reincarnation of Lee Anderson, the murderous 'hero' of *J'irai cracher sur vos tombes*.[13]

It becomes apparent as early as the opening paragraph that reincarnation is a key concept in *La Mort et l'ange*. The title itself casts a noir shadow over the dichotomy of mortality, with angel (a concept that seems to bring death to life, or to promise life after death), and not life, being opposed to death. Death itself—*la mort*—is immediately shown to refer to prisoners living out the final days of their death sentence in *le Quartier des Morts*. Thus the dead are, technically, still alive, while the living are thrust into situations where dead ends are the only possible outcome.

The novel opens with a description of Maat, whom the reader assumes to be a prison guard, ascending the stairs to death row. This clearly draws on, and inverts, the image of descending into a grave. Any heavenly, ethereal aspect that may have been indicated by the title is instantly belied by the heavy tread of Maat's boots (Stewart 1972: 9). With the tarnishing of the idea of angelic flight, the novel is cast into the shadow of the ineluctable pull towards a noir denouement. As will be made only too clear in *J'irai cracher sur vos tombes*, a noir novel is not any old novel; it is not, for example, merely defined by its own ending like that which Sartre's Roquentin aims to write on leaving Bouville. Rather, the noir novel is predicated upon, and struggles against, a 'dead end'. The dichotomy of ascent/descent, encapsulated in the climb up into death row, reveals the simultaneous birth of the novel out of *J'irai cracher sur vos tombes* and the pull of the grave that will mark *La Mort et l'ange* just as it marked its predecessor.

The narrative of *J'irai cracher sur vos tombes* is itself driven by a desire to avenge death, by a communion with the dead and finally, from the perspective of the protagonist, by the pull of the tomb. Both novels are couched in intertextuality (they interact with other texts and play on this interaction); they are also starkly aware of their own textuality: the continual use of self-referential devices in both novels points to a literary project in which both authors are conspicuously present throughout their narratives. By positing a pseudonymous author between themselves and their novels, Boris Vian and Serge Arcouët appear to distance themselves from their texts; in fact, by lying to their readers, by destabilizing epistemology—noir trait par excellence—they become one with their writing, consigning their protagonists and, in Vian's case, his project and ultimately himself as author, to the grave.

The preface to *J'irai cracher sur vos tombes* is couched in Manichaean terms: Lee Anderson, we are told, is truly black but appears completely white from the outside. Noir is, in true Vian style, taken literally: when asked to write a noir thriller, Boris Vian produces a novel with a black protagonist. This immediately makes it difficult for the reader to accept this novel as a work of noir literature. Despite its overt descriptions of sexual violence, this appears to be a comfortable read inasmuch as we are made fully aware of the truth of the story from the outset.

And yet, Boris Vian is surely too clever an exponent of his craft to produce a thriller whose very contents exclude it from the angst-ridden mood of noir. *J'irai cracher sur vos tombes* does have noir potential, and this is founded in its exploitation of the very status of truth within the novel format: the truth of Lee Anderson's racial identity is expounded in a self-consciously mendacious preface. Readers may well feel that they *know* the truth of Lee Anderson, but this is always already undermined by the fact that this novel is not written by Vernon Sullivan. It is in its destabilization of its own truth and its pivotal role within Vian's 'Sullivan project' that *J'irai cracher sur vos tombes* is able to aspire to noir, and certainly cult, status.

The preface, which confides in the reader only to lead him or her astray, anchors *J'irai cracher sur vos tombes* in a French tradition that can be traced back to *Les Liaisons dangereuses* [*Dangerous Liaisons*] via *La Nausée* [*Nausea*]. In *Les Liaisons dangereuses* Laclos uses the Publishers' note to remind his readers that the letters contained within his book are only literature; Jean-Paul Sartre, for his part, exploits the tradition of a prefatory mark of authenticity in order to make an ostensible claim that his novel is a genuine diary while, at the same time, making it obvious that his whole text will be based on a systematic challenge to concepts of truth and authenticity. Whereas Sartre's readers saw beyond his artistic deceit—Roquentin's diary was understood to be a novel (albeit, one grounded in phenomenology)—Vian's bait was taken up by his readers, however surprising this may seem with the benefit of hindsight. *J'irai cracher sur vos tombes* may not, of itself, be noir; the whole Vian/Sullivan package, however, relies on an ensnarement of the reader, a strategy exploited by both the whodunit and hard-boiled schools of detective fiction.

The interplay between reality and fiction, between literary parody and a genuine noir project is signposted by the job that Lee Anderson takes up on his arrival in Buckton. He takes over the running of the local bookshop, a position vacated by Hansen, a man who has begun his countdown to a point, in a few years' time, when he will be able to write best-sellers. Scott picks up this instance of self-referentiality, and goes as far as to suggest that this desire ('to write best sellers ... historical novels, novels where niggers will sleep with white women and won't be lynched') is satisfied in *J'irai cracher sur vos tombes*, the book that 'the reader is holding' (Scott 1996: 215). Scott recalls how affected Vian was by the failure of his novel *L'Écume des jours* to win the Prix de la Pléiade, and he considers the success of the Sullivan project to be an act of vengeance. This is amply borne out by the pride of place given in the novel to acts of revenge: 'There is only one thing that counts, and that's to avenge yourself and to avenge yourself in the most complete way possible' (Sullivan 1973: 88). This line does more than simply hark back to the failure of *L'Écume des jours* to receive the acknowledgement that it doubtless deserved; it also picks up the foreword of Vian's first novel, altering entirely its *Weltanschauung*. In *L'Écume des jours* the only things that counted were the music of Duke Ellington and making love to pretty girls. In *J'irai cracher sur vos tombes* the latter will be the means to obtain revenge, the former the backdrop against which this will be done (even if the nature of the sound track is deliberately brought in line with the affinities of a more popular audience, with Dinah Shore's *Shoo Fly Pie* replacing, for example, Duke Ellington's *In the Mood to be Wooed*—as Ben Sweed will remark in 1948, 'people like that sort of rubbish' [Stewart 1972: 148]).

There is more to the scene in the bookshop, however. It is not enough to say that Hansen will write best-sellers and that this is a best-seller so, therefore, this is the book that Hansen will write. This is not merely insufficient argumentation by virtue of its syllogistic reasoning; it is actually quite clear that the best-sellers that Hansen has in mind are the exact opposite of what Sullivan delivers. Lee Anderson *will be* lynched, and, to dash the second of Hansen's sentiments, instead of a young girl growing up pure in a corrupted environment, Anderson's arrival corrupts a previously pure environment and leads to the gruesome death of two women. This is an extravagant inversion of Hansen's best-seller, which does not so much noir his desire as blow it out of the water. This inversion is prefigured in the text by the replacement of Hansen (who is described as an archetypal Aryan) by a white man who is, in fact, black. What Sullivan is offering is a larger-than-life parody of noir, a neon-lit advertisement for this new form of literature. This scene signals the advent of the noir novel in the Latin literary tradition. Its role in the novel is at once to work fatally against Hansen's desire and to set in train an infernal descent for Lee. As Hansen counts the years that he will have to wait to write his novel, the period begins to sound more like a prison sentence, a term on death row, than a moment of sensuous anticipation; and it is precisely in terms of this period of waiting for death that Terry Stewart will, two years later, rewrite Sullivan's novel in the Série Noire. For *La Mort et l'ange* will not only condense and overwrite the ineluctability of the dead end of noir fiction, but it will also (posthumously) grant Hansen his desires: nobody will be lynched for their crimes;[14] and, more importantly, out of the carnage of a world where corruption reigns, and which surpasses the sexual violence of *J'irai cracher sur vos tombes*, a killing spree that begins with the seemingly gratuitous murder of a golden-haired innocent concludes with the sparing—salvation, even—of a young blind girl by the Ange Noir. The dark hero of *La Mort et l'ange*, Ben Sweed, hands himself in, and Jill Scott is left to grow up pure. By rewriting the story of Lee Anderson, then, Terry Stewart continues Vian's Latin erotic tradition, extending it into the mainstream of French noir.

The intertextual exploitation of this French literary tradition within this new noir framework is clearly in evidence from the moment in the bookshop scene in *J'irai cracher sur vos tombes* when Hansen comments on the fullness of Lee's voice. As a black man who looks white, Lee reworks Sartre's inversion of Sophie Tucker in *La Nausée* (in which she is portrayed as a black singer, while the writer of *Some of These Days*— the black writer Shelton Brooks—is depicted as part of the New York Jewish popular song-writing tradition).[15] Indeed, Hansen's departure from Buckton to write a best-seller bears more than a passing resemblance to the ending of *La Nausée*, which sees Roquentin leave Bouville to write a novel that will confer a little of its steely weight upon him.[16]

Furthermore, in addition to a reference to 'les vieux refrains de la Nouvelle-Orléans [the old tunes of New Orleans]' (Sullivan 1973: 21), which is a condensation of Sartre's '*refrain* [jazz tune]' and '*vieux rag-time* [old rag-time tune]' from *La Nausée* and Vian's own 'la musique de la Nouvelle-Orléans [New Orleans music]' from *L'Écume des jours*, Lee Anderson's sexuality is only one remove from that of Antoine Roquentin.

While the two protagonists have very different appetites, both use sex as a weapon: Lee is driven to sleep with young white girls in order to avenge his dead brother; Roquentin, for his part, goes through the motions with the *patronne* as a means of regaining possession of his own external reality and defeating the gaze of the Other. The question of Lee's sexuality is posed by Hansen when the latter is initiating him into the culture of the young girls hanging out in the local milk bar: 'Doesn't that interest you?' (Sullivan 1973: 21). The phrasing of this question recalls the simplicity of the Corsican's rebuke of Roquentin in the famous library scene in *La Nausée*: 'Are you a fairy too?' (Sartre 2000: 238).[17]

By bringing the implications of Roquentin's literary project to bear on the tale of Lee Anderson, we are able to take a broader view on the Sullivan case. For example, Roquentin's story has forced its readers to turn, for an explanation of its meaning, back on the novel (by considering it as *the* novel that Roquentin sets out to write) and beyond its parameters (both in Sartre's subsequent philosophical treatises, notably *L'Être et le néant*, and his biographical work *Les Mots*). To gain a wider perspective of the noir project undertaken by Lee Anderson, it is possible to see Vernon Sullivan and Boris Vian himself as protagonists. For not only is this project intertextual (existing in both earlier and later novels), it is also inextricably bound to the factual incidents surrounding the publication of the novel. If *J'irai cracher sur vos tombes* is to become a noir classic, it is clear that the protagonist will *not* be able to 'get away with it'. Lee Anderson's fate is sealed from early on in the text, and the ending comes as no surprise.

The fate of Vernon Sullivan, on the other hand, is more ostentatiously noir. One may well ask whether Vian actually achieves his ultimate success, not by dying—in what one might consider to be the ultimate act of poetic justice—at a preview of the film version of *J'irai cracher sur vos tombes*, which he had famously reviled, but by ultimately coinciding with his novel. Despite the initial success that heralded the arrival of *J'irai cracher sur vos tombes* on the bookshelves of France, any prospect of a happy ending was subverted by the court case that saw Vian lose the money that the book had brought him. Through his continual and heavily overwritten use of self-referential ploys, Vian inserts himself into the novel to the point that it is far from clear where the noir project that is *J'irai cracher sur vos tombes* ends and the real world of Boris Vian resumes. The ending of the project is a curious blend of financial failure and commercial and literary success: the ensuing court case had a serious physical impact on a man whose ill health was already common knowledge, while the novel proved ultimately to be a huge success, becoming a masterpiece of noir (meta)fiction and securing Vian's renown as an author.

The case of Lee Anderson's crossing over into the real world from a parodied America into a hotel in Paris, is well documented. Scott relates the notorious events of April 1947, during which a gruesome murder was committed that 'was seen as a 'copycat' killing, directly inspired by the scene in *J'irai cracher sur vos tombes*' (Scott 1996: 210). A copy of the novel was left by Edmond Rougé at the scene of his crime with the notorious passage that Scott goes on to quote underlined. Vian's act of literary revenge had, apparently, resulted in a murder. Furthermore, the leaving of the text by the murderer lent a literary touch to the crime, once again challenging the limits of meta-textuality. And when the same crime appears in the pages of *La Mort et l'ange*, it is not clear to the reader to which of these 'murder texts' Terry Stewart's scene is more closely related. It is our contention that, albeit via the intermediary of another parodic translation,[18] Boris Vian can finally stake a claim to have been the first French author published in the Série Noire.

If the page left by Edmond Rougé was sufficient proof to condemn Boris Vian (having initially caused sales of the book to escalate), it is in the modus operandi of our killers that proof of the link between Lee Anderson and Ben Sweed will be found.[19] The passage underlined by Edmond Rougé describes the act of strangulation, which is the method used by Lee Anderson to complete his project of revenge. Having already murdered her younger sister, Lou, Lee turns his attention to the woman who is in love with him, Jean, the elder of the two Asquith girls. It is when Lee murders Jean that the fatal word is finally used: 'She let herself be strangled without protest' (Sullivan 1973: 199). And it is this method that will become the hallmark of Ben Sweed.

In *J'irai cracher sur vos tombes* a gradual escalation of violence leads to the brutal double murder. The strangulation of Jean Asquith, the paroxysm of the sexual violence in the novel, is the culmination of a steady build-up of textual pointers. The first coincidence of sexual attraction and the impulse to murder comes in the milk bar in Buckton. The scene is couched in the parodic humour against which the whole novel is generally read and, as such, almost goes unnoticed. When Lee experiences a bout of nausea brought on by drinking a glass of cold milk, the effects are softened by the obvious allusions to Roquentin, with which Vian's readers will be all too familiar. Vian had, after all, just completed *L'Écume des jours*, whose continual references to Jean-Sol Partre and vomiting turn *La Nausée*, and specifically Vian's relationship to the text, into a standing joke. Such comic touches are, however, used within the text to inoculate the reader and to veil a more profound significance. In this case, Lee's impulse to kill comes upon him just like Roquentin's nausea, as a pathological response to the world. But whereas Roquentin finds solace from the nausea in the predefined sequence of the notes in a recording of *Some of These Days*, it is precisely an instance of listening to a record that brings on Lee's first experience of his murderous condition: 'I was just as happy for the record to stop. Two minutes more and I'd have been in no fit state' (Sullivan 1973: 29).

The reader acquainted with Vian's use of allusions, which point to an intertextual significance that is the opposite of their ostensible meaning, will spot a reference to Colin's fatal meeting with Chloé, in *L'Écume des jours*, when he both brings her into existence and consigns her to an imminent death. For Chloé is a recording and she can only live as long as the record plays. Lee's desire for the record to come to an end, whilst on one level staving off a rising carnal urge, points intertextually to the sealing of his own fate: this is the desire for death. The surprise for the reader is that Jicky, the girl with whom he is dancing, and who will be his first sexual conquest, is spared. That she lives is testimony to the strength of Lee's project. In existentialist terms—suggested by the references to *La Nausée*—Lee's nausea is the pull of his instincts, the urge to act unthinkingly. Whereas for Roquentin music functions as a release mechanism from the body's entrapment in the physical world, in *J'irai cracher sur vos tombes* it taps into primal urges and rhythms, almost as if black and white are opposed in the novel even in terms of musical traditions. As such, the erotic nature of the dancing scene in Buckton seems to strengthen the instinctual side of human behaviour.[20] The compensating factor, the project that keeps his consciousness focused, is his desire to avenge his brother, 'le gosse' [the kid]. The competing forces that constitute the viscosity of Lee's being (the ever-present, opposing pulls of pure consciousness and body) constantly vie against each other throughout the narrative; it is for this reason that his sexual gratification comes from dominating opponents rather than joining his partners in orgasm, which would expose him to the vagina dentata of the Other. Lee is in a permanent battle to control himself as well as others. The result is that his urge to strangle is expressed unconsciously (until such time as he will allow himself to combine his pleasure with the completion of his project).

The first trip made by Lee and a group of teenagers to the river synthesizes the project with an innocent side to his character. An earlier description has painted an idealized version of the river as a place where one might escape from the heat of Buckton (and become pure consciousness at the expense of carnality): 'Down by the river, it must be cool under the trees' (Sullivan 1973: 26). The solace found in the shade of these trees clearly recalls that found by Lennie and George, and the ineluctability of death of *Of Mice and Men* is clearly foreshadowed in this bucolic imagery. Lee is now heading towards this spot in a car full of teenagers, who are his prey—potential victims of his project. The idyll of the river is thus noired, bringing it into concrete existence and tainting its purity. As Lee gets the group drunk on bourbon and begins to seduce Jicky, his gestures and her response suggest that it is not only the drink that makes her cough: 'I put my arm around her neck...She made a choking sound [in French her voice is *étranglée*, or "strangled"]' (Sullivan 1973: 32–3). This first hint of strangulation is followed by the arrival at the riverbank, which lives up to his expectations and is 'cool and clear like a glass of gin' (Sullivan 1973: 35). Lee defies the limpidity of the water, however, and leads Jicky off to have sex. On their return to the river, in a gesture proleptic of the last page of the novel, Lee displays his erect phallus like a trophy. He and Jicky then have sex again in the water, suggesting how the novel itself, via this circularity, will be resurrected after Lee's apparently concluding posthumous erection.

This is a key scene in *J'irai cracher sur vos tombes* as it marks the crossing of a threshold: it is the first step in Lee's project, and as such it establishes a way of negotiating the world that allows him to act freely (i.e. he has chosen his project and can no longer act outside its parameters).[21] The result of his free choice in this case is that the purity of the river is unable to exert pressure on the project that is now fixed. The scene is also crucial in determining the handover of the gift of strangulation from Lee Anderson to Ben Sweed. For it is not by chance that the first murder in *La Mort et l'ange* takes place down by the river:

I preferred Oak River because you could swim in the clear water and dive to pick up pink pebbles and agates. That's how I taught Dora to swim...That's also how it happened [*c'est aussi comme ça que c'est arrivé*]. ... It was nice under the willows. And yet I felt down [*cafardeux*] and gloomy. My thoughts were grey in spite of the sun.

(Stewart 1972: 25)

In Ben's case, the purity of the river is noired by angst. The insistent use of the impersonal pronoun *ce*—as in the quote above ('c'est aussi comme ça que *c'est* arrivé') and Ben's earlier recollection of how it all began ('I pushed on into the fog ... *It came on* [*C'est venu*] because it [*ça*] had to happen' [Stewart 1972: 20—our emphasis]) recalls the approach of the nausea in *La Nausée*. It is also an intertextual pointer to Lee Anderson's loss of control at the end of *J'irai cracher sur vos tombes*, when he finally allows himself to give full vent to his urge to strangle. When he murders Jean, the impulse surges along his arm, seizing—and disembodying—his hand: 'Again I felt that thing coming up my back and my hand closed around her throat. There was nothing I could do to stop it; *it just came on* [*c'est venu*]' (Sullivan 1973: 199—our emphasis). This is clearly the same impulse that overwhelms Roquentin, who eventually stabs himself in the hand in a bid to regain control of his situation.

Such an inchoate submission to destiny would appear to be a sine qua non condition of the noir novel that Stewart is writing. There is, however, as in the case of Sullivan, an additional assumption on the part of the novel of its place within a Latin erotic tradition. While melancholy (*le cafard*) will be Ben Sweed's nausea—he will be unable to put a precise name to his suffering but will experience a lack of control of his destiny and an inability to appreciate the simple, sensual pleasures or to extract from them sufficient justification for his existence—there is also a rapprochement to *L'Étranger* [*The Outsider*] at work here. In Camus's novel, too, the pleasure that Meursault experiences while swimming in clear waters with Marie Cardona is followed by murder and a descent towards execution. And, as in *L'Étranger*, the cause of everything can be traced back to the death of the protagonist's mother: 'I left school the day of her funeral' (Stewart 1972: 21).[22]

Although Ben is unable to provide a motive for killing Dora, the situation in which he finds himself is hauntingly similar to that of Lee Anderson's younger brother: while the kid is lynched by the enraged father of a white girl with whom he has slept, Ben appears to murder—first the girl with whom people think he has slept and then her boyfriend—pre-emptively. Whether or not Dora's murder avenges the death of the kid, it has an important role to play in the development of Ben's character, as *La Mort et l'ange* takes the form of a *Bildungsroman*: 'Something told me that Dora was there precisely to teach me what, without knowing it, I already felt' (Stewart 1972: 26). In this case, however, the coming of age is informed by an acceptance of his existence in a previous incarnation. Throughout the text Ben and his interlocutor, Maat, join in a duel for the right to knowledge, a right that Ben and Lee will both dispute with various characters throughout their respective stories. There is a tension between Ben's quest for knowledge and the primacy within the noir novel of mood, instinct and vague sensations. Noir mood conflates the two seemingly contradictory aspects of Sartre's nausea: in *La Nausée*, the nausea stands as a reminder that life is made up of events that happen against a background of pure contingency. Roquentin's attempt to control this feeling, to stop it welling up inside him, focuses on the recording of *Some of These Days*, whose notes always produce the same tune, at the same speed, leading to the same, predictable end. As such, the song functions as a novel whose pleasure, in Roland Barthes's famous scheme, is derived from its *readerly* architecture (the way in which a novel is clear in its 'meaning' and conveys its reader smoothly to that one possible conclusion), as opposed to the blissful abandonment of the *writerly* text (the way in which the text appears to espouse the intentionality of consciousness, offering itself up to the reader as an infinity of potential 'meanings'). The pleasure of noir conflates these opposing aspects of textuality, hence the apparent bipolarity of protagonists, which maps itself onto Sartre's model of human consciousness.[23]

Noir nausea tends to come from the very ineluctability of the novel's ending; the character is pulled towards the conclusion in a novel that corresponds, self-consciously, to the type that Roquentin wishes to write in order that retrospective justification be shed on his existence. Viewed from this perspective, the control over nausea sought by Ben Sweed and Lee Anderson is merely an active assumption of an infernal machine that is already in motion. This is why Ben's project takes on aspects of Roquentin's plan to write a novel. Ben, too, wants things to correspond to a predefined sequence; only on death row can life be as hard as steel. This is why he is driven to kill; he is forcing his own conviction. In the framework of this project, Dora becomes a means to an end, a way for him to join his kindred spirit, Lee Anderson. Note, for example, the way Ben describes the sight of Dora swimming: 'It was pretty, with rhythm [*C'était joli et bien réglé*] ... It touched me to see her, and I didn't yet know how the end would come ... I didn't know, Maat. That's what shattered everything' (Stewart 1972: 26). The water initially appears to have the same nausea-averting properties as *Some of These Days*; and yet, despite his appreciation of the regulated sequence of movements offered by Dora's swimming (*'C'était...bien réglé'*), the impulse to kill surges through Ben unhindered. It is as if the weight of intertextuality deprives him of any individual consciousness—and, in this light, it is this inheritance, to which he will refer as 'the childhood accident', which renders him impotent. And from this moment on he will embrace his destiny.

Once this point in the tale is passed, Ben is able to switch in and out of his narrative, at times fully integrating his consciousness into the recollection of his past experiences (Maat observes as Ben's body plays back the gestures performed at the time of the episode that he is now recounting). Ben's past has become, in Sartrean terms, an 'adventure'. It is only possible for the life of a *being for-itself* to coincide with the sum total of his or her past actions once that being is dead; only in death, when a person finally becomes a *being in-itself,* an object devoid of consciousness and thus self-founding and sufficient unto itself, can one's life become an adventure. Hence the importance of the novel's location: on death row men seem to be able to indulge in reviewing their existence, seeking the meaning that their past can now confer upon their life, in a semblance of good faith. Although still alive physically, they are, to all intents and purposes, ontologically dead. For his part, Lee Anderson can only aspire to such a state of being: his position as a *passe-blanc,* a black man in a white man's skin, is an attempt to emulate the inverted Sophie Tucker in *La Nausée,* the being whom Roquentin envies, and who inspires him to seek to become his own adventure.[24]

Of course, the reader must question whether it is really with his own tale which Ben Sweed coincides. When he has a Proustian moment of recollection in his prison cell ('He could smell the cold water, the trees and the warm earth' [Stewart 1972: 26]), the scene is the same as that which frames Lee Anderson's first sexual encounter in Buckton. Furthermore, when Ben recalls his first murder, which he describes as his best memory, his description of Dora's complicity in the deed, in addition to not being entirely in accordance with his own previous description, is an excellent account of Jean Asquith's death at the hand(s) of Lee Anderson. Intertextuality and history become indissociable for Ben. When, for example, he first shares a tender moment with Dora, it is hardly a moment of textual intimacy. It is an intertextually woven scene that purposefully reaches beyond its own parameters. On the night of a storm, Ben and Dora take refuge in a barn. This location immediately signposts the last stand made by Lee Anderson, which is itself a scene based on the final moments of Slim Grisson in James Hadley Chase's *Pas d'orchidées pour Miss Blandish.* As if to reinforce his message, Ben describes their actions thus: 'as if we had been two other people' (Stewart 1972: 22).

The clumsy tenderness of this scene further recalls *Of Mice and Men* as Dora takes on the aspect of a vulnerable animal: 'Her arms were cool and her skin was smooth and soft. Soft like a bird's downy feathers [*douce comme un duvet d'oiseau*]' (Stewart 1972: 23). And this description, too, can be traced back to *J'irai cracher sur vos tombes*. Unlike Ben, Lee can only see women as sex objects. In this light, it is therefore unsurprising that he uses the same simile to apply to a different part of Lou Asquith's anatomy: 'I sat down and bent over her legs. I kissed her inner thighs, in that spot where a woman's skin is as soft as a bird's feathers [*aussi douce que les plumes d'un oiseau*]' (Sullivan 1973: 150).

The final proof that strangulation is hereditary comes when Ben finally snaps. As Dora swims, a familiar thought comes to him: '"Thinking of other things, as one does," said Ben, "I wondered what would happen if the movement stopped"' (Stewart 1972: 27). When Roquentin's record stops playing, the nausea returns; when in *L'Écume des jours* Duke Ellington's *Chloe* comes to an end, Chloé begins her descent into death. Ben's acceptance of his nausea comes to him like an epiphany: as if Roquentin, Colin and Lee Anderson have already spent enough time striving to come to grips with the phenomenon, he simply accepts the mantle and embraces the nothingness of his existence:[25] 'An incredible strength stirred inside me; it spread down my left arm, which had set hard like an iron bar ... As she moved towards me I felt a hollow in the pit of my stomach, like a hunger, and my back began to hurt' (Stewart 1972: 27).

As suggested, though, it is through the particularity of his modus operandi that Ben's heredity can be most clearly traced back directly to Lee Anderson:

> So, I took Dora's neck in my left hand and I squeezed gently. Just to see. I felt a life force under my fingers. I squeezed a bit harder.... I had to squeeze harder still. There was a rolling in my head, like waves or like black clouds blocking out my sun.... I realized that I didn't need to use my other hand.
>
> (Stewart 1972: 27–8)

As Maat watches the killer's hand close in his prison cell, it is clear that Ben has coincided with his, and Lee's, past: philosophically, it is as if he is finally corresponding to a *telos*. He has, in other words, become what he is.[26]

Unlike Ben, who knowingly assumes his destiny, Lee Anderson adopts an attitude of bad faith in regard to his carnal urges. He hides the full truth of his caress from both the reader and himself during the car ride to the river, at which point his hand is left to its own devices. And when he later grapples with Lou in her bedroom he again objectifies himself, allowing the nausea to take responsibility for his actions: 'I heard her drawing near; or rather, I felt her drawing near' (Sullivan 1973: 126). Once his instincts take over from his consciousness his hand, reified like Roquentin's before him, is dissociated from his understanding of self. Once more, it is up to the reader to read strangulation into the scene, where the sexual intimacy of the characters functions as an effective veil: 'I do not know what my left hand was doing during that time' (Sullivan 1973: 127). Illumination is provided by the specific focus of Lee's gaze when, immediately after leaving Lou, he moves on to her sister, Jean: 'I saw her skin tighten as I moved towards her throat' (Sullivan 1973: 132). While his left hand is the one with which he acts on Lou, he proves to be ambidextrous when she shoots him in the left arm. Having killed her while he is himself incapacitated, he leaves to complete his project: 'Even with just one arm, I was able finish Jean off too' (Sullivan 1973: 198). For both Lee and Ben, be it by strangling with one hand or killing with a gun, murder is easy.

The attitude adopted by women when confronted by Lee or Ben is one of either defiance or total disembodiment (in the latter case they effectively close down their bodies and go limp). While the first solution is active and philosophically more committed, and the second is more obviously in bad faith, both reactions prove equally useless in the face of these murderers. The vanity of these attempts to fight off assailants corresponds exactly to the failure of any attempt to avert the gaze of the Other, as examined by Sartre in *L'Être et le néant* [*Being and Nothingness*]. When she first meets Ben Sweed, Sandra Abbott, the gangster (and heroine) of *La Mort et l'ange*, appears to know instinctively that he is a killer.[27]

The initial description of Sandra recalls the entrance of the dame Carlotta into Peter Cheyney's *La Môme vert-de-gris*:

A woman appeared...An unbelievable body, I'm telling you. Imagine a tall girl with ample, curvaceous hips and a prominent chest, firm like it was set in stone....A mass of flame-coloured hair fell down to her shoulders. I was struck dumb because women like that...well I didn't think they existed. She was wearing a long gold housecoat... The material was split up the side and her bare leg was exposed with every step she took.

(Stewart 1972: 60)

This is a standard description, which slots easily into the noir tradition of Cheyney and Chase: this could be any attractive female. As such, she has universal allegorical applicability. A nautical description transforms into a fiery shimmer, which readily picks up the blazing Marianne of Paul Colin's 'Libération', and a gold dress (picking up her previously mentioned golden body); and, as if to dot the 'i's, this vision of Sandra is completed by the quasi-mandatory inspection of her legs. Her display of fear, however, is more specifically Latin in terms of its intertextual resonance. Ben and Sandra dispense early with the need to dwell on fetishized desire; their duel for epistemological superiority demands eye contact, and Sandra's gaze is accompanied by a telling gesture: as fear flashes in her eyes she brings her hand up to her neck (Stewart 1972: 60).

Sandra's gesture also allows us to shed new light on a famous passage from *La Nausée*, where phenomenology this time, not sex, tends to blind the reader to the murderous potential of the protagonist's actions. For not only can Roquentin be shown to be a role model for Lee and Ben in terms of the angst that assails him, but he can also be invested with the power of strangulation. On a dark night on the boulevard Noir, Roquentin seeks solace from the nausea. He sees a couple arguing. The man walks away, leaving the woman alone. Roquentin's description, veiled as it is in the confusion of his account, allows the reader to suspect that the woman is genuinely scared of him, and, indeed, that he does more than just stand idly by:

> I pass so close to her that I could touch her. It's... but how can I believe that this burning flesh, this face radiant with sorrow?... [I]t's she, it's Lucie, the charwoman.... I pass slowly in front of her, looking at her. Her eyes stare at me, but she doesn't seem to see me; she looks quite helpless in her suffering. I take a few steps. I turn round... She stands there, absolutely erect, holding her arms out as if she were waiting for the stigmata; she opens her mouth, she is choking.... I wait a few moments: I am afraid she is going to collapse: she is too sickly to endure this unexpected sorrow.... Lucie gives a little groan. She puts her hand to her throat, opening wide, astonished eyes. No, it isn't from herself that she is drawing the strength to suffer so much. It is coming to her from outside... from this boulevard. She needs to be taken by the shoulders and led to the lights, among people, into

the pink, gentle streets: over there you can't suffer so acutely; she would soften up, she would recover her positive look and return to the ordinary level of her sufferings. I turn my back on her. After all, she is lucky. I for my part have been much too calm these last three years … I walk away.

(Sartre 2000: 44–5)[28]

The resemblance between Lucie's reactions to Roquentin's approach and those of Sandra Abbott when she first meets Ben Sweed (the fear in her eyes, swiftly followed by the gesture of carrying a hand to her throat) is striking. It also recalls the attitudes adopted, at various stages, both by Jean and Lou in response to Lee Anderson as Other in *J'irai cracher sur vos tombes* (both girls freeze, in an attempt to become disembodied, as outlined in *L'Être et le néant*; in this way they turn his sexual advances into acts of quasi-necrophilia,[29] thereby nullifying any attempt on his part to conquer their consciousness). As one rereads the above extract from *La Nausée*, it becomes possible to read the whole incident not as a prelude to or the avoidance of an attack of nausea, but the act of strangulation, which is already being committed as early as the line: 'she opens her mouth, she is choking'. As Lucie reacts (in the same way that Dora and Lou will react in their respective novels—'She puts her hand to her throat, opening wide, astonished eyes'), Roquentin comments that the suffering that she is experiencing cannot come from inside her; instead it is the result not so much of external agency (the fact that he specifically is strangling her) as of a general mood. In this instance, '[i]t is coming to her from outside … from this boulevard.' And the name of the boulevard is Noir.

The impassive reflection that Roquentin makes on walking away (from Lucie's corpse) is picked up by the comment with which he squashes the fly when he is lunching with the Autodidact: it is an act of deliverance to relieve somebody of the burden of living. The use of insect imagery to describe people throughout *La Nausée* also serves to tighten the link between these two scenes, in the light of which Roquentin is a murderer whose nausea causes him momentarily to lose his ability to suppress the urge to kill.[30] These lapses of self-control are reflected in the syncopated diary form. Not only is the net closing around Roquentin as murderer, but there is also an increasingly strong case for considering him as the direct ancestor of Lee Anderson. Indeed, when we approach the novel from this perspective, two questions present themselves: first, just what crimes did Roquentin commit before this three-year period of calm to which he refers? And second, how many murders has he committed via his descendants in other novels?

This chapter has shown how strangulation can be read as an expression of malaise, almost as a metaphor for nausea. Before moving on to more recent avatars, let us speculate a little further on the literalness of the Sartrean text. For if Roquentin has evaded punishment for his crimes, and if his crimes have not been recognized as such, it is perhaps because his nausea has not been interpreted by his readers as a metaphor for strangulation.[31]

5
Noir Strangulation (2): Amélie Nothomb and Intertextuality

Chapter 4 showed how the motif of strangulation and the concept of literary heredity are intimately related in French noir fiction. In this light, an understanding of the heavily intertextual nature of the early French noir novel can empower the reader to reread texts from the French literary canon. This chapter continues the comparative reading of Vernon Sullivan's *J'irai cracher sur vos tombes* [*I Spit on Your Graves*] and Terry Stewart's *La Mort et l'ange* [*Death and the Angel*], placing greater emphasis on reader-based intertextual interpretation and further developing the concept of using a text to return to, and renegotiate, a chronological predecessor. While keeping in mind the importance in noir fiction of influence and consciously manipulated cross-cultural exchange between novels, an intertextual analysis allows us to read against the grain of history.

Noir closure: Open and shut endings

Chapter 4 concluded with a close-up on the neck of Ben Sweed's beloved Sandra, the heroine of *La Mort et l'ange*. It showed how the troubled feelings that this graceful neck produces in Ben recall the same sensation of being overwhelmed by the external world that besets Roquentin in Sartre's *La Nausée* [*Nausea*]. There is clearly much to be gained from an analysis of Stewart's novel in terms of the Sartrean intertext. What is equally illuminating, and perhaps more surprising, is the possibility of rereading *La Nausée* (1938) via *La Mort et l'ange* (1948), a process diametrically opposed to that of an influence-based approach. The way that Sandra Abbott instinctively raises her hand to her throat when she is confronted by Ben Sweed's piercing strangler's eyes was revealed to be retrospectively illuminating when translated on to a specific instance in

La Nausée. The subsequent reading of Roquentin as a strangler whose inspiration is generated by the oppressive mood of the foggy streets of Bouville forces us to consider *La Nausée* as a noir or perhaps proto-noir novel, depending on where one posits the beginnings of French noir literature. It certainly serves to belie such statements as the following from Conrath, which deny the existence of hard-boiled tropes in the French literature of the era that was to witness the advent of the Série Noire: 'This new type of fiction, with its rapid, incisive, slang-based style, its marginal characters, its depiction of urban decadence, its atmosphere charged with both expectancy and cynicism, had no equivalent in France' (Conrath 1995: 40). Indeed, much of the above description seems perfectly applicable to *La Nausée*, and our aim here is to pursue our reading of French noir novels through the filter of such literary works and vice versa.

As shown, Boris Vian's foreword to *J'irai cracher sur vos tombes* plays a role akin to that of the Publishers' note in *La Nausée*. On closer inspection, Sullivan's novel is also circular (*La Nausée*'s circularity lies in its ending, with the protagonist leaving the text, along with the reader, in order to write a novel that will assure his renown, and which is potentially *La Nausée* itself). The first page of *J'irai cracher sur vos tombes* prefigures its own ending. The simple comment, 'I was looking at my hands on the steering wheel' (Sullivan 1973: 13), can be read as a self-referential marker, signalling that the narrative is being guided by a 'man in control', which encourages the reader to have faith in him. It adumbrates as well the motif of strangulation. This faith in the narrator is also strengthened by the novel's opening line: 'Nobody knew me in Buckton' (Sullivan 1973: 13). This statement is a neat reversal of the tendency in the work of Peter Cheyney, whose hero Lemmy Caution begins his quest in *La Môme vert-de-gris* lost in a town where he knows nothing and nobody. For Lee Anderson, the passive reconfiguration—'not being known'—is understood as an advantage; it empowers the protagonist and, at the same time, reinforces the (natural) tendency of the reader to empathize with him. Given the subject matter of the thriller, and the ambiguous status of the protagonist in relation to the law and moral values, the narrator has to work harder than in other genres to keep the reader on side, which, as will be seen, leads to an extensive use of self-consciously literary ploys.[1] Given that this is a tale told in flashback, the reader may be forgiven for expecting a happy ending. (While Sullivan deals with the issue of the feasibility of the protagonist's recounting the tale of his own death by switching to the third person for the last three chapters, Terry Stewart manages the same situation via the role of an interlocutor.) The happy ending is, however, carefully pre-noired from the very outset.

The opening of *J'irai cracher sur vos tombes* forms a neat framing device with the last chapter narrated in the first person. Anderson is seen driving, with a close-up of his hands on the steering wheel (this will also be how he goes to his death); reference is also made to a revolver (the same type of weapon that will be used on him at the end). The whole thrust of the novel is exposed as being the need to bury a body, which prefigures Lee's own self-destruction: he not only desires to avenge his dead brother, but he must ultimately join him in death (the title of the novel, *I Spit On Your Graves*,[2] plays on this ambiguity: does it refer to the graves of Lee's victims or to those of his brother and himself?). And the law that has not shown any compassion to him as a victim of crime is the same one that will show him none when he turns perpetrator. The entire novel is thus contained in microcosm within this opening page.

The noir sting is delivered to the reader in the form of the words 'I forget', which cast a shadow over the narrator's state of mind (Sullivan 1973: 13). It turns out that the whole story is, in fact, delivered from the verge of the tomb: the events that constitute its action are the memories of a dying man. This is perhaps the most important of the links tying *J'irai cracher sur vos tombes* to *La Mort et l'ange*: both are the last visions of dying men, with the latter being much more dramatically staged as such. And yet, before the first page is complete, there is a final twist that leaves the reader perplexed and unsettled, which, insofar as it expresses the uncertainties of both a contingent universe and a writerly text, is the very mood that noir is striving to achieve: 'Perhaps I was going to get out of this.' This clearly counterbalances the assertion of control given by the hands on the steering wheel; the reader who knows nothing of the ending is left hesitating between confidence and doubt.

The ending of the novel operates on three levels: it forms a framing device via its content (Lee flees the police in a car); it offers a perfect example of noir decision-making; and finally it functions at an intertextual level, bringing into play not only another famous noir novel but also a legendary noir duo of American history.

So, *J'irai cracher sur vos tombes* ends as it begins, with Lee Anderson driving a car. This time, however, the depletion of his control over events is marked by the single hand on the steering wheel (Lou has shot him, rendering his left hand inoperative). The supreme noir moment comes when Lee is faced by a turning point in which he is entirely free to choose. This point, where the road before him bifurcates, represents a noir choice at a narrative and metaphorical level: in terms of the

Sartrean framework of free will, all that can make sense of the decision to take one direction over the other is a predefined project (otherwise, as was discussed in Chapter 4, the choice would be arbitrary rather than free). Ultimately, it is the prevailing mood that forces Lee's hand, for nowhere is a protagonist's fate more heavily pre-ordained than in noir fiction. Lee has a project—one to which he has given himself, as it were, freely—and it is noir. And yet, the key to the mood of noir is lingering doubt, and as late in the novel as the final preparations for the double murder Lee is still entertaining thoughts of 'getting away with it'. He couches his plans in enigmatic terms: 'I believe that, throughout that entire time, I had this other project, which was just then beginning to take shape, vaguely in mind, and I had in fact only then realized what it was all about' (Sullivan 1973: 169–70). That this is a Lemmy Caution-like means of making a decision (one that is caught somewhere between desire and knowledge) becomes apparent when he reaches for the bottle of rye: 'I drank a fair amount of bourbon in that period' (Sullivan 1973: 170). This noir project involves the death of the kid, and must lead to Lee's own downfall. The decision that is forced by this project is, there-fore, the only one open to the noir protagonist: when faced with the choice of left or right, Lee elects neither; he finds a third way, plunging off the road into a field.

It is precisely this direction that leads Sullivan's novel into James Hadley Chase's *Pas d'orchidées pour Miss Blandish*. As mentioned, Lee Anderson meets an intertextual death, ending up in the same barn as Slim Grisson. Slim, too, is faced with the decision either to carry on straight ahead or to take a slip road. By taking the smaller of the two roads, he narrows his prospects, condemning himself to death (Lee Anderson simply makes this decision more pointedly noir). For his part, Lee has already killed the girls; there is no chance that they may be rescued (Miss Blandish does at least outlive Slim). Vernon Sullivan thus parodies the ending of *Pas d'orchidées*, 'out-noiring' it, as Scott has sug-gested. This he does by deliberately inverting certain elements of Chase's ending: whereas the motorcycle cops dispatched to chase Slim Grisson pursue him, shooting at him from behind, those sent after Lee Anderson overtake him and shoot back at him from the opposite direction. In order to accomplish this, the two officers—Carter and Barrow—take one motorbike. While one steers, the other, held in place by a leather strap, sits facing backwards. As he watches this obvious inversion of all that is usual, Culloughs, their senior officer mutters to himself: 'That's not right [*c'est pas régulier*]' (Sullivan 1973: 203). Not only is this unorthodox pro-cedure a deliberate send-up of *Pas d'orchidées pour Miss Blandish*, but the names of the two law officers that pursue the outlaw in his car also have names that seem to ring a bell. This, too, is an inversion: whereas Carter and Barrow pursue, Parker and Barrow (a.k.a. Bonnie and Clyde) were pursued.

Terry Stewart picks up Sullivan's inversion of procedural orthodoxy by putting his law officer in the cell with the inmate. Maat's comment to Ben as to the nature of their conversation picks up Cullough's misgivings: 'It's not right [*ce n'est pas régulier*], I know' (Stewart 1972: 12). While this refers back subtly to Lee Anderson's last stand, the passing of the mantle from Lee to Ben Sweed is made possible by the very last chapter of *J'irai cracher sur vos tombes*—a short passage that reads more like a postscript than a chapter. For Lee is not hanged for his crimes but shot dead by the police while still inside the barn. His post-mortem lynching is described as being a parting shot from the locals. He is, then, strangled in death, a fate which brings together his desires for sexual revenge, necrophilia, murder, communion with a dead brother and self-destruction in a posthumous and supernumerary climax (supernumerary since he has already combined most of these elements in his murder of Jean). His sexual prowess is such that, even though already dead, his response to his lynching fulfils the legendary response of the male body to execution by hanging: he has an erection. His erection in death is passed on in inverted form to Ben Sweed, whose impotence is, perversely, the driving force of his murder spree.

The hygenics of strangulation

Ben's impotence is, we are told, the result of a childhood accident. As a result, his only access to sexual gratification comes through strangulation. While *J'irai cracher sur vos tombes* stands as a literary predecessor, in which Stewart's novel finds a pattern for combining sex and murder, comparisons of *La Mort et l'ange* and a much later text further strengthen the nexus between strangulation and the amorous act of reading. Amélie Nothomb's first novel, published in 1992, stages a battle for supremacy between a writer and his reader; indeed, as *Hygiène de l'assassin* [*The Murderer's Hygiene*][3] unfurls, it becomes increasingly difficult to separate the two characters of the novel: the reader, Nina, and the writer, Prétextat Tach, merge into each other, their borders becoming subtly noired. The passage from one stage to the other is marked by strangulation. Consider the following exchange where the author reveals the erotic combination of power and powerlessness:

[Tach:] One more word and I'll strangle you, impotent though I am.
[Nina:] Strangle? Your choice of verb seems to me revealing. . . . So, tell
  me about strangulation.

(Nothomb 1992: 101)

One of the most interesting features of Nothomb's novel is that through
its very circularity, instead of simply promoting an hermetic reading, in
which the novel held by the reader is clearly the one that the protagonist has been reading, and which is in turn becoming the one that she is
helping to finish (the classic novel within a novel à la Italo Calvino
or Georges Perec),[4] it simultaneously points outside itself. It is clear
that one of the aims of *Hygiène de l'assassin* is to twist the reading process back on itself in an ever-decreasing circle. The opening sentence
of the novel, which tells of the imminent death of a major French
writer and the media interest that this has generated, depends on the
establishment of the author, Prétextat Tach, as a member of the French
canon. And this is only accomplished by the result of Tach's final interview, thereby giving the novel an ending that appears to precede the
beginning:

When it was common knowledge that the enormous literary figure
Prétextat Tach would be dead within two months, journalists from
the world over sought private interviews with the octogenarian.

(Nothomb 1992: 7)

Following this incident there was a veritable rush to buy the works of
Prétextat Tach. Ten years later he was a classic.

(Nothomb 1992: 181)

These two lines give rise to the classic conundrum of the chicken and
the egg: the reader cannot know when the story starts, and the reading
becomes a perfect circle. And yet, even within the lines that make up
this framing device there is a push to extend the reading process outside
the circle, into an existing lineage of texts or intertext.

   When read as part of a series of novels *Hygiène de l'assassin* can be
seen to be as linear, intertextually, as it is textually circular. The fact that
the opening line couches the novel within the inevitability of noir's
dead end(ing) is strengthened by the literary reflection of the closing
lines, according to which Tach's bleak and vulgar novels are finally wel-
comed into the canon. This is the story of noir, a case of popular fiction
gaining gradual mainstream acceptance and, eventually, critical acclaim.

As Tach himself states: 'One is never the same again after reading a book, even as modest a book as a Léo Malet: it changes you, a Léo Malet' (Nothomb 1992: 57). This nonchalant insertion of Léo Malet's name into the stream of literary references has the effect of elevating the status of noir fiction, in the mind of this great author, to the level of Jean-Paul Sartre's *La Nausée* or the most famous novel of Tach's favourite author, *Voyage au bout de la nuit* [*Journey to the End of the Night*] by Louis-Ferdinand Céline. Furthermore, the list of Tach's own novels, which Nina quotes like a litany, would blend easily enough into the catalogue of the Série Noire.[5] Indeed, it would seem as though Tach has been profoundly affected by his reading. First, it is suggested that his novels owe much to writers that have gone before him: 'Had Prétextat Tach really innovated? Had he not been the ingenious successor of lesser known creative talents?' (Nothomb 1992: 9); and then it is revealed that he himself has fallen victim (although he is, in fact, delighted by this honour) to an extremely rare disease discovered only once before, 'amongst a dozen or so criminals imprisoned for acts of homicide with sexual violence' (Nothomb 1992: 8). According to Elzenveiverplatz, the man who made the discovery and who gave his name to the syndrome, the cause could be termed a genetic accident, a fate sealed before the victim's birth (Nothomb 1992: 14). At this early stage of *Hygiène de l'assassin* the line between the author Tach, his novels and those of the intertextual genealogy within which they fit is already becoming blurred.

While the book appears to form a tight circle, answering its own questions within its own pages, Nothomb's continual literary name-dropping forces readers to look outside, to speculate as to whether Elzenveiverplatz's prisoners are in fact to be found on the pages of noir novels. Although novels that contain sexual violence and murder are not uncommon, novels that conflate the acts of reading, writing, loving and strangulation (which all become synonymous over the course of *Hygiène de l'assassin*) are, like the disease itself, quite rare. Tach's own writing impulse came to him in terms that the reader has already seen in *La Nausée*, *J'irai cracher sur vos tombes* and *La Mort et l'ange*: 'It's not a vocation. It came upon me [*Ça m'est venu*] when I realized the extent of my ugliness' (Nothomb 1992: 17). Tach is referring here to writing, but it will become clear that the event that disfigured him in his own eyes, and in those of others, was an act of strangulation; and the work of the strangler will become synonymous with that of the author.

Taking into account our emphasis here on the climate of Paris in the years following the Liberation, Prétextat Tach's theory of the success of his own novels sounds uncannily like an explanation of the meteoric rise of the Série Noire:

> In fact, my most successful period began after the war....In 1945 began the great expiation: confusedly or otherwise, people felt that they had things with which to reproach themselves. And thus they stumbled across my novels...and they decided that they would constitute a punishment as outlandish as their depravity
>
> (Nothomb 1992: 58).

While the success of Peter Cheyney and James Hadley Chase clearly hinges on a need to renegotiate the past, to find a way of moving forward along a path between the misery of Occupation and the blinding light of Liberation, Tach's explanation based on guilt and masochism is compelling. He labours under no illusions as to the nature of his own writing. His readers, he will show, were able to devour his work and come out of the process unscathed precisely because they did not *read* him. The definition of the verb 'to read' is central to *Hygiène de l'assassin*, and Tach despises his readers for their bad faith. As he himself states, reading a book changes a person profoundly. His readers do not change. Ergo, they have not read him: 'Once they have read me, people ought to commit suicide' (Nothomb 1992: 55). Tach's readers may not have committed suicide; readers have nonetheless read texts and reacted to them. By his own logic, according to which the hand is the seat of pleasure for the writer in the same way that it is for the strangler, writing a novel is as sure a means of murder as seizing one's victim by the throat.

Before exposing how *Hygiène de l'assassin* can be shown to shed light retrospectively on the line of heredity joining our noir novels of strangulation, it is worth taking the time to consider Tach's line of reasoning. For Nothomb's novel is predicated on a syllogism. It becomes clear when Nina the journalist arrives to put forward her reading of Tach's unfinished novel, *Hygiène de l'assassin*, that she is getting close to what he considers to be the truth. That is to say, that he agrees with her interpretation. Tach's initial position is that in order to be said to have read a novel (and hence to be changed by it) the reader must have come to share the same opinion of its meaning as the author himself. This is a fairly simple defence of literary interpretation based on authorial power. By his own logic therefore, not only is nobody better placed than he to interpret his novels, nobody else is entitled to claim to have read him at all. Having established his position of unassailability, Tach enumerates the weapons that a writer needs to write novels in good faith: testicles (to ward off bad faith), a penis (for creativity), hands (to create and to experience orgasm) and lips (to infuse the text with sensuality). And the most important of these weapons is the hand that writes the text: 'The most specific bliss is located in the hand that writes' (Nothomb 1992: 71). It is the writer's role to use his hand to write; and it is his duty, too, to experience sexual pleasure through the actions that he writes.

As Nina pursues her reading of Tach's text, she seeks his benediction. Her assertion is that *Hygiène de l'assassin* is a work of autobiography, that every word is historical fact. This is her interpretation, but she desires the confirmation of the author. At this stage in the text, her supreme confidence in her own reading is belied by her need to force an admission from the author: her defence of reader-based interpretation will only become fully formed once Tach has verified her account. The interplay of the reader and writer and their respective roles in the interpretative process shift but remain tightly intertwined.

A turn in the tide comes as their discussion broaches the subject of strangulation. Tach concedes that the murder described in the novel actually took place. Furthermore, he declares that '[n]obody knows an individual better than his killer' (Nothomb 1992: 113). His relationship with his young cousin Léopoldine was that of writer and protagonist. Tach knew her, understood her desires as only a writer can know one of his characters. Her role was to be written by his hand; his act of strangulation was a sacred act of literary necessity.[6] It is at this point that the shift to reader-based interpretation gains credibility. Nina has learnt the truth via her engagement with the novel, not through consultation of biographical sources. Tach gradually—but actively—hands her the mantle. His initial desire to give to the one person worthy (to his mind) of the name of 'reader' the only suitable reward—strangulation at his hands, the chance to become written by the man she has read, to enter the text fully—gives way to its opposite: she knows him as well as he knows himself and has gained the right to become his strangler. The shift is ostensibly to a position where reading becomes a writerly process.[7] The movement from structuralism to post-structuralism is itself seemingly critiqued by Nothomb as Nina becomes empowered to write, strangle and, ultimately, replace as author the representative of authorial power, but only to the extent that Tach allows her to do so. Hence the location of bliss—the climax of the writerly erotic experience according to Roland Barthes's scenario, which sees authorial power abandoned to the reader—in the hands of the writer.

In terms of French noir the question of strangulation poses the question of why readers so enjoy texts of sexual violence. And indeed, should the reader or the writer bear responsibility for the production of such texts and the arousal that they produce? The following exchange poses the question of whether the writer (the strangler) or the reader (the strangled) is the one to enjoy the textual process:

> (Tach:) The hand, source of the writer's bliss.
> (Nina:) The hands, source of bliss for the strangler.
> (Tach:) Strangulation is a pleasant act, indeed.[8]
> (Nina:) For the strangler or the strangled?
>
> (Nothomb 1992: 117)

Of course, this all depends on what the gesture of strangulation really symbolizes. If to strangle a text is to construct meaning in it, then the argument returns to whether the writer or the reader is the active participant in the strangulation. And it is Tach himself who points out that '[the] strangled is far less passive than people think' (Nothomb 1992: 149); it is he who now posits the reader in the role of co-producer of meaning. Until this point he has denied the reader any possibility of producing a 'reading', while Nina has put forward the argument that all readers—and all readings—are of equal merit. In a further act of literary anarchy, she laughs in the face of Tach's sophistry (which has extended to an announcement that man's duty is to relieve women of the heavy burden of their existence):[9] 'The journalist threw her head back in a hoarse laugh that stuttered at first, but which gained in tempo, scaling octaves with each new rhythm, until eventually it became an incessant, suffocating cough. This was uncontrollable laughter, clinically hysterical' (Nothomb 1992: 129). French possesses a more succinct way of encapsulating this whole paragraph, an expression that we have already seen used as a proleptic device in *J'irai cracher sur vos tombes*. Simply put, Nina *s'étrangla*—literally, she 'strangled herself'. This paraphrased act of self-strangulation is the first sign that Tach may have been right about Léopoldine's complicity in her own murder. Nina is effacing herself, losing herself in her interpretation of Tach's text. As he suggested earlier, the act of reading a book—reading with all that this entails—is to be changed by it.

This leads to the development of an intertextual argument, whereby one text can change the reading of another. The act of strangulation, in addition to being a symbol of the meaning-making process at the heart of the reading/writing debate, is also located at the very centre of meaning in the text. The death of Léopoldine is an intertextually motivated act that makes Nothomb's—and Tach's—text a direct descendant of Vernon Sullivan and Terry Stewart; it also works backwards, informing our reading of these predecessors.

A cartilaginous reading of French Noir fiction

While Jean, in *J'irai cracher sur vos tombes*, provides the archetype of the docile victim, it is the swimming scene in *La Mort et l'ange* that prefigures Tach's actions. As shown in Chapter 4, Ben Sweed is mesmerized by Dora's strokes in the water; the rhythmic sequence of her movements forms a pattern that is comparable to the notes of *Some of These Days*—so loved by Roquentin. Ben's need to strangle is provoked by a need to impose further order to this sequence, to give it the internal necessity of a novel. He needs to author Dora's death, to know when and how it will come.

Tach's decision to strangle Léopoldine plays on the same need for order. The setting is the same as in *La Mort et l'ange*, a tranquil pool of limpid water. The act of strangulation that follows is less a dance macabre than a highly formalized lovers' ritual: 'From the moment that death was decreed, Eden...was returned to us for three minutes. We were fully conscious of having no more than those one hundred and eighty seconds left to us; it was necessary, therefore, to do things correctly, and that is how we did them' (Nothomb 1992: 149). Even the length of the act—three minutes—corresponds to the traditional length of a popular song.

In this case, the nausea that is banished by this imposition of novelistic order is that which Tach feels as he sees the blood of her first period begin to flow between Léopoldine's legs. Interestingly, while her movements are pretty [*jolis*], as are Dora's, the scene is not, in Tach's eyes, well ordered [*bien réglé*]. Tach's restoration of order plays on very the words used by Terry Stewart: *règles* means both menstruation and regulations in French. Where Tach goes further than his predecessor is in the retrospective implications that he draws out of his use of strangulation. He restores the Platonic purity of the novel by eliminating the intrusion of the natural (cyclical) order; he then decrees, in hindsight, that Léopoldine was complicit in the decision, as if the direction of his narrative was known by the protagonist as well as the author. The artificial lines of the novel, whose artifice is the precise reason for their beauty, take the place of the natural order. The author is thus only going with the flow, which in the Sartrean framework at least, frames his whole writing strategy—and his act of strangulation—in terms of bad faith, a label that Tach is at pains to avoid.

When asked why he specifically chose strangulation, Tach replies that it was in order to avoid making a reference to Victor Hugo (and the drowning of his daughter). Nina provides the obvious rejoinder: 'So, you renounced drowning in order to avoid a reference. But choosing strangulation exposed you to other references' (Nothomb 1992: 150). He admits that this is the case, but explains that it was in fact the beauty of Léopoldine's neck that inspired his decision to strangle her. This, of course, points directly back to *La Mort et l'ange*, in which a woman's beauty is gauged in terms of the slenderness of her neck.[10] For Dora, just as Léopoldine, is considered retrospectively by her killer to have died without a struggle. Indeed, Ben Sweed is delighted by the memory of strangling her, and the fact that she 'put up hardly any resistance' constitutes his best memory (Stewart 1972: 48).

It is at this point that Tach and Nina, between them, make the connection between snapping the cartilage of the neck—the most manual means of execution possible (Nothomb 1992: 151)—and the syndrome that is sending Tach to his own death, which is commonly referred to as cartilage cancer. Cartilage becomes a metaphor for a reading praxis that will allow Tach to apprehend his own life as if it were a series of interrelated texts, or intertext; a cartilaginous reading will allow him to understand the way in which the various texts that he has written (as a man for whom life and his novels are as one) confer meaning back and forth, each illuminating all the others: 'Cartilage is my missing link, an ambivalent articulation that not only permits forward movement, from back to front, but also backward movement, from front to back' (Nothomb 1992: 153). This is an elaboration of the type of intertextual interpretation developed by Michel Riffaterre, a form of reader-response theory that posits the onus for making the connections between texts at the interface of the reader and text. With the question of authorial intent put aside, intertextuality can be seen as distinct from influence-based reading praxes, which can only work in chronological order (with a text only being able to be influenced by another text that precedes it historically). Thus, the cartilaginous praxis set out in *Hygiène de l'assassin* allows the reader not only to infer the influence at work from French noir fiction, but also to renegotiate *La Mort et l'ange*, for example, from a 'Tachian' perspective.

Tach's final actions are designed to goad Nina into becoming his executioner. He confesses his love for her (i.e., his knowledge of her as text—'to love' is, as already mentioned, yet another synonym for 'to read' or 'to strangle') in such an irritating way that Nina is forced to declare her belief that love (and therefore reading) can only happen within a closed system of references: '(Tach:) Do you not understand that one can love a being outside any know point of reference? (Nina:) No' (Nothomb 1992: 172). From this point on, Nina becomes a fully intertextual being. The force that flowed from Lee Anderson into Ben Sweed, and thence into Prétextat Tach, has finally arrived inside her: '(Nina:) For pity's sake, stop talking about your love. I can feel the desire to kill rising up in me...(Tach:) The desire to kill has just died in me, and here it is being reborn in you' (Nothomb 1992: 175). This force takes full possession of her senses, until all that is left of her is Tach's avatar: 'I feel nothing, except an overwhelming desire to strangle you' (Nothomb 1992: 180). It is then she who, by her writerly reading, completes the novel that is *Hygiène de l'assassin*.

The text is a perfect example of the writerly text inasmuch as it synthesizes both reader and writer until one is indistinguishable from the other. Nina writes the ending because Tach forces her into it; and he is complicit in his own strangulation to the same extent that Nina's act of murder may be considered also to be one of suicide. For the change that she undergoes, in becoming the reincarnation of Tach, is as total as that which he experiences in death. Twice in the closing pages Nothomb uses the same pronominal verb of decision-making to describe Nina's galvanization: 'With much effort, the creature complied [*s'exécuta*]' (Nothomb 1992: 177), and, 'The journalist complied [*s'exécuta*] without the slightest slip' (Nothomb 1992: 180). Only in this extreme circumstance, where strangulation implies such ambiguity in the roles of the murderer and victim, and in which the concept of 'correct French' is pushed to pedantic extremes, can there be seen a possibility for word-play in this verb. *S'exécuter*, which to the French eye means simply 'to be moved to action', comes to suggest under Nothomb's pen the idea of 'executing oneself'. The satisfaction that Nina the avatar feels as she contemplates her strangler's hands expresses both the strength of her reading and her own authorial power. *Hygiène de l'assassin* becomes a *mise en abyme* of itself, and reading and writing collapse into each other in a circular text that is both a closed, internal system and part of an external, intertextual line of French literary heredity.[11]

It is perhaps unsurprising that a text such as *Hygiène de l'assassin*, which is so obsessed with the concepts of literary succession and intertextuality, should be constructed in such a way as to expose its own referencing. Moreover, its value in the context of this study lies in its capacity to shed light on the use of self-referentiality made in other earlier, more or less renowned, novels of twentieth-century French literature. For his part, Vernon Sullivan exploits reflexive techniques in order, on one level, to set up *J'irai cracher sur vos tombes* as a parody of noir and, more interestingly, to highlight the novel's position in an interweaving of two literary traditions—one French and one American—and the intertextuality lying at its core. And *La Mort et l'ange* is even more conscious of its dependency on a pre-established network of texts of strangulation. In concluding this discussion of intertextual and self-consciously literary noir, and the genetic predisposition of protagonists to murder with their hands—the very weapon of the author who slays the reader while, as does Tach, enjoining him or her to commit textual suicide by reading to the very end—we return to Terry Stewart's novel, examining its conclusion through the lens of self-referentiality.

One of the most intriguing instances of *mise en abyme* in *La Mort et l'ange* (by dint of its incongruity in terms of the plot and its inexplicability in terms of the psychology of a murderer) is the meeting of Ben Sweed and the journalist who has discovered and publicized his identity, Harry Renshaw. Renshaw discovers the truth by comparing murder cases that reveal traces of a common modus operandi. Like Nina, he not only plays the role of reader within the text but also points beyond the pages of the text, helping to promote an intertextual understanding of Ben's pattern of strangulation: that is, in order to understand one murder, it is necessary to go beyond it, to place it inside a pattern. Only by understanding the position of one crime within a series, can one attain knowledge of the murderer, precisely because the murders have no meaning beyond their place in that sequence. As Ben himself remarks: 'Above all, don't be surprised by the number: I work serial-style [*en série*]' (Stewart 1972: 117). There is a potential for word play here: *en série* implies *tueur en série*, or 'serial killer', but Ben is also one of a series—*une série*—of killers; he is, of course, equally a killer of the Série Noire and, as such, is part of this newly established tradition of French noir.[12]

Harry Renshaw's role is highly ambiguous in the text. By the time Ben pays him a visit, he has already understood the truth. The nature of their meeting is thus opposite to the symbiotic one that Ben has with Maat: whereas Maat wishes to extract information from Ben (and Ben wishes to get things off his chest by telling his tale to an outsider), Harry listens to Ben telling him things that he already knows. If Ben plays protagonist to Maat's reader, Harry has the omniscience of the author. The writerly reading that he offers of Ben's deeds appears to make the latter's confession redundant. And yet, this meeting must be understood within the specific context of the noir novel, in which the protagonist grimly sends himself to his doom. By murdering the man who knows his actions only too well, Ben commits—with only the barest pretence of doing so at one remove—textual suicide. Both men appear equals not only in knowledge but also in terms of their cold acceptance before death. Both men know how Ben's tale will finish. The following lines surpass the protagonists; such is the self-referentiality of the scene that they can be read as an admission made by the author to the reader:

> 'Do you know how you'll end up?'
> 'Yes,' I said, 'on the chair because no one will ever be able to
>   kill me any other way.'
> 'And that is of no concern to you?'
> 'None at all ...'

(Stewart 1972: 118)

This interview can only end in death for both Harry and Ben. For the reader, too, the stakes are high: by exposing the reader to this kind of ultimatum (close the book or face the gruesome reality of the dead ending), the author lays down the gauntlet and places responsibility for the direction of the noir novel on the shoulders of its readers. The French noir novel is not only French by virtue of the nationality of its authors (cf. the case of Cheyney and Chase) but also through the specific French climate in which it is generated, marketed and read. The complicity of reader and writer, sealed in this noir pact, and these two indistinguishable characters, leads us to consider the possibility that Harry Renshaw is in fact a mirror image of Ben Sweed. As Ben's doppelgänger, his appearance reinforces the necessity of the dead ending; as his mirror image, his murder at Ben's hands may be read as an act of suicide. This possibility is exposed by the deliberate reference to mirrors made as Ben prepares to pull the trigger: Harry begs not to be shot in the face, to which Ben replies that it shouldn't matter to him as he will not be able to see himself in the mirror (Stewart 1972: 119).[13] Killing Harry is as certain an act of suicide as killing himself because there can be no extenuating circumstances for this particularly cold-blooded crime. Faced with the blood on Ben's hands, the reader must look into the mirror, too; wherever the story goes from here, no one will remain innocent.

The meeting with Harry Renshaw is exposed as a microcosm of the whole novel when it is revealed that the interview was recorded on a Dictaphone. This revelation is made in the course of Ben's confession to Maat, which has the effect of forcing the psychologist to face the state of his own feelings for the murderer. Maat functions as another Dictaphone, recording Ben's side of the story. From an existential point of view, in order to coincide with his own past actions, the condemned man needs to confess, to tell his own adventure (or speak himself as adventure). As shown, his desire is akin to that of Roquentin's, to be read as a novel. It is important, therefore, that Ben gain the complicity of his listener/readers, thereby taking the place in the text of Stewart the author. His recollection of his interview with Harry Renshaw is given in such a way that Maat can no longer act from behind a screen of innocence. And from this point on Maat is joined in an ontological struggle with Ben, and his desire to read on is the very sustenance of the murderer's coincidence with his own recounted actions. For his part, Ben redoubles his efforts to seduce his reader, simultaneously burdening and titillating him with the truth of his acts, while at the same time laying his hands on him, soliciting from his token Other the caress, the Sartrean sign of love given freely by the beloved (and thus of the ontological victory of the lover).[14] Though he is free to walk away (in stark contrast to the incarcerated Ben), Maat, like the reader of *La Mort et l'ange* (who is free to close the book), finds himself compelled to succumb to this seduction. The reversal of positions between the prisoner and the guard (who freely enters the prison cell) neatly calques the freedom of the character in the book who, though trapped by the form of the words that give body to his tale, is given life by the reader, whose own free choice to read the book becomes an act from which he or she cannot resile.

With each subsequent page of vile deeds, the character of Ben Sweed grows less in baseness than in literariness; as the protagonist of a nearly complete novel, he now commands the perspective that readers tend unconditionally to offer to their heroes. The whole city is after this killer, but he eludes their grasp. The suggestion is that his rule is granted to him by a population (of readers, be it of detective novels or of Renshaw's scoops) that is more intrigued than vengeful. Thus, when Ben finally confronts his nemesis and equal in violent acts of murder, Charlie Rains, his position of first-person narrator is the only thing that separates the two men in the eyes of the reader. And yet, it is a crucial difference, one that Ben Sweed is quite capable of exploiting within his narrative. The violent death that he inflicts upon his fellow gangster recalls, for example, the horrific ending of Peter Cheyney's *Les Femmes s'en balancent* (published in the Série Noire in 1949), in which Lemmy Caution is seen to dispense justice with a capital 'R' for revenge. In terms of *La Mort et l'ange*, whose very construction is ultimately founded on the relationship between the writer and reader of noir fiction, this is just one more test of the complicity of Ben's reader, and as such is almost superfluous.

As the story progresses, it is the readers of noir fiction themselves who are manoeuvred directly into the firing line: 'They wanted me dead, all those representatives of society.... I fooled the police, thumbed my nose at the bourgeoisie like a wild kid, and I carried death in my pocket as my trump card. If you think about it, I wouldn't have got respect so quickly by studying' (Stewart 1972: 125). Violence is what the readers crave, in spite of themselves. And Terry Stewart's awareness of the vileness of his own writing is what he has most strongly in common with Vernon Sullivan: Boris Vian, too, would have liked good literature to have its reward, but it is not necessarily what sells.

Stewart's female lead, Sandra Abbott, like Peter Cheyney's Carlotta, is too caricatured to be anything other than allegorical. In *La Mort et l'ange*, however, this flame-haired icon (who appears as a pin-up girl on her own brand of cigarettes) can be seen not simply as an emblem of French Republican iconography but, more specifically, as Ben Sweed's literary counterpoint. Where his murder spree can be interpreted as representing the proliferation of detective fiction in post-war France, Sandra comes to stand for French literature itself. It is clear that Ben's seduction of Maat is exploitative, designed to further his own ontological redemption; his protection of Sandra, on the other hand, recalls Baudelaire's juxtaposing of poetry and prose. He venerates her, naively and tragically, as does a motley fool his Venus:

She was trembling like a little kid and it was me that had reduced her to it. You can imagine how I got off on that!... Understand this, Maat, Sandra had become indispensable to me. A habit you can't quit. *I loved meeting her, seeing her grey, mocking eyes and her silky hair. I loved breathing in her scent*: it was hot and sweet. *She was a part of me and yet, I hadn't known her long. I was happy to be around her because I knew that she would say the words I needed to calm me down in the bad moments of my life* ...

(Stewart 1972: 127—our emphasis)

The above passage describes the kind of platonic, fraternal love of which the reader no longer thought Ben Sweed capable. While at the surface level of the text this passage speaks of the love of one character for another, a surprising parallel can be found in the final revelatory page of Toni Morrison's famous novel of 1992, *Jazz*:

I envy them their public love. I myself have only known it in secret, shared it in secret and longed, aw longed to show it—to be able to say out loud what they have no need to say at all: *That I have loved only you, surrendered my whole self reckless to you and nobody else. That I want you to love me back and show it to me. That I love the way you hold me, how close you let me be to you. I like your fingers on and on, lifting, turning. I have watched your face for a long time now, and missed your eyes when you went away from me. Talking to you and hearing you answer—that's the kick.*

But I can't say that aloud; I can't tell anyone that I have been waiting for this all my life and that being chosen to wait is the reason I can. If I were able I'd say it. Say make me, remake me. You are free to do it and I am free to let you because look, look. Look where your hands are. Now.

(Morrison 1992: 264–5—original emphasis)

This famous declaration, which informs the reader that the narrative voice is that of the book itself, is one of the most powerful pieces of self-consciously literary prose of the twentieth century; its potential intertextual ramifications (as a model of the way in which a text extends beyond its own parameters, at the same time pulling the reader, and other text(s), into itself)[15] allow us a vision of Sandra Abbott as muse and/or reader, which might otherwise go unnoticed. For *Jazz* speaks its desire of the reader at a starkly physical level, which, when mapped intertextually onto Ben's love for Sandra, posits this female gangster (and descendant of Ma Grisson, the fearsome gang boss of *Pas d'orchidées pour Miss Blandish*) as reader of his tale. She soothes him by listening to him and accepting him for what he is. In this way, she parallels the reader of *La Mort et l'ange*, further embroiling him or her in the dangerous act of reading noir. But the most important facet of this intertextually revealed self-referentiality is the emphasis that it places on the two-way desire involved in the reading/writing process: whether Sandra is reader or literature itself, she is an object of textual desire, forcing us to apprehend Ben's desire for atonement and ontological survival as a powerful call to be read. And as a pure creature who happens herself to be in the wrong job at the wrong time (crime and sinister mood are only a part of her persona, not generic tropes by which she must necessarily be defined), Sandra is emblematic of literature itself, capable of lending authority and mainstream respectability to the noir novel. She is Ben's redeemer, then, at a self-referential level as well as in terms of the plot: 'When things were going well and I'd had bad dreams, she always found a way to *pull me out of my "noir" mood* [*me tirer du noir*]' [Stewart 1972: 127—our emphasis]. Being loved by Sandra is different to being respected by Maat. Sandra can confer upon Ben the status of literature, which the appellation 'noir' tends to preclude.

When read in this light, the following remark sounds like the confession of a writer who is producing noir fiction, not because he enjoys it or because he thinks it a worthy pursuit in its own right, but because it is nonetheless a form of writing, and the one that the French reading public (one more allegorical role for Sandra Abbott) is demanding:

> Nonetheless, it's for her that I did it all, sparing myself no pain, not earning a cent…I worked for free and not often for pleasure. It allowed me to come back to her side and to tell myself that she was holding up because I was defending her, because I was killing to keep her in one piece.
>
> (Stewart 1972: 128)[16]

As the novel draws to a close, however, the constraints of noir fiction come into play. The novel ends where it began, with an occlusion of binaries: Maat's objectivity loses ground to increasing empathy; and Ben loses his black-and-white realism when faced with his imminent execution. Indeed, at the very end of the novel (just before the ultimate noir twist, when it is revealed to the reader that Maat is not a prison guard at all but an FBI psychologist trained to investigate the minds of serial killers, but who has nonetheless come to understand Ben, as it were, affectively, and who has therefore moved from the position of expert reader of writerly text to that of hooked reader of the readerly), there is a brief explosion of intertextuality, as if the protagonist is preparing to join the ranks of his more illustrious peers in the French literary canon. All of a sudden, the imminence of death brings with it a desire for life to continue. There is a hopeless (and condemned) questioning of existentialist values, of authenticity in this noir novel. The grey lines of Ben Sweed's personality allow for a glimpse of something other than 'kill or be killed'. As Jill Scott, the female character with whom he finally falls in love (and who represents his first 'real'—almost sexual—relationship after the death of Sandra for whom his feelings are more pious, almost filial), remarks, 'you are fighting against yourself' (Stewart 1972: 174).

Jill Scott is a literary device, a blind girl placed at the end of the novel to demonstrate the maxim according to which, as the back cover of the book announces, 'love is blind'; her place in the text is suggestive of other literary devices and other novels. Her fragrance recalls the heroines of Boris Vian (Alise in *L'Écume des jours*) and his alter ego Vernon Sullivan (Jean in *J'irai cracher sur vos tombes*): 'She had no perfume, just the smell of her flesh, and it smelt good' (Stewart 1972: 175). Indeed, Ben's love for Jill Scott brings Lee Anderson's posthumous odyssey to a close. We may recall the sentiment of the departing bookshop owner in *J'irai cracher sur vos tombes*, Hansen, who wished for a best-seller in which a young girl would grow up pure in a world of corruption. By loving Jill Scott in his own novel, Ben Sweed lays Lee Anderson to rest and, instead of spitting, throws a flower onto his grave.

Not only are we readers led intertextually from Jill Scott back to Vernon Sullivan's Latin erotic tradition, we are also reminded that the source of these French noir novels lies also in recognized French classics. The twist Jill Scott brings to *La Mort et l'ange*, via the love (of life) that she inspires in Ben Sweed, provides a genuine bond with Albert Camus's *L'Étranger* [*The Outsider*]. Among his parting reflections are the following lines, which recall Meursault's eventual realization of the importance that sunlight has played in his life and his desire to be alive: 'The light is going to dim for me. It will blaze yellow for a few seconds, just long enough for its essence to flood my brain. And I won't see it. And it's only now that I'm beginning to love this light' (Stewart 1972: 181). While the sun for Ben Sweed has been replaced by a light bulb that glows yellow each time the power is drained from it during the operation of the electric chair, for Meursault, whose life has been lived to the sensual rhythms of the Mediterranean coast, it is replaced by a corner of starlit sky visible through the bars of his cell: 'And I too felt ready to live it all again. It was as if this great anger had purged me of evil, emptied me of hope. Before this night heavy with signs and stars, I laid myself open for the first time to the tender indifference of the world' (Camus 1990: 186–6). Such realizations are for Ben Sweed, as for Meursault, too little too late. Once judgment has been pronounced, their fate is sealed, and free will is replaced by ineluctability.

Camus's declaration that he drew his inspiration for *L'Étranger* from James M. Cain's *The Postman always Rings Twice* has long been part of literary folklore. And for his part, Sartre was famously quoted as preferring to read Hemingway over Heidegger. The influence exerted by American hard-boiled fiction on the classics of French Existentialism (for that is what *L'Étranger* has become, despite Camus's own protests) is undeniable. At the very least, then, the line of heredity between a so-called American tradition and French noir literature is indirect.

This chapter has shown not only that the origins of French noir liter-ature lie in a pre-existing Franco-French tradition but that this lineage extends forwards into contemporary French fiction, into a period where the lines between 'noir' and 'mainstream' (and, indeed, any other clas-sification) are far less clearly drawn. For Jill Scott's polysemous line 'you are fighting against yourself' (Stewart 1972: 174) has transited through the reader-*versus*-author debates of structuralism and post-structuralism, eventually culminating in the strangulation pact of Amélie Nothomb's *Hygiène de l'assassin*. It is therefore a highly delimiting practice to read French noir as a thing apart from what is often considered canonical French literature. The path of French noir, as for all noir fiction, depends on a blurring of boundaries, and those of its own origins are a case in point.

6
Jazz: Classic French Film Noir as Transatlantic Exchange

This section offers a reading of French film noir as both intertextual vector and cultural articulator of the various and often conflictual dynamics of the Franco-American relationship. Beyond multiple references in the films themselves, there are a number of good reasons for seeing French film noir as reflective of French attitudes to American culture. Since the early 1990s, leading writers on French cinema have suggested such links. Jill Forbes (1991: 48) argued that French Série Noire films from the 1950s on, 'form the principal means by which the French cinema's relationship to Hollywood has been articulated'. Phil Powrie has picked up Forbes's point, noting that the influence of both the Série Noire and classic American film noir on the French post-war *polar* (crime drama) make the latter 'uniquely placed to articulate questions of national identity in relation to the USA' (Powrie 1997: 76) and that its often sombre tone mean that 'this genre, more than any other betrays the French love-hate affair with American popular culture' (Powrie 2003: 123). The complex relationship between French and American film noir speaks of noir's constitutive hybridity: the emergence of classic noir as a French critical construct of an American film phenomenon.

In 1946, French critic Nino Frank writing for *L'Ecran français* gave the term its current usage after viewing a large number of cynical American crime thrillers made during the Second World War.[1] *Panorama du film noir* (Borde and Chaumeton 2002), the seminal work on classic noir, re-edited in translation, was of course also written by French film commentators. And even before its inception as critical construct, it has recently become clear that film noir emerged out of a transatlantic dialogue. While seen by many, including Borde and Chaumeton, as quintessentially American, since the 1990s a number of commentators have pointed out that noir also had visual and thematic roots in

European culture and cinema (Andrew and Morgan 1996): Hitchcock's British thrillers of the 1930s (Naremore 1998: 15); The Weimar Street Film (Wager 1999); German expressionism of the 1920s and French poetic realism[2] of the 1930s (Vincendeau 1992; Hirsch 1999: 67–76; Spicer 2002: 11–16), the latter heavily inflected by the former during the political upheavals of fascist-dominated Europe prior to the Second World War. The link is cemented by the group of European émigré directors and technicians behind German expressionism and/or French poetic realism and much classic American noir. Most were Jewish, many (Wilder, Siodmak, Lang, Litvak) had lived and worked in France; one, Jacques Tourneur, was French/American. Closely linked to this phenomenon is the number of classic noir remakes of French poetic realist films, including one 'original' (*Pièges/Personal Column*, France, 1939) directed by Siodmak during his stay in France and remade in Hollywood in 1947 as *Lured* by fellow ex-patriot German, Douglas Sirk.[3]

Both through and beyond its narrative and thematic focus on crime and punishment, desire and death, classic French film noir (1945–59) reproduces and highlights highly ambivalent French attitudes towards Hollywood in particular and American culture in general. As noted in Section One, the 'uneasy' historical relationship between France and the USA during the post-war period has been analysed from many angles (Ross 1995; Kuisel 1996; Gildea 2002: 8–12; Revel 2003). Marked by both emulation and increasing resistance to what was increasingly perceived as a form of cultural imperialism, French noir can be read as mirroring the general trend of relations between the two countries through the post- and cold-war periods.

This chapter provides a brief review of key films in order to demonstrate how evolving French attitudes to, and visions of, American culture have been embedded in the plots, thematics and *mise en scène* of French film noir. Secondly, we argue that the mythologized and/or demonized vision of America that seeps through much French noir, more often than not, acts as a catalyst for an examination of France's own internal tensions. However, this is preceded by our own working definition of film noir.

Defining film noir

Film noir is often defined in relation to specific historical moments, as with classic American noir, for black and white Hollywood noir-style studio films made during the 1940s and 1950s (see Hayward 1996) and neo-noir for more recent examples. When using the terms classic

American and French noir, we refer to filmic examples taken from this period, which, for the latter, encompasses films made between the Liberation (1944) and the *Nouvelle Vague* (1959). While sharing the reluctance of many writers to enclose noir within the boundaries of set definitions, particularly given that noir so often speaks of the dissolution of boundary and fixed identity (Telotte 1989; Naremore 1998; Conard 2005), we nonetheless make an attempt. We define film noir broadly, as neither a genre (e.g. Damico 1996; Hirsch 1999), a historical cycle (e.g. Schrader 1996; Silver and Ursini 1996) nor simply a style (e.g. Place and Peterson 1996) but as a trans-cultural, trans-historical, trans-genre phenomenon: the coming together of thematic and narrative concepts and visual style expressive of the noir mood (which previous chapters have examined in relation to the novel) as conveying a certain sensibility, *optique*,[4] or world view (Caputo 1990; Naremore 1998). The following summary encompasses previous canonical definitions and isolates a noir sensibility shared by American and French films alike. It establishes a corpus of works that display most, if not all of the following stylistic, narrative and thematic features:

- visually dark, unbalanced composition (at least) for key moments in the narrative; use of expressionist lighting: chiaroscuro and oblique angles
- the association of crime and eroticism, or desire, greed and death
- moral ambiguity: the problematization of conventional boundaries between good and evil, often underscored by an alternation between realism and lyrical or surreal imagery
- an underlying sense of pessimism, fatalism, existential angst and/or cynicism and paranoia, often highlighted by the use of flashback, circular narrative and/or voice-over
- the absence of positive closure: good does not triumph or merely appears to do so at a surface level. The spectator is left with a feeling of malaise.

Noir, jazz and social critique

Though they tended to underplay the left-wing political roots of the American school, French critics were the first to recognize the potentially subversive social critique implicit or explicit in much classic noir: the association of crime and lust represents the dark side of capitalism, the malaise inherent in the system. And since the 1950s, French noir in its turn has often defined itself against the 'classic American model', and not infrequently, against the culture and economic system which that model implies and often criticizes (Naremore 1998: 104; Wilson 1999: 69).

The central importance of jazz to French noir is highly emblematic here. Even more broadly popular and critically acclaimed than film noir itself (and as mentioned in Section 1, specifically in relation to Boris Vian), to the French, jazz was associated with a black counter-culture distinct from the white dominated mainstream. Jazz and film noir—and the predominance of jazz in the musical scores of French film noir—enabled the French to distinguish between a good and a bad America and to position themselves firmly on the side of the 'good': anti-racist and/or anti-capitalist corruption. As Elizabeth Vilhen has pointed out, through the use of jazz:

> French cultural critics could both embrace and renounce different aspects of American culture and society. In appreciating jazz, French men and women on the cultural left criticized American racism, consumerism, and global authority, yet they also supported a unique American art form and its wide-reaching potential. Jazz made it possible for those French to assert their identity in the face of an American threat.
>
> (Vilhen 2000: 150)

France/USA: odi et amo

As we have seen, the period following the Second World War, which saw the baptism, if not the birth of classic noir, also corresponds to the confirmation of the USA as global super-power, both politically, economically and in terms of film production. It marks the beginnings of a passionate love–hate relationship between France and the USA that endures to this day: consider, for example, French opposition to the war in Iraq and the ongoing Franco-European battle for *l'exception culturelle* (the exclusion from international free trade agreements of cultural products, notably cinema and televisual production, considered vectors of local and national identities), without which American attempts to extend the global free market to the audio-visual sector would see a swift end to French and European national cinemas.[5]

From 1945, after the euphoria of the Liberation subsides, French attitudes towards the USA oscillate between gratitude (for American military intervention), bitterness (over the late arrival and blatantly self-interested motivation of the transatlantic ally) and, above all, anxiety over the ultimate price of American liberation and economic aid. In terms of the film industry, fears of a Hollywood invasion appeared chillingly well founded. The infamous Blum-Byrnes agreements of 1946, supposedly designed to safeguard French film, reserved a mere 13 weeks per annum for local production, with the remaining 39 weeks open to wholesale dumping by the Hollywood studios. Historians have largely vindicated Blum-Byrnes as a necessary evil, an unavoidable sacrifice to the greater national interest: in return, France obtained the conversion of wartime debts to interest-free loans, essential to the reconstruction of a war-ravaged economy.

But, however well-intentioned and justifiable Blum's decision, he unwittingly provided the far left, led by the French Communist Party (which enjoyed the support of more than one in four French voters) with a perfect opportunity to fan the fires of nascent anti-Americanism: the agreements were universally condemned by French film industry players as an act of vile betrayal. Between 1947 and 1949, more than one in two films screened in France were American, while only one in four were French (Hubert-Lacombe 1996: 153). Official records (CNC: *Centre national de la cinématographie*) show that the opening up of the French cinema market did indeed result in a drop in French production's market share: from 51.16 per cent (of total spectators) in 1946 to 42.43 per cent in 1949, while American market share rose from 39.26 per cent to 44.53 per cent over the same period.

Nonetheless, as a number of commentators have pointed out, the preponderance and popularity of American films on French screens during the post-war period did not lead French cinema-goers to desert local production and a preference for the national cinema remained strong (Hubert-Lacombe 1996: 165–74). French market share never drops below 30 per cent and American films decline progressively in the early 1950s, enjoying a smaller share than the French until 1986 (Hugues 1999: 60). During the classic period of the late 1940s and 1950s, the American invasion is contained owing to three factors that serve to sustain the national preference. First, the French film industry picks up and produces a number of impressive box-office hits such as *La symphonie pastorale* [*The Pastoral Symphony*] (Jean Delannoy, 1946) 6,373,12 entries, *Monsieur Vincent* (Maurice Cloche, 1947) 7,055,290; *La chartreuse de parme* [*The Charterhouse of Parma*] (Christian-Jacque, 1948) 6,151,521; *Le salaire de la peur* [*The Wages of Fear*] (HG Clouzot, 1953) 6,944,306. In the ten-year period from 1946 to 1956, of the one hundred films that made up the top ten annual box-office list, 65 were French productions or co-productions.[6] Second, film industry unions and much of the French critical establishment remained virulently anti-American at this time, especially the Communist dominated *L'Ecran français*. As a measure of the effectiveness of leftist anti-American sentiment in the industry, massive PCF-backed demonstrations of cinema workers in January 1948, headed by famous actors and directors (including Jean Marais, Simone Signoret and Jacques Becker) managed to scare the Americans, fearful that France might 'go Communist', into expanding the local quota by a further four weeks per year (Sowerwine 2001: 262). And finally, from 1948 to 1952, French government measures providing state aid to its national industry, most notably from a tax on box-office, enabled French production to keep pace with the constantly growing wave of American imports.

As in the broader economic and military spheres, French admiration for American technological know-how, military and economic might often goes hand in hand with repressed envy, jealousy, resentment and fear. Thus, in spite of the fact that, by 1948, an overwhelming 73 per cent of the French population declared itself in favour of the Marshall Plan (Roger 1996: 164), the concomitant process of modernization—inextricably linked, in the Gallic mind with America— also represented, for many, a form of cultural imperialism or 'coca-colonisation' (Kuisel 1996: 52–69; Sowerwine 2001: 279–282) and a phenomenon of future shock. From the late 1940s on, French film-makers, particularly those making French noir, more often than not drawing on noir fiction, have expressed aspects of this ambivalence in their work.[7]

America between the lines of classic French noir

The quintessential French noir thriller of the early 1950s, Clouzot's *Le salaire de la peur* [*The Wages of Fear*] (1953) is a scathing indictment of American new-world capitalist exploitation and the debilitating greed that it engenders. Set in a squalid outback town in an unnamed, economically depressed Latin American banana republic, the film features a ruthless American oil corporation whose name, Southern Oil Company, or SOC, is a thinly veiled reference to Standard Oil. The company's arrogant, exploitative shadow falls over the wretched townsfolk as they struggle to eke out an existence: half starved and mostly unemployed, they can only stand by and watch as their country's wealth is literally siphoned off and away via a heavily policed company pipeline. The local American boss, tellingly portrayed as a corrupt ex-gangster, hires the film's four 'heroes', the most desperate of the town's sorry bunch of nothing-left-to-lose ex-pats, to drive two truckloads of dangerously unstable nitroglycerine up-country over treacherous mountain roads, to extinguish a raging oil fire. The men are chosen specifically because of their desperate greed and marginal status: if they do not make it, and the oil boss figures at least half of them will not, there will be no family members, no consular authorities and no pesky unions to ask embarrassing questions or cause legal problems.

In the Cold-War context of the film's initial reception, Clouzot's unambiguous condemnation of American big business practices did not escape notice. When *Le salaire de la peur* was first released in the USA in 1955, some 50 minutes of footage were excised from American versions of the print. The majority of the deleted scenes highlight the unscrupulous greed and imperialist exploitation of the SOC: such a stance was deemed anti-capitalist (the left-wing political stance of the film's star and director were noted with suspicion) and therefore anti-American.[8] It must be added that during this period, the French were equally sensitive to negative constructions of their national image, as evidenced by the reception in Belgium of *Paths of Glory* (1957). Kubrick's uncompromisingly cutting portrayal of high-ranking French army officers (whose arrogant and senseless incompetence inflicts futile battle casualties and unjust executions on their own men) was condemned as a scandalous affront to the nation and French authorities saw to it that the producers did not seek to have the film released in France.[9]

A number of highly popular, noir-inspired French spy comedies of the period display a lighter, potentially mocking stance towards American might. The films of the Raymond Rouleau trilogy directed by André Hunebelle and scripted by Michel Audiard, *Mission à Tanger* [*Mission in Tangier*] (1949); *Méfiez-vous des blondes* [*Beware of Blondes*] (1950) and *Massacre en dentelles* [*Massacre in Lace*] (1951) are pure parodic noir. The Lemmy Caution series, after Série Noire author Peter Cheyney, also headed by *La môme vert-de-gris* (Bernard Borderie, 1953) and starring American crooner Eddie Constantine, presents a tongue-in-cheek, Gallic vision of the ultra-cool American spy hero. Most interesting to note here is the way in which the screen adaptation transfers the symbolic, national-allegorical dimension added by Duhamel's translation from Cheyney's female protagonist (see Chapter 3) to the person of Lemmy/Constantine himself. The film cleverly offsets Caution's physical and economic superiority by means of comic exaggeration (he is constantly seducing dames, roughing up gangsters, out-drinking even the most hardened drunks and shelling out wads of dough) and by endowing him with a gaucheness that occasionally borders on stupidity. When he first arrives undercover in Casablanca, Yankee super-spy Lemmy has trouble even remembering the name of his cover identity: Perry Charles

Rice, a Texan bumpkin from Dallas. By humorously exaggerating and offsetting the swaggering machismo of its hero, the film ensures that the spectacle of total American superiority presented through his person is, at least partially, comically defused. Paradoxically also, Constantine's lack of experience and limited talent as an actor unwittingly contributed to the series' ironic, offbeat tone, catapulting its unlikely star and Borderie's Cheyney adaptations to a cult status that would endure several decades.[10]

Fast cars, clean bodies, chic sofas...

During the same period, an 'anti-Lemmy', Franco-French noir tradition is upheld through screen adaptations of Simenon and writers of the French hard-boiled school (most notably Auguste Le Breton and Albert Simonin) and through the physical presence of that icon of Gallic masculinity, Jean Gabin. As Marc Vernet (2007) has observed, the character of Max, the ageing gangster boss played by Gabin in *Touchez pas au grisbi* [Grisbi] (Jacques Becker, 1954) and the spaces he inhabits, can be read as a clever attempt to negotiate between tradition and renewal as a means of reappropriating modernity for Frenchness. Max's car is the French response to the *belle Américaine*: a latest edition, top-of-the-line Simca V8 Vedette, hot off the factory floor in Poissy, just outside of Paris. At a time when the housing crisis was at its most acute, when inside toilets were rare, when most French still used public baths and many houses lacked even running water, Max's spacious, ultramodern, chicly appointed apartment, complete with chrome furnishings, electrical appliances and own bathroom is almost shockingly opulent. *Grisbi* offers a spectacle of technological progress and consumer-capitalist abundance to which few French of this post-war decade had access.[11] And its hero, Gabin/Max is the archetypal champagne-drinking, pâté-eating French patriarch and entrepreneur—moreover, one who has attained mastery over the iconic objects and tools of modernity, right down to a beautiful, young, wealthy English-speaking mistress and an American jukebox that plays a jazzy harmonica theme.

A not dissimilar dynamic is found in *Bob le Flambeur* [*Bob the Gambler*] (1955),[12] scripted by Le Breton and the first in a long line of American-inspired French gangster noir movies by self-confessed Americanophile, Jean-Pierre Melville. In *Bob*, American culture, equated not with capitalist greed and corruption but with technological progress combined with the ultimate cool of jazz, blends harmoniously with the more classically bohemian chic of post-war Paris, between the 'heaven and hell' of Montmartre and Pigalle. As his name suggests, the film's eponymous hero, Bob Montagné, is a charming blend of the two cultures. Wearing the classic trench coat, driving an enormous yet sleek American convertible (conspicuously filmed by Melville to contrast with the heavy black 1940s-style Renaults and comical Tati-esque *Deux Chevaux* that line the Parisian streets), frequenting ultra-trendy night-clubs complete with black jazzmen, Melville's Bob is a nostalgic *clin d'oeil* to the protagonists of Hollywood gangster movies and noir B-films. Yet Melville also frames his hero as the quintessential Parisian, born and raised a mile from Pigalle and the Moulin Rouge. As noted by Ginette Vincendeau in her recent monograph on Melville, 'Bob reverberates with a celebration of the American gangster iconography, but it is couched in the French slang of the Série Noire author Auguste Le Breton…this Franco-American dynamic is key to both the Série Noire and the film' (Vincendeau 2003: 100). The music score echoes the cultural blend, moving smoothly throughout the film from jazz to traditional French accordion, strings and three-beat waltz. Likewise, despite the film's unmistakable air of nostalgia, the process of modernization appears as a generally positive and harmonious one: American sailors, neon signs, and mechanized street sweepers seem to invest the old-world Parisian streets with even greater, if more wistful charm.

Not that the film is obsequious in its admiration for things American. Bob and his safe-cracking partner in 'left-handed-endeavour' are portrayed as professionals whose technical skill and mastery of new technologies is a key factor in the high-tech casino heist that drives the plot. The military precision with which the operation is planned is explicitly likened to a commando operation, perhaps an allusion to the role of de Gaulle's Free French airborne divisions during the Second World War and the Liberation. In this and other scenes, Melville's *mise en scène* and Le Breton's dialogues set the record straight on who owes what to whom in the field of innovation, technical progress and skill, thus restoring a level of Gallic pride. A casual comment by Bob's partner to the latter's young protégé, reminiscing about their early gangster days, points out that it was the Americans who copied Bob's elegant methods (which enabled successful and bloodless robberies), and not the other way around, as was generally thought. The lines are clearly meant to be read on several levels, the underlying aim being to reappropriate noir filiation by reminding the *cinéphile* viewer that many so-called Hollywood inventions, including much of the classic American gangster noir, like Huston's *Asphalt Jungle* (1950), which Melville draws on for this film and others, are themselves based on French or hybrid European models: the Anglo-American pulp fiction of Cheyney, Chandler and Chase, French poetic realism and German expressionism, as outlined above.

Later in the decade, Louis Malle's *L'Ascenseur pour l'échaffaud* [*Lift to the Scaffold*] (1957) goes even further than Becker's *Grisbi* and Melville's *Bob* in combining evocations of modern architecture, technological progress and upward social mobility with the exotic sensuality of jazz, in this instance provided by Miles Davis's original score (incidentally, the only one Davis ever composed for the cinema). Significantly, though, in *L'Ascenseur*, processes of technology-driven modernization are a source of both admiration and malaise. The film was shot almost exclusively in modern locations filled with high-tech gadgetry. Concrete office blocks, equipped with electric elevator, telephone switchboard and state-of-the-art electric pencil-sharpener(!), neon-lit streets and France's first motel, situated just outside Paris, off the equally new motorway: these are all signifiers of modernity that constitute a source of both fascination and futuristic alienation.

The film's ambivalence towards American-style modernity is particularly evident in the fate of the male protagonist. Seemingly at home in this environment, Julien Tavernier is, nonetheless, ultimately betrayed by it, inadvertently trapped for two days in the ultra-modern lift, which in turn almost leads to his being caught for the perfect murder he has just committed. Meanwhile, the war hero's racy new convertible is stolen by a teenage wannabe James Dean, a poignant example of French youth 'led astray by the movies' (Buss 1994: 52) who ends up committing another murder in which Tavernier is wrongfully implicated. And finally, when it seems Tavernier and his mistress (whose evil husband he has eliminated) will get off scot-free, they are implicated by yet another tragically modern twist of technological fate when a series of incriminating photos taken with the hero's state-of-the-art camera fall into the hands of the police. In an ironic, existential reversal of their supposed role at the service of the agency of the individual subject, iconic objects of modernity serve instead as malicious agents of blind fate.

What is most striking about all these French noir film texts are the ways in which they mobilize America to signify fetishistic French ambivalence towards processes of capitalist-driven modernization and a refusal to accept its declining status as a global economic, colonial and military world power. And beneath French film-makers' unfeigned admiration for Hollywood, one reads varying levels of mistrust, along with a need to reassert national pride and maintain a foothold in an increasingly competitive local and global market.

While much of French noir set in France is obliquely 'about' America and French fears over processes of modernization, the converse is also true, with classic French noir set on the American continent acting as a catalyst for an examination of France's own internal tensions. Melville's *Deux Hommes à Manhattan* [*Two Men in Manhattan*] (1959) shot largely on location in New York, ultimately evokes the Occupation and Resistance. Two French journalists, Moreau (played by Melville) and Delmas (Pierre Grasset), head for The Big Apple on the trail of a hot story: the mysterious disappearance of a French diplomat and former Resistance hero, now working for the recently formed United Nations. After roaming through the city, following dead-end leads and questioning the various women in the diplomat's life, the two eventually discover him dead at his mistress's apartment. In true paparazzi style, Delmas wants to cash in on the situation but Moreau refuses, partly out of compassion for the man's daughter, but more importantly, so as not to tarnish the glorious reputation of the Resistance, in which Melville himself had taken part. As Vincendeau observes, 'Melville empties the American referent of its social content and fills it with his own aesthetic and cultural concerns. *Deux Hommes* is a personal odyssey which marries cultural pilgrimage with sexual narrative.…embedded at the core (of Melville's preoccupations) is the Myth of the Resistance' (Vincendeau 2003: 121).

The shadows of the Occupation, Dien Bien Phu and Algeria fall over other French noir of the period, notably constituting an additional subtextual layer of *Lift to the Scaffold*: first, and most directly, through the couple of German tourists, whose high-tech car and camera symbolize Germany's spectacular, and for France, somewhat humiliating rebuilding and modernization after 1945. The husband boasts of having been a member of the Occupying Forces before he is shot dead, a reminder of how fresh the wounds of history were for French people of this time, and how fragile the new European alliance intended to heal them. Second, the figure of Carala, corrupt businessman involved in exploiting France's colonial conflicts, is a clear reference, not only to the recent defeat at Dien Bien Phu and the current Algerian crisis but, inescapably, to recent memories of the role played by some of France's leading industrialists as pro-Vichy collaborators.

J'irai cracher sur vos tombes

We have suggested that even when the action of French noir takes place on the American continent, the noir narrative acts as a catalyst for an examination of France's own internal tensions. Perhaps the most compelling example of this specific type of transatlantic dialogue is provided by Michel Gast's much-maligned screen adaptation of Vian's *J'irai cracher sur vos tombes* (1959).

As in Vian's novel, the Joe Grant[13] of Gast's film (Christian Marquand) is a mixed-race black American from Memphis whose fair skin enables him to pass for a white Man. When his brother is lynched for wanting to marry a white girl, Grant leaves town, moves north and starts a new life managing a small-town bookstore. The town is run by the unscrupulous Stan Walker—aided and abetted by his gang of young delinquents—who uses the bookstore as a front for an extortion racket. To take revenge on white society for his brother's death, Joe seduces several white girls, including two wealthy sisters. He half intends to murder one, the pure and beautiful Lisbeth Shannon (Antonella Lualdi), heiress to the family fortune, engaged against her will to marry Walker. But, in stark contrast with the novel (though in keeping with Vian's screenplay), Joe falls in love with Lisbeth and is incapable of carrying out the final act of his revenge-plan. When Lisbeth learns that Joe is black, she suggests they run away together to escape the posse organized by her enraged fiancé. In the final scene, they almost reach the border when they are tragically gunned down by police.

The first point to note about Gast's film is that it constitutes a triple 'narrative of passing'.[14] We have seen that Vian's novel—about a black American attempting to pass for white—replays its central thematic, being originally published as a French translation, purportedly written by black American writer Vernon Sullivan, in fact, a pseudonym of Vian's invention. The film, like the novel, is a French production[15] attempting, in a sense, to pass for American. Moreover, Gast's screen version is engaged in a second narrative of passing in claiming to be a daring filmic rendition of Vian's scandalously successful 1946 novel: *the film no one dared make*, declares an Opening Title, echoing the introduction to the book as *the novel America didn't dare to publish*. In fact, the film was the object of a long series of acrimonious exchanges and lawsuits between Vian and the production company: the script was quite extensively rewritten (from Vian's original screenplay and dialogues), by the director and co-writers and subsequently disowned by Vian himself. The extremely fraught situation surrounding the film's genesis (see Arnaud 1974), compounded by Vian's untimely death from a heart attack at a press screening of the film, sealed its critical fate. Without the blessing of its literary auteur, accused even of having caused his demise, Gast's film could not hope to 'pass' for Vian's in the eyes of the highbrow critical establishment. Despite a number of favourable reviews in the popular press, it became something of a *film maudit*, being more or less lynched by the Parisian literati. Nonetheless, Vian's name remained atop the opening credits and *J'irai cracher* did very respectably at the box office in France. It totalled almost three and half million entries in 1959, making it the ninth biggest selling French film of that year, just behind Truffaut's *400 Blows*. Moreover, the saga of Joey Grant spoke directly to black Americans—according to Michel Gast, the purchaser of the American distribution rights made millions from largely black audiences by touring the film throughout the South.

Like Vian, first-time director Michel Gast had never been to the United States when he undertook the project, and for budgetary reasons, the entire film was shot in France: on location near Fréjus and in the Victorine Studios in Nice. The streets of Trenton were built on the very set that had once recreated the famous *Boulevard du Crime* of Marcel Carné's *Children of Paradise* (1945), one of Gast's most loved films. Sets and decors were reconstructed from still photos of American towns, giving rise to a number of unintentionally humorous cultural gaffes. Among the signs adorning the town's buildings, for example, one finds such odd misnomers as BROTHER—presumably intended to stand for a family-run business—or the even more puzzlingly apocryphal ZERO FOOD LOCKER. Tellingly, the one noticeably correct sign, so ubiquitous that even Frenchmen who had never set foot in the United States could not help but get it right, somewhat ironically proclaims: It's the real thing! And in terms of its decors, the film's various locations fly blithely in the face of geographical logic. Joey's saga begins in Memphis, where his brother is lynched. He supposedly flees north to Trenton. But although the sets for the town could conceivably 'pass for' middle America, the Shannon plantation is pure, deep South, from the colonnaded architecture of its central mansion, and lush, sub-tropical gardens to the anachronistic liveried splendour of its black servants.[16] Not that such details detract significantly from the film's interest, nor would they have mattered in the slightest to its original target audience. For the America of the film is an intentionally stylized, mythologized America. Mythologized, in the sense of Cocteau as much as of Barthes: myth as a means to express displaced social realities and deeper levels of human truth. Mythologized also through Alain Goraguer's haunting jazz-blues score, the most convincingly American element of the film, one of the few to meet with Vian's approval, and perhaps its most impressive feature. Mythologized and noired, both literally and figuratively as Vian had originally intended.

While Vian's novel is supposedly parodic and excessive, Gast's *J'irai cracher* is, on the other hand, a 'straight' noir portrayal of the dirty underbelly of a modern society eaten away by capitalist corruption, greed and violence, fed by the twin hypocrisies of class prejudice and racism. And the society Gast ultimately seeks to describe and critique is not so much America as it is contemporary France. Firstly, the evocation of white youth culture, following Vian, is both voyeuristically sensationalist and slightly patronizing. However, Gast goes much further in representing middle-class white youth as driven by peer-group pressure, bullying gang mentality and cowardice, as well as greedy hedonism and promiscuity: sex, booze and rock-and-roll. The threat represented by nascent 1950s youth culture is expressed in *mise en scène* and highlighted by camera work and editing. We are introduced to the gang members in a high-angle crane shot as they swoop down the main street riding oversize motorbikes whose engines invade the soundtrack. After terrorizing the ageing bookstore owner, the youths proceed to take over the town drugstore, jiving to loud jukebox music, drinking, kissing and fighting while its pot-bellied, middle-aged proprietor can do no more than protest lamely before being unceremoniously shoved out of the frame. Much as in Carné's *Les tricheurs* [*The Cheats*] (1958) and Chabrol's *Les cousins* [*Cousins*] (1959), American pop culture is represented as having an intoxicating and corrupting influence on the young.

J'irai cracher's overt theme is white American racism towards blacks. The trailer opens with a clear announcement of the film's central project:

> Still today, as unthinkable as it may appear, the law is different in the USA for Whites and for the 40 million Blacks who live there. The Black Man is the object of contempt and often hatred, which can go as far as the horrifying and still common practice of lynching. And such violence engenders violence...

But again, the real target here, for the film's director, is racism within the French Republic. In a discussion session that followed a re-screening of the film in Paris in June 2004, Gast traces his desire to expose racial prejudice and injustice back to a childhood spent in French Algeria, during which time he was constantly outraged at the banality and ubiquity of French racism towards Algerians. The film-maker notably recounts how his father, principal of a *lycée*, or senior high school, had a major battle with the authorities (which he eventually won) when he refused to pass the son of a French colonel into the next class, since 'It was unthinkable that the son of a (French) colonel should fail while even one Arab child in the class should be allowed to pass.' At the time the film was made, the war in Algeria was the major issue facing France, but, as during the Occupation, censorship meant that it was a taboo subject for French cinema.[17] And, as in Occupation cinema, censorship necessitated a recourse to allegory. In *J'irai cracher*, Gast uses Vian's parodic-noir evocation of racism in the United States to raise the questions of racism, class prejudice and military torture within the French Republic. Despite controls on print media[18] and a national reluctance to criticize the country's army, major newspapers like *Le Monde* and *l'Observateur* had run reports openly denouncing the practices of General Massu's paratroopers (heroes of the Liberation!) during the Battle of Algiers in 1957, comparing their methods to those of the Nazi occupiers.

Gast weaves a number of oblique references to the Algerian question into the plot of *J'irai cracher*, adding two scenes that foreground specific torture practices known to be common in Algeria: electric shock and drowning. In the drug-store scene mentioned above, amid a surreal party-like atmosphere that announces *A Clockwork Orange*, two rival gang members engage in ritual self-torture termed 'the electric chair': one volunteering, the other being forced[19] to undergo a prolonged electric shock of mounting intensity. The round ends when the volunteer 'talks' by screaming out in pain. In a later, noirish, night-for-night torture scene, Walker's gang extorts the key information on Joe's identity from Chandley by repeatedly holding his head down in a tank of water.

In these as in other key scenes, content, *mise en scène* and camera work—low key-lighting, deep focus wide shots alternating with close-ups and extreme angles, night-for-night exteriors—evoke the violence and paranoia of classic noir. Unlike Melville, Michel Gast strenuously rejects the notion that he might have been attempting to emulate films from the recently consecrated classic American noir canon. Though he admits to being inevitably influenced by classic noir, the film-maker cites instead, as his major aesthetic frame of reference, French poetic realism, in particular *Le jour se lève* [*Daybreak*] (Carné, 1939). And indeed, in its tragic plot structure, social analysis and doomed hero character, *J'irai cracher* is very much in the poetic realist mode. As Joey Grant, Christian Marquand has something of the Gabin of the late 1930s. Though much taller than Gabin, Marquand's body language and diction are similar: his movements lithe but restrained, his speech direct, minimalist. Both play the quiet man of the people, the tragic hero driven to violence and death through social injustice and unhappy fate. Like

Gabin's deserter in *Quai des brumes* [*Port of Shadows*] (Carné, 1938), Joe is fleeing from his past. Like Pépé (*Pépé le Moko*, Duvivier, 1937), he is trapped in exile and dies attempting to escape. Like François of *Le jour se lève*, he kills an evil adversary and is hunted down by police. His sick desire for revenge is reminiscent of Jacques Lantier's mental illness (*La bête humaine* [*The Human Beast*], Renoir, 1938) but unlike the latter, it is based on lived experience and choice not genetic fate. And unlike Lantier, Joe falls for a 'good woman' who convinces him that if they are happy together, his brother will be avenged. Most significantly, like all the Gabin characters, the Joey Grant of Gast's film reacts violently against hypocrisy, injustice and exploitation. In a notable departure from Vian's novel and screenplay, Joe responds to Stan Walker/Dexter's offer of sex with an under-age black girl with a Gabin-like outburst. Punching and beating Walker with a length of rope, Joe runs him out-doors through the crowded bar and pushes him half conscious into the river.

Gast's reluctance to see his film defined as noir (i.e., according to a term that, during the 1950s was applied almost exclusively to American productions), though understandable in terms of national pride, is somewhat disingenuous, particularly given Vian's original literary project. Moreover, as well as drawing heavily on noir visual style, as mentioned, Gast adds references to hard-boiled fiction that are not to be found in Vian's Queneau-esque screenplay. The film's bookshop décor notably includes a prominent stand full of classic-sounding noir titles like *You Asked for It* and *Man Trap*. And in one scene, an elderly Miss Marple-like spinster and fervent consumer of detective fiction declares: '*The detective novel is an inferior genre but it teaches us perspicacity.*'[20]

Conclusion

In a similar spirit, this chapter has sought to demonstrate the various ways in which a careful analysis of classic French film noir can shed light on the Franco-American love–hate relationship and the tensions within French society that fuelled it. Notably, we have seen that while the majority of French noir of the 1950s is set in France and is ostensibly about France, it speaks between the lines of French attitudes towards the United States: American cinema, culture, economic and military power. Conversely, it is when French noir is set in the United States that the ultimate object of investigation tends to focus most closely on France's own internal tensions.

In *J'irai cracher sur vos tombes*, we have examined ways in which America functions as a sign of modernity and capitalist greed and indexical signifier of displaced, repressed contemporary French political and social reality: anti-social youth culture, racism, class prejudice and military atrocities in Algeria. In both cases, America functions to crystallize French ambivalence towards a capitalist-driven modernity equated with the promise of freedom, progress and consumerist utopia but in constant danger of succumbing to insatiable greed, loss of values, and class or race-driven violence.

7
Fatal(e) Crossings: Figures of the Feminine in French and American Film Noir

Cherchez la femme! the age-old French adage that unambiguously singles out Woman as the underlying cause of man's woes. Whenever there is trouble, particularly whenever a serious crime is committed, in order to find the cause or reason or culprit: look for the woman! Emblematic of the noir attitude to the (often darker) fairer sex, the phrase, *Cherchez la femme,* sees in every woman, a potential *femme fatale.*[1]

American vs French *femme fatale*

Similarly, the *femme fatale* is at the heart of both classic and contemporary American noir-style cinema. Classic American fatale is the alluring yet ruthless spider woman who seduces the hapless noir hero before seeking to dispose of him, and who is generally killed or imprisoned for her sins. She appears in a multitude of noirs, most notably as Brigid O'Shaughnessy in *The Maltese Falcon* (Huston, 1941), Phyllis Dietrichson in *Double Indemnity* (Wilder, 1944), Cora in *The Postman Always Rings Twice* (Garnett, 1946), Kitty in *The Killers* (Siodmak, 1946), Kathy in *Out of the Past* (Tourneur, 1947) and Elsa Bannister in *The Lady from Shanghai* (Welles, 1948).

While much has been written on *femme fatale* in American film noir, generally from a feminist and/or psychoanalytical perspective (e.g. Place 1980; Doane 1991; Kaplan 1998; Wager 1999, 2005), there has been little comprehensive research into feminine figures in French film noir, or French *fatale*, if indeed such a creature exists. Robin Buss's monograph, *French film Noir* (Buss 1994), the only work entirely devoted exclusively to this area, is almost entirely silent on the question. The subject has been broached through a number of recent studies of women in French film (Burch and Sellier 1996, 2001) and of film-makers (Vincendeau

2003) and actors (Hayward 2004) involved in French noir. Yet no specific studies of French *fatale* have been published to date. Such a lacuna is puzzling, particularly given the central importance of the *femme fatale* in American noir, but it is equally understandable. A close examination of feminine figures in classic French film noir reveals that the spider-woman fatale is almost entirely absent. As surprising as this may seem given the both latent and blatant misogyny of mid-twentieth-century French culture, in French film noir, when one looks for the woman, the lethal temptress of so many noir classics, the lady more or less vanishes.

Classic American *fatale*: The sociological thesis

It is useful at this point to outline the widely accepted sociological explanation for the emergence of the American spider-woman fatale. According to this thesis, the negative portrayal of woman in much classic American noir can be seen as reflecting a crisis of masculinity aggravated, if not precipitated, by the nation's traumatic experience of the Second World War. This is not to suggest that Pearl Harbor constituted a point of absolute origin in terms of American cynicism and mistrust of women. After all, the first *fatales* of American noir classics (notably *The Maltese Falcon*, 1941) predate American entry into the war, reminding us that the roots of noir reach back into the economic and social turmoil that accompanied women's enfranchisement (1920), Prohibition (1920–33) and the Great Depression of the early 1930s. Nonetheless, the profound psychological impact on millions of American servicemen of the trauma of war cannot be overlooked. And, as always in wartime, the constant physical threats of armed confrontation would have been doubled by the threat (no doubt equally horrific for some) of sexual infidelity on the part of wives and girlfriends left at home. Moreover, these factors and the consequent difficulties in readjusting to civilian life—re-entering the family and workforce, sufficient in themselves to unsettle masculine identity—were compounded by the radical transformation of both social spaces. American men, already emotionally scarred by the direct experience of war, suddenly faced massive competition from those whose role had previously been strictly limited to serving their needs as wives and mothers. As Thomas Schatz was among the first to point out:

> Changing views of sexuality and marriage were generated by the millions of men overseas and by the millions of women pressed into the workforce. The post-war return to 'normalcy' never really

materialized—the GIs' triumphant home-coming only seemed to complicate matters and to bring out issues of urban anonymity and sexual confusion.... These concerns tinged Hollywood's traditional macho-redeemer hero and domesticating heroine with a certain ambiguity and brought two other character types into the midst of the Hollywood constellation: the brutally violent, sexually confused psychopath and the aptly named *femme noire*, that sultry seductress who preys on the hero and whose motives and allegiance generally are in doubt until the film's closing moments.

(Schatz 1981: 113–114)

This chapter outlines and attempts to explicate the cultural specificity of French fatale in terms of the 'American model.' In doing so, we test the sociological thesis behind the emergence of American fatale by applying it to the French situation.

Feminine figures in classic French film noir

The figure of the vamp, the mysterious, dangerous sexual woman is, of course, no stranger to French cinematic and literary culture. As early as 1915, Feuillade drew on this figure in the creation of his silent screen anti-heroine Irma Vep (*Les Vampires*). Similarly, French cinema of the 1930s has more than its fair share of alluring vamps, epitomized by Mireille Balin in *Gueule d'Amour* (Jean Gremillon, 1937) and *Pépé le Moko* (Duvivier, 1937) and treacherous *garces* (gold-digging bitch figures) as played by Janie Marèse in *La chienne* (Renoir, 1930) and Viviane Romance in *La belle équipe* (Duvivier, 1936). And to take but one example from the French literary tradition, the ruthlessly ambitious Milady of Dumas' *Les trois Mousquétaires* (written in the nineteenth century, set in the seventeenth) is every bit as powerfully seductive, far deadlier in fact, than the Hollywood *femmes fatales* of more recent times.

Neither is the vamp absent from classic French noir. The 1940s and 1950s see a number of compelling examples of sexually assertive female characters who combine intelligence, ambition, seductiveness and power. Like her American homologue, French *fatale* 'gets men into bed and into trouble' (Marie Windsor, quoted in Horowitz and Schon 1994). The fundamental difference between the two figures, however, as we argue, lies in motive. Although she is most often, either directly or indirectly, the cause of the male protagonist's fall (and often her own), rarely does French *fatale* consciously plot his demise. In this sense, she is more a *fatalitaire*, the unwitting and tragic instrument of doom, than the utterly self-seeking *fatale*, the devouring spider-woman typically at the centre of classic American noir, whose punishment or death is presented as just and desirable.

French *fatale* may possess all the seductive qualities and powerful agency of the classic *fatale*. However, though she may be ambitious and unscrupulous, whether she is out to murder her lover's wife (as in Clouzot's *Diaboliques*, 1955) or her husband (as in Malle's *Ascenseur pour L'Echaffaud*), whether she is prepared to cuckold the man she loves for material gain (Clouzot's *Manon*, 1949) or pin a murder on an innocent victim to save her guilty lover (Duvivier's *Panique* [*Panic*], 1947) what most often sets French *fatale* apart from the American figure is her overriding and unshakeable emotional attachment to a male protagonist. French *fatale* is almost always an *amoureuse*, a woman in love whose basic aim is to get and/or keep her man. The man is still her ultimate object of desire, not merely a tool to be used in the quest for power and independence, used, abused, then discarded, as tends to be the case in classic American noir: 'what she's after is not the man. He's another tool. What she's after is something for herself' (Janey Place quoted in Horowitz and Schon 1994).

Clouzot's diabolical *fatale* character, Nicole, played by Simone Signoret, whose treacherous betrayal and quasi-murder of the film's *ingénue* places her among the most powerful and monstrous French *fatale* figures of the period, is nonetheless revealed to be doing it all for love or at least unfeigned passion. After *Celle qui n'était plus* (1952) by leading French crime-writing duo Boileau-Narcejac, the film is set in a second-rate private school, in a small, drab country town. Virtuous, psychologically battered wife Christina (Vera Clouzot), is persuaded by her husband's disillusioned mistress, Nicole (Signoret), to get rid of the cause of their misery. They drug the unsuspecting husband, drown him in the bathtub then throw the body into the swimming pool. But next day the body has disappeared and later a number of uncanny events suggest supernatural intervention or foul play. The wife, who suffers from a bad heart, is sick with guilt. The climactic sequence sees the husband rise zombie-like from the bathtub, causing his wife to drop dead from a cardiac arrest. At this moment the mistress rushes in to embrace her lover, awakening the spectator to the full monstrosity of the crime: the pair had been plotting the death of the gullible wife all along. In this penultimate scene, when the spectator is finally let in on the secret of the film's plot, the camera focuses briefly but intensely on the passionate embrace of the murderous lovers. Unlike her American sisters in the noir classics mentioned above, there is no hint here that

Signoret's *fatale* is planning to ditch the male or eliminate him and go it alone.

Even Signoret's ruthless gold-digger, Dora, in Yves Allegret's somewhat misogynistic *Manèges* (*The Cheat*, 1949), ends up falling in love. But the handsome, debonair young man she chooses (over her doting, middle-aged husband, whose meagre fortune she has ruthlessly dissipated) turns out to be a heartless gigolo, an *homme fatal* of even more dubious morals than her own.

Signoret is the single most prominent female star of French noir realism of this period. Previous to *Diaboliques*, she had played the classic French *fatalitaire* five times, once, in *Thérèse Raquin* (Carné, 1953) as a desperate young wife trapped in a sterile and stifling marriage, but most often in her explicitly sexualized form as the proud and fundamentally good-hearted prostitute. In *Les démons de l'aube* [*Dawn Devils*] (Yves Allegret, 1945), *Macadam* (Marcel Blistène, 1946), *Dédé d'Anvers* (Yves Allegret, 1947) and *Casque d'or* [*Golden Marie*] (Jacques Becker, 1952) Signoret's prostitute figure falls in love and risks everything to save her man. In all these films, assertive feminine sexuality and agency are coupled with both intelligence and moral integrity, in what Susan Hayward has described as Signoret's 'erotics of power' (Hayward 2004). The complexity and ethical values that Signoret brings to her characters contribute massively to the construction of French *fatale* as a largely positive figure, certainly much more than a heartless and treacherous *garce*. As Hayward points out 'Signoret's characters […] exude an intelligence about life (and being in it) in ways that the superficial, stereotyped *femme fatale* is never allowed to enjoy' (Hayward 2004: 77).

In a none too dissimilar vein, the character played by New Wave icon Jeanne Moreau in Malle's *Ascenseur pour l'Echaffaud*, is prepared to risk her reputation, status and freedom, not simply to rid herself of an unwanted husband and pocket his fortune, but to be with the man she loves. The investigative agency of Moreau's *fatalitaire*, envisioned by her character's relentless search for her lover through the rain-soaked Paris streets (her unswerving efforts to find and free him momentarily rewarded, only to be thwarted by the final twist in the plot that implicates them both), is doubled linguistically by her poignant voice-over narration. Her command of both sound and image-track is further accentuated by Miles Davis's hauntingly sensual jazz score as it becomes indelibly associated with Moreau's image.

Here as elsewhere, the construction of the *fatale* ultimately turns on the question of loyalty, which may or may not be associated with sexual fidelity. In her unflinching loyalty to her man, French *fatale* of this period remains a generally positive though often tragic figure, more *fatalitaire* than mysterious vamp or cold, unfeeling *garce*. It is largely the *fatalitaire*'s loyalty that enables the construction of the common French noir couple of the ill-fated, star-crossed lovers,[2] in stark contrast to the *femme fatale*/fall guy combination of much American noir.

Classic noir is very much about treacherously false surfaces, with the spider-woman as the ultimate embodiment of this theme. *She looks like an angel, but she's a devil in disguise*, as the song goes. French *fatale*, while also being very often the signifier of misleading appearances, is generally the reverse. She is a kind of angel in devil's disguise, demonstrating how the falsely mercenary or promiscuous surface (the prostitute or adulteress) can conceal a passionately genuine heart. In terms of *mise en scène*, this aspect is nowhere better illustrated than in Signoret's costuming in Becker's *Casque d'or* [*Golden Marie*].

Loosely based on a true story, *Casque d'Or* is set in the Paris demi-monde of 1900. Georges Manda (Serge Reggiani) an honest carpenter with a criminal record and underworld connections, falls for Marie (Simone Signoret), the good-hearted prostitute 'moll' of minor crook Roland, himself under the thumb of evil gangster boss Leca, who also lusts after Marie. When Manda kills Roland in a duel over Marie, Leca has his closest friend arrested, knowing that Manda will surrender to save him, thus leaving Marie alone and unprotected. When Georges discovers he has been set up, he escapes from police custody and kills Leca but he and his friend are rearrested. The film ends tragically as Marie watches their execution.

Meticulously analysed by Susan Haywood (2004: 112–19), costume plays a crucial role in constructing and reflecting Marie's status as *fatalitaire*. We extend the complex reading offered by Hayward of Marie's most significant costume: the black and white striped taffeta ball gown, trimmed with white lace ruffles and which she wears with a black feather boa that in turn conceals a black onyx choker.

> The dangling pieces of the necklace look like long, sharp teeth. The fetishistic value of the plumed female body is a common enough stereotype of the devouring *femme fatale*, as is the notion of the plumed female as dangerous and predatory, which the necklace serves to enhance.
>
> (Haywood 2004: 112–13)

Hayward shows how this costume can be read variously, either marking Marie as a predatory black widow or as a sign of genuine mourning, since she wears it on the night of her lover Manda's fateful shooting of Roland, just after discovering that she has lost Manda to another woman, and before consequently deciding to sell herself to the evil gang boss, Leca. We would add that this ambiguous layering of signification is part and parcel of the film's construction of Marie as *fatalitaire*. The costume, which appears straight black in long shot, is revealed to be more complex on closer-framing: black and white stripes, indicating Marie's potential for both good and evil and emphasizing the uncertainty of the spectator as to which side she will choose. Moreover, the white lace at the throat softens and offsets the cutting jaggedness of the necklace. The costume is therefore partly a question mark: will Marie reveal herself to be black widow or loyal mistress? *Garce* or *fatalitaire*? The question will be answered by the progression of the narrative, which will expose the spider-woman costume as a masquerade. Marie's tough exterior is a survival mechanism, concealing a heart that is not ruthlessly treacherous but fiercely loyal.

In this sense, as a romantic and/or misunderstood figure, set up as false appearance or falsely accused, classic French *fatale* resembles more closely the good-bad-girl false *fatales* of melo-noirs like *Laura* (Preminger, 1944) and especially *Gilda* (Vidor, 1946). Signoret's prostitute characters use sexual promiscuity as a front, as does Vidor's eponymous heroine. Like Carlotta, the eponymous 'heroine' of *La Môme vert-de-gris*, all are victims of the patriarchal tendency to *Look for the Woman*, or *Put the Blame on Mame*, as Rita Hayworth sings. And all are ultimately morally vindicated.

What sets classic French *fatale* apart from the American spider-woman is that she lacks the latter's lethal combination of physical seductiveness, powerful agency and ruthless, selfish ambition. Not that we would therefore consider French cinema to be less misogynous or more emancipated in its portrayal of the feminine than American cinema. Burch and Sellier's influential analyses of post-war French Cinema argue that the *sale garce* or evil bitch is a central feminine figure, present in 25 per cent of all French films made between 1945 and 1955 (Burch and Sellier 2001). However, as we have argued, and as Hayward's study of Signoret clearly demonstrates, neither should the power and ubiquity of the *garce* be overstated. While not opposing the fundamental position of Burch and Sellier (1996), Hayward (2004) shows that Signoret's post-war roles (with the exception of *Manèges*) do not conform to stereotypical notions of the *fatale*, more specifically they do not feed into the demonization of sexual women perpetrated through the figure of the *garce*.

Nonetheless, one must not overlook the fact that French noir of this period does indeed contain some very negative images of women. In *Touchez pas au grisbi* [*Grisbi*] (Jacques Becker, 1954) several of the female characters are indeed classic *sales garces*: little more than treacherous, petty gold-diggers. But these are minor characters, *petites garces* with nothing of the *fatale*'s breathtaking power and narrative agency. Even the central character of Dora in *Manèges* who corresponds more closely to the classic *fatale*, has been rendered powerless from the opening moments of the film, through an accident which has left her physically paralysed. In other cases, the various elements of the classic *fatale* exist, but fail to crystallize in a single character, as in Melville's *Bob le Flambeur*. *Bob* figures two apparently ambitious, treacherous females, the domineering wife of a minor character who ultimately turns informer, and a young blonde temptress, Anne (introduced by Melville's sardonic voice-over narration as 'very advanced for her age') who seduces the main character's naive young sidekick, then unwittingly betrays him to a police nark.

Neither of these characters ultimately qualifies as true *femme fatale*. The more powerful former figure, filmed in distorting low-angle close-ups, is a *mégère*, an unattractive, henpecking shrew entirely lacking in the physical appeal that enables the *fatale* to command the gaze, attaining her powerful subjectivity through the paradoxical status as ultimate object of desire. The younger, seductive temptress ultimately proves too young and inexperienced to wield the *fatale*'s power. Crucially, the eponymous hero figure, Bob, deflects her kittenish sexual advances (repressing his desire by pushing her into the arms of his protégé) thereby retaining the patriarchal status and power to drive the male-centred heist narrative. Soon after spilling the beans about the gang's robbery plans, Anne redeems herself by confessing to the father-figure, then meekly accepting her punishment (a swift slap) like the little girl she clearly is, at which point she is literally forced off-screen and is barely seen again. French *fatale* at this time, it would appear, is yet to come of age. *Jeune fille fatale*, perhaps; *femme fatale*, she is not.

The socio-cultural origins of French *fatale*

What then, might be the possible socio-cultural explanations for the specificity of French *fatale*? Why does French noir, the product of a resolutely patriarchal society and heavily inspired by classic American noir, fail to import what may arguably be defined as the latter's central figure? To what extent does the sociological thesis that sees the emancipation of women and ensuing crisis of masculinity at the heart of American noir also hold for the French situation?

We suggest, firstly, that the specificity of French *fatale* involves differing cultural attitudes towards sexuality. One is tempted to evoke a certain French Catholic sensibility, which may be more accepting of 'weaknesses of the flesh' (that can be confessed away) and more open in allowing the expression of both male and female sexuality than the more puritanically repressed attitudes of traditional Anglo-Saxon culture. More pertinent perhaps is France's strong secular tradition dating back to the Enlightenment, and which, to a considerable extent, counterbalances prohibitive religious attitudes to sex. French cinema, although subject to censorship, never had a Hays Code; relatively explicit references to sex abound and female sexuality is not necessarily portrayed as inherently threatening. From the 1930s, French film offers no shortage of female characters who are at once sexually assertive, independent and positive, non-monogamous yet emotionally loyal, notably those played by Arletty (in Carné's *Hôtel du Nord*, 1938; *Le jour se lève* [*Daybreak*], 1939; *Les Enfants du Paradis* [*Children of Paradise*], 1944) and later Signoret as mentioned.

Non-monogamous yet emotionally loyal: this is a combination that appears unthinkable in terms of American noir of the period. There, we suspect, is the rub. For it seems clear that it is the duplicitous exploitation of sexual appeal that is condemned in French film noir, rather than assertive female sexuality per se, as has been generally argued in relation to classic noir: 'The sexual, dangerous woman…is the psychological expression of his (man's) own internal fears of sexuality, and his need to control and repress it' (Place 1980: 41). Signoret's prostitute roles are a key case in point. Similarly, are *Thérèse Raquin* and *Ascenseur*, where the adulterous woman seeks to escape the negatively portrayed, corrupt or weak patriarchal husband for a younger lover of cleaner moral values and of whom she is clearly the equal. Adultery is not seen as immoral in these films; it is rather presented as a more ethical and more valid existential choice. And despite, or perhaps because of, her tragic demise, the desire of the fatale can be read here as an open challenge to patriarchy.

Let us take the case of *Ascenseur*: the ending, when the lovers are unmasked, is designed to evoke pity, sadness and revolt, when the detective insists that the woman's punishment will be heavier than the man's. For the law, the real crime is not so much Tavernier's elimination of a (corrupt employer and) rival, it is Florence Carala's refusal and attempted subversion of the patriarchal order in plotting the elimination of her husband. But although the voice of the law of the narrative punishes her, the voice of the film is clearly on her side. In presenting Florence Carala as a loyal, courageous mistress, throughout the film, and in stressing her dignity and honesty even as she stands accused, Malle calls on the spectator to condemn not the *fatale* but the injustice of society's verdict. Rather than a reconfirmation of the law, therefore, we can read the film as exposing its basic injustice, thereby calling on the spectator to reject, or at least question its authority. The ultimate emotional response of the spectator in reaction to the *fatale* here is one of sympathy, not the horror and revulsion evoked by her treacherous American sister-figure. We may admire Phyllis Dietrichson (*Double Indemnity*) and Elsa Bannister (*Lady from Shanghai*) for their unashamed sexual assertiveness and sheer energy in having the pluck to disentangle themselves from claustrophobic marriages, but their ruthless duplicity in deceiving their hapless lovers leaves us cold.

Following, and indeed, in confirmation of the sociological thesis, a major determining factor underlying the specificity of French *fatale* can be seen to lie in the social status of French women at this time, and in the two countries' differing experiences of the Second World War. For, and this is our first point, although the Occupation undoubtedly had traumatic and transformative effects on the French as a nation, it did not produce the sudden, considerable and durable gains in independence and economic status experienced by American women. Apart from a few key industries exploited to feed the German war machine, France's economy was largely in tatters during this period, which did not therefore involve women's large-scale accession to professional life. Moreover, historical sources suggest that French women's priorities following the Liberation, after years of physical deprivation and danger, were often centred on rebuilding the family rather than liberating themselves from it: 'Men returned to work, women retired to the home to have children' (Gildea 2002: 145). And for those women who had acquired a measure of autonomy during the war years and desired to hold on to it, their hopes were often frustrated by the weight of French conservatism (Diamond 1999).

Neither was this conservatism confined to men: apart from the Communist-influenced *Union des Femmes Françaises*, few women's organizations of the period defended women's right to work, focusing instead on bolstering women's procreational role as wives and mothers within the patriarchal family unit (Burch and Sellier 2001: 49). Only being granted the vote in 1944, still regarded legally as minors by the *Code civil*, more or less entirely absent from positions of power, comprising a mere 1.3 per cent of the National Assembly in 1958, French women of the post-war period were hardly in a position to pose a major economic or political threat to the Gallic male psyche. It is understandable, therefore, that French *fatale* is yet to entertain the thoughts of economic independence from the male partner that make her American sister of post-war classic noir so heartlessly and so magnificently ruthless. Understandable also, that French noir film-makers of this period, following Melville and Becker, seem relatively untouched by the type of crisis of masculinity that can be said to precipitate the construction of the classic American *fatale*-fall guy dyad.

We have suggested that the construction of various types of classic French *fatale* turns on notions of fidelity and betrayal, which brings us to our second point. There is a clear connection to the Occupation, where the major threat posed by woman involved perceived sexual infidelity coupled with betrayal of the nation: not simply sleeping around but sleeping with the enemy or 'horizontal collaboration'. Among the minor characters in *Les démons de l'aube*, part of the cycle of resistance films that followed the Liberation, is a doubly treacherous adulteress, who not only takes a lover while her husband is in a German POW camp, but when he is freed (as part of an STO exchange of French workers for prisoners), knowingly sabotages his resistance efforts, almost resulting in his death.[3]

Films like this illustrate the extent to which the Liberation made French women the principal scapegoats for the nation's shame. Public head-shavings, estimated by recent historians to number as many as 10,000, were daily affairs 'in grotesque carnevalesque scenes by men who had been unable to protect either their country or their womenfolk...' (Gildea 2002: 67). The phenomenon is first referred to in the opening scenes of Clouzot's *Manon* (1949) whose young eponymous 'heroine' narrowly escapes such a fate for having fraternized too openly with the occupying troops. A decade later it is represented explicitly in Resnais and Duras's *Hiroshima mon amour* (1959), in which the female protagonist is shorn then locked away in the family cellar by her father for having had a love affair with a German soldier, whom she hoped to marry. A poignant, non-fictional case in point is the cinematic heroine of the Occupation, Arletty, whose Garance (*Les Enfants du paradis*) had been seen by many as symbolic of the enduring presence of French liberty of spirit. Arletty was nonetheless censured by the nation (sentenced to several months house arrest and prevented from working for three years, from which her career never recovered) for her quite public affair with a German officer. In neither case, fictional nor actual, was there any suspicion of adulterous personal betrayal or political treason.

Given the historical context, it is hardly coincidental that in French noir of this period and beyond, the pervading sense of paranoia is induced first and foremost by instances or suspicions of treacherous dishonesty or outright betrayal, sexual or otherwise. And as we have seen, it is French *fatale*, in her various (dis)guises, who serves as the central repository of evocations of fear, suspicion, horror or—very often—sympathy. Crucially though, the *fatale* of classic French film noir is almost never the powerful but heartless spider-woman. Though often tough, sometimes ruthless, her attachment to the male protagonist remains unshakeable. This may well be a symptom of the enduring misogyny of French society: a sign that the French patriarchy is yet to feel sufficiently threatened to result in the emergence of a totally sexual, totally powerful, totally independent female. Even so, this does not preclude our more positively feminist reading of classic French *fatale* as *fatalitaire*: passionately sensual woman, loyal mistress and tragic heroine who serves to reinforce and extend the signification of feminine agency and integrity.

French film noir of the 1970s

The post-May '68 decade in France is marked by the growing emancipation of French women. The sexual revolution, generalized availability of contraception and legalization of abortion, the popularization of feminist discourse and creation of the *MLF* (Women's Liberation Movement) meant that women became increasingly present, not just in the workforce but in positions of power and in sectors of the economy previously open only to men: higher education, politics, even the film industry.

Following the American example, one might expect this period to witness the sudden emergence of dominant fatale-like figures in French film noir as French men struggled to adjust to women's increasing gains in economic power and social status. And yet, curiously, it is almost the opposite that one observes. Out of a corpus of twenty films, the majority are also gangster movies or *polars* whose central focus is on male relationships. In almost all of these, the basic thematic is constructed out of familiar polar/noir tropes: honour among thieves, friendship, loyalty and betrayal. In keeping also with the political focus of the post-May '68 decade,[4] new themes emerge which reflect a growing mistrust of structures of authority: political and police corruption and police internecine rivalries. Women are most often given only minor roles, as mistresses, girlfriends, wives, widows, more often than not as loyal supporters, innocent suspects or victims of various forms of male corruption, violence or oppression. Thus, the 1970s would seem to present almost a trivialization of feminine tropes in French film noir.

However, a general overview is, here as often, somewhat misleading. For when woman does take centre stage in 1970s noir police thrillers and psycho-dramas, as film-maker or central narrative focus, it is not only as supporter or victim. In Yannick Bellon's *L'amour violé* (arguably more psychological drama than film noir, though included in Buss 1994), woman appears (not as *femme fatale* but) as victim turned survivor, accuser and seeker of justice. The film seeks to expose, not only the physical and emotional devastation of rape, but the horror of its normalization under the existing patriarchal system. During the period, woman as active protagonist can also be seen in the appearance of the *femme-flic* (female cop) in *La guerre des polices* (1979). Director Robin Davis, while admitting that the role was somewhat of an afterthought, nonetheless claimed that it was created in recognition of women's changing place in French society (Tchernia 1989: 50).

What is interesting here is that in 1970s France the accession of women to positions of power does not appear to result in the immediate demonization of feminine figures in film, as has been so convincingly argued for classic American noir. The period appears to constitute a kind of hiatus or watershed. It is partly that in French cinema, the threat of the strong, independent woman is not primarily articulated through noir style, as has traditionally been the case in the United States. The appearance of such a virulently misogynous comedy as Blier's *Calmos* in the mid-1970s lends weight to such a hypothesis.

Generally speaking, 1970s French noir is notable for its lack of strong feminine figures. Even the emblematic *Série Noire* (Alain Corneau, 1978, after Jim Thompson's *A Helluva Woman*) contains a fatale-like figure who is not so much a vamp as a victim, whom the hero (Patrick Dewaere) attempts to rescue from sexual exploitation at the hands of an evil aunt who keeps her locked in her bedroom and pimps her off to creditors. In the search for a thoroughly seductive, ruthless, narratively powerful French *femme fatale*, the period that sees the beginnings of the emancipation of French women, paradoxically figures a kind of *mise en abyme* of absence. The exception that proves the rule, we now argue, is provided by Claude Sautet's *Max et les ferrailleurs* [*Max and The Scrap Merchants*] (1971).

Max et les ferrailleurs

Michel Piccoli plays Max, a professionally frustrated, sexually repressed, ex-judge turned police inspector bent on pulling off a *flagrant délit*. He sets up an elaborate and perverse scheme involving a prostitute, Lilly (charismatic German actress, Romy Schneider), the mistress of an old friend (Bernard Fresson as Abel Maresca) now turned small-time crook. Posing as a banker, Max becomes Lilly's regular 'client', paying handsomely for the pleasure of her company though constantly refusing any form of sexual or physical contact. Slowly and deliberately, he manipulates her into persuading her lover and his gang to hold up his bank. Completely taken in, both fascinated and repelled by the banker's sexual disinterest, Lilly plays straight into his hand, pushing Abel and his gang of *ferrailleurs* into organizing the heist. According to Max's plan (though not without bloodshed), the gang is caught red-handed and arrested. Victory is short-lived, however, as a rival inspector (François Perrier as Inspector Rosinsky) is determined to make the *fatale* pay, as it were, by ensuring Lilly is charged for incitement to robbery. In order to protect the woman he has fallen in love with, Max is left with a single option. He guns down the colleague, letting himself be caught, *en flagrant délit*, arrested, and taken away under armed escort, as Lilly watches.

Whereas in American noir it is most often the femme fatale who is cast as sexually and morally perverse, ensnaring her prey out of ulterior motives, here the roles are very largely reversed and it is the male, representative of the law, who is presented as corrupt. For the greatest evil in noir, particularly in French noir, we would argue, is not crime or violence or even sexual promiscuity, it is emotional duplicity and betrayal. Of course, Max is ostensibly working for the greater good. However, as in many other French (and American) noir *polars*, the film questions to what extent the end justifies the means, pointing out the contamination of good by evil as the law employs methods that are more morally suspect than those of its opponents. This is in line with post-Occupation themes and with the renewed attitude of mistrust and radical questioning of existing power structures crystallized by the aborted revolution of May '68. The trend is evident in other noir films of the period, not all of them *polars*.[5]

In *Max*, Sautet takes the classic noir scenario, which sees the woman manipulate the gullible male 'hero' for her own selfish ends, and turns it on its head. Here it is the fatale who is set up as the pawn in an all-male power game: Lilly initially interests Max only as an accessory, through her relationship to Abel, to be manipulated and used as a tool, the unwitting agent of her lover's downfall. This apparent trivialization of her role is expressed, both in terms of plot development and *mise en scène*, by the fact that she is not introduced until some twenty minutes into the film, in a point-of-view shot as Max spies on her and Abel through a miniature telescope. An iris shot establishes Max as manipulator, predator and sexual voyeur, with Lilly as potential victim. Visually, Lilly and her lover are singled out as prey and surrounded by darkness, suggesting the couple's eventual demise.

As the relationship between Max and Lilly develops, however, her character takes on an increasing degree of complexity and narrative importance. This is no surprise of course: the star status of actress Romy Schneider is sufficient to cue spectator response as to the importance of her role and relationship to the male lead. In the central segment of the film, their 'friendship' becomes the central focus. Crucially, the predator/prey dynamic central to their interaction continually shifts, and it is never entirely clear who will ultimately be the hunter, who the hunted. The shifting power dynamics between them are literalized in the card games they play: first Lilly wins, then Max. Lilly's startled reaction when she first loses a game to her banker, foreshadows her shock when she discovers the truth of his identity. In both cases, she loses the game because she underestimates her adversary's capacity for deceit.

Narrative control, for Max/Félix, depends on the control of desire. Lilly, too, is faced with a very similar dilemma since successfully using Félix for her own ends (to enable Abel to pull off the heist) depends on similar denial. The perversity of the situation is thus intensified as for the two central characters, male and female, it is based not only on duplicity but also on the repression of desire. Emblematic of the attraction of noir, it is precisely this perverse combination that provides much of the film's dramatic tension.

Lilly bears the surface marks of the gangster's moll: reformed junkie and prostitute. However, brilliantly portrayed by Schneider, she appears as a complex and fascinating figure, simultaneously independent modern woman, loyal mistress, seductive manipulating femme fatale, exotic vamp and innocent victim. But unlike the romantic prostitute figures of French poetic realism and classic noir, she is more than just another hooker with a heart of gold. Neither financially nor emotionally dependent on her man, Lilly's loyalty is genuine though not unshakeable. Modern woman, almost a material girl, her first lines of dialogue are an explicit sign of her frank economic ambition: to a client's 'How much do you want?' she responds simply, 'As much as possible.' And it is her material ambition that leads her straight into Max's trap. Lilly's attraction to her banker is understandable in that he represents masculine power and control. Moreover, his displays of sexual disinterest and wealth, in sharp contrast to Abel, make him an *homme fatal* object of fascination and desire. Her divided sympathies are made clear when she almost fails to tip off the gang as to the appointed date for the bank robbery. Whether this is out of emotional attachment to her banker, physical desire, pure venality or a combination of the three, remains uncertain, adding to the enigmatic, *fatalitaire* aspect of her own character.

Visually, Lilly is cast as oscillating between *fatale* and *ingénue*. As befits her profession, she inhabits dark urban spaces which are a 'normally' masculine preserve. Highly sexually coded, long flowing hair and smoky eye make-up, slinky dresses under vampish, tightly-belted black vinyl raincoat (sexualized, feminine version of the classic noir trench coat), Lilly is reminiscent of the most seductive of classic Hollywood screen sirens. On the other hand, the ribbon choker she wears around her neck is more indicative of her role as sacrificial victim to Max's ambition than the fatale role. Moreover, her public persona is contrasted with another, more private self, which is presented as natural, uncontrived and innocent. Shots of her in domestic daytime situations use high-key lighting, showing her in simple clothes, with little or no make-up, thereby reinforcing the girlish spontaneity of her body language and actions. Significantly, it is this Lilly who appears in the climactic heist sequence, reinforcing her naive ignorance and shock when Max reveals the full extent of his duplicity. But when we see her for the last time, as Max is being driven away under police escort in the closing scene, she is once again dressed in her trademark black trench coat and ribbon choker: it is this imagined image of Lilly as *fatalitaire* that both Max and the spectator retain.

The 1970s are a transitional period in terms of feminist issues in France. Although marking the beginning of French women's accession to positions of power, the decade is precisely that, a beginning. As very clearly attested by Coline Serreau's landmark documentary *Mais qu'est-ce qu'elles veulent?* [*What do women want?*] (1973), the experience of many French women at this time is still one of very real oppression, whether in the domestic sphere or in the workplace.

Looking ahead to the next decade of the 1980s, which sees a consolidation of women's status and a concomitant crisis of masculinity (Powrie 1997), one also notes the appearance of a number of more inscrutable and ruthless fatale figures in French noir. Most notable are Isabelle Adjani's role as seductress and serial killer in *Mortelle Randonnée* [*Deadly Circuit*] (Claude Miller, 1983), Isabelle Huppert's vindictive sadomasochistic orphan turned career woman in *La garce* [*The Bitch*] (Christine Pascal, 1984) and Sophie Marceau's enigmatic temptress in *Police* (Maurice Pialat, 1985).

The character of Lilly is both a distillation and a displacement of classic French *fatalitaire* of the 1940s and 1950s French noir. Our archetypal 1970s fatale's fierce independence, material ambition and divided loyalties point forwards towards the ruthless, independent vamp, while her ultimate loyalty and natural spontaneity, contrasted with the more perverse manipulation on the part of the masculine figure, remain aligned with the ingénue and the 'classic' French fatale. In this, she is both exceptional and emblematic of the place of the feminine in French film noir of this transitional decade.

Conclusion

In defining pre-1980s French fatale as *fatalitaire* in contrast to the spider-woman of American noir, we have provided confirmation of the sociological thesis for the construction of classic fatale. That France remained a more solidly patriarchal society, which did not experience a wide-reaching crisis of masculinity until well after the mid-twentieth century can be seen to explain the relative absence of strong, ruthlessly independent feminine figures in French noir until this time. We hope also to have demonstrated that the *fatalitaire*, far from being a patriarchal puppet or scapegoat, very often serves to expose and critique the sexist social structures that seek to contain her.

8
Americans in Paris

Section One put forward the argument that Duhamel's Série Noire translations of Peter Cheyney appropriated the author for French noir fiction. This chapter discusses the relatively more straightforward contribution of two American film-makers to the canon of French film noir: Jules Dassin (1911–2008) and Bob Swaim (1943–).

Dassin was already respected in France as a noir director, so his influence would have been significant even without his forced sojourn on French soil (having moved to Europe after being blacklisted under McCarthyism). Dassin's first French film, the gangster-noir *Du Rififi chez les hommes* (*Rififi Means Trouble*, 1955) was immediately hailed by leading critics as the best example of its genre. Paradoxically, American exile Dassin makes a decisive (arguably the most decisive) contribution to the revitalization and reterritorialization of the French *polar* in the mid-1950s. First, in being the first adaptation of Le Breton, the success of Dassin's feature lent a major impetus to the former's career as both novelist and screenwriter, authoring a long series of thrillers whose titles began with Rififi.[1] Second, as Ginette Vincendeau argues, *Rififi* (along with two other polars of the same year, *Touchez pas au Grisbi* [*Grisbi*] (Jacques Becker, 1954, after Albert Simonin) and *Razzia sur le Chnouf* [*Razzia*] (Henri Decoin, 1955, after Le Breton) offered a home-grown counter to the excessively Americanized Lemmy Caution series and 'domesticated the cosmopolitan genre into a familiar, more "realistic" village-like Paris, creating a highly successful and influential generic matrix which added yet another Franco-American mix to the earlier Série noire films' (Vincendeau 2003: 103). Finally, along with Clouzot's *Diaboliques*, *Rififi* played a major role in raising the profile of French films across the Atlantic during this period. It was released in the United States in 1956 where it played for twenty weeks and was ranked by influential *New York Times* critic, Bosley Crowther, among the best foreign films of the year (Schwarz 2007: 115–16).

A generation later, Francophile expatriate, Bob Swaim, who had come to Paris as a student, made two works of major relevance to this study: a cinematic revival of Léo Malet, *La Nuit de St-Germain-des-Prés* [*The Night of St-Germain-des-Prés*] (1977) and the immensely popular police thriller *La balance* [*The Nark*] (1982). Our discussion of *St-Germain* reads this film in the light of French efforts to assimilate American culture during the post-war period. With *La Balance*, we review critical and academic discourses around the film with the aim of repositioning it within French film history as occupying a similar position to Dassin's *Rififi*.

Jules Dassin: From noir auteur to blacklist resister

Dassin began his career in New York, in left-wing Yiddish theatre, before moving to Hollywood where he obtained a contract with MGM. Soon frustrated by the minion status of director within the studio system and disgusted at the manipulative and exploitative methods of MGM patriarch L.B. Mayer, Dassin moved to Universal, then to 20th Century-Fox, directing three social noir classics: *Brute Force* (1947), *The Naked City* (1948) and *Thieves' Highway* (1949). During these years, with the beginnings of the Cold War and McCarthyism, Dassin's leftist political leanings (he had been a member of the Communist Party during the 1930s) singled him out for scrutiny. In 1950, he was only able to direct *Night and the City* by filming it in London, thanks to the support of Fox's Darryl Zanuck. Subsequently named as a communist (by former comrades, Ed Dmytryk and Frank Tuttle) at a 1951 House Un-American Activities Committee (HUAC) hearing, Dassin was blacklisted and his passport revoked. He found himself unable to work not only in Hollywood, but also in Europe. In 1953, he had managed to obtain a contract to direct *L'Ennemi public numéro 1* (*Public Enemy Number 1*) a high production-value vehicle for French comic star Fernandel (alongside Zsa Zsa Gabor) but was dismissed within days of shooting following pressure from Hollywood. Known as *l'affaire Dassin*, the incident transformed Dassin into something of a cause célèbre in France, with French noir director Jacques Becker (*Casque d'Or, Touchez pas au grisbi, Le trou*) setting up an industry support group and making Dassin a member of the French directors' guild.

L'affaire Dassin highlights both the extent to which the Motion Picture Association of America (MPAA) was 'occupied' by HUAC collaborators at this time and the strength of the alliance between Hollywood and the State Department. After the studios had succeeded in removing Dassin from *Public Enemy*, American authorities also attempted to prevent him from working in Italy unless he 'collaborated', as Elia Kazan, Dmytryk, Tuttle and other 'friendly witnesses' had done: publicly repenting their communist sympathies and 'naming names'. Dassin refused. After winning the Best Director Award at Cannes for *Rififi* (as a French film) in 1955, he again 'resisted' American diplomatic attempts to bribe him back into the fold. As he confided to Patrick McGilligan:

> So some guy from the U.S. Embassy was assigned to come and visit and talk to me and it looked as though he wanted to give me my passport back. That would have fixed things but you know the manner in which they wanted to fix things, so it didn't happen.
>
> (McGilligan 1996)

Social Noir and the Hollywood Left

> I have no politics, only sympathies, and my sympathies are for the underdog.
>
> (Marxist blacklistee, Abe Polonsky)[2]

In his overview of contemporary French noir, Phil Powrie states that since the function of the *polar* is 'to maintain order by defining who should be included in the dominant social formation, and who should be excluded, it is by nature a conservative genre' (Powrie 2007: 55). While we agree that the crime drama's emphasis on issues of morality—good vs. evil—speaks of defining who should and should *not* be included in a given social formation, we do not see this as necessarily the mark of conservatism, which consists in reaffirming existing power orders. Most commentators oppose conservative crime dramas, in which the representatives of the law are good and great and prevail over criminals who are bad and justly punished, and those noir texts in which such conventional divisions between good and evil are blurred, thereby calling the existing social order into question. In such noir, as noted in Chapter 6, the association of greed, crime and lust represents a growing sense of malaise within American society: 'this general sense of jeopardy in life, which is what exists in all film noir, is a correct representation of the anxiety caused by the system' (Polonsky, in Horowitz and Schon 1994).

As James Naremore (1998: 103–35), Andrew Spicer (2002: 71–3) and others have noted, the bulk of noir reflected the lost ideals of the 1930s collective American left: a New Deal, Popular Front emphasis on absent social justice, 'a left-liberal critique of American democracy as sick and corrupt' (Spicer 2002: 71). In social noir, crime may be presented as understandable if not justifiable; in other cases, the greed and/or social dysfunctionality of the criminal is seen as the product of the socio-economic formation: the alienating excesses of free-market, consumer capitalism. Buhle and Wagner's recent studies of progressive left-wing film-makers in Hollywood (2002, 2003) corroborate this view, highlighting the radicals' contribution to classic noir and serving as a reminder of the social dimension and progressive message (often coded to escape industry self-censorship) of many of their films. Blacklisted film-makers well known for their involvement in noir include writers Dashiell Hammett, Dalton Trumbo, Vera Caspary, Clifford Odets; directors Dassin, Polonsky, Edward Dmytryk, Frank Tuttle, Joseph Losey,[3] Robert Rossen; actors Sterling Hayden and John Garfield; and producer Adrian Scott. Among blacklist sympathizers from the noir canon, one notes such names as Fritz Lang, Billy Wilder, Edgar G. Ulmer, Anatole Litvak, Robert Wise, John Huston, Orson Welles, Nicholas Ray and Joseph H. Lewis, to name the most prominent.

Social noir often used the genre to cloak its messages beneath layers of extended metaphor. Buhle and Wagner note, for example, that 'Polonsky's *Body and Soul* (1947) was a "fable of the streets" in the reverse Aesopian sense in that its humans took on the behaviour of jungle animals...and *Force of Evil* (1948) was an elaborate metaphor for the predations of Wall Street' (Buhle and Wagner 2003: xvii).[4] And Andrew Spicer observes that Dassin's *Brute Force* 'uses the prison film to mount a critique of totalitarian institutions. Its allegory is both social and existential...a generalized revolt against entrapment and persecution' (Spicer 2002: 71).

So often in the studio system, social contextual factors were watered down in the editing process, while conservative moral messages were played up, inserted into the script or added during post-production. With the exception of *Night and the City*, such production factors made Dassin dissatisfied with his American noir (*Brute Force*, *The Naked City*, *Thieves' Highway*). Nonetheless, his films were generally well received in France for their extensive use of location settings and social focus:

the privileging of milieu, relationships and nuance over action and gratuitous violence.[5]

Dassin's adaptation of Le Breton

> Out of the worst crime novel I have ever read, Jules Dassin has made the best crime film I have ever seen.
>
> (François Truffaut)[6]

The basic plot of *Rififi*—a group of sympathetic crooks succeed in pulling off the perfect jewel robbery but do not live to enjoy the proceeds—is very much in the classic noir mode, like Huston's *Asphalt Jungle*, though without the sermonizing, Code-imposed police peroration.[7] *Rififi* the film, is also far removed from Le Breton's novel (1953), which Dassin detested for its seediness and racism: Le Breton's protagonists, of North African Maghrebi origin, are pimps, sadists and perverts. Ignoring his producer's suggestion to pander to certain sections of the French audience by making the rival thugs American, Dassin instead made them French, though with the Germanic (read Nazi) sounding name of Grutter.

The screenplay rewrites its source text to such an extent that Le Breton, who claimed real-life underworld connections, is said to have threatened Dassin with a firearm over it (after which they became firm friends until Le Breton's death in 1999). Dassin's adaptation, written in just six days, radically transforms the novel, moving the emphasis away from Le Breton's unsavoury rival gangsters to focus on a) the intricate details of the robbery itself; b) the close bonds among the four heist members, in particular the surrogate father-son relationship between the film's hero, Tony le Stéphanois and protégé Jo the Swede; and c) the tragic undoing of this 'community'.

From a minor, ten-page incident in the novel, the caper becomes the central narrative event, whose preparations and execution occupy a third of the film's 118 minutes. In a sense extending and improving on *Asphalt Jungle*, it was a cinematic first that revolutionized the heist genre and earned the film an enduring place in the noir canon. The dramatic intensity of the sequence, still the quintessential reference in the genre, is wrought from an almost surgical attention to detail (the transformation of everyday objects into professional, precision tools), taut direction and camera work (cross-cutting between the closely framed action in the room, ticking clock on the wall, and the street below) and, of course, the Bressonian soundtrack, entirely without dialogue and music for 25 minutes.[8] In fact, Dassin eliminates dialogue for the entire duration of the heist and getaway: 31 minutes, over 200 of the film's 832 shots.

In this sequence as elsewhere, Dassin uses editing, shot-scale and *mise en scène* to emphasize the collaborative nature of the heist: the visual presentation of Tony's team is relatively egalitarian, with roughly equal screen time devoted to each member. This aspect is highlighted by the extensive use of group shots: the first discussion of the 'job', with Tony, Jo and Mario, is filmed using deep focus, as a three shot (the three in a café, with the jewellers, Mappin & Webb, behind them, across the street); the heist preparations (in which Tony devises a way to foil the state-of-the-art alarm system) are filmed almost entirely in group shots and the heist itself plays on the complicit looks and silent gestures between the four men that enable them to work in unison without the need for language.

'Rififi' as double allegory

Though far from original in this respect, *Rififi* is notable for its emphasis on crime as work and the role of skill and cooperation in transforming labour into art. In this, as in *Asphalt Jungle* which preceded it, and in the scores of films that have drawn on it (notably Melville's *Bob, Le Flambeur* and *Le Cercle Rouge* [*The Red Circle*], 1969), *Rififi*'s heist cries out to be read as an allegory of the film-making process itself as collective craftsmanship. This theme did not escape France's more astute critics: François Truffaut, supreme champion of the director as auteur, devotes an entire article to it (Truffaut 1955a). According to this self-reflexive, symbolic logic, Tony as gang leader, symbolic father figure and heist mastermind, can be read as a stand-in for Dassin as director.

Dassin's 1940s American noir emerges out of a climate of leftist disillusionment with the failure of the New Deal, and against a background of the HUAC hearings (the first of which was held in 1947). By the time of *Rififi*, the film's washed-out palette and the even darker, existentialist angst of its final segment, clearly mirrors Dassin's experience of the Hollywood blacklist as being one of Occupation, Resistance and betrayal, as he and others were named, shamed and professionally annihilated by colleagues and friends.

When he was offered *Rififi*, Dassin had not worked in almost five years. Not unlike Harry Fabian (Richard Widmark), the protagonist of his previous feature, *Night and The City*, shot more or less as an exile in London, Dassin was *an artist without an art, groping for the means to express himself.* If geographical exile was not painful enough, being locked out of his chosen profession—for refusing to collaborate with HUAC—was tantamount to prison. His personal situation undoubtedly contributed to the moving portrayal of his washed-out hero, Tony le Stéphanois. When the film opens, Tony is sick in body and in soul, broke and branded a loser, having just done exactly five years for refusing to squeal (taking the rap for his surrogate son, Jo the Swede).

Dassin's feelings of personal betrayal at the HUAC witch-hunts and his despair at the reactionary political turn his country had taken clearly find symbolic expression in *Rififi*, which can be read as a cathartic, therapeutic working through of this process. Though the gang succeeds in pulling off the *biggest heist since the rape of the Sabines*, their defeat is precipitated by the betrayal of the Italian, César le Milanais, who inadvertently puts the rival gang on their trail then cracks under the threat of torture, before being executed by Tony. That Dassin ended up playing his traitor adds a supplementary layer of meaning and pathos to the film, strengthening the case for an allegorical reading. The execution's surreal staging among the theatrical props in the basement of the cabaret, *L'Age d'Or*, named in homage to Buñuel's early masterpiece, makes such a reading compelling.

The film's hapless safe cracker is (like a number of the friendly witnesses) a master craftsman whose cowardice and vanity lead him to betrayal. The execution scene is all the more effective since Dassin's persona is doubly distributed between both the talented but weak traitor and the washed-out gang boss and heist orchestrator, Tony le Stéphanois. With the film's *auteur* standing in for his ex-comrades, while also standing behind their judge and executioner, the scene reads as pure allegory. Dassin's theatrical, almost expressionist *mise en scène* gives weight to symbolic readings and injects the scene with an element of dream-like, projection-displacement. César is executed amid a bric-a-brac of surrealist symbols: naked mannequins evoking the ghosts of old comrades, masks and a guitar for dissimilation and 'singing' betrayal, daisies for happy illusions and (broken) ideals. The tying of César/Vita/Dassin's hands before his face in a gesture of supplication, face and body slashed by shards of truth as light and the weak but sincere admission of guilt—*Forgive me. I was afraid*—complete the tableau. In interviews, Dassin states explicitly that he drew on personal memories of the blacklist in order to play the scene. His own experience of betrayal: 'We would follow them and weep and suffer over every friend that succumbed' (McGilligan 1996) is revealed as a combination of sympathy and empathy that are given visible expression in this scene.

Significantly, Dassin avoids making his traitor a villain, and the justice that is meted out here by Tony/Dassin as director comes with no self-aggrandizing sense of contempt, satisfaction or even relief, but with dark melancholy and profound humanity: *I really liked you, Macaroni, I really liked you.*

Dassin/Melville: the *'Rififi'* legacy

Occupation, Resistance, betrayal: all this, of course, gestures towards another interesting parallel with French noir, particularly with the work of Melville, for whom the Occupation and Resistance provide a central hermeneutic key. For Dassin, particularly in *Rififi*, we have argued that 'resistance' against McCarthyism and despair at the cycle of betrayals it precipitated, plays an analogous role.

We also see other parallels between these two key figures in French gangster noir that have not been fully acknowledged. As much as *The Asphalt Jungle*, we see Dassin's American noir trilogy and particularly *Rififi* as direct precursors to Melville's *Bob le Flambeur* (discussed in Chapter 6) and to Melville's subsequent polars. *Rififi* is notably the major reference for *Le Cercle Rouge* (*The Red Circle*, 1969), which features a long, silent heist sequence, gang warfare and tragic ending.[9] When comparing *Rififi* with *Bob*, Vincendeau (2003: 105) brackets Dassin's film with *Grisbi* and *Chnouf* for their higher production values and more studio-bound aesthetics. While this is certainly true of the latter films, we do not see the description as applicable to *Rififi*.

First, *Rififi* was a low-budget project: according to Dassin, it was made for a mere $200,000. It has neither a star-studded cast nor a large number of elaborate sets, which contributes to its rougher, more spontaneously 'realist' feel, and its sparing use of dialogue further contributes to its relatively paired-down aesthetics. Unable to afford Gabin or any A-list French star, Dassin chose an actor whose career was in decline and whose drinking problem and visibly poor health serendipitously added to the existential angst of the character he would play. Jean Servais's etched, world-weary features and hacking smoker's cough served his character perfectly, especially when compared to the stout bourgeois appearance of Gabin, whether in *Grisbi* as upwardly mobile Max le Menteur, or in *Chnouf* as the Pasha, Henri le Nantais.

Second, it seems to us that Melville's *Bob* follows *Rififi* (though not derivatively so) in the extensive use of location exteriors, again, in contrast to the relatively studio-bound *Grisbi* and especially *Chnouf*, and both Dassin's and Melville's films alternate between real interiors, sets and location exteriors. At the time of *Rififi*'s first release, a number of French commentators noted Dassin's quasi-neo-realist use of Parisian locations,[10] drawing parallels with his American noir work and seeing the film as another episode to a trilogy of dark, city symphonies: New York in *The Naked City*, San Francisco in *Thieves' Highway* and London in *Night and the City*. Borde and Chaumeton's chapter on French noir,[11] which judges *Rififi* the 'only authentic film in the French noir series' (Borde and Chaumeton 2002: 137), also notes the constant presence of Paris: 'not the Paris of smart comedies, but a mist-shrouded and hostile big city' (2002: 136). To this, we would add, firstly, the Paris of community, evident in the bistro scenes and the dawn cameos of ordinary Parisians going off to work, a florist, a newspaper vendor, and a mechanized street sweeper that Melville reprises in the opening sequence of *Bob le Flambeur*.

Finally, *Rififi*'s Paris, created by Dassin and his French team, led by cinematographer Philippe Agostini and poetic realist designer Alexandre Trauner, hovers between the real and the imaginary in ways we have argued to be the very essence of noir fiction. The combination of realist and expressionistic decors, real locations and haunting use of natural light revealed to French audiences a starkly beautiful, almost surreal Paris on the brink of modernity, a Paris that is both poetic and concrete, by turns hostile and alluring, evoking the photography of Brassaï and the poetry of Baudelaire. By day, the city's river banks, architecture and boulevards, its stairways and colonnaded walkways are that of the quintessential, centuries-old European capital. But the night exteriors create surreal juxtapositions of dimly lit cobblestone alleys with a new Paris of slick automobiles and neon lights reminiscent of *The Naked City*. And the gangsters' half-built villa in the southern suburbs is another, somewhat grim reminder of encroaching modernity.

Bob Swaim: from Lévi-Strauss to Léo Malet

Unlike Dassin, and like so many American writers and artists before and since, Bob Swaim came to Paris by choice, arriving in 1965, at the age of 21, as a graduate student of social anthropology, to study towards a doctorate with Claude Lévi-Strauss at the prestigious Collège de France. Instead, the young anthropologist found himself spending most of his time at the Cinémathèque Française, favourite haunt of the New Wave directors and the subsequent generations of French film-makers, where he discovered the classics of French and European cinema, rediscovered American cinema and, in the process, discovered his own calling. Fatally bitten by the film bug and desperate to get into movies, Swaim enrolled at the Ecole Nationale de la Photographie et Cinématographie, where he spent two years learning film technique, graduating in 1970. After a long apprenticeship spent working as a TV cameraman, editor, sound technician and maker of documentaries and short films, in 1977 Swaim was able to make his first feature, *La Nuit de Saint-Germain-des-Prés* [*The Night of Saint-Germain-des-Prés*].

'*La Nuit de Saint-Germain-des-Prés*'

As a nostalgic glimpse back into a past he had never experienced first hand, Swaim's film has the express project of reviving the work of Léo Malet, an author he felt had been scandalously neglected by the French literary and film establishment.[12] The retro-noir intentions of Swaim's poetic evocation of post-war Paris are signalled in the credit sequence: a series of black and white production stills of Saint-Germain nightlife over a wistful French chanson entitled '*Les amoureux de Saint-Germain*', sung by one of the best-loved exponents of the genre, Serge Reggiani.[13] The last still morphs into a moving shot, black and white segueing into sepia-toned colour, bringing to life the sombre raincoated silhouette of Malet's detective as he approaches the Café de Flore.

As much as Malet, the ghost of Vian hovers over Swaim's *Saint-Germain*, which, for all its flaws, has the merit of being faithful to its author's creation of a Paris bathed in the noir atmosphere, 'posited in an interstitial space, caught between the realms of the real and the imaginary' (Durozoi 1984: 175). The credits are preceded by an opening title quotation from Vian on the role of the imaginary as the key to the unconscious: *If you have such a need to free yourselves from your darkest passions, know this, that the novel, poetry, fiction, simple fantasy are there to guide you and that in the field of the imagination, there are no rules, no limits.*[14]

The fantasy takes us back to Paris, 1951. Nestor Burma, private detective, is hired by an insurance company to recover a stash of stolen jewels. Burma's investigations lead him to return to the cafés and basement clubs of Saint-Germain-des-Prés, in search of black American jazz trumpeter Charlie McGee. When Burma arrives, McGee has been stabbed to death. We, the audience, know from the pre-credit sequence that McGee has been slain by a lover, which leads us on a false track in search of a femme fatale. The enquiry throws Burma into a surreal Paris where the impossible intellectual mix of existentialism, situationism and lettrism and the sensual hedonism of jazz and rock and roll leads inevitably to murder. Not until the final act do we discover (with Burma) that the barely glimpsed assassin of the opening scene is in fact a young man: bisexual psychopath and failed poet, Rémy Brandonnel, played by Daniel Auteuil in his first screen role.

Fiat lux, proclaims a singularly unconvincing plaque on the door of the detective's dimly lit office. Though Burma will recover the jewels and eventually solve the central enigma, what little light is shed, as his workplace suggests, will be overshadowed by a lingering sense of greater mystery.[15] The enquiry sees Burma led down a number of labyrinthine back alleys in which, in true noir style, he will be tricked, misled and beaten, finding that the answer to a question is either a hermeneutic dead end or merely reveals a new question. With Burma powerless to prevent two more murders, the film's final scene will have him narrowly escape death before witnessing, at first hand, the execution of the murderer (at the hands of his police inspector father). The final freeze frame as Burma exits the scene is a perfect encapsulation of the dilemma of the noir detective: the solution of the mystery reveals, more than anything, an unfathomable darkness at the heart of the human soul.

Swaim's fully assumed voyeurism and uneasy attitude towards the modernity that his culture of origin has foisted onto the culture of his choice was already apparent in his critically acclaimed short film *Self-Portrait of a Pornographer* (1971), a retro black comedy, which chronicles the death of French craftsmanship in post-war Paris through the vicissitudes of a struggling soft-porn photographer. Burma, in many ways, faces a similar predicament. In one jazz club scene, the detective exclaims: *I don't feel quite with it*. His frank admission to feeling out of place in this new Paris of basement clubs and pay phones is telling, and his naturalness contrasts markedly with the affected posturing of the film's literary characters. Burma's sardonic humour appears to be partly a defence mechanism against a prevailing feeling of cultural alienation, a slight out-of-place-ness. As such he is more world-weary than cynical. As an incongruous literary creation (a French private detective), he constantly battles to assert his authority. Swaim's dialogues self-consciously foreground this aspect of Malet's unlikely sleuth, having another character exclaim: *What? You are a private detective* and *French? That's rare!*[16] Moreover, Swaim follows Malet in frequent self-reflexive references to American hard-boiled film and fiction, notably highlighting the gap between the film's somewhat drab looking investigator and his suave transatlantic counterparts: *I'm no Gary Cooper,* says paunchy, down-at-heel, middle-aged Burma (somewhat redundantly). Brilliantly underplayed by Michel Galabru, Swaim's Burma manages to capture

Malet's idiosyncratic, Surrealist-influenced, Gallic blend of noir, with his iconic detective alternating (discussed in Chapter 1) between the cold objectivity of the whodunit sleuth and the emotionally involved, hands-on approach of the hard-boiled private eye.

Swaim sees the film as a flawed first feature that suffers from an excessive desire to foreground its Frenchness.[17] While this may be true, for us, it is precisely *Saint-Germain*'s self-consciousness that makes it most interesting and relevant to our project. In line with our discussion of noir as transatlantic exchange, the film can be read partly as a self-conscious American attempt to chronicle equally self-conscious French attempts during the 1950s to adapt to modernity by adopting the hip youth culture of their saviours and occupiers.

The sense of the temporal dislocation and culture shock articulated by Burma and mirroring that experienced by post-war France is already present in the lyrics of the title song: *The young lovers of St-Germain-des-Prés cannot say whether it's tomorrow or today. When you live by night you lose sight of the times / the present fades away.*[18] Swaim's *Saint-Germain* sits uneasily in its existentialist Franco-American garb. Following the credits, the film opens in a café, on a young French woman leaning against a jukebox. The camera follows as she slowly and somewhat self-consciously saunters over to the bar to request American cigarettes. The proprietor responds by saying he has *Lukey Streek*, which a French audience would recognize, through the impossibly thick accent, as Lucky Strikes. This cultural incompetency is echoed in a number of scenes in which young French extras are shown wearing American-style clothing, dancing rock and roll, attempting a song in American English. These eager, heartfelt, half-competent but not yet entirely convincing attempts to master iconic aspects of American culture (contrasted with the easy grace of their black American homologues) mirror the awkward, ambivalent stance of the French nation to American-induced modernity discussed previously, and which Swaim himself would later highlight in a TV documentary charting the American presence in France from 1944 to 1965: *France, Made in USA* (2007).

The pre-credit sequence opens on a shot of a neon hotel sign reflected in a pair of dark glasses worn by Charlie McGee, playing trumpet, a slow husky jazz tune.[19] Black musicians, who appear in a number of scenes, seem strangely more at home in the film than many of the French characters, who appear to be rehearsing a role. This is most conspicuously true of the literary figures, even the fully bilingual Saint Germain. For this character, American-born composer Mort Schuman, in a reverse mirror of Vian-Sullivan, plays a Jewish American, Stephen

Jacobs, a flamboyant Oscar Wilde-like figure masquerading as a Parisian writer 'Germain de St Germain'. As Burma remarks: *that's not a name, it's a pleonasm...*

The crisis of identity underlying the film is epitomized by its bisexual assassin, Auteuil's Remi Blondonnel, whose psychopathy can be read as an extended metaphor for cultural anxiety. Enamoured of both black American musician, Charlie McGee and Taxi, French Queen of the Saint-Germain basement clubs, the threat of losing possession of either leads the failed existentialist-surrealist poet to eliminate each in turn.

La Nuit de Saint-Germain-des-Prés was screened at the Directors' Fortnight in Cannes, where it was a critical success. Critical acclaim did not, however, translate into box-office success, and Swaim went back to doing odd jobs.

'La balance': An opportunity to explore a world

In 1980, still without a feature in sight, Swaim accepted the invitation of a young police inspector Mathieu Fabiani[20] to visit his Belleville unit of the Territorial Brigades, recently constituted plain-clothes units set up to combat increasingly violent urban crime. Swaim would spend twelve months[21] with the group, studying their work methods and the criminals and prostitutes they frequented, with the express aim of writing a feature, although with no pre-existing storyline. As a graduate in social anthropology, Swaim was well aware that his presence among the members of the unit would alter their behaviour and that he would need to stay with them for many months in order for his fieldwork to have real documentary value. He states that the first six months were largely spent on becoming invisible, the next six gradually enabling the observation of spontaneous, authentic behaviour. The ethnographic research underpinning the film,[22] including Fabiani's role, was widely publicized and was undoubtedly a major factor in the film's commercial success, particularly given its uncompromising portrayal of police methods.

La Balance signals its documentary project from the opening shot, an introductory title appearing over a Belleville street scene punctuated by Arab market voices. The title explains the work of the Brigades: *the only squads infiltrating the underworld* and the signification of its central *argot* term, hitherto unknown in everyday French: *Each unit relies on its own network of informers without whom they cannot function. The informer is called a 'balance' by the underworld.*[23] When the Brigade's key *balance* is murdered by thugs working for local underworld boss, Roger Massina (Maurice Ronet), the squad, led by Inspector Palouzi (Richard Berry), is under pressure to find a replacement. They decide on Dédé Laffont (Philippe Léotard), variously described as hoodlum or pimp, who has an old score to settle with Massina over Dédé's girl, streetwalker Nicole Danet (Nathalie Baye). When Dédé and Nicole refuse to collaborate, Palouzi uses every brutal, manipulative trick in the book to press-gang the lovers into service. Though unsuccessful in playing them off one against the other, he eventually coerces Dédé into helping the Brigade to bring Massina down. When police plans go horribly awry, there is a bloodbath on the streets and Dédé ends up shooting Massina in self-defence. Before he can flee, Nicole turns him over to Palouzi, as the only way of saving him from the underworld.

'*La Balance*': French re-invention or 'American turn'?

The film was an enormous box-office success, totalling 4,192,189 entries, making it the fifth most popular film in 1982.[24] The film also had nine César nominations in 1983, winning Best Picture, Best Actor (Philippe Léotard), and Best Actress (Nathalie Baye). It was the first and only noir police drama to have won the César for best film until joined in 2006 by Jacques Audiard's *De battre mon cœur s'est arêté* [*The Beat That My Heart Skipped*] (2005, see Chapter 10).[25]

On one hand *La Balance's* 'wide appeal, critical acclaim and Mr. Swaim's exoticism as an American in Paris rendered him a celebrity' (Insdorf 1983), on the other hand, the film has been the object of some harsh criticism, notably from intellectual film circles and academic commentators. Given the divergence of views and the frequent mentions of the film's American influences, we structure our discussion around the film's critical and academic reception, as an outline of and response to existing discourses.

On its release, *La Balance* was generally well received by the French press.[26] Of the 31 reviews we have been able to access,[27] only 4 were very negative,[28] 3 were mixed[29] and 23 generally positive or very positive. The harshest criticisms came from the intellectual left-wing newspapers and film journals, who were either scathing about the characterization (*Le Monde*) or found the film's frank portrayal of police brutality to be fascist (*Libération* and *Le Canard Enchaîné*), a serious charge, to which we shall return. *Libération* and the film journal *Positif* labelled the portrayal of Arab drug dealers as racist, a criticism that would also be levelled at Pialat's *Police* (1985) and Tavernier's *L.627* (1992). (In all three cases, the film-makers would invoke the demands of realism as sole determinant of the choice of ethnicity for their gangsters, dealers and petty delinquents.) Other recurrent criticisms concerned Swaim and Fabiani's dialogues, particularly the cops' wise-cracking, gallows humour, which some reviewers applauded for its street-wise immediacy, while others found the repartee forced and/or clichéd.

Olivier Assayas reviewing the film for *Cahiers*, although among those unconvinced by the dialogues, nonetheless thought the film an improvement on most French *polars* of the day, notably Robin Davis's *La guerre des polices* (1979), which deals with internecine strife among French police and which had been the first film to show French cops wearing contemporary, casual dress. Neglecting to mention Swaim's background research, Assayas considered the film's greatest strength was that although it recalled television rather than cinema, its major inter-textual reference was not the usual humdrum French TV detective series but the American series *Starsky and Hutch* (of which Swaim says he was unaware at the time). A decade later, the comment was taken up by British academic Guy Austin, whose section on the film is entitled 'Starsky and Hutch in Belleville' (Austin 1996: 108–9). Phil Powrie picks up the argument, also seeing *La Balance* as heralding a worrying trend towards the Americanization of the French polar (Powrie 2007b: 63), a point to which we shall return.

Nonetheless, and as mentioned, the film obtained many positive reviews. These came from newspapers and weeklies across the political spectrum, from the conservative *Figaro*, the libertarian *Le Matin*, through centre-right *Le point* and centre-left *Nouvel Observateur* to the left wing *Quotidien de Paris*, *Révolution*, communist *l'Humanité* and its weekend edition *l'Humanité dimanche*. There was a similarly enthusiastic response from popular film magazines *VSD* and *Pariscope*, the literary weekly *Les nouvelles littéraires*, financial daily *les Echos* and the French-based English-language publication, *International Herald Tribune*, whose reporter thought 'it is not the sensationalism but its cool objectivity that is uncommon, bestowing an authenticity on its incidents and dramatis personae' (Quinn Curtis 1982). Many reviewers (*Le Matin, Le Monde, Le Point, VSD, L'Aurore, La Croix*) congratulated Swaim for his realistic portrayal of the police and for having revitalized the *polar à la française*. Swaim's updated, realist approach was often contrasted with the more heavily codified, archetypal portrayal of the police in French cinema: the lone, trench-coated superstar cop played by Delon and Belmondo or the middle-aged, pipe-smoking detachment of the quintessential French detective, Maigret.

As a fast-paced (by French standards), hard-hitting, American-style police procedural, the film was generally regarded favourably (*L'Aurore*,

Le quotidien de Paris, La vie ouvrière, Télérama); Swaim was seen to have injected an element of *cinéma vérité* into the polar, his realistic portrait of Belleville was admired (*Cinématographe*),[30] and the unprecedented level of ethnographic research was frequently noted. In highlighting Swaim's American origins and academic background, positive reviews suggest that the film is the happy product of a rich bicultural legacy, dubbing it 'an ethno-western about the Territorial Brigades' (*Les nouvelles littéraires*); 'somewhere between Lévi-Strauss and Dashiell Hammett' (*Pariscope*). *L'Humanité* also particularly liked the film's avoidance of over-dramatization and its complex character construction, avoiding more conventional divisions into 'goodies and baddies', and the even treatment given to the police and the central couple on the wrong side of the law.

Critical reception among Anglophone reviewers was also largely positive. *Sight and Sound* reviewer Tom Milne (1984: 153) thought the film even-handed, its *cinéma vérité* illusion perfect and its twin references to contemporary American action cinema and French poetic realism effective. The *New York Times* also appreciated the film for its combination of (American) punchy rhythm and typically Gallic attention to cultural details extraneous to the central action: notably the emphasis on food (both Dédé and Massina are shown to be gourmet cooks) and the multi-layered construction of the main protagonists (Maslin 1983).

Influential, Pulitzer Prize-winning film critic, Roger Ebert praised the film for having absorbed and transcended the stereotypical plot and characterization of the Hollywood gangster movie, shifting the focus from the crimes to the lives of the characters, noting the symbolic weight of the love story 'about a man and woman who are desperately trying to hold everything in the balance: their lives, their commitments, their self-destructive lifestyles' (Ebert 1983). Ex-Yale professor, Annette Insdorf, who interviewed Swaim, notes the film's combination of realism, arising from the fact that 'the filmmaker did indeed study his milieu' and its 'gritty, sensual and stylized tone' (1983), the latter of which she also sees as a salient feature of the earlier *Saint-Germain*.

The worrying 'American turn' in the French polar that Powrie (2007b: 63) sees as exemplified and announced by *La Balance* is not generally regarded as such outside highbrow Parisian film circles. Our research has revealed that the vast majority of French reviewers saw the film as a positive development: a welcome breath of fresh air, re-injecting a level of realism into the codes of the *polar* and constituting a powerful, French reappropriation of the contemporary American action thriller. Subsequently, the French *polar* became faster in pace, sartorial codes more contemporary and Swaim's ethnographic approach would be taken up by numerous French film-makers, most notably by Pialat for *Police*, although the latter's 'research' was somewhat less rigorous,[31] and Tavernier for the more crusading and more starkly realist *L.627*, scripted by drugs' squad investigator, Michel Alexandre.[32] Swaim's approach in *La Balance* was so influential that by the early 1990s it was hardly think-able to envisage a *polar* as a simple literary adaptation, without it being underpinned by a level of direct, on-the-ground experience, whether in the form of a police scriptwriter-adviser or by spending time among police (Philippe 1996: 179).

Obviously, this method is no guarantee of objectivity or authentic-ity, but we feel it is important to note that, in this sense, *La Balance* signals a genuine realist turn as well as a change in pace and move in the direction of the more spectacular, American-style thriller. We thus position ourselves with those who saw *La Balance* as 'reinventing the polar', that is, inventing new codes. Of course, these are then repeatedly copied, and in turn over time, become ultra-codified. As Olivier Philippe (1996: 33–4) has observed: 'The very real transformations that *La Bal-ance* brought about in 1982 have since been widely taken up, imitated to the point of becoming clichéd.' If some commentators looking back a decade later saw the film as being 'ultra-codified' (Powrie 1997: 77, 97), we would suggest that it is to a large degree, precisely because the new codes it invented had been so widely copied and, in the case of films like *Police* and *L.627*, updated, extended and taken in new directions.

Despite describing *La Balance* as ultra-codified, Powrie nonetheless sees Dédé's multilayered character construction worthy of serious dis-cussion, as a complex example of the 'discomfited male' of 1980s French cinema:

> complex object of erotic contemplation . . . he is coded as the archety-pal macho male of the polar, with his rugged face and rolling gait, his reticence with language, and his bouts of frustrated anger directed towards his lover or objects such as rubbish bins. But he is also coded as the feminized lover. . . . Dédé strides towards the camera in a mid-distance low-angle shot, the effect of which is to emphasize the authority of rugged male beauty. He chooses a rose from a stall, intro-ducing the feminized lover, just as Palouzi is saying in a voice-over that you can't work with a man who's in love.
>
> (Powrie 1997: 100)

Powrie (1997: 101) goes on to argue that Dédé's character is rendered more complex still by the fact that he is frequently the masochistic object of physical violence and must constantly fight back to reassert his autonomy and masculine pride. For us, this discussion highlights the ways in which Dédé's characterization, in its juxtaposition of several different, sometimes opposing codes (the macho, by turns rugged and degraded, the vulnerable lover, the brutal male, the loyal partner, the street-smart hoodlum, the domesticated gourmet, the beleaguered underdog and so forth) wonderfully served by Léotard's performance, transcends the stereotypical and attains a level of depth and authenticity that is beyond the ultra-codification that Powrie claims to be a salient feature of the film.

Neither do we share Powrie's conclusion, that (since Nicole turns him over to the police for his own safety) 'Feminization, as well as women, are [therefore] established as potential threat, ready to disfigure the ruggedness of a "real man"' (Powrie 1997b: 102). For us, the central factor working against such a reading is the construction of the character of Nicole, who, in being cast as fatalitaire rather than femme fatale, is a positive if ultimately tragic figure. Nicole recalls the many good-hearted prostitute characters of poetic realism and subsequent French noir, as discussed in Chapter 7. Her frank, gutsy defence of her profession—*I'm a hooker. So what? I'd rather get laid for five hundred francs than for a sandwich, like your wife*—recalls Lily in *Max et les ferrailleurs* when the latter declares to her 'banker': *My profession is as good as yours*.[33] And Nicole's resolute, if doomed attempts at saving her man recall Signoret's Marie in *Casque d'Or*. Far more than just a love interest or object of the gaze, Nicole possesses a high degree of individual agency and integrity.[34] That she is ultimately forced into betraying Dédé to the police is yet another testimony to the difficulties faced by marginalized individuals inexorably caught between powerful, more ruthless forces on both sides of the law.

The most vitriolic criticisms levelled at *La Balance* concerned the film's depiction of brutal police tactics, which were labelled by some as constituting a fascist endorsement of a reactionary right-wing law-and-order agenda because police engaging in morally and legally suspect behaviour (roughing up drug Arab dealers, 'lynching' an apprehended psychopathic murderer) are not presented as evil monsters or punished for their actions. Undeniably, the film's opening title and expository scenes position the spectator on the side of the law. However, Swaim reverses the spectator's allegiances when Palouzi and his squad use coercive force against Dédé and Nicole. Robin Buss notes how the moral focus of the film shifts, suggesting that we question our instinctive sympathy with the forces of law and order, and consider whether Dédé's code may not represent a higher morality ... more principled because it defines the limits of behavior within which Dédé can respect himself. Dédé's values are intrinsic while those of the police are extrinsic: the uniform and the legal code that it represents legitimize their behavior, relieving them of their responsibility for their actions.... We may approve of their struggle against crime, but when they are ready to use Dédé and Nicole to get at Massina, we start to perceive them as we might soldiers who would excuse any action on the grounds they were merely obeying orders.

(Buss 1994: 145)

And yet the film also reminds us that as citizens, we depend on such soldiers. The moral complexity of *La Balance* as noir lies precisely in the ways in which Swaim's characters cannot be simplistically categorized as good and evil; right and wrong are not the exclusive province of one or other individual(s); black and white blend inevitably and often painfully into varying shades of grey. For us, the importance of *La Balance* lies in the way its combination of frank realism, complex characterization, contemporary, stylized visuals and fast-paced rhythm served to renew and complexify the codes of the *polar* by also drawing on archetypal sources in French noir. In so doing, the film reminded audiences, as good noir so often does, of the problematic moral state of contemporary French society, the price of law and order, the gap between the law and substantive justice and the impossibility of easy moral distinctions.

Conclusion

In terms of the present study, we consider both *Rififi* and *La Balance* as landmarks in French film noir, saluted by many critics for their realism, hailed as revitalizing the *polar* and revealing little known sides of Paris to the French. Again, reflecting the passionate ambivalence with which France views its transatlantic big brother, perceived American influences in both *Rififi* and *La Balance* were variously praised and critiqued by reviewers or subsequent commentators. We conclude by saying that the work of these Americans in Paris further demonstrates the oft-contested double legacy and hybrid status of French noir, defining itself against, inextricably entwined with, profoundly indebted to yet proudly distinct from its transatlantic counterpart.

9
From Honest Thief to Media Sociopath

This chapter follows Chapter 6 in examining the ongoing evolution of the love–hate relationship between France and the United States as seen through the refracting prism of late twentieth-century French film noir. A brief, diachronic survey beginning from the New Wave outlines the continuing paradox of a French noir cinephile tradition that draws inspiration from, and pays homage to, American noir while presenting increasingly negative images of the United States. The main thrust of the argument is presented through an analysis of Bertrand Tavernier's 1993 feature, *L'Appât* [*The Bait*], a film which has been read as a scathing indictment of American media-materialism and cultural invasion. This chapter attempts to resituate canonical readings of the film and concludes by relating the film's particular mobilization of noir anxiety back to broader issues in Franco-American relations. These centre around the French-led European resistance to American-dominated globalization and monopolization of the world's film industries that began during the General Agreement on Tariffs and Trade (GATT) negotiations of 1993.

The 1960s: *nouvelle vague* Americanophilia and its limits

The almost unmitigated Americanophilia of the Cahiers' film critics who went on to form the French New Wave was evident in their work and has been widely documented since. As Ginette Vincendeau points out, 'Love of American cinema was the cement of their generation, and in their cinematic landscape, film noir occupied a special place' (Vincendeau 2007: 40). It is also important to note that for these 'Hitchcocko-Hawksians', and for Chabrol and Truffaut in particular, American cinephilia operated within a generational struggle: American cinema was both an aesthetic tool and a weapon. It was a stick with which to beat the hated older generation of French film-makers that the Young Turks wished to supplant and a stylistic toolbox which (together with Anglo-American titles from the Série Noire) could be selectively drawn on in order to construct a fresher, faster-paced New French cinema. Melville, himself a precursor of the *nouvelle vague*, continues throughout the 1960s to develop the Franco-American noir gangster genre centred on honour (and betrayal) that he had helped to initiate in 1956, with *Bob Le Flambeur* and its quintessential honest thief protagonist. Melville's Americanophilia is particularly evident in *L'Aîné des Ferchaux* (*Magnet of Doom*, 1963), largely set and partly shot in the United States, in which the two protagonists (played by rising New Wave star, Jean-Paul Belmondo and veteran Charles Vanel) go on a pilgrimage to the home town of Frank Sinatra.

Despite the overwhelmingly positive tone of the *nouvelle vague* as a series of idiosyncratic, Gallic hymns to American cinema, there were—unavoidably perhaps—a few dissonant tones. Though dedicated to Monogram pictures and, on the whole, nostalgically celebratory of modernity and American culture, Godard's first feature, the anti-noir classic *A bout de souffle* (*Breathless*, 1960), nonetheless displays elements of ambivalence and unease. It is difficult to escape reading the erotically charged but troubled relationship between the central couple of Michel and Patricia as a 'transatlantic exchange' (Wilson 1999: 71). Their somewhat hesitant, *I love you, I love you not* interaction and Patricia's final, generically predetermined betrayal point towards the aggressive, Maoist-inspired anti-Americanism of much of Godard's later work.

The 1970s: Anti-Americanism in the French noir political thriller

One must not forget that on a broader socio-political level, the first decade of the Fifth Republic was also marked by the determined Anti-Americanism of its founding father. De Gaulle's often openly-displayed 'sovereignist' hostility (Meunier 2005: 3) towards the increasing geopolitical domination of France's erstwhile ally, is evident in the General's withdrawal from NATO and dismantling of American army bases on French soil in 1966. Anti-Americanism is the one factor shared by the Gaullist right and the intellectual left, with the consequence that the anti-authoritarian, left-wing civic cinema of the 1970s that followed the socio-political upheavals of May '68 very much continues the Anti-American tradition. The two film-makers most associated with the French leftist political noir thriller during this period are Greek-born Constantin Costa-Gavras (*Z*, 1969; *L'Aveu* [*The Confession*], 1970; *Etat de siège* [*State of Siege*], 1973) and Yves Boisset (*L'Attentat* [*The Assassination*], 1972;[1] *Le juge Fayard dit le Shérif* [*Judge Fayard, aka The Sheriff*], 1976). This chapter looks at just one of these films, for the ways in which it both draws on American cinematic traditions while playing on anti-American sentiment across the French political spectrum.

Yves Boisset's *L'Attentat* is a thinly disguised reconstruction of the Ben Barka Affair, a political scandal that had rocked the Gaullist regime prior to May '68. Lured from his safe haven exile in Switzerland to Paris with offers of a film on third-world leftist protest movements, Barka was kidnapped outside the famous Brasserie Lipp on the Boulevard St Germain on 29 October 1965. Almost certainly tortured and murdered by Moroccan authorities with the complicity of the French police (in turn, aided and abetted by gangster-informers), Barka was never seen alive again and his body was never found. The affair represented one of the biggest scandals of de Gaulle's reign, resulted in two trials that occupied the nation for over two years, had serious consequences for diplomatic relations between France and Morocco (the Moroccan Interior Minister was found guilty of the murder and sentenced to death by the French courts) and forced the General to make a public statement in which he was at pains to downplay the situation.

L'Attentat is based on a screenplay by Ben Barzmann, blacklisted expatriate, friend and collaborator of Jules Dassin, with dialogues by Spanish leftist writer, exiled Anti-Franco militant (and future Spanish Minister of Culture) Jorge Semprun (*Z*; *L'Aveu*). Given the credentials of its various authors, it is hardly surprising that the film's conspiracy theory plot rewrites the Ben Barka affair as masterminded by the CIA playing the role of Big Brother with the collaboration of the French state. In its staging of French and American politicians secretly planning the kidnapping of the film's dissident hero, Sadiel/Barka, and its sting in the tail ending wherein a supposedly radical American journalist turns out to be a CIA assassin, the film explicitly accuses the American secret service as being behind the affair. And despite there being no real historical evidence for such a claim, both Boisset and Semprun openly defended their thesis in press interviews.

L'Attentat did well at the French box office, totalling almost 1.5 million entries, making it the sixth biggest grossing *polar* to be released in 1972. Somewhat predictably, given its controversial, political subject matter and mainstream treatment, the film polarized the critics.

The right-wing *Figaro* reviewed it favourably, confirming criticisms emanating from a number of left-wing papers (including the communist daily *l'Humanité*) that the CIA hypothesis suited the Gaullist regime. The existentialist newspaper *Combat* was among the film's most fervent admirers. By and large, however, the intellectual film establishment was unenthusiastic, judging the film's glossy, pop-art American-style visuals, fast pace, emphatic music (by Ennio Morricone) and star-studded international cast[2] as seriously undermining the film's political message. Given the number of French people who saw it and repeated attempts by French authorities to censor it,[3] one wonders to what extent this argument really holds. It would appears that this type of criticism, common among academic commentators and 'serious' critics, confuses issues of taste and style with political impact. One may well critique a film on aesthetic grounds, but this has little bearing on popular audiences' ability to comprehend and/or be receptive to its political or social message, which can only be ascertained through detailed studies of audience reception, too rarely included in film studies' panoply of analytical tools.

Stylistically gesturing towards the New York gangster films of Coppola and Scorsese, *L'Attentat* draws on, and contributes to, both French and American noir traditions of the spectacular as a means to socio-political comment. The film displays a post-May '68 mistrust of the State, the media and technology (Powrie 2007b: 58–9), linked to a characteristically French left-wing, anti-American imperialism while simultaneously flattering the anti-Americanism of certain sections of the French Gaullist right.

The 1980s: A new American turn?

As shown in Chapter 8, the 1980s *polar* is increasingly marked by the American action thriller. The other new popular development of the decade, equally American-influenced, is the youth-oriented, postmodern pastiche noir of *le cinéma du look*. Continuing the spectacularization of violent crime and mistrust of authority but without a parallel realist context or political engagement, the *polars* of Beineix[4] (*Diva*, 1981; *La lune dans le canniveau* [*The Moon in the Gutter*], 1983), Carax (*Mauvais Sang* [*Bad Blood*], 1986) and Besson (*Subway*, 1985; *Nikita*, 1990) have been termed post-modern for their playful self-referentiality and privileging of style or look over meaning. The first of these films, *Diva*, is of particular interest to this study for its novel construction of its eponymous character. By casting an African-American opera singer (Wilhelmenia Wiggins Fernandez) as a diva struggling to uphold the highest form of western music and the integrity of artistic live performance,[5] Beineix can be said to confer new cultural capital on her country of origin, hitherto associated almost exclusively with less highbrow, popular forms of music: rock and roll and of course, jazz.

Tellingly, even in the relatively pro-American period of the 1980s, American influence was still felt by (presumably older sections of) the French public to be excessive in the areas of cinema and television in particular (Kuisel 1996: 225). Cultural anxieties associated with television surface in a number of French films of this period. Even Luc Besson's *Subway* ends with a laconic pop song whose lyrics proclaim, in English: *Why do we keep on watching this fucking TV?* Yves Boisset's 1983 sci-fi thriller, *Le Prix du Danger* [*The Prize of Peril*] features a macabre reality-TV game show set up as a human foxhunt in which the main contestant must evade a posse of killers in order to claim the grand cash prize. In parallel with Godard's increasingly negative, avant-garde explorations of things American, Chabrol's 1986 mainstream suspense drama, *Masques* [*Masks*], released during the same year that marked the beginning of the dismantling of French national television and its rapid replacement by American-style consumer-capitalist models, can be read as an indirect indictment of this process. In *Masques*, Philippe Noiret plays Legagneur (The Winner!), a cloying, overbearing TV game-show host whose affable mask hides a manipulating, cruelly contemptuous, sociopathic monster.

Two years earlier, *La triche* (Yannick Bellon, 1984) presented Annie Duperey as a top oenologist from a wealthy Bordeaux wine-making family whose talents had been solicited by Californian interests. In referencing the United States as the source of a brain drain, which is equally cultural and economic, this film anticipates globalization debates, here displacing on to the context of the wine industry, the burning issue of Hollywood and its long-standing tactic of luring European talent away from national cinemas.

From the celebratory gangster films of Melville, from Malle and Godard's ambiguous first features, through the political noir-thrillers of 1970s civic cinema to the new-look police thrillers and post-modern pastiche *cinéma du look* films of the 1980s and beyond, it is clear that as the century drew to a close, the love–hate relationship that we have traced in French noir remained as strong as ever. Although we do not suggest a simple, linear progression, by and large, images of America in French noir had become increasingly negative, in step with American domination of international politics and the progression of American share of the domestic film market in France.

Bertrand Tavernier: From reluctant lover to Gallic resister

In line with our central theme of paroxystic French noir ambivalence, Bertrand Tavernier, the film-maker who would most embody French resistance to Hollywood hegemony over the next decade and into the new millennium, is also one of its most passionate and most knowledge-able admirers. Author or co-author of a number of books on the subject, most notably the panoramic study, *Fifty Years of American Cinema* (Tavernier and Coursodon 1991), Tavernier's knowledge of Hollywood and independent US film-making is second to none among French film-makers and cinephiles alike. Ex-film writer for all the main journals, including *Cahiers* and *Positif*, founding director of the *Institut Lumière*[6] in his native Lyon, Tavernier more than any other French film-maker today, displays a characteristically Gallic fascination with and mistrust of American consumer culture and cinema, an 'amorous repulsion that seeps through the thousands of pages of passionate writing he has devoted to it' (Raspiengeas 2001: 384).

Two of Tavernier's films of the 1980s (though not categorizable as French noir) can be productively read in terms of issues raised in the previous section, namely French cultural unease at the increasingly prominent role of television (Ostrowska 2007: 30). In *Une semaine de vacances* (*A Week's Holiday*, 1980) the film's schoolteacher protagonist (Nathalie Baye) sees excessive TV watching as the probable cause of her pupils' anti-social behaviour. Released in the same year, shot in Glasgow, and starring Harvey Keitel, Romy Schneider and Harry Dean Stanton, *Death Watch* (*La mort en direct*, 1980), like *The Prize of Peril*, questions the venal motives and unbridled voyeurism of televised entertain-ment (somewhat problematically contrasted with cinema). A journalist (Keitel) hired by an American television producer (Stanton) has a cam-era implanted in his eye so that he may secretly film the dying moments of a famous writer (Schneider) suffering from an incurable illness. Unbe-known to the writer, the footage will be broadcast live on the weekly hit show, *Death Watch*.

We have noted how, a decade later, Tavernier's *L.627* (1992) takes Bob Swaim's insider view of the French police in ever more realist, anthropo-logical directions and with an increasingly clear socio-political agenda. Three years on, the film-maker's mistrust of a certain type of televi-sion, for its increasingly consumerist game-show mentality, and the mind-numbing effects of American action films on French youth will (re)surface and coalesce with a broader critique of globalizing culture in the social noir thriller, *L'Appât* [The *Bait*].

L'Appât [*The Bait*] (1995)

The screenplay is loosely adapted from Morgan Sportès's novel of the same name, recounting a news story (the Valéria Subra case) that had shocked the French nation in 1984. The film relates how three fairly ordinary French teenagers, Eric, his aspiring model girlfriend Nathalie and not very bright sidekick, Bruno, become sucked into a downward spiral of criminality and cold-blooded murder. Apparently drugged on a cultural diet of American thrillers and an Americanized consumer-driven French media, their one ambition is to move to the United States and make their fortune in the rag trade. However, they have a problem: money. The boys are both unemployed and Nat's present salary as a 'salesgirl-model' barely keeps them in food and cigarettes. They resolve to use Nat's contacts and charm to gain entrance to the apartments of wealthy middle-aged Parisians, whose bulging safes they will empty, all the better to finance their own American Dream. The dream, of course, turns into a nightmare: they end up torturing then murdering the victims, making next to nothing out of the 'jobs' and are finally arrested.

On the surface, Tavernier's film reads as a biting critique of American globalizing media-culture. Anglo-Saxon critical discourse around the film, in noting this, has generally fallen into two camps, according to whether or not the critic finds the characters plausible and the indictment worthwhile or justified. Chris Darke, reviewing the film for *Sight and Sound* thinks not:

> Tavernier's teenagers are identikit victims of modern consumer society, and when it comes to assigning symptomatic reasons for their casual criminality it's a matter of rounding up the usual suspects. American cinema, video culture and game shows are proposed as perpetuating a culture of celebrity and hyper-acquisitive capitalism. However, Tavernier's take on these hardly qualifies as an analysis, condemning a soulless, international (read American) visual culture for having corrupted youth is more of a knee-jerk reflex of symptomatic moralism.
>
> (Darke 1995: 43)

Stephen Hay, on the other hand (who devotes a chapter of his monograph on Tavernier to *The Bait*) heaps praise on the film-maker for

> his most devastating attack on the alliance between commercial television and American capitalist culture, depicting a society in which the saturation of French youth with Hollywood's message had created a generation whose identity relied totally on beliefs formed through conformist materialism masquerading as individualism.
>
> (Hay 2000: 170–1)

We argue that his film, beyond (rather than simply against) the critical discourse, reveals itself to be much more than an anti-American pamphlet. Careful analysis reveals that the film's social critique targets elements that are every bit as European, as French in origin, if not universal, as they are products of American cultural imperialism.

Undeniably, *The Bait* points the finger at American mass culture. From a surface reading, Eric, Nat and Bruno have been corrupted by Hollywood, by its images that seem to promote the normalization of violence and the unscrupulous pursuit of individual gain. For the three, America represents the ultimate object of desire: things American are seen as always, already infinitely bigger, better, hotter, cooler than things French. Julia Roberts earns more than Isabelle Adjani; Budweiser is superior to French beer; hip-hop is naturally hipper than French rock; no doubt, Stephen Siegal would be seen as a better film-maker than Bertrand Tavernier. And over there, where there is no pesky bureaucracy to impose taxes on business, anyone with a few smarts and a bit of capital can make it rich. Hay's chapter is deft and thorough in exposing the ridiculousness and superficiality of the characters' belief systems. On another level, though, the author seems blind to his text's own internal contradictions. At several points, the media-driven consumerism of contemporary French society depicted in the film is described as an imported American capitalist conspiracy or disease:

> The society they survive in is infested with a commercial ideology that equates success with the possession of specific items, driving French youth to buy, wear, eat, drink and watch, in particular, American goods, under the clear advertising warnings that lacking them represents a failure to acquire the only image which confirms your position as an accepted member of society.
>
> (Hay 2000: 172)

And yet, when one lists the many status objects mentioned in the film: Mont Blanc pen, Piaget watch, Mercedes cars, Hermès scarf, Cartier jewellery, Rolex, Porsche, Ferrari, Maserati, one cannot help noticing that all are quite conspicuously, well, un-American...

In Hay's analysis, America functions as a sign for the perceived ills of media-driven consumer capitalism. (In this respect, we are more in agreement with Darke. However, we hope to show that the film is ultimately less reductionist than this critic claims.) Moreover, this sign is in many ways a projection. First, of certain fears on the part of the French film industry at the prospect of a totally American-dominated world film market, a point to which we return in the final section. Second, this fetishized America is a target for the projection of undesirable, aspects of French society, or, dare we say, of human nature. Hay's constructivist reading sees the protagonists' preoccupation with beauty, wealth, power and status, as produced by American-inspired consumer-capitalism. But to do so is to confuse cause with effect. Such preoccupations are the underlying *causes* rather than the products of the consumerism and image-consciousness of contemporary society, on both sides of the Atlantic. In its enumeration of European status symbols, the film clearly reveals this.

We propose instead, a neo-Darwinian reading of this aspect of the film,[7] one which would see it—probably beyond conscious authorial intention—as posing consumerism and image-consciousness as the ultimate products, not of American capitalism, but of a universal human desire for beauty, wealth, power, status and its symbols. The basic plot highlights the fact that what underlies these obsessions is none other than the age-old human socio-sexual system built on the sexual division of labour: exchange of wealth by dominant males for sexual access to young, desirable (i.e. healthy and fertile) females. Men seek power, wealth and status because these are the prime attributes that will increase their chances in the mating game. Conversely, women are obsessed with their image because in almost all human cultures, it has been beauty, above all, that increases a woman's chances of attracting a superior mate and gaining access to resources that have traditionally been controlled by men. Economic resources for sexual favours: this is the dynamic that enables Nathalie to play *The Bait*, setting the trap for her victims, apparently turning the patriarchal power game to her, and her boyfriend's, advantage. The irony is twofold. First, the three friends will be caught in their own trap. Second, even if they had succeeded in their plan, the wealth they seek, their American Dream, is also shown to be the bait in another more universal trap.

So, Nat feigns attraction to further her career; the men feign an interest in her career and welfare to get sex. It is a grotesque, banal, inherently dishonest commerce, each party attempting to dupe and exploit the other, each wanting to get out of the transaction more than they are prepared to put in. It is a game in which all parties are cheats. Because she is young, inexperienced and relatively powerless, not so much a fatale as a corrupted ingénue trying to survive and make her mark in a still male-dominated society, Nat gains a certain amount of initial audience sympathy. This is counter-balanced by her somewhat vain superficiality. Still, to what extent can we blame her for using the only weapon she has? In the expository restaurant sequence, where we see Nat and her friend 'at work', making contacts, Tavernier's dialogues, camera-work and *mise en scène*, all underline the fact that the young women are viewed by the men exclusively in terms of their physique (and the men exclusively in terms of their wealth and status).

In the relationship between the young protagonists, Nat and Eric, the dynamic is different, much more equal, in terms of age, economic status (both come from middle-class backgrounds and have yet to make a career) and sexual terms (the attraction is mutual). Nonetheless, Nat must struggle to assert herself against Eric's often paternalistic, macho comments and behaviour. In one scene, he casually enquires of her boss whether 'the kid is doing a good job'. In another, he takes his ironing to his grandmother's, who enquires 'Doesn't Nathalie know how to iron?' Eric defends Nat, pointing out the fact that she works full time; however, it never once occurs to either the young man or his more understandably traditionalist grandmother that perhaps he might start ironing his own trousers! In scene after scene, the young couple are shown to be caught up in age-old patriarchal socio-sexual power structures. It is these structures, coupled with employment difficulties, breakdowns in their family relationships and societal failures that lead to their succumbing to the media-driven materialism that will ultimately lead them to murder.

First among the contemporary socio-economic issues depicted in the film, is the dissolution of the family, signalled by the fact that Nat's parents are divorced, and her lack of contact with her father. The emotionally dysfunctional nature of her family life is further indicated by scenes with a mother portrayed as, primarily, interested in physical appearance and status, and a younger sister who is too often left home alone. Second, the film highlights the issue of youth unemployment: Eric and Bruno's slide into crime is precipitated by their failure to keep down a job. Their situation is tragically reflective of national trends, with the early 1990s witnessing record highs in French unemployment: 11.8 per cent by the end of 1993, second only to Italy in the developed world. Third, *L'Appât* foregrounds the effects of globalization on the French economy and the uncivic reactions of its capitalist classes. The French clothing industry is portrayed as being in decline owing to perceived excessively high taxes and wages which drive companies to manufacture offshore in the Third World. Eric mentions *Naf Naf*, the French label that has made a killing in the United States by following the same practices. The film thus alludes to the fact that French companies also have a stake in global capitalism and to their role in aggravating unemployment and by extension, crime, in the developed world.

The dialogues further highlight French capitalist greed and dishonesty by informing spectators that Eric's father (a businessman in the 'rag trade') is facing tax evasion charges. Finally, an allusion is made to the corruption and scandals that dogged French political life in the 1990s, through the televised images of the flamboyant and controversial Bernard Tapie. A prominent public figure, Tapie rose to fame in the 1980s as an entrepreneurial whizz-kid, later becoming involved in politics, and more recently, television, cinema and theatre. From 1992 to 1993 he had been a minister in Pierre Bérégovoy's socialist government. But in 1993, his political immunity was rescinded and his career nosedived when he was accused of match-fixing on behalf of his Marseille Soccer Club. At the time of *The Bait*'s release, Tapie's name and image had become synonymous with media glitz, financial and political hubris, dishonesty and scandal. Here again, we see that the gangrene eating away at the fabric of French society at this time was, in many respects, home grown.

To return to the film's protagonists, the three's fixation with the United States as the land of opportunity and their adulation of American cinema crystallize in their obsessive video-viewing of de Palma's *Scarface* (1983). De Palma's remake of Howard Hawks's 1932 classic is set in 1980 when Castro used an amnesty for would-be emigrants to empty out his prisons. Starring Al Pacino as Tony Montana, the story tells of the rise and fall of such a Cuban emigrant, a small-time criminal who arrives in Florida with nothing but his wits, and manages to claw his way to the top as a gang boss and drug lord. The extract we see in *The Bait* comes at a pivotal moment in the protagonist's rise to power. Realizing he has been double-crossed by his gang leader, he will turn the tables, have him eliminated and take his place. For audiences unfamiliar with de Palma's film, the reference signifies the boys' desire to fulfil their own American Dream by emulating a violent and unscrupulous

American gangster. The extract would thus appear to function as a *mise en abyme* or miniaturized reflection of Tavernier's film. We argue that the relationship between the two is far more disjunctive and that the significance of the *Scarface* reference, in its points of contrast with Tavernier's text, is to underline the protagonists' misreading of their fetish film and the culture it embodies.

Indeed, the element of misreading is already implied by the mode of viewing. The three watch a dubbed French tape, that is, an inferior third-hand (even subtitles are never perfect) version of the original. In France, English language films are generally available in both dubbed and subtitled versions, so the choice indicates a level of ignorance, pointing towards the protagonists' failure to accurately read the film. Moreover, there happens to be a translation error in Nat's favourite line, which she repeats in one scene. Pacino says in French: '*Je suis, comment vous dites…paranoiaque*', which the English subtitles faithfully render as 'I'm, how do you say…paranoid.' But in the original, what his character says is '*I ain't* how you say…paranoid' (our emphasis). A detail perhaps, especially since the character clearly *is* paranoid—he has to be to survive—but the point of de Palma's dialogue in this scene is Montana's denial and lack of self-knowledge. So, the French text of the dubbed extract, blithely assimilated by the three, is shown to be inherently subject to cultural mistranslation.

It is a misreading that extends to the film as a whole, namely that *Scarface* is an illustration of Hollywood glorification of crime and violence. Anyone familiar with this film will remember it as an unequivocal critique of the falseness and emptiness of the American Dream when it is: a) reduced to wealth, image and status, since even when the character has it all, happiness eludes him; and b) built on crime and violence, since he who lives by the sword will inevitably die by the sword.

This brings us to the central character, Tony Montana. Given that he is the principal role model for our protagonists, what is it that makes this character a hero? It is neither his overwhelming ambition nor the fact that he is a violent gangster. Following a familiar noir trope, what makes Tony Montana the hero of *Scarface* is above all his courage and sense of honour. As the character puts it: 'I got two things, my balls and my word.' These are the qualities that set him apart: guts, streetwise intelligence, loyalty and personal values, an integrity that his adversaries in the film blatantly lack. Tragically, it is this integrity that will be his undoing. The downward spiral that ends with Montana's death is set in motion when he refuses to go ahead with a bomb attack because the intended victim is accompanied by his wife and children. Our point, in relation to *The Bait,* is that when the film's aspiring gangsters are put into situations in which they face similar existential and ethical choices to those of their hero, they fail entirely to live up to his example. Neither smart nor brave, Eric does not really have the stomach for murder, preferring to let his partner Bruno do the dirty work. But in the end, Eric will stab to death, in cold blood, a fellow Jew, a 'brother', and father of a young child, who has done him no personal harm. Finally, the three also fail to see the moral lessons implicit in their Hollywood screen hero's trajectory: money as the greatest trap of all. Even when crime does pay, it does not buy love, happiness and peace of mind, as noir so often reminds us.

Hay's reading of *The Bait*'s protagonists is that 'they have been anaesthetized by their cultural diet' (Hay 2000: 172). For cultural diet, read American-driven consumerism. For American-driven consumerism, read American cinema, namely, violent action and horror movies and noir-inspired thrillers like *Scarface*. But *Scarface*, as we have seen, is not a film that would anaesthetize in this way, unless misread by spectators already in some way lacking in knowledge and/or moral values. As Tavernier explains in *Le Nouvel Observateur* of 2 March 1995:

> I try to show that there is no single culprit. No single explanation. The fascination with American images wouldn't be such a problem if it didn't go hand in hand with a certain impression of collective disengagement and loss of values... We live in a world that has lost its safeguard mechanisms: education, religion, political commitment, trade unionism, family.
>
> (Quoted in Dehée 2000: 278)

What we hope to have shown is that Tavernier's portrayal of both American culture, and the underlying causes of contemporary French social malaise, is indeed more complex, more nuanced and less self-righteously moralizing than has been recognized. We have outlined ways in which the film highlights the difficulty in accurately reading and representing the cultural Other. Just as the protagonists' vision of *Les States* is a fetish, a fantasy projection of their own desires, the negative vision of American culture portrayed in *The Bait* is as much a projection of certain fears and failings of French society itself as it is an analysis of the impact on that society of American consumer capitalism. The film suggests that while coca-colonization remains a major concern, a number of the ills that plague contemporary France are anchored deeper within its own society, perhaps even in the human condition. We do not mean in any way to suggest that these issues are therefore irresolvable. But no real progress is made by their wholesale projection on to mythified images of American crime and violence or American-led globalization, as Tavernier states.

Finally, we move on to examine briefly the reasons behind the indisputably noir vision of American mass culture offered in *The Bait*. As we have suggested, this clearly relates back to broader issues in Franco-American relations, namely French (and European) fears of American-dominated globalization and monopolization of world markets, notably in the audio-visual sector. Since the end of the Second World War, the popularity and sheer mass of American film product has been a constantly growing threat to national film industries in Europe. And as European film industry leader, indeed, as the only European nation to still possess a national film industry, France has been particularly sensitive to Hollywood domination.[8] The French response has been a multi-pronged defensive counter-attack: a series of fiscal measures including taxes on box office, compulsory funding of local film production by French television companies, quotas, subsidies and trade barriers that continue to support and protect its local film industry to this day (Fournier Lanzoni 2002: 351–7). Without state support, in a totally free-trade environment, the French film industry could not hope to maintain its position. Indeed, it would hardly be an overstatement to claim that its very survival would be jeopardized: witness the decline in the British film industry following the dismantlement of its state-funded financial support system during the late 1970s.

French film-makers are acutely aware of their dependence on state support and (like their counterparts in farming and agriculture) have periodically gone into battle when it has been threatened, arguing that although cinema is an industry, it is not simply a marketable commodity but also a form of personal, cultural and political expression, central to French identity. Tavernier himself has played a particularly active role, notably during the GATT negotiations of 1993, as active campaigner for *l'exception culturelle*, the French-inspired European demand for the exclusion of film and other cultural products from global free-trade agreements. As de facto spokesperson for the French film industry, Tavernier of course had a clear vested interest in opposing the liberalization of the European audio-visual market. Nonetheless, his view of GATT liberalism as a Trojan horse, a covert vehicle for American ideology whose entry into the French economy would ultimately signify nothing less than the end of the French way of life,[9] was overwhelmingly representative of the industry and enjoyed wide popular and political support. Both socialist President, François Mitterrand and his successive culture ministers, socialist Jack Lang and Gaullist Jacques Toubon made impassioned speeches in favour of cinema as a 'creation of the spirit' and *l'exception culturelle* as essential to preserving European cultural identity against the stultifying, homogenizing forces of American-led globalization (Jeancolas 1998: 57; Strode 2000: 65). In the face of French-led EU opposition, the 1993 GATT round ended in a stalemate that was claimed as a victory for cultural exception.[10] But if a battle had been won, the war was far from over and Tavernier continued to be at the forefront.

Less well known than his participation in the GATT debates, but arguably more significant, is his intervention in 1997, to mobilize French opinion against the planned Multilateral Agreement on Investment (MAI), aimed at facilitating international corporate investment into local economies. In press conferences and rallies, Tavernier and colleagues were quick to point out the threat to the French and European socio-economic model represented by the secretly prepared OECD project. In granting multinationals the same rights as local investors in national markets without the attendant social responsibilities, the MAI would not only threaten cultural industries such as cinema, it would seriously undermine the ability of France and other European nations to maintain their distinctive systems of social protection, notably in the fields of health and employment. 'This treaty is leading us towards an insidious change of civilization. From the rights of peoples to self-determination, it takes us to the rights of investors to determine the fate of peoples,' the film-makers declared (Raspiengeas 2001: 497). On 16 February 1998, an anti-free-trade film industry protest meeting, held in the Quartier Latin, at the legendary Odeon Theatre and attended by the French Minister of Culture, had as its rallying cry: 'Cultural exception in the MAI: A question of survival' (Véron 1999). Cultural exception had been reframed in terms of national autonomy and survival, in the name of human rights and cultural diversity. In October 1998, faced with fierce industry protests, media interest and public opposition, and following a negative parliamentary report on the likely impact of the MAI on French sovereignty, socialist Prime Minister, Lionel Jospin withdrew from the negotiations.

Tavernier's personal battle with Hollywood continued long after the making of *The Bait* and after these initial free-trade furores had died down. In 1999, he was involved in a very public dispute with Steven Spielberg, neatly summarized by Australian critic Neil MacDonald as:

pretty spectacular, nothing less than a complaint from the American that French support for their film industry violated the principles of the free market. Tavernier's reaction had been explosive. He pointed out that France had only a fraction of its own market, which was swamped by American product. Tavernier was a formidable adversary.

(McDonald 2001: 65)

Conclusion

The battle for French and other European cinemas to maintain their national specificity and cultural integrity against the Goliath that is Hollywood is thus a very real one and in the present authors' opinion, one well worth fighting for. While less simplistically anti-American than has been argued, Tavernier's agenda in *The Bait*, conceived during a period of GATT negotiations, when American share of the French box office had almost reached 60 per cent, almost double that of local production, when cinema attendance in France was at an all-time low (116 million entries in 1992 as against almost 202 million a decade earlier), is thus explainable in terms of national cinemas' fight to survive in an increasingly free global-market context. We agree that it is also defensible in terms of cultural diversity, in that the loss of national cinemas, as the cultural equivalent to the extinction of species, would result in the further impoverishment of our global cultural heritage. And finally, *The Bait* is a prime example of the way noir anxiety has been mobilized by French cinema as a vehicle for the expression of national anxieties—from the coca-colonization debates of the post-war period to its contemporary form as globalization at the turn of the millennium— and also as a weapon in the ongoing battle against the main sources of this anxiety.

10
Double-Crossings: Reversing the Remake

As shown in Chapter 9, exponents of French noir have been at the forefront of recent European attempts to counter the increasing presence of American productions on its national TV and cinema screens and the overwhelming dominance of Hollywood as an irresistible global force. Ways in which French film-makers have remobilized and reinvented the crime drama genre in an attempt to reverse this trend, range from explicit critique of the Americanization of French cinema and society (*L'Appât*) to an increasingly Americanized approach to the genre (e.g. *Les rivières pourpres*, Kassovitz, 2000, *36 Quai des Orfèvres*, Marchal, 2004). Since the 1990s, resorting increasingly to an 'if you can't beat 'em, join 'em' strategy has seen a significant number of French film-makers (most notably, Luc Besson: *Nikita, Leon, The 5th Element, Joan of Arc*) making the Atlantic crossing to produce and/or direct films in American English, with somewhat mixed results, both in terms of critical reception and popular appeal. The twin tropes of emulation versus resistance and the issue of Hollywood hegemony that have been shown to lie at the heart of French noir, are perhaps nowhere more evident than in the phenomenon of the transnational and transcultural remake, particularly given the number of American remakes produced since the 1990s, many involving films from the French noir canon.[1] While a number of academic film analysts have pointed out the need for a re-evaluation of Hollywood reprises of French 'originals' as rich sources of cinematic intercultural knowledge, others, Francophile film critics and industry players in particular, have tended to see the remake in a more negative light. For the latter groups, American remakes of French comedies and noir crime dramas generally represent little more than an aesthetically debased form of cultural cannibalism.

It is only very recently that the French have themselves begun to adopt the practice of the transcultural remake, reappropriating the

Hollywood strategy for their own national cinema. This chapter focuses specifically on Jacques Audiard's ground-breaking *De battre mon coeur s'est arrêté*, after James Toback's *Fingers*, to our knowledge the first French language noir remake of an American 'original'. We argue that Audiard's neo-noir crime thriller is an original and productive adaptation in the ways it expands on, departs from or reverses the postulates of its source-text. Audiard's film both reminds us of the positive creative potential of the remake and offers the tantalizing possibility of a reversal in the trend towards total Hollywood domination of the world cinema stage.

Franco-American transcultural remakes: A brief history

We begin by discussing briefly the history of the transcultural remake's poor reputation in France. As early as 1938, industry sources had signalled the economic threat to French cinema exports represented by the remake.[2] We have already noted how on a broader level of aesthetic critique, the equation: French originality vs. American formulaic repetition was common parlance, notably articulated by Boris Vian/Sullivan in his preface to *J'irai cracher sur vos tombes*. In terms of cinema, it was *Cahiers'* founder and spiritual father, André Bazin (Bazin 1951: 52–6, 1952: 54–9) who publicized the debate in the early 1950s, notably bemoaning the lack of originality of Hollywood remakes. Ever since, critics and film-makers on both sides of the Atlantic have claimed, and indeed proclaimed, that remake rhymes with fake. The polemic raged anew in the early 1990s, fuelled by Hollywood's escalating use of the transcultural remake, drawing particularly on French originals (see Cohen 1994). During the 1980s and 1990s there were a total of 41 transcultural Franco-American remakes (Moine 2007: 195–8), compared with only three in the two preceding decades.[3] Until the late 1990s, practically every discussion of the remake constitutes a two-pronged attack that is highly revealing of the economic stakes underpinning its expansion.

On the one hand, the remake is held up as further evidence of Hollywood's aesthetic poverty, its lack of creative inspiration. Unable to creatively renew itself, bereft of new and original ideas, it is charged with vampirizing European national cinemas' best-loved originals, of which it churns out cheap production-line copies that are either luridly sensationalist or superficially insipid. But of course there is nothing intrinsically 'bad' about transcultural remakes, which figure in many official canons of world cinema and loom large in the corpus of American film noir. To cite but one example, Tay Garnett's *The Postman Always Rings*

Twice (USA 1946) remade by Bob Rafelson (USA 1981) was in fact the third screen adaptation of Cain's hard-boiled novel. Pierre Chenal had been the first to adapt *Postman* as French poetic realist *Le dernier tournant* (France 1939), followed by Visconti's neo-realist *Ossessione* (Italy 1942). Bazin himself recognized the creative potential of remakes in transposing one cultural narrative into a different cultural setting. And as a number of commentators have since pointed out, creative remakes of other French poetic classics, directed by ex-patriot European film-makers working in Hollywood in the post-war period made a major contribution to the classic noir canon, confirming noir as an indicator of cultural specificity and a powerful vector of intertextual and cultural exchange (Moine 2007: 149). Such French-inspired noir classics include Fritz Lang's *Scarlett Street* (1945) after Jean Renoir's *La Chienne* (1931), Lang's *Human Desire* (1954), after Renoir's *La bête humaine* (1938) and Anatole Litvak's *The Long Night* (1947) after Carné's *Le jour se lève* (1939).

Despite the undisputed aesthetic merits and intercultural richness of films such as these, charges of mercantilism levelled at Hollywood remakes, particularly those made since the 1980s, are difficult to cast aside. For like the series, sequel and prequel, the remake is primarily used as a means of cashing in on a past commercial success, recycling a proven formula, and/or saving the time and money required for the development of new ideas: story line, screenplay and script. It is the economics of the remake that leads to its dismissal as a debased form. This is particularly true when failure to acknowledge the source equates to an act of plagiarism. It must be added that Hollywood is not the only perpetrator here. One notable European example is Sergio Leone's *Fistful of Dollars* (1964), somewhat infamously lifted from Kurosawa's *Yojimbo* (1961), but which the Japanese master had himself 'stolen' from the novel *Red Harvest*, written by none other than Dashiell Hammett.[4]

Cases of European remakes notwithstanding, whether plagiarized or legitimate, in terms of Franco-American cinematic exchange, the remake has been and remains, overwhelmingly, a Hollywood practice. The end result has been that, to the French and Francophile members of the Anglo-American critical establishment, the remake has long been seen as indexical signifier of Hollywood greed, one of the cornerstones of its Machiavellian plan for global market monopolization, the most insidious current form of coca-colonization. Along with financial enticement of talented overseas film-makers (actors, directors and cinematographers), the remake is one very visible way that Hollywood is seen to extend its tentacular grip on world film markets to the detriment of other national industries, via the wholesale plundering of national cinemas for its own commercial gain (see Forrest and Koos 2002: 6–7). A few facts and figures suffice to explicate this position. We have seen how during the 1980s and 1990s, American market share in France rose to almost 60 per cent, while the French share of the American market stood at a mere 1 per cent (half the total share for foreign/European films).

In the mid-1980s Disney's Touchstone cashed in on the success of *Trois Hommes et un Couffin* (Serreau, France 1985), which had earned $3.5 million in the United States in its subtitled French version, by remaking it as *Three Men and a Baby* (Nimoy, USA 1987), which went on to earn $170 million. Later in the decade, Touchstone and other American production companies sought to make even bigger profits by withholding the release of the French originals to which they had purchased the American distribution and remake rights, to the understandable rage of the French camp. As Sharon Waxman (1993, quoted in Forrest and Koos 2002: 6) points out, there is little incentive for Hollywood producers to release a foreign original if they can safely assume more money is to be made by remaking it with American stars and according to American tastes.

These economic facts demonstrate why the transcultural remake has become emblematic of the souring of the Franco-American relationship and why it has served to focalize France's incessant struggle for survival as a film-making nation. Conversely, over the last decade, academic theorists looking into the phenomenon have also pointed out the sociological value of the transcultural remake as a privileged site for examining representations of national identity, cultural difference and intercultural dynamics (see Durham 1998; Nacache 1999; Mazdon 2000; Forrest and Koos 2002; Moine 2007). The discussion following attempts to address both sides of this vexed, fascinating and crucial question.

Jaccques Audiard's *De Battre mon cœur s'est arrêté* after James Toback's Fingers

In 2005, Jacques Audiard directed *De battre mon cœur s'est arrêté* [*The Beat That My Heart Skipped*] (hereafter *Beat*) adapting James Toback's 1978 first feature *Fingers*, and realizing the first French-language remake of an American production.[5] Despite its modest budget even by French standards (€ 5.3m) and equally modest distribution (210 copies on first release), *Beat* did very respectably at the box office, with over a million ticket sales and was a huge critical success, inspiring a plethora of positive press reviews and winning a host of awards at the 2006

César Awards, including best director, best film and (most significantly perhaps) best adaptation.

The low-budget independent production *Fingers,* a disturbing, mafia-noir psycho-drama, provides Audiard with *Beat*'s central concept. Shot in three weeks on the streets of New York by first-time director James Toback, *Fingers* is the story of Jimmy 'Fingers' Angelelli, with Harvey Keitel in a sadly underrated early performance. Jimmy is the only son of a small-time Mafia hood (Michael V. Gazzo), who attempts to escape his father's world of greed and violence through classical music. Seeking to follow in the footsteps of his concert pianist mother, now in a psychiatric clinic, Jimmy appears in the opening shot, practising Bach's Toccata in E minor for a make-or-break audition at Carnegie Hall (with his mother's ex-impresario, Mr Fox). But the obstacles facing him prove insurmountable. Jimmy's own insecurities, which include a clear suggestion of repressed homosexuality, lead him into a destructive relationship with an alluring sculptress (Tisa Farrow, sister of Mia) and render him incapable of resisting the pull of his father and his brutal, materialistic world. Almost in one breath, the audition is a failure, he doesn't get the girl and his father is shot dead by a Mafia boss. Though, in the next scene, Jimmy runs to avenge his father, it is a hollow victory. He has lost everything and is still no closer to discovering who he really is.

Resituated to present-day Paris, *Beat* centres on 28-year-old Thomas Seyr (Romain Duris), a dealer working the sleazy, criminally ruthless end of the high-stakes property market, with his associates and mates, Fabrice and Sami (Johnathan Zaccai, Gilles Cohen). The trio specialize in trading old or derelict buildings, using a combination of live rats, baseball bats and demolition crews to evict the poor tenants or immigrant squatters who occupy them. As in *Fingers,* Tom's profession is a paternal heritage: his father, Robert, is in much the same game. Despite being recently engaged to a young photo-model and aspiring actress (Chris/Emmanuelle Devos), the father is too old now to play the heavy and increasingly calls on his son to lean on creditors. Then, 18 minutes into the film, a chance meeting sees Tom rethink his life options. He bumps into Mr Fox, impresario to his deceased mother, a successful concert pianist who committed suicide after a long mental illness. Mr Fox remembers Tom as a promising young talent and invites him to audition.

Wishing to refresh his skills (having abandoned the piano after his mother's death) but turned away by the Conservatoire, Tom is introduced to Chinese pianist Miao Lin (played by Vietnamese actress

Lin-Dan Pham), recently arrived in France on a music scholarship, who is happy to act as tutor. His father is not impressed. Likewise, business partner Fabrice, who regularly uses Tom to provide alibis for his extra-conjugal escapades. Fabrice's wife, Aline, guesses what is going on; she and Tom become lovers. With daily lessons from Miao Lin, Tom's playing improves though his associates complain that his mind is not on the job. Robert calls Tom: this time he needs Tom to 'deal with' a Russian gangster, Minskov (Anton Yakovlev), who has cheated him and had him beaten up. Tom goes to Minskov's hotel and, in one of the few scenes taken directly from *Fingers*, spots him by the swimming pool, heavily guarded. After verbally threatening him over the phone, Tom follows Minskov's young mistress into the changing rooms and charms her into having sex with him in a toilet cubicle. Again, his father is not impressed. The night before the audition, Tom's associates drag him off to a building site to close an important deal. Predictably, the building has been overtaken by squatters and the two employ the usual methods to evict them. This time, Tom watches on, no longer having the stomach to join in. The next day the audition is a failure. Seeking solace, Tom goes to Robert's flat and finds him shot dead. Cut to two years later: Tom is Miao Lin's partner and agent, managing her concert career. Driving to a concert, he spots Minskov in the street, follows him and a violent fight ensues. Tom gains the upper hand but cannot bring himself to finish off the gangster. Bloodied and dazed, he staggers back to the concert.

Fingers, *Beat* and intertextual noir

Audiard's inventive approach to his hypotextual source-film is a positive reminder of the ontological status of noir as intertextual nexus, born out of, nurtured by, reinvented through an ongoing process of bi-directional transatlantic exchange. While both Audiard and Toback draw on American noir 'traditions', notably the 1970s New York crime drama of Scorsese and Coppola, it must be remembered that these film-makers owe much to European traditions, specifically Italian and French New Waves. The *nouvelle vague* is also a major point of reference for younger exponents of this American genre. Quentin Tarantino in particular, openly acknowledges his debt to French cinema, from Dassin's *Rififi* to the self-reflexive *nouvelle vague* gangster films of Truffaut (*Shoot The Pianist*) and particularly Godard (*Breathless*, *Band of Outsiders*), to whom Tarantino paid homage in naming his Production Company, Band Apart.

The influence of Scorsese on Toback's *Fingers* is clear, in the New York mafia setting, graphic violence, cinematography (Director of photography (DOP) Mike Chapman had worked on *Taxi Driver*) and the disjunctive co-presence of classical and pop music. And, of course, Scorsese's early work is also given a physical, intertextual presence in *Fingers* through Toback's casting of Keitel. In keeping with the mean-street 'tradition', both *Fingers* and *Beat* combine documentary realism (location shooting, naturalistic lighting and acting style) with highly stylized camera angles, editing and soundtrack. Stylistically, *Fingers* uses more static camera and smooth tracking shots to observe and track its protagonist and underscore his nervous, performance anxiety. Also clearly drawing on Scorsese (Dobson 2007: 183–4), Audiard makes greater use (than Toback) of the hand-held camera, often moving *with* the protagonist and creating a greater sense of empathy. Editing and music generate an intense, discontinuous rhythm (scenes are cut mid-way through a shot, phrase or song sequence), which parallels Tom's hyperactive nervous energy. Audiard also adds a small number of slower, dream-like interludes that punctuate the film, providing an element of contrast that invites reflective, symbolic readings.

In *Fingers*, graphic depictions of sex and violence and the construction of Keitel's character as unlikely gangster turned would-be classical pianist obsessed with outdated, 1960s popular music, both reference Scorsese and prefigure the post-modern neo noir of Tarantino. Twenty-five years on, *Beat* references both, calling explicitly on its spectator's awareness of musical and filmic genre. The ritualistic costume—black suit, white shirt, slim black tie—that Tom chooses for the showdown audition beg to be read intertextually, referencing both *Reservoir Dogs* and *Pulp Fiction* as much as *Fingers*. More spectacularly, the chillingly ironic use of music in the final eviction scene is evocative of *Reservoir Dogs*' (in)famous torture sequence. In the scene from *Beat*, Fabrice and Sami brutalize yet another group of immigrant squatters, with Sami dancing to Grand Funk's *Locomotion* as he and Gilles gleefully destroy the living space of their hapless 'tenants'. Shot with jerky hand-held camera and lit by eerie, diegetic torch-lights that pick out discontinuous, flashing details of the action, lighting and camera-work highlight Tom's new sense of alienation as he now observes with horror his workmates going about their routine business.

Fingers, Beat and problematic filiation

The most striking similarity between the two films consists in the father-son relationship as a painful but necessary Oedipal trajectory.

This filial narrative and thematic strand[6] is what drew Audiard to *Fingers* initially and he makes it both more central and more explicit. *Beat* opens with an expository prologue in which Tom's friend and business associate describes his passage to adulthood in classic Oedipal terms, outlining the rivalry, power struggles and gradual role reversal that took place between himself and his father. Sami tells Tom how he began reluctantly responding to his father's requests for advice, then progressed to making decisions on his behalf before finally caring for him physically when he fell terminally ill. And of course, *Beat* sees Tom go through an uncannily similar process.

In both films the father figures are aging patriarchs from whom their sons must liberate themselves if they are to attain authentic subjectivity and individual agency. Though both fathers are strangely likeable in their vulnerable, retrograde masculinity and clumsy expressions of paternal affection (both are engaged to much younger women but desperately need their sons' approval), both are arch manipulators, ruthless in their use of rejection and emotional blackmail to persuade their sons into doing the dirty work that is part and parcel of their world, and of which they are now physically incapable. Tom's father resorts to getting himself beaten up to force his son to act on his behalf. In *Fingers*, when Jimmy refuses to confront head-on the Mafia boss who has cheated his father, the latter's retort and chilling last words to his son are: *I shoulda strangled you in yer crib.*

Beat as creative reversal. I: Cultural transposition

But what interests us most in *Beat* is that, despite hewing quite close to the original in terms of broad characterization and plot, Audiard's film is in no sense an imitation nor even simply a cultural transposition, but a creative reworking of *Fingers*. While we have no wish to cast the two films in Manichean terms, as good and bad cinematic objects, we argue that on several crucial levels, *Beat* is a creative reversal of its American source.

In transposing *Fingers* geographically, Audiard wisely recontextualizes his film culturally, modifying the Italian Mafia setting, non-existent in Paris. The little Italy crime world of *Fingers* is replaced by the shady, though officially legitimate, world of Parisian real estate brokerage. Cultural transposition is doubled by a greater emphasis on sociological context that is broadly characteristic of French cinema and often downplayed in American remakes. Though less overtly criminal than the Mafia backdrop of *Fingers*, the dealer milieu of *Beat* is equally dubious in moral terms, and very explicitly portrayed as sharing the strong arm, extortionist tactics, dishonesty and official bribery aspects of organized crime. *Beat*'s authors add details of plot and *mise en scène* that attest to ethnic and class tensions and other socio-economic issues specific to France as a post-colonial power and founding member of an ever expanding Europe. Whereas in *Fingers*, Jimmy's adversaries are of the same ethnic background, in *Beat*, the restaurant owner is Maghrebi while the squatters and poor (illegal?) immigrant families who occupy the trio's apartment blocks (one group backed by a French civil rights agency) are of African and Eastern European origin.

The influx of single eastern European women into western Europe, many of whom end up in the sex industry, is referred to briefly in the dialogues, when Tom casually asks his father's model girlfriend whether she isn't finding things tough, 'with the competition from all those Eastern European girls'. Finally, the choice of a Russian gangster comments on the recent infiltration of the French crime scene by Eastern European and Russian mafias (Pasquier and Blanc 2004).[7]

Audiard effects a highly significant cultural and linguistic transposition in his lengthy French title, *De battre mon cœur s'est arrêté*, more or less literally (if, perhaps, clumsily) translated as *The Beat that my Heart Skipped*. A surface reading evokes the adrenaline-like energy of the film's protagonist and the life-transforming experience the narrative will take him through. As is often the case, intertextual knowledge enables a more productive reading, providing a clear reference to Audiard's thematics. A good percentage of the film's French target audience would have recognized *De battre mon cœur s'est arrêté* as a line from the 1966 hit single, *La fille du Père Noël* (Father Christmas's Daughter).[8] The lyrics are an encapsulation of *Beat*'s central theme of filial struggle: a symbolic account of the transformative power of sexual love to overcome the destructive effects of a violent patriarchal heritage.

'Beat' as creative reversal. II: Characterization and narrative trajectory

Beat's most striking reversal in terms of plot development lies in the protagonist's narrative trajectory: though Tom is in a similar situation to that of Jimmy Angelelli, his trajectory is reversed so that *Beat* offers a light at the end of the noir tunnel, offering a possibility of redemption while Jimmy's is more relentlessly noir: a no-exit downward spiral. In this sense, *Beat*'s less bleak narrative resolution also represents something of a reversal in the general trend of the Franco-American remake, in which American reprises of darkly fatalistic French originals have tended to comply with Hollywood's requirement for a morally satisfying outcome or conventional happy ending, sometimes to the point of operating a genre shift that almost entirely erases the source-film's status as noir (Moine 2007: 155–62). But, of course, *Fingers* is unrepresentative in that it is an independent production not a studio product: its uncompromisingly dark vision would have been unthinkable in 1970s Hollywood.

The crucial difference introduced by Audiard and his co-writer Tonino Benacquista, unmotivated in terms of cultural transposition (this is clearly a personal authorial choice) and which drives the plot of *Beat* in the opposite direction to *Fingers*, centres around Tom's more positive relationships with women, enabled by a more positively coded maternal image. He still has idyllic memories of childhood, presumably before his mother's illness: in his father's flat he gazes nostalgically at old photos which show him as a small boy, happy and smiling within a warm, protective triangular family unit. It is precisely because his mother is dead (and despite clear suggestions of her madness and suicide) that she can and does operate as a fond and positive memory. Her photo, recorded voice and piano playing continue to serve as inspiration and emotional support. The fact that recordings of her rehearsals underline her somewhat obsessive perfectionism—she is never satisfied with own performance—might perhaps be read as undermining her son's chances of success. We would argue instead that Audiard's construction of this figure as marked by emotional fragility and self-doubt plays a positive role, bringing a sense of intimacy to the relationship with her son. An accomplished and supremely confident, phallic mother-figure would risk becoming a castrating image of cold perfection and madness.

This is approximately the image Toback provides in *Fingers*. Jimmy's mother is alive but provides no inspiration or solace: the one scene he has with her brings him face to face with the harsh, alienating reality of her mental illness and reinforces his sense of abandonment. After the failed audition he goes to her for support but, of course, she is in no position to help anyone. When Jimmy needs her most, his mother pushes him away in horror.

In both films, the protagonists' relationship with their respective mothers can be seen to impact on subsequent relationships with women. The expository scenes show Tom as a relatively carefree single man engaging enthusiastically in regular casual sex. But when he has an affair with his partner's neglected wife, Aline, their relationship is presented as being based on emotional as well as physical attraction and their love-making scenes, though not sexually explicit, are played and shot as moments of sensual intimacy. This is in sharp contrast to *Fingers*, which charts its protagonist's sexual inadequacies through colder, more graphic representations. The clearest example is the bathroom scene, in which Jimmy has sex with the girlfriend of his father's most deadly adversary, one of the few narrative details which Audiard includes in *Beat*. In *Fingers*, Keitel half forces himself onto the girl and into the act, oafishly performing sex on her as if it were a mildly distasteful filial obligation, leaving her unsatisfied and angry. In *Beat*, the tone of the scene moves from tender to playful and there is no depiction of sex nor suggestion of rape: Audiard cuts away from the scene on the couple's laughter as Tom tumbles over the wall of the toilet cubicle, presumably into the welcoming arms of the gangster's girlfriend.

Both Jimmy and Tom are complex characters for whom a love of classical music represents a deeply lyrical, poetic side with an emotional/spiritual aspiration toward transcendence. Jimmy Angelelli's surname attests to this search for transcendence through art, though the film also uses it to underline the cruel irony and somewhat schizophrenic nature of his situation and personality: the song that plays as he is about to administer a vicious beating to one of his father's recalcitrant creditors is the 1968 hit, *Just Call me Angel in the Morning* (Merrilee Rush and The Turnabouts). As the name, era and ironic positioning of the song suggest, Jimmy is a dark angel; an outsider, friendless despite his easy charm, out of touch with the times and with himself, unable to face his own repressed homosexuality, ultimately rejected by both parents and by the woman he falls in love with. Clumsy as a lover, he is uncomfortable with women despite chasing them; desperately wanting love and approval, capable of playing the macho heavy but, as James Toback's DVD (2002) commentary explains, not yet a man. This fact is made cruelly evident when Tisa, the object of his desire, ultimately prefers a 'real man': ultra-macho black nightclub owner, Dreems, played by ex-football star Jim Brown as the quintessential, even stereotypical black stud. Audiard removes this most deeply problematic aspect of Toback's film, which functions as a *mise en scène* of white masculinity in crisis, upstaged and rendered impotent by a disturbingly triumphant and sadistically misogynous black male sexuality.

Both films present conventional masculinity as marked by an overriding will to power that manifests itself in violent, ruthless materialism and misogynistic acquisitive/exploitative attitudes to women. But *Beat* offers the possibility of an alternative: the redemption of masculinity through a positive encounter with feminine agency. Like Jimmy

Fingers, Audiard's protagonist also goes through a type of identity crisis, but one which is resolved by a process of metamorphosis enabled by the presence of a strong, positively coded femininity. Unlike Jimmy, Tom's relationship with the piano involves a learning process (with his mother and Miao Lin as teachers), which extends to the whole of his existence. Being forced reluctantly into the position of student allows him to learn and therefore to change, to outgrow his old skin, to find himself and finally to grow up, and to invent himself as an authentic agent. The film's ending clearly implies that it is because Tom's relationship with Miao Lin has empowered him to negotiate his own space within the world of music and high art, effecting a positive integration of feminine musicality and masculine business acumen, that he is able to liberate himself from his father's world of base materialism and violence. He is thus able to escape the destructive consequences of a dependent over-investment in either parental pole: the internal, intimate, emotional world and music, equated with the mother, madness and suicide; and the external, social world of action and money, associated with the father, violence and murder.

This all sounds rather trite and pompous, not very French and certainly more melo- than noir. In less expert hands the film might easily have gone down this path, but Audiard avoids the trap in two moves that constitute the final act. He begins by setting up the classic Hollywood ending, only to dismantle it and reveal a quite different and, we argue, quite revolutionary scenario. After Tom's failed recital and the violent discovery of his father's murder, Audiard fades to black, followed by an elliptical title announcing a chronological leap: *Two years later*. We cut to a concert hall, to an overhead shot of Tom at the piano, framed by dream-like, deep red velvet curtains, as if preparing to give a recital. But we subsequently discover it is not his original dream that we see realized: he is not here to perform but to set the stage for the real star, Miao Lin, for whom he is now manager and romantic partner. We cut to the penultimate sequence in which Tom will confront the demons of his past in the form of the Russian gangster, Minskov. In a stairwell scene which closely mirrors that of *Fingers*, the two are locked in a brutal, bloody fight to the death.

In each film, the protagonist (Tom/Jimmy) finally gains the upper hand by emasculating his adversary (crushing the testosterone-driven power of the father's world) and holding a gun to his head. But while the two scenes are identical thus far (in terms of *mise en scène*, lighting and framing), the outcomes diverge. Where Jimmy pulls the trigger

and remains psychologically trapped within the structures of violent filiation, Tom's inability to kill paradoxically enables him to walk free,
shakily reaffirming his will to live a different life, according to different
values. The subsequent and final scenes of the two films are reverse mirror images: in the final shot sequence of *Fingers*, Jimmy sits naked at his
piano, staring bleakly out into the street then to camera, like a caged
animal, while Bach's Toccata plays on without him. In *Beat*, Tom sits in
the concert hall, bloody and bruised, still trembling from the trauma of
this forced rebirth, yet enraptured as Miao Lin performs, his fingers tap-
ping out the notes. The final close-up on Tom's face as he watches her
play captures a look that has finally encountered the sublime.

This brings us to Audiard's second reversal: his masterful construction of the Miao Lin character, beautifully served by Vietnamese
actor, Lin-Dan Pham. First, in making Tom's piano teacher Chinese,
the film-makers introduce a language barrier that serves to contain
the matriarchal element inherent in the teacher role. Moreover, and
even more importantly, the language barrier adds emotional depth
and dramatic interest to the interaction between the two characters
by forcing them to communicate sensually rather than intellectually,
through music, sight and touch. The Word of the Father, associated
with materialism and violence, can have no currency in their relationship. Even more importantly, Audiard and Benacquista reverse the
classic race-gender matrix where the exotic(ized) Other (whether Asian,
African, Indigenous, or simply Woman) is either reduced to a sexualized body of power (Jim Brown as Dreems in *Fingers*) or placed in a
subservient position of mistress, lover, wife, servant or pupil to the western protagonist. An inability to communicate in the language of the
dominant culture can be severely undermining in terms of subjectivity
and power. But *Beat*'s construction of Miao Lin reverses this structure:
her agency is asserted from the outset. She refuses to occupy the subordinate position that might be implied by the political, commercial
and gendered nature of their relationship: she is a foreign musician
on a scholarship, an Asian woman in need of money, and he is an
affluent western male paying for her services. Instead, she is quietly
assertive, as evidenced by her first hesitant words to Tom (in English):
No smoking!

Any incipient exoticism/eroticism is contained by Audiard's camera
work and *mise en scène*. Pham is barely made up, her hair is worn naturally and costuming is unfashionably simple: thick, roll-neck sweaters
over dark trousers. It is Miao Lin's professional status, talent and knowledge that are foregrounded, contributing to her construction as subject,

or if one prefers, as an autonomous agent, one worthy of a respect and admiration that is not primarily sexual. Wide framing highlights Tom's initial lack of interest: he not only shows no sexual attraction, he is also uninterested in Miao Lin as a person and irritated rather than fascinated at her lack of French and prissy health concerns. Whenever Audiard cuts to a close shot of her during the first lessons with Tom, an absence of eyeline match makes it clear that the intimate glimpses we get of her reactions are not his point of view: too focused on his own performance, he is not looking at her at all.

Unused to taking orders, unwilling to occupy the subordinate position of student and object of the gaze, he initially refuses to let her watch him play. Predictably perhaps, the relationship is the site of a subtle power struggle. When Miao Lin quietly and somewhat reluctantly tells him his playing is bad, Tom's masculine pride is wounded to the point where he must get even with her: in the next scene he reverses the roles, teaching her a few words in French, delighting in telling her she is 'Bad, Very bad!' when her pronunciation is predictably less than perfect, and simultaneously striking a match to light a forbidden cigarette. We see their interaction evolve from purely instrumental and confrontational to more personal as Tom grows to admire and respect Miao Lin's professional expertise and authority. In a later short scene, the camera frames them as a couple, in a static full shot through the kitchen doorway, silently sharing tea in a calm, domestic space. Around this point in the film, Audiard filmed scenes that provide more explicit signs of a developing sexual attraction and intimacy but these were wisely discarded. The most explicit is a single shot framing Tom as he casts a furtive glance at Miao Lin's underwear hanging in her bathroom. By resisting the temptation to cater to audience expectations for the conventionally voyeuristic *mise en scène* of male desire, Audiard maintains a level of dramatic tension which borders on the erotic (viz. Tom's reaction when Miao Lin first touches his hands, her startled look when he kisses her on both cheeks before leaving for the audition), and situates the relationship above and beyond the purely physical, on a more equal and more emotionally intimate level.

In this way, Audiard and Benacquista construct the relationship that is revealed in the final act, where we see that Tom has realized his dream vicariously, through her, by becoming her impresario and lover, as a true partnership. Classically, this type of relationship would have been set up in terms of unequal power structures, either in the patriarchal Pygmalion mould (*My Fair Lady, A Star is Born*, etc.) or with Miao Lin acting as an all powerful, pre-Oedipal mother figure. Instead, *Beat* presents a positive resolution to the inevitable power struggle between masculine and feminine: Tom's learning to alternate between subject and object positions constitutes a process of becoming that finally enables him to experience a relationship based on complementarity, mutual affection and respect. The film's convincing construction of the central couple is refreshingly positive, indeed revolutionary, in terms of its disruption of traditional gender politics: an unambiguously heterosexual western-European 'alpha' male finds personal and professional fulfilment in serving the career of an Asian woman whose beauty and ethnic Otherness is eclipsed but not occulted by her personal qualities and artistic talent.

The final scene evokes both the strength and the fragility of this relationship, reinjecting an element of noir anxiety into what might have been an unambiguously idyllic and upbeat ending. As Tom gazes intently at Miao Lin on stage, her face and his are bathed in light. But his bloodied hands are a stark reminder of the continued existence of the brutal world in which he once belonged and which, like Minskov, remains 'out there'.[9] So that, while Audiard ends his adaptation on a very different note to Toback's black malaise, his eschewal of a straight happy ending returns the film to its noir roots.

Beat as creative reversal. III: Reversing the remake

Reversal III has to do with the broader context of the remake. In line with a long-standing Gallic film-making tradition, *Beat* negotiates skilfully between auteurist expression and commercial considerations. Moreover, the choice of a somewhat obscure, dated, critically unacclaimed, low-budget independent source-text[10] is integral to Audiard's project to adapt rather than transpose or reproduce, and breaks with the Hollywood tendency to remake copies of recent foreign hits to more purely mercenary ends. After an extremely positive reception in France, *De battre mon coeur s'est arrêté* was subsequently released in New York and Los Angeles as *The Beat my Heart Skipped*, to similar critical applause. In stark contrast to the Hollywood studio remake practice of suppressing and supplanting French originals, the American distributor, Wellspring, ran successful back-to-back subtitled screenings with *Fingers* (since labelled a cult classic), followed by discussion sessions with James Toback comparing the two films. In this case the remake was made to function as part of an alternative marketing approach, one commonly used with proven success in literary-based screen adaptations, in which each work brings added value to the other. The question which immediately springs to mind, one which a number of critics and commentators on both sides of the Atlantic have indeed posed, is whether *Beat* will prove the first in a line of successful French remakes, and whether such a prospect might assist in reversing local and global market trends, helping to stem the tidal wave of Hollywood and swing the balance of the long-standing love–hate Franco-American romance back in a more positive direction.

> [C]ould we just possibly be looking at the first frisky sparks of a rekindling of the traditional Franco-American love affair? Are we witnessing a daring re-eroticising of the tired old transatlantic bedroom routine of decades past? Instead of flabby Hollywood retreads of Gallic box-office hits, can we anticipate fresh revivifyings of those seminal but flawed movie classics of the US counterculture, all modishly spruced up in smart new *gilets*?
>
> (Kemp 2005: 45)

Conclusion

We hope to have demonstrated that Audiard's film is indeed a 'fresh revivifying' of its hypotextual source. We have argued for the film as a textbook case in favour of the rehabilitation of the transcultural remake as creative adaptation. We have noted ways in which its successful marketing in conjunction with its American source signals the possibility of a more inclusive, mutually beneficial relationship between original and remake. And although one swallow does not a summer make, it appears to us that *Beat*'s reversal of the long-standing Hollywood monopoly of the transatlantic remake both renews with a positive tradition of cultural cross-fertilization at the heart of noir and introduces the enticing possibility that the ongoing Franco-American film story might again come to resemble a true exchange.

Notes

Introduction

1. David Bellos, for example, is loath to pin down Tati as a symptom of French-ness. David Bellos, *Jacques Tati: His Life and Art* (London: The Harvill Press, 1999).
2. We might think of David Harvey's *Paris, Capital of Modernity* (New York; London: Routledge, 2003) or Patrice Higonnet's *Paris, capitale du monde: Des Lumières au surréalisme* (Paris: Tallandier, 2006).
3. We should like to acknowledge our debt here to Ross Chambers, whose work on *Loiterature* has had such an impact on our conceptualization of modernity, and whose language (of 'dogging' and 'haunting') is so difficult to go past.
4. James Naremore, *More Than Night: Film Noir in its Contexts* (Berkeley, Los Angeles and London: University of California Press, 1998).
5. Woody Haut, *Pulp Culture: Hardboiled Fiction and the Cold War* (London: Serpent's Tail, 1995), and *Neon Noir: Contemporary American Crime Fiction* (London: Serpent's Tail, 1999).
6. Geoffrey O'Brien, *Hardboiled America: Lurid Paperbacks and the Masters of Noir* (New York: Van Nostrand Reinhold, 1981).

1   Fetishistic Noir: Charles Baudelaire and Léo Malet

1. We are deliberately using fetish terminology as expounded by Ellen Lee McCallum, whose work we return to in later chapters.
2. For the Surrealists, Objective Chance describes an event that appears to be random when considered objectively, that is from an outsider's perspective. When considered subjectively, however, it is deemed to be driven by unconscious desires that are eventuating in the 'real world'.
3. *Le Chagrin et la pitié*, Marcel Ophuls's documentary of the Occupation, was first released in Paris on 5 April 1971.
4. If one did not know better, one might be tempted to see in Deleuze's use of the term *vert-de-gris* a Freudian slip, an unconscious acknowledgment that Malet's novel has somehow been made relevant by the retrospective light of Duhamel's translation of Cheyney.
5. Gorrara deals with the following: French fiction vs. American fiction, France vs. Germany, rich vs. poor, occupied vs. non-occupied and the everyday vs. the oneiric.
6. For the fetishist-heroes of post-war French noir fiction, the phallic woman will not turn out to be real; rather there is a real woman and a fetish, and to solve the mystery, the truth must be taken out of the abstract realm and brought into the existential world. Likewise in Baudelaire's prose poems the statues remain mute before the townsfolk, the dream and reality interlocking but resisting communication.

7. The basic shift in perspective in Baudelaire's poetry is from the objective narrative position of his verse, which is generally written by a poet who has observed his subject matter and has returned to his garret in order to 're-present' what he saw at a later stage (as such, his objectivity relies not only on an elevated position but also on the passing of time), to a mitigated perspective in the prose poem form, which is that of the flâneur, who simultaneously presents and represents his subjects (that is to say, that he is both part of the crowd and separate from it, both pulled in and critically objective). The development of literary Modernism hinges on this mitigated position becoming that of the reader, who is both pulled into the text (by a compelling narrative) and repelled by it (forced to read critically by the text's own reflexive gestures, its tendency to remind the reader of its status as literary text). As flâneurs we read more actively, we re-read. Ross Chambers is one of the most eloquent voices to lament the contemporary move away from such 'loiterly' reading as we submit increasingly to a culture of speed.
8. The Surrealists became famous for making art out of anything, and then (e.g. in Marcel Duchamp's case) denying that it was art at all, preferring to justify the importance of their installations in terms of the objects themselves. For his part, Baudelaire operated a poetics of neutrality; all objects were worthy of his glance. And as soon as a goddess is on the same level as a street, she or any other object can be the subject of the most intense scrutiny.
9. References here are to Louise Varène's 1931 translation of the *Petits Poèmes en prose* as published by New Directions under the title *Paris Spleen* (New York, 1970), in this case 'Evening Twilight', p. 45.
10. There are perhaps in this image of the doctor, with blood still on his apron, overtones of Baudelaire's interest in Edgar Allan Poe as well as a premonition of the infamous Whitechapel murders that would follow twenty years after the publication of the prose poems.
11. Charles Baudelaire, 'To a Woman Passing By', in *The Flowers of Evil*, trans. by James McGowan (Oxford: Oxford University Press, 1993), p.189.
12. It will be shown how Boris Vian's work draws on the fashions of the day as well as literature of the past; Nestor Burma too is an avid reader of such publications as *Vogue*, which strike a contrast with Baudelaire and Poe.
13. In cinematographic terms a MacGuffin is a device that drives the plot, but which is otherwise considered of little relevance to a film's overall meaning. It was a term often used by Hitchcock and one that is generally associated with thrillers. Malet's use of the term is potentially both coy and cleverly deceptive: the dwarf is a small and insignificant character; his insignificance, however, is precisely how he drives the main plotline. Here he is a pointer to the novel's articulation with Baudelairean prose poetry and, as such, his cameo role is of crucial relevance to the production of meaning in the work.
14. This southbound flight and derailment, of course, recall the retreat of the French government at the beginning of the Occupation.

2 Liberation Noir: Boris Vian and the Série Noire (1)

1. In Chapter 1 it was seen how poetic objectivity is provided by the distancing quality of time (a poet's verse is formulated belatedly, to use Ross Chambers's

term). Here, the objectivity necessary for successful allegory is provided both by physical and linguistic distance. To this more traditional idea of latitude is then added the extra remove of translation, which allows what is, effectively, a disingenuous appearance of objectivity (that is to say, that Marcel Duhamel writes his allegory of France via a body of text that he translates at times loosely, and which is there only to lend credence to his story).

2. We should be less tentative than Boris Vian in our praise; indeed, the importance of Marcel Duhamel's translated version of *La Môme vert-de-gris* will be the subject of Chapter 3.

3. Raymond Chandler himself, though born American, was in fact naturalized British.

4. 'One day Boris Vian will become Boris Vian,' he enigmatically wrote in his famous foreword to the last of Vian's novels, *L'Arrache-cœur* (Paris: Vrille, 1953).

5. Boris Vian's work has been gaining an increasingly widespread popular following in recent years; this is due in no small part to the publication of many new (and retranslated) titles in English translation by TamTam Books in California. The title of Dan Halpern's review article in *The New Yorker* (25 December 2006) gives a feel for the aura that still envelops Vian the author: 'The Art of Extinction: How Boris Vian brought Cool to Paris.' (www.newyorker.com/archive/2006/12/25/061225crbo_books1   [accessed 1 May 2008]).

6. This construction of noir's development would typically show it being christened in France, and more specifically in Paris, travelling back to the United States where it grows up, flourishing under its French identity, before being translated back into French—in all its Americanness—and recapturing the Parisian imagination.

7. *L'Écume des jours* has been variously translated into English as *Froth on the Daydream* (by Stanley Chapman—London: Rapp and Carroll, 1967), *Mood Indigo* (by John Sturrock—New York: Grove Press, 1968) and, most recently, *Foam of the Daze* (by Brian Harper—California: TamTam Books, 2003). Given the difficulty of translating Vian's work, the French title is used throughout (as is the case for most of the works discussed in this study) and all quotations are translated by the authors.

8. In the last decade of his life Vian's production shifted away from novels (apart from his notorious noir parodies, his novels met with no real commercial success until after his death) towards poems, songs and jazz journalism.

9. For a more detailed reading of the fine line between free will and determinism in the novel, see Rolls (2000).

10. For a whodunit interpretation of *L'Écume des jours*, see Rolls (2004).

11. Clearly, the passer-by in Baudelaire's poem, 'À une passante', to which Vian appeals in this depiction of leg fetishism, is not wearing nylons. Indeed, as was seen in Chapter 1, Baudelaire's figure of the woman passing by is an iconic image and a necessary point of reference in all Parisian literary instances of this kind. Vian's choice of material here marks an unmistakable modernization of the Baudelairean Ur-text, which is ironic given the importance of Baudelaire's woman passing by in the development of modernity and the mourning of a lost Paris in the mid-nineteenth century.

12. Virtually no mention is made of the nylon stocking in the pages of such fashion publications as *Elle* in the years immediately following the Liberation. Indeed, given that advertisements for leg-tinting products continued to appear in the fashion press for some time after the end of the Second World War, we might suggest that rumours of nylon's appearance at the time of Liberation have been greatly exaggerated.

13. While it is important to note that it took some time for the French to become used to all things American, it should also be noted that the French still remain markedly ambiguous in relation to the Americanization of their culture. In the twenty-first century brands such as McDonald's are still feared in France as symbols of the decay of traditional French cuisine, and this despite their ubiquitous footprint—and huge popularity—on French soil, which now dates back well into the last century.

14. When viewed from this perspective, *L'Écume des jours* is a tale of tragic defeat, and the status of the individual becomes shrouded in ambiguity. The poem, 'Elle serait là, si lourde', on the other hand, in which Vian chooses a small bird over a modern train, is a perfect example of his rejection of the tide of modernity in the face of intimate and timeless beauty (Boris Vian, *Je voudrais pas crever* [Paris: Pauvert, 1962]).

15. For a more detailed account of Isis as potential bawd, see Rolls (1999).

3 Allegorical Noir: Boris Vian and the Série Noire (2)

1. Excellent recent studies of this relationship include Colin Nettelbeck's *Dancing with de Beauvoir: Jazz and the French* (Melbourne: Melbourne University Press, 2005).

2. Speculation as to whether this incident was a spontaneous and genuine expression of public exasperation or a stunt staged entirely for the benefit of the media, far from nullifying its significance, serves merely to increase the symbolic value of the event as an indicator of the prevalent mood of the day.

3. Cf. Rolls (1999, 2000).

4. In such a reading, the removal of her hair stands as a symbol of revenge, the heart that Alise snatches from her victims recalling the wave of purges that saw the hair shorn from thousands of alleged collaborators and the heart taken out of the celebrations that marked the end of the Occupation.

5. We should like to thank our colleague Toni Johnson-Woods of the University of Queensland whose thoughts on this issue have been a source of inspiration.

6. Those translating Cheyney's early novels for the Série Noire collection include Marcel Duhamel (*La Môme vert-de-gris* (1945) / *Poison Ivy* (1937) and *Cet Homme est dangereux* (1945) / *This Man is Dangerous* (1936)), Jean Weil (*Comment qu'elle est!* (1948) / *I'll Say She Does!* (1945)) and Michelle and Boris Vian (*Les Femmes s'en balancent* (1949) / *Dames Don't Care* (1937)).

7. In addition to the work by Marc Lapprand to which we refer here, we might mention J. K. L. Scott's 'Imagined Americas: Boris Vian, Vernon Sullivan and the Franco-American Thriller' (*Cincinnati Romance Review*, 17, 1998, 137–47) and Geoffrey Harris's edited volume of essays, *Through the Anglo-French*

Looking-Glass: Essays in Translating French Literature and Film (New York; Amsterdam: Rodopi, 1996).

8. The novel was published in translation in Paris in 1949.

9. Accordingly, we have chosen to translate the French text of *La Môme vert-de-gris* ourselves throughout, rather than reverting to Cheyney's 'original English' because our emphasis is on the former, and specifically, on the translation choices made in the production of the French version of the novel, some of which would not be clear if our analysis were supported by Cheyney's own words.

10. The films to which Borde and Chaumeton are referring are: John Huston's *The Maltese Falcon*, Otto Preminger's *Laura*, Edward Dmytryk's *Murder, My Sweet*, Billy Wilder's *Double Indemnity*, and Fritz Lang's *The Woman in the Window*.

11. As captured, for example, by Robert Doisneau in photographs such as 'Au Saint-Yves, Saint-Germain-des-Prés, 1947', which is featured in the collection *Doisneau – La Fête*, published by Tana éditions.

12. Jill Forbes and Michael Kelly describe this poster as 'one of the most striking images of the period'; they go on to offer a comprehensive analysis of the ambiguity of the symbolism at work in Colin's image (1995: 103–4).

13. In the Freudian schema, the fetish is adopted by a man who wishes to keep alive his myth-based view of his mother as phallic despite his knowledge that this is not the case.

14. It is interesting to note that geographical setting is not in itself a valid excuse for seeking to exclude texts authored by non-French writers from the canon of French noir fiction. For whilst non-French authors occasionally set their texts in France, the first French authors to be included in Duhamel's series do the reverse, as shown in Chapter 4.

15. Indeed, Conrath deems the Série Noire to function as a popularized form of Existentialism. It should be noted, in passing, that Georges Simenon's Maigret novels, for example, which may be considered traditional French detective stories, whilst far from gritty, are just as nostalgic and allegorical insofar as the resolution of the crime is rarely more than a pretext for lamenting the gradual disappearance of 'essentially' French customs. Indeed, the very classification of detective stories according to a binary opposition of whodunit and hard-boiled can be rather misleading; only a small leap on the part of the reader is required in order for the authorial power over 'truth' of the classic sleuth to collapse and for the whodunit to become just as noir as any hard-boiled text.

16. We are, of course, the first to admit that detective fiction is, almost necessarily and by its very nature, an overwhelmingly self-referential genre, be it the whodunit or the hard-boiled variety. Our discussion of Lemmy Caution's referencing of the art of detection and detection fiction is predicated on a simple question of degrees: he is particularly 'lost at sea' and his satire is particularly acerbic.

17. San Reima's foreign accent, and the fact that it appears to enhance the story, is just one more sign of the novel's suitability for allegorical translation.

18. Harberry Chase's hand, of course, symbolizes the body part with which the author orchestrates the plot of the thriller.

4   Noir strangulation (1): Terry Stewart and Vernon Sullivan

1. Lennie's actions are all the more powerful, even graceful, for their simplicity: 'And then she was still, for Lennie had broken her neck.' John Steinbeck, *Of Mice and Men* (London: Penguin, 2000), p. 90.
2. Ian Fleming, *Casino Royale, Live and Let Die, Moonraker* (London: Penguin, 2003), pp. 56–7.
3. One might note the number of articles (academic and otherwise) whose titles bear the '*Des...et des...*' ('Of...and of...') structure of *Des Souris et des hommes*, the French translation of *Of Mice and Men*. We should suggest that this use is rarely unconnected to Steinbeck's novel.
4. It should be noted in passing that at the time of the successful market release of *J'irai cracher sur vos tombes* Boris Vian was proud of one of his novels alone: *L'Écume des jours*. That his Sullivan novels have become as famous as those written in his own name would undoubtedly have been a source of consternation for him.
5. In a deliberately ironic twist, Boris Vian himself 'translated' *J'irai cracher sur vos tombes* into English as *I Spit on Your Graves*. This version (as translated by Vian and Milton Rosenthal) was republished in the United States in 1998 by TamTam Books. Here as elsewhere, all references to the text are our own translations of the French version.
6. It is no coincidence that *Tropic of Cancer* was first published in Paris; Samuel Beckett and many black American writers had also found outlets there for their works. Miller would have been far too scandalous for the American market, a point that strengthens Vian's claim for his disturbing tale to be more Latin than American. For a full account of Paris's role in the publication of works by white Anglo-Saxon and African American writers in exile, see James Campbell, *Paris Interzone* (London: Vintage, 2001).
7. As is shown in the introduction to the present volume, Boris Vian's preface to *J'irai cracher sur vos tombes* is deliberately steeped in contradiction: while drawing on familiar American sources to validate his novel's credentials, he simultaneously paints the picture of a French literary tradition whose hallmarks are originality and subtlety. Vernon Sullivan will thus display subtlety beneath a veneer of violence and originality under a veil of familiar resonances.
8. Such a literary hierarchy within the ensemble of writings referred to as noir has to sit alongside a debate as to the merits of all noir, which writers such as Thomas Narcejac considered to be not only a para-literary phenomenon but non-literary and liable to degrade literature (e.g. his work *La Fin d'un Bluff.* Paris: Le Portulan, 1949).
9. These three authors can be classified in other ways: for example, both Boris Vian and Jean Meckert specify in their first novels that they are translating the works of Vernon Sullivan and John Amila, respectively; Serge Arcouët's name, on the other hand, makes no such appearance in *La Mort et l'ange*.
10. Gorrara, for example, is quite candid on this issue in the introduction to *The 'Roman Noir' in Post-War French Culture*. Whilst she mentions the possibility of establishing a link to the eighteenth-century Gothic tradition

(2003a: 24), she nonetheless locates her entry into noir in the United States of the inter-war years.

11. Gorrara, for her part, is categorical in giving this title to Léo Malet for his novel of 1943, *120, rue de la Gare*. This she calls the first French *roman noir* (2003b: 592).

12. Both the English and French editions post-date *J'irai cracher sur vos tombes*, appearing in 1947 and 1948 respectively.

13. These names lend themselves to the concept of passing on traditions. Lee Anderson's surname is extremely close to the second most common surname in Sweden: Andersson. Patronymic names, which expose the bearer's descendancy, are much used in Sweden. Although Stewart's character is named Sweed, and not Swede, there are clear grounds to suspect a passing on of certain homicidal literary genes.

14. While Ben Sweed is indeed executed, this is done with all due process. As for the role of a sexual motive in Sweed's crimes, this lies precisely in his impotence or the very inversion of the sex drive as exploited in *J'irai cracher sur vos tombes*.

15. It is interesting to note that Tucker, herself Jewish, often appeared on stage, in an overt show of inversion, in black make-up. For a more extensive reading of the role of inversion, and specifically in relation to the song *Some of These Days*, see Rolls (2003).

16. In addition to Pestureau's suggestion that Buckton is a town where one can make a buck (1977: 349), it is also an English rendering of *Boucville*, only one letter away from Sartre's fictional town.

17. References throughout are to Robert Baldick's famous 1963 translation of *Nausea* (London: Penguin, 2000).

18. To borrow a term used by Marc Lapprand in his analysis of the methodology adopted by Vian when translating such texts as Chandler's *The Lady of the Lake* for the Série Noire. See Lapprand (1992).

19. The case of Edmond Rougé was only one factor in the eventual banning of the novel. For a detailed account of events surrounding the publication of *J'irai cracher sur vos tombes*, see Noël Arnaud *Le Dossier de l'affaire 'J'irai cracher sur vos tombes'* (Paris: Bourgois, 1974).

20. The dancing in the milk bar in Buckton—a scarcely veiled reference to the zazous and bobby-soxers of Saint-Germain-des-Prés—provides an explanation of the origins of the *biglemoi*, the dance favoured by the characters of *L'Écume des jours*. When Lee returns exhausted from dancing, he is asked: 'What have you been doing? The shag with a Negress?' (Sullivan 1973: 58). Dancing the *biglemoi* in the style of black dancers is prohibited by Colin's manservant Nicolas because it has sexual connotations. The shag is a frenetic dance, which corresponds closely to the explanations outlined by Nicolas. Hence the sexual overtones here are primarily intertextual in origin, although the sexual connotations of the term 'shag' had become part of English colloquial usage by 1946. As further proof of this link to *L'Écume des jours*, Lee later explains that he was taught to dance by his grandfather, and that he has spent time in France in domestic service. This suggests that Nicolas is Lee's (intertextual) grandfather.

21. As Neil Levy explains in his work on Sartre, to make choices in the absence of parameters is not to act freely but to act arbitrarily. So, perverse as it may

seem, it is the very limits imposed by the chosen project that allows us to activate our freedom; in the same way, it is the nothingness, the negating film that distances us from the world, which binds us inexorably to it (Levy 2002: 109). The curiously fixed freedom of the project suggests that Lee freely embraces the intertextual weight of such texts as *Of Mice and Men*, which serve to taint clear water with the memory of age-old murder.

22. The death is also intertextually bound to *J'irai cracher sur vos tombes*; it refers to the death of the kid, which combines a 'coming of age' with the need for murder. There is additionally a potential allegorical significance, according to which the death of Ben's mother may be seen to symbolize the loss of control that followed the disempowerment of the French Republic under the Occupation. For evidence of intertextual links between Camus's *L'Étranger* and Boris Vian's *L'Automne à Pékin*, see Rolls (1999). The transatlantic literary exchange is complex here, however, as *L'Étranger* was also inspired by the American hard-boiled tradition. Camus himself admitted that James M. Cain's *The Postman always Rings Twice* had had a direct influence on his novel.

23. The pleasure of Roland Barthes's *Le Plaisir du texte* (*The Pleasure of the Text*) also juxtaposes, merges and seems to synthesize these same drives: *plaisir*, the pleasure felt in the consolidation of the ego (one transparent identity), and *jouissance*, the bliss felt in fragmentation of the ego (dissolution of identity).

24. Although Lee Anderson does not share the same privileged situation—the narrative shifts definitively to the third person once he is dead whereas Ben's narrative is throughout his story a first-person soliloquy within a third-person framework—he does manage to outlive himself, to borrow an expression from Anny in *La Nausée*, when undergoing a brief post-mortem adventure (he is lynched by the good burghers only after his death), which allows him to pass on into the form of Ben Sweed.

25. The nothingness that distances me from myself and me from others is here the same void that lies between Ben Sweed and his predecessors in other texts. Intertextuality itself can be seen to function in much the same way as human existence: the membrane that simultaneously separates and joins man and his situation is akin to the difference (uniqueness of all 'texts') and similarity (interconnectedness of all 'text') expressed in all textual relations, the multiplicity and oneness of the intertext.

26. Sandra Abbott refers on various occasions to the inevitability of Ben's condition, as if he has another's blood in his veins: 'You are possessed, Ben' and 'I can only think that it's in your blood' (Stewart 1972: 64, 72). And this is an opinion that Ben comes to share: 'I don't know how it came about [*c'est venu*]...Perhaps it's just the way I am. Perhaps I got it at birth' (Stewart 1972: 81).

27. Although it is true that she has already been informed of this fact, her eyes immediately allow her to feel the reports to be true.

28. Our thanks here to Meg Vertigan from the University of Newcastle, who first alerted us to the possibility of reading this scene from the perspective of strangulation.

29. Necrophilia ceases to be metaphorical at the end of the novel when Lee finally synthesizes his sexual and homicidal impulses by possessing Jean's dead body while it is still warm, at which point he remarks that 'shining

things passed before my eyes' (Sullivan 1973: 200). The shooting stars that accompany this synthesis of apparent binary opposites comes close to signifying Sartre's underlying value (the impossible being for-itself-in-itself) or the surrealist *point suprême*—one may call to mind, for example, the vivid images of the merging of death and sexual desire in Buñuel's *Un Chien andalou*, which is accompanied by a convulsion of the eyes.

30. Roquentin's Nausea with its capital 'N' is not necessarily any different to the noir nausea that dominates Ben and Lee; in this light, it is an urge to murder that has caused him to isolate himself in Bouville.

31. Parallel to this is the most common misapprehension about Nausea, which is that it can be read as a metaphor (e.g., for the drudgery of existence). In fact, all concrete instances of nausea, such as vomiting, are metaphors for the fundamental nature of our existence, the realization of which is Nausea.

5   Noir Strangulation (2): Amélie Nothomb and Intertextuality

1. As a tale told from the perspective of the criminal, *J'irai cracher sur vos tombes* can be compared to works such as Horace McCoy's *Kiss Tomorrow Goodbye* (1948) (published in the Série Noire in 1949 as *Adieu la vie, adieu l'amour*) and the works of Boileau-Narcejac (although their narrators tend to be both criminal and victim).

2. The translation is Vian's own. Indeed, Vian translated the whole novel into English in order to provide the proof, a posteriori, that *J'irai cracher* was indeed a translation of an American novel. As noted in Chapter 4, the quotations used in the present volume are our own translation of the French 'original'.

3. This is an approximate translation of the French title. Strangely, Amélie Nothomb's first novel is one of the few not to have yet appeared in English translation.

4. David Gascoigne offers an excellent analysis of the functioning of what he calls 'embedded narratives' in his recent study *The Games of Fiction: Georges Perec and Modern French Ludic Narrative* (Bern: Peter Lang, 2006), Chapter 11.

5. For example, *Viols gratuits entre deux guerres* (*Gratuitous Rape Between the Wars*), *Les Sales gens* (*Dirty People*), *Sinistre total* (*Total Black-out*), *La Mort et j'en passe* (*Death, etc.*), *Le Désordre de la jarretière* (*Garter Trouble*) and *Le Poker, la femme et les autres* (*Poker, Women and the Rest*). Despite Nothomb's obvious satirical edge, these titles pass muster as possible noir novels. The obvious exception is *Perles pour un massacre* (*Pearls for a Massacre*), which picks up Tach's stated debt to Céline, one of whose most notorious texts is entitled *Bagatelles pour un massacre* (*Trinkets for a Massacre*); it also reminds the reader of one of Amélie Nothomb's favourite expressions—*margaritas ante porcos* (pearls to swine) (Nothomb 1992: 26): instead of high literature for unworthy readers, these titles suggest low quality writing that has been read by an expert reader in Nina.

6. 'Writer, killer: two aspects of the same profession, two conjugations of the same verb' (Nothomb 1992: 115).

7. Akin to the structuralist reading of Honoré de Balzac's *Sarrasine* offered by Roland Barthes in *S/Z*.
8. The jousting between pleasure (*le plaisir*) and bliss (*la jouissance*) reflect the battle between the readerly and the writerly. The pleasure of reading and writing, for Nina and Tach, seems to combine both, just as it does in Barthes's *Le Plaisir du texte*. Cf. Chapter 4, note 23.
9. In addition to being redolent of Roquentin's world-view in *La Nausée*, the confrontation of Tach and Nina allows for the establishment of a dichotomy that sees man as author opposed to woman as reader. In such a binary Tach's misogyny can be read as a metaphorical defence of the readerly text, Barthes's ironic definition of literature in *S/Z*.
10. Sandra Abbott, the muse of Terry Stewart's dark angel, can thus be considered a noir prototype for Léopoldine.
11. The way the cartilage is snapped—by strangulation—also simultaneously breaks and founds the intertextuality linking *Hygiène de l'assassin* to earlier novels.
12. This double meaning has the added result of promoting *J'irai cracher sur vos tombes*, where, genetically speaking, Ben's serial killing begins, into the Série Noire.
13. Hermann Hesse's Harry (a.k.a. the Steppenwolf), knows only too well the danger of seeing his reflection in 'that mirror in which he has such bitter need to look and from which he shrinks in such deathly fear', for the reflection in the mirror awaits only death, a death whose arrival is imminent (Hesse 1965: 237).
14. The way Ben lays his finger on Maat's arm (Stewart 1972: 124), as if he is confiding in him, functions as an allusion to the diary-style tropes of the modernist novel, which serve to implicate the reader in the production of (unpalatable) meaning. By this stage of the novel such contact is made, in Sartrean terms, with a body already frozen beyond consciousness as adventure-text.
15. Intertextuality depends on the borders of books being simultaneously fixed in place (allowing for one work to be distinguishable from another), which is the fixity craved as a means of calming existential angst by Sartre's Roquentin in *La Nausée*, and permeable (allowing text(s) quasi-infinite scope for interpenetration).
16. Readers of Boris Vian will recognize in this type of admission the words of an author for whom formulaic detective fiction (à la Vernon Sullivan) is a *gagne-pain*, a way of making a living, a way of nourishing the man in order to make the writing of 'real literature' a financial possibility.

6 Jazz: Classic French Film Noir as Transatlantic Exchange

1. These included *The Maltese Falcon, Double Indemnity, Laura, Murder My Sweet, The Lost Weekend, The Woman in the Window*.
2. This term refers to a body of French noir-precursor films of the 1930s, marked by dark fatalism, featuring tragic popular heroes (usually played by Jean Gabin), and combining 'realist' working-class settings with highly evocative, symbolic use of props, décor, lighting, music and dialogues adapted from

contemporary Francophone writers like Georges Simenon, Pierre Véry and Pierre Mac Orlan, or written for the screen by the supreme poet of simplicity, Jacques Prévert). For the most informative and insightful work on poetic realism, see Andrew (1995).

3. The remake phenomenon is discussed in detail in Chapter 10.

4. We have borrowed this term from Dudley Andrew, *Mists of Regret: Culture and Sensibility in Classic French Film* (New Jersey: Princeton University Press, 1995).

5. The burning issue of *l'exception culturelle*, in which Franco-American rivalry plays out on and through the cinema screens of the world, is discussed in greater detail in Chapters 9 and 10.

6. All box office statistics from official and industry sources, accessed through CBO Box Office online, www.cbo-boxoffice.com (12 May 2008).

7. In the comic mode, Jacques Tati's anti-modernization works, *Jour de Fête* (*Holiday*) (1949); *Mon oncle* (*My* Uncle) (1958); *Playtime* (1967) explicitly associate a sterile, consumerist modernity with the American Way.

8. The full, uncut version of the film would not be available in the States until 1991. For a brief review and selection of deleted scenes, see The Criterion Collection 2DVD Edition.

9. For a thorough review of the affair, see Veray (2002).

10. Constantine's most notable reappearance as Lemmy Caution is in Jean-Luc Godard's off-beat sci-fi feature *Alphaville* (1965).

11. Living spaces inhabited by protagonists of Jules Dassin's *Du rififi chez chez les hommes* [*Rififi Means Trouble*] (1955; see Chapter 8), while less ostentatious, also display the iconic features of modern consumer comfort, including modern kitchens, baths, showers and vacuum cleaners.

12. More recently (and disappointingly) remade by Neil Jordan as *The Honest Thief* (a.k.a. *The Good Thief,* 2001).

13. The film is based on Vian's original screenplay (Vian 1989), in which he modified much of the plot and changed the names of the novel's three central characters and main town. Thus, the Lee Anderson of the novel became Joe Grant; Lou and Jean Asquith became Lisbeth and Sylvia Shannon; the town of Buckton was renamed Trenton. Michel Gast and his co-writers also renamed and remodelled the characters of Dexter, who became Stan Walker, and the bookshop owner Hansen, whose role was greatly expanded as Horace Chandley.

14. Narratives that centre on protagonists attempting to pass for racially other, generally black or mixed-race passing as white, as in Nella Larsen, *Passing* (2002). First published in 1929, Larsen's seminal work tells the story of two such women, one of whom has successfully crossed the 'color line' in 1920s New York.

15. The film was a Franco-German-Italian co-production but with a majority French interest.

16. Though there is no such décor in Vian's screenplay, the latter's geography is equally muddled since in the final scene, Joe and Lisbeth flee over the border to Mexico.

17. Godard's *Le petit soldat,* made in 1960, was banned until after the conflict, not being released until 1963. Recall also the role of the French authorities in the non-release of Kubrick's *Paths of Glory,* as mentioned above.

18. Henri Alleg's autobiographical account of being tortured by French paratroopers caused such a stir that it was banned and withdrawn from circulation weeks after its release (see Alleg 1958).
19. In fact, Joe Grant intervenes surreptitiously to save the second reluctant volunteer (played by a very young Claude Berri) by short-circuiting the electrical mains just as the torture is about to begin.
20. (Le roman policier est un genre inférieur mais il nous apprend à être perspicace!).

7 Fatal(e) Crossings: Figures of the Feminine in French and American Film Noir

1. The adage is explicitly evoked in Melville's *Deux hommes à Manhattan* (1959) and reprised in Polanski's neo-noir classic, *Chinatown* (1974).
2. The figure of the ill-fated lovers or *amants maudits* is a hallmark of late 1930s poetic realist classics such as *Le quai des brumes* (Carné, 1938), *La bête humaine* (Renoir, 1938) and *Le jour se lève* (Carné, 1939).
3. The behaviour of this figure is offset by Signoret in the role of Lili, a good-hearted and much adored barmaid and prostitute, whose sexual generosity tragically precipitates the suicide of a desperate young Resistance fighter. Like *Bob le Flambeur*, therefore, the film also sees the classic *fatale* figure split between two characters, in this case: the wife as *garce* and Lili as *fatalitaire*.
4. For a discussion of militant and civic cinema, see Hayward (1993), pp. 241–3.
5. See Chapter 9.

8 Americans in Paris

1. The film also inspired a number of parodies, including Mario Monicelli's celebrated Italian caper movie *I Soliti ignoti (Big Deal on Madonna Street, 1958)* and Dassin's own *Topkapi* (1964).
2. In Buhle and Wagner (2003), p. xvii.
3. Regrettably, space does not allow us to discuss Losey's contribution to French noir, most notably for *Mr Klein* (1975), starring Alain Delon in a sombre Occupation drama of mistaken identity, foregrounding the Vichy deportation of French Jews.
4. See also Humphries (1996).
5. In *Rififi*, Dassin continues this somewhat un-American approach. Anecdotally, he recounts how his producer, Henri Bérard, was frustrated by the film's lack of 'Rififi' à la Lemmy Caution. 'He'd keep insisting, "Where are the fights, where are the fights?" and I'd say, "Well, next week, next week!"' (Borger 2003).
6. Truffaut (1955b).
7. Dassin has claimed in interviews that he had not seen *Asphalt Jungle* when he made *Rififi*.
8. The latter was Dassin's choice, for which he famously had to work hard to convince his collaborators. Veteran composer, Georges Auric had wanted to score the entire sequence and author Le Breton (who wrote the dialogues) had planned to insert a single word referring to the key prop: *Umbrella*.

9. If Melville preferred to cite Huston rather than Dassin as major stylistic influence, it was no doubt in large part out of pique at producer Bérard's decision to drop him from the direction of *Rififi*. See Borger (2003).
10. Dassin was a fervent admirer of neo-realism, particularly of Rossellini's *Rome Open City* (1945).
11. Written in 1955, thus pre-dating *Bob le Flambeur* (1956).
12. The dialogues include a specific homage to the writer, with Burma declaring at one point: *We must call Malet*.
13. Reggiani also had a successful acting career, playing leading roles in two French noir classics: as Georges Manda in Becker's *Casque d'or* [*Golden Marie*] (1952) and as Maurice Faugel in Melville's *Le doulos* [*The Fingerman*] (1962).
14. '*Que diable, si vous avez tant besoin de vous libérer de vos instincts sournois, rendez-vous compte que le roman, la poésie, la fiction, la simple fantaisie sont là, prêts à vous accueillir, et que, dans ce domaine, tout est permis*', Boris Vian, preface to *Manuel de Saint-Germain-des-Prés* (Paris: Pauvert, 1997), p. 32 (text first published by Éditions du Chêne, 1974).
15. This is also signalled by the use of a film fragment as *mise en abyme*. During a late-night party, Saint Germain organizes a projection of *Les chasses de Count Zaroff* [*The Most Dangerous Game*] (Pichel, 1932), a King Kong-like horror thriller starring Fay Wray. The fragment, a menacing shot of swamp waters evokes monstrous desires about to surface from the murky depths of the psyche (the film is about a sadistic count, a keen hunter whose favourite prey are fellow humans).
16. French *polars* typically figure servants of the state, police inspectors or commissioners (like Maigret) in the detective role.
17. Unless otherwise indicated by a bibliographical note, opinions attributed to and quotes by Bob Swaim are taken from two unpublished interviews with Deborah Walker, conducted in Saint-Germain-des-Prés, Paris, June 2007.
18. '*Les amoureux de Saint-Germain ne savent plus si c'est demain. A force de vivre la nuit, on ne sait pas quel temps on vit.*'
19. This opening close-up is a clear reminder that the prominence of jazz and blues in French noir was due in large part to the physical presence of so many Black musicians in post-war Paris. Historians estimate their numbers to have been around five hundred. Their collective story was later told through Bertrand Tavernier's *Autour de minuit* [*Round* Midnight] (1986), starring jazz saxophonist Dexter Gordon.
20. Fabiani later co-wrote the dialogues for the film and acted as set adviser.
21. Numerous sources erroneously state six months.
22. Both Berry and Baye spent time among police and streetwalkers respectively.
23. In standard French, *une balance* is a set of scales. The verb *balancer*, meaning to swing or rock to and fro, also has a colloquial sense of to throw or 'chuck' which gave rise to the slang expression meaning to 'dob in' or nark.
24. Behind Spielberg's *E.T.* and three French comedies.
25. Claude Zidi's *Les Ripoux* [*My New Partner*]) (1984), which won best picture in 1985 is more a black comedy.
26. Powrie (1997b: 98) claims the film was 'panned by the critics'. This is only true of a small section of the press, as we demonstrate.
27. Press reviews were obtained from the *Bibliothèque du film* in Paris. These are not currently available online from this source.

28. *Libération*, 13.1.1982; *Le Monde*, 13.11.82; *Le canard Enchaîné*, 17.12.1982; *Positif* 263, January 1983.
29. *Les Echos* found the film's violence somewhat brutal and commercially spectacular but praised the roles of the three main protagonists. Influential *France-Soir* critic Robert Chazal was unsure whether *La Balance* was good or simply 'all right' (*passable*). Somewhat sceptical as to the film's central premise (the search for a replacement informer) and documentary foundation, and less than enthusiastic about the casting of Baye and Ronet, Chazal nonetheless praised Léotard's performance as Dédé. Assayas's review for *Cahiers* is discussed within the text.
30. Swaim's skilful location shooting fooled most reviewers, who commented on the film's documentary revelations of Belleville. In fact, apart from two opening establishing shots filmed with a hidden camera, locations were done on the outskirts of Paris, in Puteaux. Ironically, Swaim's locations are visually more convincing than another popular *polar* released earlier the same year, *Le grand pardon* (Arcady, 1982), about the Jewish Pied-Noir mafia, which was shot on location in Belleville.
31. Pialat spent three months with the *Brigades Territoriales*.
32. The film is a highly effective, sombre exposé of France's overworked and under-resourced drugs' squad units.
33. The film's final freeze frame, a close-up of Nicole through a rain-spattered car window as Dédé is handcuffed and led away, also recalls the ending of Sautet's *Max* (see Chapter 7).
34. Strong female protagonists are a feature of Swaim's work, most notably in *Half Moon Street* (UK/USA, 1986, starring Sigourney Weaver) and *Nos amis les flics* [*Cheap Shot*] (France, 2004).

9   From Honest Thief to Media Sociopath

1. Interestingly, the film was later released on video in the United States under the title *The French Conspiracy*.
2. Jean-Louis Trintignant as a hapless journalist, Jean Seberg as his left-wing liberal wife, Gian Maria Volonté as the doomed revolutionary Sadiel (Barka), Michel Piccoli as an evil North African General, Roy Schneider as a CIA operative.
3. See Powrie (2003), p. 61.
4. For the most detailed and insightful reading of Beineix's work, see Powrie (2001).
5. Her character has always refused for her voice to be recorded, leading to the film's music-buff hero 'stealing her voice' by making a clandestine recording during the opening concert. Also of note, the nationality of the film's villains has shifted: the ruthless exploiters of art here are no longer Hollywood producers but Taiwanese gangsters specializing in the burgeoning international trade in pirated music.
6. Tavernier played a key role in setting up the Lumière Institute, film library and archives, raising subsidies and persuading the Lyon municipal authorities to set aside and renovate the one remaining building of those that had once housed the firm of the French inventors of the *cinématographe*.
7. See also Walker (2007).

8. For a detailed analysis, see Jeancolas (1998).
9. Academic commentators have also recognized the role of cultural industries in the construction of national identity. See, for example, Goff (2000), pp. 537–8.
10. Although cultural products were not specifically excluded from the 1993 agreements, European nations made no commitment to move their audio-visual sectors in the direction of free trade.

10 Double-Crossings: Reversing the Remake

1. *Point of No Return* (Badham, 1993) after *Nikita* (Besson, 1990); *Diabolique* (Chechik, 1996) after *Les Diaboliques* (Clouzot, 1955); *Eye of the Beholder* (Elliott, 1999) after *Mortelle Randonnée* (Miller, 1982); *Under Suspicion* (Hopkins, 2000) after *Garde à vue* (Miller, 1982); *Unfaithful* (Lyne, 2001) after *La femme infidèle* (Chabrol, 1968); *Original Sin* (Christofer, 2001) after *La sirène du Mississippi* (Truffaut, 1969); *The Good Thief* (Jordan, 2003) after *Bob le Flambeur* (Melville, 1955). At the time of writing, Dassin's *Rififi* is being remade by Stone Village Pictures, with Al Pacino in the lead role.
2. Cf. Pierre Harlé's article 'Attention aux remakes!' [Beware of Remakes!] published on 23 September 1938 in *La Cinématographie française* (quoted in Moine 2007: 74).
3. It must be noted that seven of these American reprises were made with some level of French involvement (in terms of direction, production or casting).
4. A 1996, Hollywood version, *Last Man Standing*, starring Bruce Willis, credits Kurosawa as writer though not Hammett.
5. Audiard's producer, Pascal Cocheux, had just completed an English-language remake of John Carpenter's *Assault on Precinct 13*, directed (after much resistance from the film's American backers) by French *banlieue* film-maker, Jean François Richet, but filmed in the USA as a conventional American-style action thriller with an all-American cast.
6. For a persuasive, Deleuzian exploration of this theme, see Dobson (2007).
7. Poor Russian illegal immigrants and criminal elements also feature in Xavier Beauvois' *Le Petit Lieutenant* (2005).
8. The song is by Jacques Dutronc, lyrics by Jacques Lanzmann. Disappointingly, the scene including the title line was cut from the final version of the film, as were others featuring diegetic popular French music. The consequent absence of 'indigenous' musical references in favour of exclusively Anglo-American tracks is without doubt reflective of a certain cultural reality: as is the case with cinema, English pop music has overtaken local productions. But whatever the reasons behind this choice, in terms of cultural transposition alone, we feel it constitutes a regrettable error in an otherwise outstanding work.
9. We may recall here the confrontation of the existential protagonist and the reification of abstract beauty in *Nestor Burma contre CQFD*, which was our focus in Chapter 1 above. Here again, we see a trope reminiscent of Baudelaire's famous Venus and the Motley Fool.
10. Retitled *Mélodie pour un tueur* (Melody for a Killer), the film opened in Paris in August 1978, to very mixed reviews, with the conservative press predictably charging Toback with gratuitous use of sex and violence.

Bibliography

Agulhon, M. and Bonte, P. (1992) *Marianne: Les Visages de la République*. Paris: Gallimard.

Alleg, H. (1958) *La Question*. Paris, Editions de Minuit.

Andrew, D. (1995) *Mists of Regret: Culture and Sensibility in Classic French Noir*. New Jersey: Princeton University Press.

Andrew, D. and Morgan, J. (eds) (1996) *European Precursors of Film Noir. Iris* n 21, Spring.

Arnaud, N. (1974) *Dossier de l'affaire «J'irai cracher sur vos tombes»*. Paris: Christian Bourgois.

Austin, G. (1996) *Contemporary French Cinema: An Introduction*. Manchester and New York: Manchester University Press.

Baudelaire, C. (1970) *Paris Spleen*, trans. Louise Varène. New York: New Directions.

—— (1993) *The Flowers of Evil*, trans. James McGowan. Oxford: Oxford University Press.

Bazin, A. (1951) 'A propos des reprises', *Cahiers du cinéma*, September: 52–6.

—— (1952) 'Remade in USA', *Cahiers du cinéma*, September: 54–9.

Beevor, A. and Cooper, A. (1995) *Paris after the Liberation: 1944–1949*. London: Penguin.

Borde, R. and Chaumeton, E. (2002) *A Panorama of American Film Noir 1941–1953*, trans. Paul Hammond. San Francisco: City Lights Books. (This book was originally published in France as *Panorama du film noir américain 1941–1953* by Les Éditions de Minuit in 1955.)

Borger, L. (2003) 'Rififi. Rialto Pictures LCC'. Available 28/12/2007: www.filmforum.org/archivedfilms/rififipress.html.

Bridgeman, T. (1998) 'Paris-Polar in the Fog: Power of Place and Generic Space in Léo Malet's *Brouillard au Pont de Tolbiac*', *Australian Journal of French Studies* 35 (1): 58–74.

Buhle, P. and Wagner, D. (2002) *Radical Hollywood: The Untold Story Behind America's Favorite Movies*. New York: New Press.

—— (2003) *Hide in Plain Sight: The Hollywood Blacklistees in Film and Television, 1952–2002*. New York: Palgrave Macmillan.

Burch, N. and Sellier, G. (1996) *La drôle de guerre des sexes du cinéma français*. Paris: Nathan.

—— (2001) 'Evil Women in Post-War French Cinema' in Sieglohr, U. (ed.) *Heroines without Heroes: Reconstructing Female and National Identities in European Cinema 1945–1951*. London; New York: Cassell.

Buss, R. (1994) *French Film Noir*. London; New York: M. Boyars.

Camus, A. (1990) *L'Étranger*. Paris: Gallimard. (First published by Gallimard in 1942.)

Caputo, R. (1990) 'Film noir: You sure you don't see what you don't hear?' *Continuum* 5 (2): sin pag.

Chambers, R. (1999) *Loiterature*. Lincoln and London: University of Nebraska Press.

Cheyney, P. (1945) *La Môme vert-de-gris*. Paris: Gallimard. (Text quoted: Gallimard's carré noir series, printed in 1982.)

Cohen, R. (1994) 'Aux Armes! France Rallies to Battle Sly and T. Rex', *New York Times*, 2 January, Late Edition (East Coast edn), sec. A: 1.

Conard, M. (2005) 'Nietzsche and the Meaning and Definition of Noir' in Conard, M. (ed.) *The Philosophy of Film Noir*. Lexington: University Press of Kentucky, pp. 7–22.

Conrath, R. (1995) 'Pulp fixation: Le Roman noir américain et son lecteur français d'après-guerre', *La Revue générale* 12: 37–45.

Covin, M. (2000) *L'Homme de la rue: Essai sur la poétique baudelairienne*. Paris: L'Harmattan.

Damico, J. (1996) '*Film Noir*: A Modest Proposal' in Silver, A. and Ursini, J. (eds) *Film Noir Reader*. New York: Limelight Editions, pp. 95–106.

Darke, C. (1995) 'The Bait (L'Appât)', *Sight and Sound* September: 43–4.

Dehée, Y. (2000) *Mythologies politiques du cinéma français*. Paris: Presses Universitaires de France.

Deleuse, R. (1997) 'Petite histoire du roman noir français', *Les Temps Modernes* 595: 51–87.

Diamond, H. (1999) *Women and the Second World War in France 1939–1948. Choices and Constraints*. London: Longman.

Doane, M. (1991) *Femmes fatales: Feminism, Film Theory, Psychoanalysis*. New York: Routledge.

Dobson, J. (2007) 'Jacques Audiard and the Filial Challenge', *Studies in French Cinema* 7 (3): 179–89.

Duchateau, J. (1982) *Boris Vian ou les facéties du destin*. Paris: La Table Ronde.

Duhamel, M. (1972) *Raconte pas ta vie*. Paris: Mercure de France.

Durham, C. (1998) *Double Takes: Culture and Gender in French Films and their American Remakes*. Contemporary French Culture and Society. Hanover, NH and Dartmouth: University Press of New England.

Durozoi, G. (1984) 'Esquisse pour un portrait anthume de Léo Malet en auteur de romans policiers', *Revue des Sciences Humaines*, 64 (193): 169–78.

Ebert, R. (1983) '*La Balance*' (Review), *Chicago Sun Times*. Available 12/01/2008: http://rogerebert.suntimes.com/apps/pbcs.dll/article?AID=/19831223/REVIEWS/312230301/1023.

Film Noir (1994) Video recording directed by Jeffrey Schon. New York Center for Visual History.

Forbes, J. (1991) 'The *Série Noire*' in Rigby, B. and Hewitt, N. (eds) *France and the Mass Media*. London: Macmillan.

—— (1997) 'Winning Hearts and Minds: The American Cinema in France 1945–49', *French Cultural Studies* 8: 29–39.

Forbes, J. and Kelly M. (eds) (1995) *French Cultural Studies: An Introduction*. Oxford: Oxford University Press.

Forrest, J. and Koos, L. (2002) *Dead Ringers: The Remake in Theory and Practice*. SUNY series, cultural studies in cinema/video. Albany: State University of New York Press.

Fournier Lanzoni, R. (2002) *French Cinema from its Beginnings to the Present*. New York: Continuum.

Freud, S. (1961) 'Fetishism' in *The Standard Edition of the Complete Psychological Works of Sigmund Freud*, vol. 21. London: The Hogarth Press and the Institute of Psychoanalysis, pp. 147–57. (This essay was first published in 1927.)

Frodon, J.-M. (1995) *L'Âge moderne du cinéma français: De la Nouvelle Vague à nos jours*. Paris: Flammarion.

Gildea, R. (2002) *France Since 1945* (2nd edition). Oxford: Oxford University Press.

Goff, P. (2000) 'Invisible Borders: Economic Liberalization and National Identity', *International Studies Quarterly* 44 (4): 533–62.

Gorrara, C. (2001) 'Malheurs et ténèbres: Narratives of Social Disorder in Léo Malet's *120, Rue de la Gare*', *French Cultural Studies* 12: 271–83.

—— (2003a) *The 'Roman Noir' in Post-War French Culture*. Oxford: Oxford University Press.

—— (2003b) 'Cultural Intersections: The American Hard-Boiled Detective Novel and Early French *Roman Noir*', *Modern Language Review* 98 (2): 590–601.

Hamilton, D. (2000) 'The roman noir and the Reconstruction of National Identity in Postwar France', in Mullen, A. and O'Beirne, E. (eds) *Crime Scenes: Detective Narratives in European Culture since 1945*. Amsterdam and Atlanta: Rodopi, pp. 228–40.

Handley, S. (1999) *Nylon: The Story of a Fashion Revolution*. Baltimore, Maryland: The John Hopkins University Press.

Harlé, P. (1938) 'Attention aux «remakes»!', *La Cinématographie française*, 23 September. sin. pag.

Harrison, M. (1954) *Peter Cheyney – Prince of Hokum*. London, Neville Spearman.

Hay, S. (2000) *Bertrand Tavernier: The Film-Maker of Lyon*. London; New York: I.B. Tauris.

Hayward, S. (1993) *French National Cinema*. National Cinemas Series. London and New York: Routledge.

—— (1996) *Key Concepts in Cinema Studies*. London and New York: Routledge.

—— (2004) *Simone Signoret: The Star as Cultural Sign*. New York and London: Continuum.

Henry, G. (2004) 'L'âge d'or de Saint-Germain-des-Prés', *Paroles* (Alliance Française) 25 May 2004. www.alliancefrancaise.com.hk/paroles/numeros/187/02.html (15.11.07).

Hesse, H. (1965) *Steppenwolf*. London: Penguin. (First published in Germany by S. Fischer Verlag A.G. in 1927.)

Hirsch, F. (ed.) (1999) *Detours and Lost Highways: A Map of Neo-Noir*. New York: Limelight Editions (1st Limelight).

Horowitz, M. and Schon, J. (1994) 'Film Noir.' (Video recording, in the series: *American Cinema*. New York Center for Visual History.)

Hubert-Lacombe, P. (1996) *Le cinéma français dans la guerre froide: 1946–1956*. Paris: L'Harmattan.

Hugues, P. (1999) *L'envahisseur américain: Hollywood contre Billancourt*. Lausanne: Favre.

Humphries, R. (1996) 'The Politics of Crime and the Crime of Politics: Postwar Noir, the Liberal Consensus and the Hollywood Left' in Silver, A. and Ursini, J. (eds) *Film Noir Reader*. New York: Limelight Editions, pp. 227–45.

Insdorf, A. (1983) 'An American is France's Hot Director' (Review), *New York Times*, 13 November, late edition (East Coast edition): A.17.

Jeancolas, J.-P. (1998) 'From the Blum-Byrnes Agreement to the GATT Affair', in Nowell-Smith, G. and Ricci, S. (eds) *Hollywood and Europe: Economics, Culture, National Identity 1945–95*. London: British Film Institute, pp. 47–60.

Jones, C. (1999) *Boris Vian Transatlantic: Sources, Myths, and Dreams*. New York: Peter Lang.

Kaplan, E. A. (ed.) (1998) *Women in Film Noir*. London: BFI Publishing.

Kemp, P. (2005) 'Shoot the Pianist', *Sight & Sound*, November: 44–5.

Kuisel, R. (1996) *Seducing the French: The Dilemma of Americanization*. Berkeley, Los Angeles and London: University of California Press.

Lapprand, M. (1992) 'Les Traductions parodiques de Boris Vian', *The French Review* 65 (4): 537–46.

Larsen, N. (2002) *Passing*. New York: Modern Library. (Text first published in 1929).

Le Breton, A. (1953) *Du rififi chez les hommes*. Paris: Gallimard.

Levy, N. (2002) *Sartre*. Oxford: Oneworld.

McCallum, E.L. (1999) *Object Lessons: How to do Things with Fetishism*. New York: State University of New York Press.

McDonald, N. (2001) 'Fidélité et Maladie (The French Film)', *Quadrant* 45 (5): 65–7.

McGilligan, P. (1996) 'Jules Dassin', *Film Comment* 32 (6): 34–49.

Malet, L. (1985) *Les Enquêtes de Nestor Burma et Les Nouveaux mystères de Paris*. Paris: Robert Laffont. (This edition, overseen by Francis Lacassin, contains both the Malet novels referred to in the present volume, i.e. *120, Rue de la Gare* (1943) and *Nestor Burma contre CQFD* (1945)).

Maslin, J. (1983) '*La Balance*' (Review), *New York Times*, 20 November.

Mathy, J.-P. (1989) ' "L'Américanisme" est-il un humanisme? Sartre aux États-Unis (1945–46)', *The French Review* 62 (3): 456–66.

Mazdon, L. (2000) *Encore Hollywood: Remaking French Cinema*. London: British Film Institute.

Meakin, D. (1996) *Vian: 'L'Écume des jours' (Glasgow Introductory Guides to French Literature)*. Glasgow: University of Glasgow French and German Publications.

Mesplède, C. and Schleret, J.-J. (1996) *Les Auteurs de la Série Noire: Voyage au bout de la Noire 1945–1995*. Paris: Joseph K.

Meunier, S. (2005) 'Anti-Americanisms in France', *European Studies Newsletter* 34 (3/4) January: 1–4.

Miller, H. (1993) *Tropic of Cancer*. London: Flamingo. (The text was first published in Paris by Obelisk Press in 1934.)

Milne, T. (1984) '*La Balance*' (Review), *Sight and Sound*, Spring: 148.

Moine, R. (2007) *Remakes: Les films français à Hollywood*. Paris: CNRS Editions.

Morita-Clément, M.-A. (1985) *L'Image de l'Allemagne dans le roman français de 1945 à nos jours*. Nagoya: Presses Universitaires de Nagoya.

Morrison, T. (1992) *Jazz*. New York: Signet.

Nacache, J. (1999) 'Comment penser les remakes américains?' *Positif*, June: 76–80.

Naremore, J. (1998) *More than Night: Film Noir in its Contexts*. Berkeley, Los Angeles and London: University of California Press.

Nothomb, A. (1992) *Hygiène de l'assassin*. Paris: Albin Michel.

Ostrowska, D. (2007) 'France: Cinematic Television or Televisual Cinema' in Ostrowska, D. and Roberts, G. (eds) *European Cinemas in the Television Age*. Edinburgh: Edinburgh University Press, pp. 25–40.

Pasquier, S. and Blanc, H. (2004) 'Les mafias russes menacent l'Europe' L'Express, 28 June.

Pestureau, G. (1977) in Noël Arnaud and Henri Baudin (eds) *Boris Vian: Colloque de Cerisy/2*. Paris: Union Générale d'Éditions.

—— (1978) *Boris Vian, les Amerlauds et les Godons*. Paris: Union Générale d'Éditions.

Philippe, O. (1996) *Le Film policier français contemporain*. Paris: Cerf.

Place, J. (1980) 'Women in Film Noir' in Kaplan, E.A. (ed) *Women in Film Noir*. London: BFI Publishing, pp. 47–68.

Place, J. and Peterson, L. (1996) 'Some Visual Motifs of *Film Noir*' in Silver, A. and Ursini, J. (eds) *Film Noir Reader*. New York: Limelight Editions, pp. 65–76.

Platten, D. (2002) 'Polar Positions: The Theme of Identity in Contemporary Noir Fiction', *Nottingham French Studies* 41 (1): 5–18.

Pons, J. (1997) 'Le roman noir, literature réelle', *Les Temps Modernes* 595: 5–14.

Powrie, P. (1997) *French Cinema in the 1980s: Nostalgia and the Crisis of Masculinity*. Oxford: Clarendon.

—— (2001) *Jean-Jacques Beineix*. Manchester, UK: Manchester University Press.

—— (2003) 'Cinema' in Dauncey, H. (ed.) *French Popular Culture: An Introduction*. London: Arnold, pp. 119–34.

—— (2007) 'French Neo-Noir to Hyper-Noir' in Spicer, A. (ed.) *European Film Noir*. Manchester, England; New York: Manchester University Press (distributed exclusively in the USA by Palgrave), pp. 55–83.

Quinn Curtis, T. (1982) '*La Balance*' (Review), *International Herald Tribune*, 30 November: sin. pag.

Raspiengeas, J.-C. (2001) *Bertrand Tavernier*. Paris: Flammarion.

Revel, J.-F. (2003) *Anti-Americanism*, trans. Diarmid Cammell. San Francisco: Encounter Books.

Rivière, F. (1995) 'Léo Malet: Un noir jeu de l'oie', *Magazine Littéraire* 332: 61–63.

Roger, P. (1996) *Rêves et cauchemars américains*. Villeneuve-d'Ascq: Presses Universitaires du Septentrion.

Rolls, A. (1999) *The Flight of the Angels: Intertextuality in Four Novels by Boris Vian*. Amsterdam and Atlanta: Rodopi.

—— (2000) 'Boris Vian's *L'Écume des jours*: The Pulls of Froth and Days', *Nottingham French Studies* 39 (2): 203–12.

—— (2003) ' "This Lovely, Sweet Refrain": Reading the Fiction back into *Nausea*', *Literature and Aesthetics – The Journal of the Sydney Society of Literature and Aesthetics* 13 (2): 57–72.

—— (2004) 'Of Mice and Murder: Playing Cat and Mouse with Boris Vian's *L'Écume des jours*', *Australian Journal of French Studies* 41 (1): 48–58.

Ross, K. (1995) *Fast Cars, Clean Bodies: Decolonization and the Reordering of French Culture*. Cambridge, Mass. and London: MIT Press.

Sabatier, R. (1990) *La Souris verte*. Paris: Albin Michel.

Sartre, J.-P. (2000) *Nausea*. London: Penguin. (First published in the original French by Gallimard in 1938.)

Schatz, T. (1981) *Hollywood Genres*. New York: McGraw-Hill.

Schrader, P. (1996) in Silver, A. and Ursini, J. (eds) *Film Noir Reader*. New York: Limelight Editions, pp. 53–63.

Schulman, P. (2000) 'Paris en jeu de l'oie: Les fantômes de Nestor Burma', *The French Review* 73 (6): 1155–64.

Schwartz, V. (2007) *It's So French! Hollywood, Paris, and the Making of Cosmopolitan Film Culture*. The University of Chicago Press.

Scott, J. (1996) '*J'irai cracher sur vos tombes*: A Two-Faced "Translation"', in Geoffrey T. Harris (ed.) *On Translating French Literature and Film*. Amsterdam and Atlanta: Rodopi, pp. 209–25.

Silver, A. and Ursini, J. (eds) (1996) *Film Noir Reader*. New York: Limelight Editions.

Smith, S. (2000) 'Between Detachment and Desire: Léo Malet's French *roman noir*', in Mullen, A. and O'Beirne, E. (eds) *Crime Scenes: Detective Narratives in European Culture since 1945*. Amsterdam and Atlanta: Rodopi, pp. 125–36.

Sowerwine, C. (2001) *France since 1870: Culture, Politics and Society*. New York: Palgrave.

Spicer, A. (2002) *Film Noir*. Harlow, UK and New York: Pearson Education.

Stewart, T. / Arcouët, S. (1972) *La Mort et l'ange*. Paris: Gallimard. (First published by Gallimard in 1948.)

Strode, L. (2000) 'France and EU Policy-Making on Visual Culture: New Opportunities for National Identity' in Ezra, E. and Harris, S. (eds) *France in Focus: Film and National Identity*. Oxford: Berg, pp. 61–75.

Sullivan, V. / Vian, B. (1973) *J'irai cracher sur vos tombes*. Paris: Bourgois. (First published by Éditions du Scorpion in 1946.)

Tavernier, B. and Coursodon, J.-P. (1991) *50 ans de cinéma américain*. Paris: Nathan.

Tchernia, P. (1989) *80 Grands Succès du cinéma policier français*. Paris: Casterman.

Telotte, J. (1989) *Voices in the Dark: Narrative Patterns of Film Noir*. Urbana: University of Illinois Press.

Truffaut, F. (1955a) 'Du Rififi à la compétence', *Arts*, 18 May.

—— (1955b) 'Du Rififi chez les hommes de Jules Dassin', *Arts*, 20 April.

Veillon, D. (2002) *Fashion under the Occupation*, trans. Miriam Kochan. Oxford and New York: Berg.

Veray, L. (2002) 'Le cinéma américain constitue-t-il une menace pour l'identité nationale française?' in Barnier, M. and Moine, R. (eds) *France/Hollywood: échanges cinématographiques*. Paris: L'Harmattan, pp. 175–2001.

Vernet, M. (2007) 'Le nationalisme du film policier français des années 50' *Popular European Cinema Conference (PEC) 5: European Crime Drama*. Paris: Université Paris X Nanterre. (Conference Address)

Véron, L. (1999) 'Hollywood and Europe: A Case of Trade in Cultural Industries – The 1993 GATT Dispute' (Working Paper). School of International Relations, University of Southern Carolina. Available 12/11/2007: www.ciaonet.org/wps/vel02/.

Vian, B. (1956) *L'Automne à Pékin*. Paris: Union Générale d'Éditions. (First published by Minuit in 1947.)

—— (1989) *Rue des ravissantes et dix-huit autres scénarios cinématographiques*. Paris: Christian Bourgois.

—— (1999) *Œuvres romanesques 2*. Paris, Fayard.

Vilhen, E. (2000) 'Jammin' on the Champs-Elysées: Jazz, France and the 1950s' in Wagnleitner, R. and Tyler May, E. (eds) *"Here, There and Everywhere." The Foreign Politics of American Popular Culture*. Hanover; London: University Press of New England, pp. 149–62.

Vincendeau, G. (1992) 'Noir is also a French Word' in Cameron, I. (ed.) *The Movie Book of Film Noir*. London and New York: Studio Vista, pp. 49–58.

—— (2003) *Jean-Pierre Melville: An American in Paris*. London: British Film Institute.

—— (2007) 'French Film Noir' in Spicer, A. (ed.) *European Film Noir*. Manchester, UK and New York: Manchester University Press (distributed exclusively in the USA by Palgrave), pp. 23–54.

Wager, J. (1999) *Dangerous Dames: Women and Representation in the Weimar Street Film and Film Noir*. Athens: Ohio University Press.

—— (2005) *Dames in the Driver's Seat: Rereading Film Noir*. Austin: University of Texas Press.

Walker, D. (2004) 'From Honest Thief to Media Psychopath: American Culture through French Film Noir', *Post-Scriptum 4*, (http://www.post-scriptum.org/sin.pag.).

—— (2007) 'Reversing the Remake: Jacques Audiard's *De battre mon cœur s'est arrêté*', *AUMLA-Journal of The Australasian Universities Language and Literature Association*, Special Issue: 301–310.

—— (2007) 'Re-Reading the Femme Fatale in Film Noir: An Evolutionary Perspective', *Journal of Moving Image Studies* 4: 25.

—— (2008) 'European Dialogues with Hollywood: Classic French Film Noir', *New Zealand and the EU: Perspectives on European Cinema, New Zealand Europe Institute Research Series*, Special Issue: 1–16.

Waxman, S. (1993) 'A Matter of Déjà View: Cry Faux over US Film Remakes', *Washington Post* July 15, sec. C: 1+.

Wilson, E. (1999) *French Cinema since 1950: Personal Histories*. Lanham, MD: Rowman & Littlefield.

Index